MOONLIT DESIRE

"This moon, all I need is you," Bright Arrow murmured in a heavy voice.

"I need you too," Rebecca responded.

Lifting her in his arms, he carried her to an expanse of thick grass and, kneeling, he gently placed her on the soft covering. For a time, he was content to visually explore her face in the moonlight. Then slowly he came forward until his body was touching hers. Reaching out his hand, he fondled her cheek, then ran his fingers through silky hair. Finally, all restraint disappeared as his mouth closed over hers.

Bright Arrow's lips deftly and hungrily captured Rebecca's. It had been so long since they had felt such passion searing their flesh. In this heady moment, nothing and no one else existed. It was a time for total possession, for complete giving and taking and sharing. Their hearts pleaded and their desires soared.

The Sioux warrior covered her face with kisses, and rained them down her throat. His eager fingers untied the fastenings of her dress and slid it from her shoulders to expose her satiny flesh to his greedy senses. Rebecca didn't stop him as he removed her clothes; she shifted to assist him.

His eyes swept over her with barely controlled desire, and she could not contain the low moan that escaped her lips. "Bright Arrow, please . . ."

Without hesitation he drew her into his possessive embrace. Soon they were rapturously entwined in their private haven . . .

THE FIERY PASSION, EARTHY SENSUALITY, AND THRILLING ADVENTURES OF THE McLOUGHLIN CLAN

Book I, CARESS OF FIRE (3718, $4.50/$5.50)
by Martha Hix

Lisette Keller wanted out of Texas. The stubborn beauty was willing to work her way north, but first she needed a job. Why not hire on as trail cook with the McLoughlin outfit? To virile rancher Gil McLoughlin, a cattle drive was no place for a lady. Soon, he not only hired her, he also vowed to find out if her lips were as sweet as her cooking . . .

Book II, LONE STAR LOVING (4029, $4.50/$5.50)
by Martha Hix

The law at her heels, smuggler Charity McLoughlin had enough trouble without getting abducted by a black-haired savage called Hawk. When he fired her passion, were her fortunes looking up or down? But she wouldn't try to get away just yet, even though he would deliver her to a fate worse than death. For one night, she'd surrender to those dark eyes and his every desire . . .

Book III, WILD SIERRA ROGUE (4256, $4.50/$5.50)
by Martha Hix

Sparks flew when Rafe Delgado teamed with starchy and absolutely desperate Margaret McLoughlin on a rescue mission to save her mother. It irked Margaret, depending on the very rogue who'd wronged the family to lead her to the legendary Copper Canyon of Chihuahua. She condemned the rake's lack of redeeming values, while he meant to take the starch out of her drawers. They didn't count on falling in love . . .

Available wherever paperbacks are sold, or order direct from the Publisher. Send cover price plus 50¢ per copy for mailing and handling to Penguin USA, P.O. Box 999, c/o Dept. 17109, Bergenfield, NJ 07621. Residents of New York and Tennessee must include sales tax. DO NOT SEND CASH.

JANELLE TAYLOR

Stolen Ecstasy

ZEBRA BOOKS
KENSINGTON PUBLISHING CORP.

ZEBRA BOOKS

are published by

Kensington Publishing Corp.
850 Third Avenue
New York, NY 10022

Tenth printing: December, 1994

Printed in the United States of America

To my very good friend Fred Mertins, III.

And to Carin Cohen, my ex-Zebra editor, whom I shall miss greatly.

And lastly to Elaine Duillo, for this and many other exquisite bookcovers. Thanks for your talent and accurate expression.

Acknowledgments:

My thanks to Joe Taylor, Jr., for his assistance with many outdoor/hunting facts.

And again I thank my good friend and helper Hiram C. Owen of the Sisseton/Wahpeton (Dakota Sioux) Tribe from the Lake Traverse Reservation.

If you can look into the seeds of time,
and say which grain will grow and which will not . . .

—Shakespeare, *Macbeth*

But stronger than all . . . is . . . fury,
Fury that brings upon mortals the greatest evils.

—Euripedes, *Medea*

[Yet], they that sow in tears shall reap in joy,
. . . bearing precious seeds.

—*Psalms* 125:5-6

Prologue

Dakota Territory
April, 1804

Rebecca Kenny moved quietly along the forest path. She usually took great delight in feeling the cool, moist earth beneath her bare feet. But, she reflected, how could she enjoy nature when her world was falling apart? She halted abruptly, then slipped behind a spruce to observe her husband as he sat beside a narrow stream. How he had changed since he had been exiled from his people six-and-a-half years ago. Where was the man she had loved and married, the indomitable Sioux warrior Bright Arrow, son of the legendary Chief Gray Eagle? Her beloved had become a stranger, a man she didn't know or understand.

Rebecca inwardly raged at the sight before her tawny eyes. It was as if her husband had lost all interest in himself, in life, and in his family. Self-pity and resentment had been more destructive than the ravages of revenge. Gone were his former energy and enthusiasm; instead, he had become lazy, gloomy, listless, and melancholy. His lackadaisical behavior proclaimed he had nothing and no one to live for any more. Her angered mind screamed at him, *What about your family? What about your pride?*

Undesirable emotions implanted themselves within

11

her each day like wild seeds, and she wondered how long she could prevent them from germinating, from becoming seedlings which could grow into strangling vines. If only she could look into the future and determine which emotional seeds would grow and which would die. And the most destructive seed was fury, fury directed not only at her love but at her own helplessness. She had to find a way to unearth and destroy those powerful seeds . . .

Each month—no, week—the situation worsened. They were becoming as estranged from each other as he was from his tribe and parents, and his apathy was taking its toll on Rebecca. She felt she was to blame for his detached state, for he acted as if he no longer found her desirable, as if his love and passion for her were gradually vanishing. He never exercised or honed his skills and instincts. Hunting was difficult, for his keen senses and quick reflexes had become dulled through lack of use.

Why must he travel this self-destructive course? She wondered. Why did guilt gnaw at him until he was willing to do anything to benumb its anguish and power? As the days passed, it became clear to Rebecca that he was losing his prowess and his special appeal. His deterioration was a travesty of his former greatness, and sometimes she feared she would grow to hate him for allowing himself such a slow and agonizing defeat.

When they had met, Bright Arrow's body had been a sensual blending of black and bronze, a healthy body of exceptional beauty and appeal. He had been so handsome and virile that she had lost her wits and will before him. His presently drab hair had been the shade of a crow's wing beneath a full moon; his eyes had gleamed like highly polished jet. Now they were as lifeless as his company. His coppery brown body had once been hard and strong, but now it was fat and flaccid to the touch. He moved sluggishly and without his former gracefulness. At one time he had moved as invisibly as a soft breeze across a cloudless sky, yet now he trudged awkwardly and loudly through the forests which had so often before yielded its treasures to his silent mastery.

A mere glance from him had once sent ripples of desire and happiness over her body. Rebecca had believed then that no matter what blows fate dealt them, she would never love or desire another as she did this majestic creature. But the unique man she had met, loved, and wed no longer existed. In his place was a pale and pathetic ghost.

He sat cross-legged and slump-shouldered on the stream's bank, so lax and still that she almost thought he was dozing. He was so deeply ensnared by his moody thoughts that his no-longer-keen instincts failed to detect her approach and intense stare. If she had been an enemy, she silently mused, he would be dead and scalped at this very moment!

Rebecca envisioned the mental path he traveled, a trail he had walked too frequently during these many years. She knew that path by heart, for she had journeyed it at his side. Tears blurred her golden brown eyes and sadness filled her heart, for she felt there was nothing she could say to ease his suffering and nothing she could do to alter his intolerable condition. Perhaps it was too late to save Bright Arrow from himself.

She wanted to scream at him, to force him to see what he was doing to both of them. She had tried that ploy, and it had failed. She had pleaded, cried, reasoned, argued, and threatened; nothing had reached him in his self-imprisoning world of indifference. Many nights she had imagined daring ways to catch his attention or to shock

13

him back to reality, but in the light of dawn she had seen how futile and foolish they were. First Bright Arrow had to care; he had to want to change, to live again.

His parents had been accurate when they had warned of the demands and perils of a mixed marriage between a white girl and a Sioux Indian. If she were going to be fair, she would have to admit that her beloved had not realized the extent of his sacrifices before he had claimed her as his wife. He had never imagined that his tribe would banish him for his choice, not when his father was chief, not when he was a dauntless warrior with numerous *coups!* But what could a loving father or powerful chief do when the council voted against his son, the son who would have become the next Oglala chief if Fate had not intervened? How foolish for the council to deny the tribe his enormous skills and prowess. How sad and cruel for fate to demand such a high price for love.

Rebecca knew all too well that a short distance to the north the Cheyenne River flowed swiftly. To the south was the summer camp of Brave Arrow's family and tribe, and the sacred Black Hills, the *Paha Sapa*—winter encampment of the Oglalas and other tribes—were to the west. There were three divisions in the Sioux Nation: Lakota/Teton, Nakota/Yankton, and Dakota/Santee. In each division were many tribes and bands, and all tribes were members of the Seven Council Fires of the Sioux, *Dakota Oceti Sakawin.* Her husband had been a member of the Oglala tribe in the Teton branch. His people were all about him, but they seemed forever beyond his reach.

She leaned against the tree and permitted her mind to roam through the past. Bright Arrow had been a courageous and daring warrior when they had first met in 1796, she as his white prisoner. In spite of their differences and the objections of others, they had fallen

14

in love, a love too potent to resist or deny. Even after she had saved Bright Arrow's life and proven her mettle and value, the council had demanded she live as his *kaskapi*, his captive; but that had meant being considered nothing more than his *witkowin*, his whore. Her beloved would not permit such a degrading role for her, nor would he allow any future children to be viewed as "half-breed bastards." His pride and love had been so strong that he had rebelled against his people's orders. He had bravely vowed that if they could not live as honorable mates in his camp he would take Rebecca and leave. That had been almost seven years ago; and nothing had changed— nothing but her handsome and virile husband . . .

With these memories still filling her thoughts, the auburn-haired beauty of twenty-five returned to their cabin, a home which they had built together in those early days before he had allowed this wasting disease to attack his mind and body. Within its confines, three small girls slept peacefully. With all her heart, Rebecca believed she would have forced her husband to return to his people if not for the children; she loved him that much, and each day it became more unbearable to watch his disintegration. But it was the children who would suffer most, for their appearances were unmistakably Indian and, without their father, they would be forced into the white world or be trapped between two warring cultures.

As for Rebecca, her olive flesh and deep brown eyes falsely suggested she might be part Indian. Except for her flaming chestnut curls, her looks did nothing to attest to her white blood. She had often thought that her misleading appearance had been the reason Bright Arrow had accepted her so easily. If only his people could also over- look her white heritage. They had adamantly refused and, in doing so, Rebecca felt they were partly responsible for this predicament.

At first she had been loyal, understanding, and patient. She had comprehended that what Bright Arrow had lost was consuming him as viciously as a fatal disease. His tribe had taken away his rank, his honor, his customs and ways, his adventures, his family, his people. Worse, they had stolen his spirit and his destiny; they had severed his life-circle. He could not adjust to such losses. The more time that passed, the more her husband changed, and the more he resisted their present life together. Tears ran down her cheeks as she wept for what had been and for what she despaired could never be again.

Rebecca sat down on the bench that Bright Arrow had constructed near the cabin door. Time had not lessened his displeasure at living inside a "white man's dwelling." But they had been alone in the wilderness and such a dwelling had been necessary for the protection of his family against harsh winters, wild animals, and bitter enemies. As she sat, she reflected that the name Bright Arrow—a name once feared and admired and envied— had vanished from before the eyes of his tribe and foes. But had they forgotten his existence? Could they have forgotten? At twenty-six, he should have been at the peak of physical prowess. No man had possessed more valor, cunning, or daring! While her girls napped, she would give herself time to think. There had to be something she could do.

Rebecca recalled the awful days following her parents' deaths from a fever and those two years with her menacing uncle, Jamie O'Hara. It was that vile creature who had brought her into the Sioux domain, and his dreams of riches and his greed had gotten him killed, along with a small troop of soldiers. Following a raid on her uncle's camp, Bright Arrow had taken her captive. From the moment their gazes had fused, she had been enchanted by the handsome and masterful warrior who had rescued her from a soldier's brutal attack, but she had fled in fear as he battled another warrior for her possession. Bright Arrow had pursued and captured her.

From the night he first took her innocence upon his mat, her heart and body had been enslaved by him. He had been so gentle and tender for a man of such strength. In the forest that first night, their hearts, bodies, and spirits had become as one forever. And if a great warrior could love her, respect her, and accept her, she could not understand how his people could be so set against her and their union. Was it such a horrible crime that her skin was white? she had wondered. If it had been possible, she would have become an Indian!

They had endured many hardships and perils, and they had savored countless moments of passion and joy. But they had not heeded the warnings of his family and the objections of his people. They had been young and in love, refusing to see beyond their forbidden emotions and need for each other. It was as if some mystical arm of revenge had been extended over the land to seize and punish them.

During Rebecca's captivity, Bright Arrow had been taken prisoner by white soldiers, who threatened to execute him unless he could be traded for his father. She had risked her life to secure his escape. And beyond this courageous deed she had been an obedient slave. But no matter what she did, the Sioux would not look past her white skin and allow her to marry Bright Arrow. She had often wondered if it might have been different had he not rejected so many Indian maidens in favor of a white slave or not been the son of Chief Gray Eagle.

At fifty-three, Gray Eagle still sparked fear in his enemies and respect in his people and allies. It was said that no greater warrior than Gray Eagle had ever ridden the open Plains. If Bright Arrow had not been banished for marrying her, this would no longer be true, for at nineteen Bright Arrow had been close to equalling his father's prowess. He would have made a great chief one day, if he had not rejected the laws and customs of his people. He had done the unforgivable; he had refused his heritage and defied the council—all for a white love.

Rebecca could not forget Gray Eagle's ominous words as she had left his side to help rescue her imprisoned love. "If you help him escape . . . I will return you to my son. Even so, a slave is all you can ever be to him. Is this enough for you?" he had challenged her. Her naive response had been, "Yes, Gray Eagle. Even a small part of him is better than none. I will do nothing to dishonor him before the eyes of his people." But she had done worse; she had loved him and enchanted him, then stolen him from his people and his fate. She had allowed him to believe that love was an unbeatable force, that it could conquer their foes. Just as sadly, she had also believed their love could triumph over all obstacles. But years had passed and he was still an outcast.

Now her husband was being destroyed. He could not live as half a man, a man without his life-force, his honor, his very reasons for existence. He lived neither in the white world nor the Indian world. He was a warrior without a war, an arrow that couldn't fly. He was lonely for his Indian family and culture; he was hungry for the lost days of adventure and danger. He yearned for the life which he had left behind him. He had not been born to be a trapper, living in a wooden enclosure, existing alone with only his wife and children. They could have joined

18

another friendly tribe, such as the Cheyenne, but his pride would not allow it.

Bright Arrow was like a captured eagle leashed to a post. His keen abilities were being weakened by inactivity while his mind was allowed to imagine a state where he could revel in his freedom and prowess, where he could test himself against other forces. He had been tricked by Fate, and his bonds were those of love and responsibility. To break his leash would cost him dearly. And although he had not complained or spoken of such denials and losses, Rebecca knew he missed the ceremonies, the hunts, the raids, the suspense, the victories. He had broken his life-circle, and he could not find an acceptable way to repair it.

Until recently, Rebecca had not doubted Bright Arrow's love for her and their children, for he had proven it many times. But she had feared the uncontrollable resentment that could sprout and grow within him, seedlings of fury born of frustration and bitterness toward himself and his tribe. She would do anything to keep their love from being destroyed. Despite all their troubles, they had been happy until his exile. But from the changes demanded of him ensnaring vines had germinated; it seemed as if he were being slowly and painfully choked.

Something would have to be done to rescue her love once more—but what and how? She couldn't force his tribe to recall him. She couldn't free him by demanding he leave her or by running away. Was there no way? She was all too aware that time was running out for him, for them. Yet she was helpless to stop its inevitable passage.

Rebecca thought about the innocent children inside their cabin, children denied their grandparents and their heritage. Although they were living between two worlds, the girls had been given Indian names. Little Feet was six, Moon Eyes was four, and Tashina was sixteen months. As if Fate were determined to further punish Bright Arrow, it had denied him a son that could ride with him and train at his side, a boy to share that special bond between father and son. And that same Fate had given his parents another son just before Bright Arrow had left home. Sun Cloud, now seven, would one day become the Oglala chief in his place. Perhaps the birth of another son had given the council the courage to banish her defiant love. Perhaps it had given Gray Eagle the heart to accept such a foul deed. But even without his birthright, Rebecca knew Bright Arrow would gladly return to his people.

Surely her husband had been punished enough by now? Surely his family and tribe missed him, perhaps needed him? He was a warrior, a protector of his people and lands. He should be at his father's side! He had been condemned to a life of nonexistence. Surely they could find forgiveness and acceptance in their hearts? Was love such a mysterious emotion that they could not comprehend it? Didn't they realize what they were doing to him? Didn't they care?

Perhaps if she went to Gray Eagle and Shalee and pleaded with them to send for their son . . . No, her husband would be furious with her. It was not the Indian way for a woman to interfere in a warrior's affairs. His people would not respect one who begged or groveled or rejected the vote of the council. Yet she knew he couldn't go on like this. It was his haunting silence and the increasing distance between them that frightened Rebecca. She dreaded to imagine what another year in the cabin would do to her husband, to their marriage. Fate owed them something, for Fate had thrown them together! In her Bible it said, "They that sow in tears shall reap in joy . . .

20

bearing precious seeds." They had shed more than their share of tears and endured more than their portion of pain; they had borne three precious seeds. It was time for the seeds of fury and denial to blow away; it was time to reap a much deserved harvest of joy and peace.

Rebecca rested her head and shoulders against the wooden surface behind her. She closed her eyes and recalled blissful moments from their bittersweet past. Bright Arrow had captured her during a raid on her uncle's wagon train. He had stood proud and powerful before her after slaying a soldier who was trying to rape her. She had been mesmerized by his handsome physique and drawn to his gentle manner. He had appeared as a earth-bound god before her absorbing senses, a provocative blending of blacks and bronzes. His body had been sleek and hard, and his jet eyes had shone with victory and intrigue. It had seemed as if no power in existence could prevent their attraction to each other.

Abruptly, another warrior, a cruel and hostile brave, had laid claim to her. Yet a magical and mystical bond had been forged between Rebecca and Bright Arrow in those brief moments when they had gazed into each other's eyes. As he fought the challenging warrior to retain her, she had escaped into the forest. She had run and walked for hours, trying to be free of the grim sight left behind in the clearing. Bright Arrow had pursued her and captured her. Despite his awesome strength and power over her life, he had awakened a never-ending passion within her as he claimed her body later that night. In the following weeks, many hours of sensual pleasure on his mats had deepened the bonds of that first rapturous night. Soon she not only belonged to him in body, but also in heart and spirit as well.

Bright Arrow's parents, especially his father, had

resisted their union. The dauntless Sioux chief had done all within his power to influence his son to part with her. Other tribe members had tried to encourage him to send her away, to sell her, even to slay her. Nothing and no one could persuade him to be rid of her.

He had loved and desired her so greatly that no taunts, jests, reasons, or pleas could compel her departure. Rebecca remembered how hard she had worked to prove her value and loyalty to her captor and his people, but nothing had obliterated the fact that this object of their future chief's forbidden desires was white. Bright Arrow had been advised and threatened by the council; still he had held fast to her. How could she have resisted or denied such love and sacrifice on his part? She could not.

The time her love had been captured by the soldiers to ransom for Chief Gray Eagle, she had risked her life to save her love's. Later, when her ruse had been uncovered, he had returned to the fort to rescue her! When his council had realized that Bright Arrow's feelings were growing stronger and bolder with each day, they had attempted a desperate and final measure "to free him from the evil white spirit who enslaved him and blinded him to his duty and destiny." The council had demanded her departure, by trade or death or release. Otherwise, Bright Arrow would be exiled, banished until he could sate his lust for her and return to his people free of her distracting magic and evil allure. Bright Arrow had tried to call their bluff. For years he had waited for his tribe to call him back; but not a word had been sent.

In the beginning, here, at their cabin, they had been happy; they had been free of insults and demands. Oh, they had loved and shared a passion and zeal to make the gods envious! They had experienced a burning love a man and a woman could hope to find only once in a lifetime.

22

How could anyone have expected them to sacrifice such feelings?

Born a creature of nature, Bright Arrow had been eager to make love in any place and at any time. He especially enjoyed lovemaking beneath the stars and moon or in the sheltering forest in early morning or mid-afternoon. As Rebecca drowsed on the bench in the warm sun, her dreamy mind recalled one such delightful union . . .

It was shortly after the noon meal and the girls were napping. Tashina was seven weeks old, and they had not made love since the month before her birth in mid-January. It had been a mild winter, and early March seemed almost like spring. Bright Arrow had suggested a walk while the girls slept. He grinned mischievously as he tossed a blanket over his right arm and held out an invit-ing hand. His dark eyes twinkled with lights of promise, and Rebecca smiled and tingled as she slipped her smaller hand into his large one.

Together they strolled a short distance from the warm cabin. The air was crisp and refreshing. Nature was taking on a new face of supple greens and birds sang joy-fully as they realized that winter was past. Bright Arrow halted his movements and dropped the blanket to the ground. He stood within inches of her, yet he didn't touch her physically. His softened eyes seemed content to roam over her flushed features, engulfing her in waves of anticipation his magnetic gaze always evoked. As if she were a prize filly, he appreciatively examined her. A warm glow covered her body, chasing away the slight chill in the air.

Bright Arrow lifted his finger to touch her lips, to ever

so slowly move over them. His hands captured her face and tilted it for a full view. The dam that had held back their desires for so many weeks was shattered, allowing a surge of passion to spill forth. And still his probing gaze caressed her face with a matchless tenderness, which caused her heart to race with her respiration. His hands moved at a snail's pace down her throat to lightly grasp her shoulders. Deftly he unbuttoned her dress and removed each of her garments. Without taking his eyes from hers, he cast the clothing aside. His fingertips drifted sensuously over her bare flesh, enticing tremors throughout her body.

Bright Arrow leaned forward and fastened his eager mouth to hers. His tongue darted between her lips and played tag with hers. He kissed her eyes, then tormented her earlobes. Leisurely his lips traveled down her neck and teased the flesh over each shoulder and across her collarbone. When his seeking mouth found a taut nipple on a passion-sensitive breast, a moan came from Rebecca's parted lips. Soon warm breath and moisture tormented both points until she shivered with longing and pleasure. Strong bronze hands journeyed down her sides and eased around her hips to take hold of firm buttocks. He carefully kneaded them as his mouth worked at her breasts. Rebecca's head swayed from side to side as the tension mounted within her hungry body. She was aware of each caress, each kiss, each stirring movement. They produced glorious sensations which only birthed a longing for more, an aching which drove her senses wild.

Bright Arrow's lips wandered down the cleft between her breasts, halting briefly to tease her navel before continuing along a deliberate path in search of another peak which mutely demanded his attention and talents.

He laid his coppery chin against the auburn softness which surrounded the precious mound like a lush forest. His smooth cheek caressed it. As exploring interlopers, his fingers parted the reddish brown forest which guarded her most private territory. His tongue skillfully invaded the smooth area and lovingly labored to bring her to the height of eagerness, and it was with gloriously agonizing difficulty that he held back from sending his nearly uncontrollable shaft into her enticing cave of wondrous magic.

Rebecca's body quivered with delight. Her breath came in quick, short gasps as his tongue and hands brought tantalizing sensations to her. Soft moans and pleas escaped from her mouth as her tongue moved over her dry lips again and again. For a time, she thought she might faint as the sensual provocation increased.

Suddenly the blissful torture ceased as Bright Arrow straightened to remove his garments. He hastily spread out the blanket and turned to reach for her. Rebecca's golden brown eyes were glazed with a fierce craving that matched his own. As she started to kneel to take possession of the tempting treat which beckoned to her to sample its nectar, Bright Arrow gently grasped her shoulders and shook his head. He breathlessly warned, "Not this sun, little heart. I fear my hold over him is strained too much." As her hand encircled the torrid flesh, he shuddered and hoarsely whispered, "Later, when our passions do not burn as wildfires."

Rebecca understood and accepted his precaution. It had been so long since they had been together like this, and both were starving for this sensual meal. She lay down without modesty or hesitation. Her eyes journeyed up the full length of his iron-muscled body. While he took a moment to cool his flaming senses, Bright Arrow observed her intense study of him.

His legs were firm and smooth. His hips were narrow and his stomach taut and flat. His manhood stood erect and proud, a large, smooth staff displaying its readiness and greedy appetite. His hairless chest bespoke his immense physical strength, as did his muscular arms. His was a body honed to perfection, for agility, for victory. His arresting face with its ebony eyes, full lips, and magnificent bone structure enchanted her. Shiny, midnight black hair teased the nape of his neck. His bronze flesh was stretched tightly over his splendid frame like a hide staked for tanning, its smooth lines broken only by rippling muscles. He was such a stimulating male, and Rebecca knew he belonged to her. Her pulse quickened with joy and love.

Rebecca's gaze fused with Bright Arrow's, her tawny eyes speaking messages of love and urgency to his ebony ones. He joined her on the blanket, and the chilly breeze was ignored in the heat of shared passion. Again he lavished his attention upon her lips and breasts until she begged for their union. His finger tempted her lower peak to stand rigid and quivering beneath his caress. Finding her ready to accept him, he lay atop her, and gently slid his hard maleness into her receptive body, creating a sensation of bliss which almost erupted into a blazing, all-consuming fire.

Rebecca's body arched upward, taking his entire length. As he moved with care and experience, she matched her rhythm to his. Bright Arrow whispered raggedly, "I love you, little heart. I have missed this closeness with you. You have enslaved my heart and body."

At such moments, Rebecca knew he didn't resent the sacrifices he had made in order to have her. As they fondled each other, they hungrily sought fulfillment. It was joyous to share such a special union. Each was aware of the other's needs, giving and taking for mutual satisfaction. Wildly and skillfully they rode the waves of titillating desires. The world receded for a time as Bright Arrow and Rebecca Kenny came together to blend bodies and spirits.

From many days and nights of lovemaking, signals had been learned and now were given mutely, given with responses and touches. Each sensed how close to rapture the other was, and they adjusted their loving attentions to meet at the peak of passion simultaneously. Prisoners of desire and enchantment, they remained bound together as ecstasy assailed and consumed them. Their bodies blended time and again until every blissful spasm ceased and they were enveloped in the warmth of contentment and sated senses.

Bright Arrow's lips brushed over Rebecca's mouth several times. He kissed the tip of her nose and each closed eye. He trailed kisses over her cheeks and brows. He whispered words of love and satisfaction into her ears. He was always tender and sensitive after making love, as if he hated to release her until compelled to do so. And, as they had so many other times after a union, they lay entwined on the blanket, silently and lovingly holding each other, savoring their triumphant joining . . .

As Rebecca shifted her numb buttocks on the wooden bench, reality came back in shocking force. She opened her eyes and glanced around the clearing. Bright Arrow had not returned from the stream. She felt so lonely, so frustrated, so dejected. The dreamy recollection had stirred in her body fierce hunger. It had been so long since they had made love passionately, uninhibitedly, thoroughly. She longed for such feelings and experiences to be shared again.

Why had Bright Arrow lost all interest in lovemaking? Why did he pretend to be sleeping many nights or too exhausted other nights? Why did he turn a deaf ear or cold shoulder to her whenever she became amorous? He had created her sensual appetite and had fed it for years! Why starve her now? Why did he refuse to share this special part of himself? The distance and coolness between them tormented her. She squeezed her eyes tightly as tears ran down her cheeks. She feared it would never be that way between them again.

The early spring weather was still cool, but the afternoon sun felt warm and relaxing. Rebecca sat in deep thought for another hour, then arose to enter the cabin and begin their evening meal. If a change was to be made in their lives, the decision would have to come from him, she decided. All she could do was show Bright Arrow how much she loved him and needed him, for she did still love and desire him. Yet she couldn't help but pray for the return of the man he had been long ago; she couldn't help but resent his faded image.

Lately he had become quieter, more remote. He had lost all interest in making love to her, in talking with her, in sharing her company. He paid little attention to the children or to his chores. He spent hours alone in pensive study. What was he thinking and feeling?

A storm was brewing within him. Icy fingers seemed to grasp her heart and to squeeze it painfully as she comprehended that love was not enough for a man like Bright Arrow. She asked herself how long it would be before he confronted this same reality? How long before his dissatisfaction erupted into a violent explosion? When that time came, how would he deal with the situation? Would he hold her responsible for his living death? Would he betray and desert her? Would he sacrifice all he possessed to regain his past glory?

She wept, for by asking herself such questions and by experiencing such feelings, the heartrending state of their relationship was finally revealed to her.

Chapter One

June 22, 1804

Despite the mild breeze from the forest which encircled the cabin and clearing, the summer heat and mugginess encouraged the small children to be fretful. Rebecca couldn't recall a year when it had been so hot this early in the season. She wished Bright Arrow would return home and take them to the nearby pond for a swim and picnic, or at least for a refreshing walk in the woods. Surely that wasn't too much to expect from a dutiful husband and father! This downward spiral of Bright Arrow's was drawing her to depressing and perilous depths which she didn't want to visit. She was rapidly approaching the point where her maternal and survival instincts would compel her to make a drastic choice: her children and herself or her misguided mate.

When Bright Arrow went hunting, he always insisted that Rebecca and the girls remain inside, with windows and doors barred. Today she was too vexed to obey his orders. These last few months, atop the past few years, had been as merciless and demanding on her as they had been on him! He wasn't the only one affected by their predicament. She was as torpid and gloomy as he. Besides the cabin chores and caring for her girls, there was little else to feed her emotions or to challenge her mind. It was becoming harder to conceal her ill feelings, contain her resentment, or retain her hope.

It was lonely and depressing here in the wilderness, especially with a husband who hardly seemed to notice his wife's presence. Rebecca yearned for her love's touch and smile, his tenderness and attention. For months he had been making love *at* her, not to her, making love as if it were a duty he wanted over as quickly as possible. And lately he hadn't touched her at all. At first she had tried playfully and sensuously to seduce him; he had pretended to misread her signals. With this added tension, she accepted the fact that it was only a matter of time before her own simmering fury exploded, only a matter of time before she no longer tried, or cared.

Banishment had been a difficult and heavy burden for each of them! In the beginning, she had believed he was unintentionally making it worse for himself and his family. But could she say that now? No. Were his bruised pride and bitterness causing him to punish all of them? Had he made any attempt at reconciliation with his people? Did he erroneously believe that he deserved this cruel treatment? Had he selected this nearly deserted area to insure their safety, or to prevent contact with his past friends and allies? They had done nothing wrong! Who were his people to judge and to ostracize them! How long would it be before Bright Arrow admitted that his tribe would never send for them! Frustration and anger chewed at Rebecca, and she became furious because his exile was destroying their happiness and she felt utterly helpless.

Rebecca couldn't even recall the last time she had seen or spoken with another female. As for their girls, only their eldest daughter had seen another child since birth—once! If they couldn't attend school, she wanted

32

books with which to teach them. How could they survive if Bright Arrow were injured or became gravely ill? What would happen to her family if she fell ill or died, or to her children if she and her husband were both taken with a fever as her parents had been? This isolation could be fatal for all of them. It was lonely and unnecessary, and the winters locked inside the cabin were an added burden.

She had been patient, loving, supportive, and understanding. But now these emotions and traits were strained. They needed friends for emotional nourishment. They needed neighbors for diversion and for assistance in times of hardship or peril. They needed supplies. This life of barely existing was aging them too quickly. How could her husband ignore these emotional and physical necessities? How long could they go on this way? She had been willing to deny herself to live with his people. Why shouldn't he do the same for her, as it was his people who had rejected them? Could she demand a better life for them, a life near a white settlement or with another friendly tribe? Would that demand lance this festering boil? Would it excise and cleanse its putrid infection? Did she dare?

As the humid day sluggishly crawled toward late afternoon, Rebecca's nerves became frayed from the stuffiness and the girls' whimperings. Any attempt to entertain them was met with defiance and fussiness. Annoyingly low on supplies, she could not distract them with a treat. Even if he despised the whites, Rebecca told herself, her husband would soon have to trade for their needs. He had been so strange these last months, refusing to go near any white for any reason. Yet his blunted hunting skills had brought home little meat, and they had great need of other supplies, supplies which were vanishing as rapidly as her spirits.

The heat of the cabin seemed only to increase her smoldering ire. Rebecca tossed aside caution and opened the door for fresh air. That action served to enlarge her misery, for the two older girls darted past her to play chase outside. Even Tashina bubbled with laughter and rapidly toddled in the direction of freedom and her sisters' giggles. For the first time, she almost wished she didn't have any children, children who prevented her escape from this soul-draining place. She immediately chided herself for thinking such evil and selfish thoughts.

Rebecca sighed heavily and pursued them. When she attempted to force them back inside, she was met with screams and rebellion. Clearly the children were as moody and bored as she was. She could hardly blame them, for Bright Arrow had been away since dawn. It was nearing five, and the locked cabin was unbearable.

Surely he would return at any moment. Besides, they rarely saw anyone out here, friendly or hostile, other than a few men passing by on their way westward past the Black Hills or eastward to the Lake Traverse Trading Post. At those times, all she was allowed to do was serve refreshments or a brief meal. If an amiable man spent the night, it was outside with her husband on sleeping rolls. How she missed polite or stimulating conversation, warm smiles, exciting news!

Surely there was no harm in taking the girls to play and to cool themselves in the nearby stream? Someone had to be concerned with their happiness and health! As a precaution, Rebecca took the loaded gun which Bright Arrow had bought from Jean Truteau of the Spanish Trading Company, where her husband made most of his purchases or exchanges.

Because he had been taught from birth to kill the Great Spirit's creatures only for food or clothing or other necessities, Bright Arrow had refused to trap or shoot more animals than necessary for their survival. Instead, he traded the "shiny yellow rocks," which he found along the riverbanks near the Black Hills, or the lovely rose quartz for any necessities that they could not make or find. Though he had been offered many supplies in exchange for red stone, he had refused to give the white man the special stone which was used for pipes and other objects. The red stone grounds were sacred, but neutral, territory for any tribe. Rebecca had tried to explain such matters to her husband, but Bright Arrow had claimed he couldn't understand why the white men were so greedy for colored rocks. He had declared that the whites were a strange and devious breed who no doubt thought the rocks held Indian magic and power. He could be such a superstitious creature at times! she had mused.

When they had first moved into this area years before, Bright Arrow had been determined to prove they could survive without his people, survive on his courage and cunning. For the defense of his family, he had bargained for two guns, ball, powder, flints, two hatchets, and several sturdy knives. For his home and wife, he had traded for sewing implements, cooking kettles, salt, flour, blankets, cloth, and personal items which had brought smiles to her lips and doelike eyes. To make his home safer and stronger, he had purchased two hammers, a saw, an awl, nails, and other tools. In order to gather the coveted yellow and pink rocks more easily and rapidly and hurry home to his family, he had traded for a pickaxe. Then early this year, he had changed drastically. He began avoiding all whites and had refused to trade with them. She wondered why.

As Little Feet and Moon Eyes splashed and laughed beside her, Rebecca held Tashina's hands while she wiggled her toes into the sand at the bottom of the creek. When the shadows began to lengthen, Rebecca firmly told the girls it was time to return home. Fatigued and refreshed, they all complied without a fuss. Rebecca lifted Tashina into her arms and headed down the path with the other girls trailing her closely. She sighed happily, for it had been a pleasant outing.

Once inside, Rebecca fed Tashina while Little Feet and Moon Eyes gaily feasted with their fingers on the last of the wild berries that she had gathered. That was one distracting task she had sorely missed, for in the past when she had gone to gather wild fruits and vegetables, Bright Arrow had been compelled to go along and spend time with her. She couldn't go alone, and lately he had appeared reluctant to escort her. No doubt, she mused bitterly, because such outings had been fun, even romantic, in the past!

She was grateful that her girls were good eaters and that they hadn't rebelled at the lack of variety in their diets. As soon as the meal was consumed, Rebecca put the girls to bed, smiling and kissing each child. To her surprise and relief, all three were asleep within minutes, and love surged through her as she watched them.

Her children were deeply ensnared by slumber, their faces glowing in the soft light of the lantern burning low in the back corner. Suddenly she was assailed by terrible loneliness and a fierce hunger that had nothing to do with food. She wished as she had so many times before that Bright Arrow would not spend so much time avoiding her or so much energy pretending nothing was wrong. Once winter had passed, he had spent as many hours outside as possible, feigning masculine chores. At night, only his

36

body lay beside her, for his spirit and mind roamed territories which she wasn't allowed to share. He might as well leave and return to his people, she thought, for he wasn't here with her.

Rebecca walked to the doorway and gazed outside. As surely as the moon was shining, the end was near for them, if some drastic act didn't stir him from his daze. As her tawny eyes surveyed the view, she rested her smooth cheek against the door jamb. A full moon illuminated the clearing around the cabin, reminding her of the many nights she had shared a sleeping mat with her love as the moon shone down upon them.

Concern edged into her overcrowded mind. She mellowed as she pondered her life without Bright Arrow, despite his present state. There had been so much love and passion between them, and she wanted it back. Would it ever be the same between them again?

Rebecca wanted and needed to talk for she yearned to solve their problems. She wondered what was preventing her husband's return; it was unusual for him to remain away after dark. Unless he went to retrieve more gold or to bargain with the traders, he was never late. If he had been any man except Bright Arrow, she would worry. Then again, she reasoned, he hadn't been himself in a long time . . .

It was past nine. The lovely hues of sunset had faded to a dull glow beyond the treetops. Every few minutes the shade of blue above her deepened. Soon it would be dark, save for the full moon that tonight resembled a pale sun. From the noises nearby, she knew that night creatures were moving about in search of food and exercise. Nocturnal insects, frogs, and birds were beginning their musical serenade. Trees moved sleepily in the mild breeze, creating ghostly shadows upon the earth. It was as if Nature were issuing an irresistible, provocative invitation to join her merry and carefree adventure.

Rebecca was not a timorous person. She had courageously confronted danger many times. Having lived in the wilderness with her parents until age fifteen, she had then endured the harsh life in a bawdy roadhouse with her uncle. She had lived as a prisoner in an Indian camp and had survived a brutal sojourn at a fort. In spite of her slim size and sex, she was strong and agile. She possessed guts and mettle. She could fire a gun, use a knife, and fight like a wildcat. And although she was normally a sensible person, concern and tension were building inside Rebecca, emotions which belied a clear head and caution.

Without thinking of peril, she strolled outside. Humming softly, she began to whirl and dance in the moonlit clearing with an invisible partner, freeing her mind and body. Time and troubles fled. Floral scents drifted to her on the currents of night air, and an aura of sensual romance and daring filled the surroundings. She removed the thongs on her long braids and loosened her chestnut hair. She ran her fingers through it until it hung free and wavy around her shoulders. Her bare feet seemed to caress the ground. Within her fanciful mind, she imagined the music from the roadhouse in St. Louis. She envisioned how the laughing girls had melted over the lusty customers like butter beneath a blazing sun.

Erotic messages filtered through her dreamy senses as she mentally searched for a means of cooling her fiery passions. Her hands yearned to glide over her husband's virile body as it had been years ago. Imagining it, her body tingled and warmed with rising desire. She thought back to the past, and, as she called his face and frame to mind, her respiration quickening at that potent vision of masculinity, such a heady blend of strength and gentleness. Recalling his skills upon the sleeping mat, she allowed a soft moan of desire to escape her lips. She longed for her love to join her, the love whom she had met and wed . . .

As if capturing and sharing her sensations, the moonlight played upon Rebecca's head with shimmers of silvery red. Despite the fact that she had borne three children, her body was sleek and firm. Her breasts were supple beneath the faded blue cotton dress. Her sunkissed complexion was unmarred by illness or the weather and her golden brown eyes were gentle, concealing her inner turbulence. Any male, Indian or white, would consider her a breathtaking creature. Time had increased her beauty and shaped her body, as it had increased her sensual appetite and skill. Her body and mind were alive with need and she vowed she would not permit him to ignore or deny her when he came home! She would refresh his memory of the nights they had known together! As she swayed and dreamed with her eyes closed, her eagerness for Bright Arrow mounted and her annoyance with him disappeared.

Abruptly a dirty, moist hand clamped her lips and a strong arm securely banded her chest, pinning her arms to her sides and stifling her instinctive scream. Her eyes opened and her head jerked sideways in an attempt to see her attacker. She struggled futilely as the man's grip tightened unnecessarily. Terror seized and cleared her dreamy mind. She knew it was not her husband trying to teach her a lesson, for it was not his distinctive and heady odor which filled her nostrils. The stench of filthy clothes and a sweaty body warned her of danger. Her horror increased as her senses registered the presence of another male standing in the shadows, motioning for his partner to drag her into that stygian dimness where he seemed to lurk as Evil Incarnate.

Her heart pounded wildly, playing havoc with her wits and respiration. She kicked at the male behind her, though her bare feet caused him no pain. She squirmed feverishly to free herself from his grip, until his muffled threat stilled and silenced her.

"If'n you wants yore chilluns and half-breed man to keep safe, you best hold your tongue and arms mighty quiet, squaw," he warned ominously. "If'n yore pretty mouth brings anybody out that door, big er little, they's dead. You savvy?" he sneered, shaking her.

Rebecca nodded and complied with his frightening order, but her trembling legs balked as she was taken into the darkness of the trees. The foul-smelling villain chuckled wickedly as he detected her quivering. She heard him smack his lips in anticipation of some dark deed.

Once enclosed by the forest, his pudgy fingers released her. She was prevented from fleeing, for she was trapped in a triangle of two males and a sturdy pine. She stifled the shriek that tried to slip between her clenched teeth. Her children, her sweet and innocent girls, were in danger. With Bright Arrow gone, she knew she must protect them herself, but she was still too shocked and alarmed to think clearly or quickly.

"Billy Culpepper ain't lied, Jess; she's prettier 'an a flower in full bloom. Shame we got us 'mportant business in these here parts." As the man spoke, his left hand boldly moved over her breasts, halting to cup and squeeze each one in turn. "Don't you worry none, pretty squaw; we ain't here to hurt no one. Soon's we gits some of them yeller rocks, we'll be gone quicker 'an a rabbit outruns a hawk. You just do as yore told." Lester Paul was aroused by the beauty and allure of the young woman before him. His eyes glazed and his hands quivered with lust. "Course, if'n I had time, you might like what I has right here," he whispered close to her ear as he forced her hand to caress his hardened manhood. "I heard them half-red studs er somethin' to keep around if'n you got real fire in yore privates," he teased crudely. "Ain't that right?" he demanded, a nipple trapped between each of his thumbs and forefingers. Lester chuckled as she tried to shove away his hands. "A man don't take kindly to sharing his goods."

Rebecca remained stiff and alert, mentally cursing these two men and condemning them to death and Hell. But his words alerted her to his motive for being here tonight—robbery. She had feared that someone would come looking for them and the gold, but her husband had sworn he had never left a trail or clue for anyone to follow.

Who was this Culpepper who had told them about Bright Arrow, his family, and the gold? What would they do when they learned he wasn't home and she had no gold or valuables to give them? Obviously, they thought her husband was inside the cabin; that meant they had not ambushed him earlier to carry out their crime. What would they do if they learned that Clay Rivera was actually the exiled Sioux warrior Bright Arrow? Where was her husband when his family was in danger? Why had she rashly left the cabin? She anxiously waited and listened for a chance to escape.

"Jess, you go fetch that half-breed Rivera. If'n he wants his squaw returned, he'd best turn over his bags and tell us the location of his gold diggings. Cain't be much of a man anyways with that Spanish and Crow blood in 'im. Yep, we's gonna be rich men afore this night's o'er. You be careful now. Some men don't hold they's squaws high. Course this'un's somethin' to fight and die fur. If'n we hafta, we'll plug 'em all and take ever nugget," the man stated coldly, although Rebecca didn't believe they would actually carry out such pernicious threats, which surely had been spoken to terrorize and intimidate her.

"Listen 'ere, Lester Paul, don't be sending me into a dark cabin. This here's yore plan; you take the cabin while I holds this she-cat. You know them Crow snakes is sneaky," Jess argued tensely. "You remember what Culpepper tol' us? Clay Rivera nearly chopped off his hand when he tried to sneak just one gold nugget off his pile."

"Billy Culpepper's a fool, Jess. He's tough and sly, but he gave Rivera the drop on 'im. You know them crazy ideas he has. 'Sides, we got us something to trade," he remarked smugly as he pinched her cheeks. He laughed as she winced and jerked away. "These here hands are gonna be touchin' gold or blood before I leave," he vowed irritably.

"What if'n it's yore blood?" Jess speculated. "What's Martha gonna do then? You's the leader; you fetch 'im."

It was plain to Rebecca that at least the younger man was afraid of "Clay." And she prayed that the other was more talk than action. Unfortunately, Rebecca had been away from civilization too long, and she had forgotten the depth of some men's evil and brutality.

"You yeller, Jess Thomas? He's got babies and his woman to protect. He ain't gonna fight us. Git going, boy. We got us a long ride. Think of all the women and whiskey we kin buy with his gold," Lester hinted to sway his partner, whom Lester knew to be somewhat lacking in intelligence. Lester had seen the sullen Rivera in a fight at the trading post, and he wanted no part of him.

Rebecca didn't know what to think about these two ruffians and her unpredictable situation. It would be foolish to call their bluff and behave boldly. If she were careful not to provoke them to violence, she might compel them to back down and leave. Was there any remote chance of persuading them to alter their iniquitous plan? What if she made matters worse? Everything hinged on how these villains would react. She realized that men so close to the edge of lust, greed, and cruelty shouldn't be pushed over the precipice without careful deliberation. She couldn't bear for her children to be harmed or frightened. She was determined to discover the best way to handle this precarious situation, and until then, she would merely watch and wait.

Rebecca suddenly recalled the extent of some men's base natures and evil acts from days long past. If these men were ensnared by wickedness, she was doomed to face it. Yet, if there were a small light hidden in this dark moment, she would try to seek it out and reveal their sins to them. The beast called Lester seemed to enjoy ordering women around and fully expected to be obeyed without question or resistance. She promptly concluded that arrogance and boldness on her part would be unwise. Even so, she couldn't behave as a terrified, weak-willed, groveling female, or Lester's sense of power over her would increase. She had to walk an extremely fine line. If she physically fought him, he would become rougher with her. For now, she had to ignore his gropings and insults. If at all possible, she would use logic and reasoning to end this matter. Often ruffians were confused and rebuffed by genteel ladies . . .

She decided to use partial truth and an unspoken plea for mercy. Her goal was to protect her children. No matter how much she despised being touched and intimidated, it was vital that she appear calm and pleasant, as if in control of this ominous situation. Perhaps her mood and manner would take them off guard and she could escape, for they wouldn't be expecting such behavior.

Using her most educated and ladylike tone, she told them, "My husband is hunting and trading near the Black Hills. Clay trades furs to the Cheyenne for the gold, but they'll only give him a small bag once a year. He doesn't know where they get it, so he couldn't tell you even if he were home. We've used all of it, and we're almost out of supplies. He's gone to trade all of last winter's furs for more gold or food." Her tone became firm as she stated, "Don't go in that cabin and frighten my children. If you have any God-fearing decency, you'll leave us alone. And I'm not a squaw; I'm white," she announced fiercely, hoping that this news would inspire a change of heart if they bore ill feelings toward Indians. Her voice had not exposed her panic or lies, and it was obvious that her news didn't sit well with either man.

"You 'ear that, Lester?" Jess stormed angrily. "We done come all this way for nuthin'. Now how we's gonna git rich? We cain't ride into no Cheyenne camp," he scoffed. "I said it was a dumb plan. Let's git outta here afore someone comes."

The wily Lester was deep in thought. He casually asked, "When's yore man coming back? When'd he leave?"

Rebecca didn't want them hanging around waiting for her husband's return, which she assumed they wouldn't do if they believed he would be gone for many days. Jess's voice and reaction gave her hope, for he had sounded ready and eager to give up and depart. She pressed her presumed advantage. "Early this morning. I suppose he'll be gone for a week," she replied carefully. "We're poor folks, Lester. We have nothing worth stealing. You can't harm little children."

"What'cha think, Jess? Think we should leave empty-handed?" he asked, winking surreptitiously at his disgruntled cohort.

"She said she don't have nuthin' worth nuthin', Lester. I ain't killin' no woman and babies, least not if'n they ain't Injuns." He chuckled and his eyes rolled dreamily, as if recalling some exciting event.

Rebecca almost sighed aloud with relief. Surely she had reached that tiny spot of conscience and had won her battle. She cautioned herself not to say or do anything to tarnish her success. She patiently waited for Lester to agree and order their departure. He did neither.

"I say she's got somethin' worth somethin'," Lester announced, grinning lewdly at Rebecca. "If'n she's so poor, we'll just put our best treasure in her little bag," he suggested, stroking his erect maleness. "Yep, we'll just make a little trade—their lives for a little fun and relief. You 'member when we caught us that Pawnee squaw? Boy, was she e'r a fighter, but good on them blankets. She had nice tits like these. What a good time we had us! And that squaw got to liking it. Took us three days to tire her. Martha don't hafta know about men's dealings. I ain't sent you down no wrong path yet. Old Clay ain't here to stop us. You want some of this squaw?" he enticed his friend, yanking Rebecca's arms behind her and holding them at an angle that made her full, firm breasts jut out temptingly.

Rebecca had gone rigid and pale. She now realized that these disgusting men, especially the nefarious leader, were not going to withdraw peacefully. She was alone, at their mercy and whims. She squirmed in Lester's iron grip and shrieked, "Let go of me, you sorry bastard! My husband will kill you for this!"

Lester howled with amusement, knowing she was helpless. "Feel them soft tits, Jess," he coaxed, a fiery wildness controlling his senses.

As the lusty episode with the Pawnee woman flashed through Jess's mind, spittle left the corner of his wide mouth and eased down his chin. His eyes were large and glittery with eagerness. He wiped the saliva away before it could drip onto his dirty shirt, then fondled her breasts as gently as if they were made of some fragile material. Touching her kindled his blinding passion and his emotions quickly shifted from apprehension to lust. "Kin I be first this time?" he asked, sounding like a child speaking of a harmless game. "You always git the best part. Let me take her down first. I know lots of tricks. After I take my piece, I'll git her ready and begging fur you."

"You wouldn't dare harm me!" Rebecca screamed, her terror mounting. "I have children inside that cabin. Only an animal would do such an evil thing," she bravely reasoned, yanking free.

Jess's mood was revealed when he grinned and barked like a wild dog, then panted comically. Lester seized her arms and cruelly pinned them behind her before she could flee or gain any advantage. When she tried to knee Jess in the groin, he threatened maliciously, "Fur every time you hurt me balls and stick, I'll make another cut on one of them half-red nits inside. You gonna fight me?" he snarled.

Lester answered for her. "I bet she's gonna be nice to us, Jess, even nicer'n that Pawnee whore. She don't want her babies all cut up. And she ain't gonna scream and bring 'em out here to watch Mama get rammed by two horny stags." He turned to Rebecca and continued, "It's been a long time since we had us a female, 'specially a good looker like you. Ole Jess here has a bad temper when he's riled. He don't like folks refusin' us nothin'," he informed her with a cruel laugh. "She's gonna let us take our fill and be on our way without no trouble. Right, squaw?" When she didn't respond, Lester demanded, "You best do as told, woman, or I'll head inside that cabin and bring out somethin' to convince you."

Rebecca knew if either man entered the cabin the truth of her children's parentage would be revealed, for all three girls were unmistakably Indian in looks and coloring. She had to keep them out, no matter what. "I don't trust you, you varmits," she gasped, struggling to gain time.

"And we don't trust you, Ma'am. We ain't leaving here without some reward fur our troubles. I give you my word we'll leave after you let us take our fill. 'Sides, we kin do as we please without your say. Course if we gits mad, we could be rough on ever'one."

"Reward?" she sneered sarcastically. "I should reward you for trying to rob us and attack me? Like a fool, I should believe you?" she scoffed, stalling for time to plan, time for her husband to return.

The evil-minded Lester drawled, "We's taking your word about no gold inside. We gotta be paid some way. Like Jess said, we don't kill females er little'uns, less theys savages. But we don't mind hurtin' 'em a bit to gits our way. Ole Jess here's nice unless you goes against us and our wants." He clasped one of her hands over his stiff manhood and the other one over Jess's matching condition. Then he informed her, "And right now, we wants these hards to go real soft and happy. Then we'll just mount up and be gone, real friendly like. We won't even wait on old Clay to return with the gold. Might be best fur all of us if'n he don't know how you paid us to leave his family alive. What'cha say, woman? Won't take long. We got us a deal?"

Rebecca's eyes eased over the man called Jess. She marked his age at a little over twenty. He was tall and lanky, but surprisingly strong. His dull brown hair hadn't been washed, combed, or cut in months, and his wide mouth exposed bad teeth and a lecherous grin. Oddly, it appeared he had shaven within the last two weeks, yet the garments he wore were ragged and smelly. Rebecca saw in his light-colored eyes a weakness of character that could easily lead him down a path of crime. Once Jess had understood they had the upper hand, all fear and hesitation had vanished. Standing before her now, he seemed to possess no morals or kindness. He would obey Lester's orders and heed the sexual urgings of his body.

She focused her attention on Lester. She estimated he was about nine inches over five feet, only three inches taller than Rebecca. As she observed his girth, she decided she could almost consider him fat. Dark, wet stains at his armpits revealed his previous exertions in the heat, as did the moisture gleaming on his face. His jowls moved as if he were chewing a cud. Lester's pale complexion was presently flushed pink, and she couldn't determine his age, for his face was boyish and his thinning hair had streaks of gray at the temples. His nose and lips were large, but his eyes brought tremors to her very soul. They were stone cold.

Without a doubt, Lester Paul was a mean and immoral man. Although stocky and short, he had bullish strength, and she knew he was not adverse to using it on her or her children. She could not trust him, for she felt he would not leave witnesses to his cruel acts of greed and lust. She wisely realized that Jess would do almost anything Lester suggested, but she sensed that Jess had a violent, crazy streak in him, and an unpredictable male was more dangerous than a menacing one like Lester. Rebecca was repulsed by both men, and she felt she would rather die than submit to either of them. She had made love to only one man—Bright Arrow. Until recently, those times had been filled with passion, love, and pleasure. If these dirty beasts touched her, would she ever be clean again? She could not allow them to invade her body, to stain her soul. Somehow, she had to catch them off guard. They had to be foiled or killed . . .

"You trying to pull some trick on us?" Lester questioned as she remained silent and pensive, though eyeing them keenly.

"How could I possibly defeat two strong men?" she responded softly. "If Jess is going to be first, we could place his bedroll over there," she suggested timidly, pointing to a thick growth of trees. "It would be easier for me in the dark," she suggested cleverly. She had to separate them, to disarm the most deadly one! Then she would be able to sneak back into the cabin, bolt the door and obtain a weapon.

For a few minutes, Lester Paul and Jess Thomas debated who was going to have Rebecca first. She dared not run toward the cabin, knowing they could overtake her before she reached the door and bolted it. She would have to be clever and patient. Her anger and apprehension gave her courage and willpower. As she listened to the men argue over their imminent rape, rage burned brighter and brighter within her. All fear was seared away, leaving only confidence and determination.

When it appeared that Lester was winning their argument, Rebecca intervened. Such precarious times called for desperate and daring measures. She asked demurely,

"Who was first the last time?" When Jess quickly told her it was Lester, she asked, "And the time before that?" She knew the answers before Jess spoke them aloud. It was evident that Lester gave the orders and Jess normally followed them. Smiling innocently at Jess, she concluded, "Then it seems fair for Jess to be first this time. You promised you won't hurt me, so I'll trust you." Having felt both men's grips, she knew Jess would be easier to battle. She was amused and astonished by the effect of her silky voice and radiant smile on the dim-witted Jess. Even so, she realized he would never free her or help her fight Lester.

Lester's eyes narrowed. He glared coldly and vengefully at Rebecca, who pretended not to notice his silent threat. She had won; Jess refused to yield to Lester's demands for the first time in their relationship. "Go on then! But don't take too long or I'll toss you off 'er," Lester growled. "I'll wait me turn," he said, his tone implying more to her.

While Jess was fetching his sleeping roll, Lester snarled, "Think you's smart, don't you? You cain't turn Jess 'gainst me."

Rebecca craftily smiled at Lester and boldly placed her hand upon his barrel chest. She whispered softly as if to prevent Jess from hearing her words. "The best should always come last, Lester, like dessert. He's only a boy. I'm sure you know more about pleasuring a woman than he does. Let him ease his needs; he'll be quick. Then we can take our time. You just wait here and I'll give Jess a good time . . . But a fast one," she crooned provocatively, smiling at him once more.

"Yep, just like I thought, fire in them regions," he jested, rubbing one hand over her furry mound through her dress as the other caressed her right buttock. He was pleased when she groaned softly and arched toward him. His eyes sparkled with eagerness and merriment as he taunted, "I got you hot just touchin' you. That breed of yours ain't no good or he cain't give you enough."

"He got hurt in May, strained himself there. He can't . . . you know, Lester," she hinted saucily, lowering her lashes flirtatiously. "I'm glad you came by while he's gone. A woman doesn't see a real man out here often. It gets lonely while he's gone. He's been talking about moving closer to the settlement. If he does, we might be able to see each other on the sly. That is, if you don't have a woman who keeps you too busy or too tired. This Martha that Jess mentioned? Think you can keep us both satisfied?" she brazenly asked, working on his immense ego.

"No woman's enough fur Lester Paul. 'Cept you might be. Martha Thomas has just as many rocks in 'er head as her brother Jess. It makes Jess happy fur me to see his sister. I been planning to rid myself of both of 'em. Me and you got some plans to make. You git Jess to be quick. He's young and won't last long if you work on him good. I'll be ready fur you when you finish him off."

Rebecca nodded as if in full agreement. She knew she had this lecherous, vain creature fooled. She forced herself to endure his gropings but prayed he wouldn't try to steal a kiss. If he did, she would surely be sick. Fortunately Jess returned at that moment. Winking conspiratorially at her, Lester dropped his hands to his sides, anticipating a lusty bout with her soon. He sat down and leaned against a tree, drinking from the whiskey botle which Jess had given him.

Rebecca led Jess into the thick cluster of cottonwoods where Bright Arrow had discarded the rocks from his last campfire. She told him to spread out the sleeping roll and undress. Jess was too excited to obey her instructions. He insisted on unbuttoning her dress and removing it. "I wants a good look at'cha afore we lays down."

Rebecca stifled her pride and controlled her anger. She couldn't reach one of the rocks in the bushes until they were on the mat. Even though she was close to a weapon, she dared not act rashly and risk being bound. While Jess was distracted, she would seize one and clobber him senseless. Then she could sneak through the dark treeline and return to the cabin by the other side. There she would get a weapon to use on Lester if he followed her.

Jess called joyously as he removed the dress, "She's naked under this dress, Lester. Look at them beauts."

Because of the heat in the cabin, Rebecca had not worn anything beneath the dress. She had no choice but to suffer through Jess's stares and touches. She gritted her teeth in revulsion when he spread kisses over her breasts, then fastened his mouth to one nipple and sucked noisily on it. "Lawd, she tastes good, Lester," he called out as he moved to her other breast. When Rebecca didn't struggle with him, he told Lester, "She's ready and willing, Lester. She wants this, man."

In the full moonlight, Rebecca could watch Lester through the leaves, but Lester could not see them in the dark shadows. She saw Lester grin each time Jess whistled or spoke. She knew Lester was becoming highly aroused by the way he was fondling himself through his pants. To cover her impending attack on Jess, she pretended to send Lester verbal clues. "I'm giving him a good time like I promised, Lester. He's burning for me over here."

As Jess's hands started to wander over her body from the neck down, he declared hoarsely, "I don't think I kin go long, Lester. Hell, I ain't never been first."

Rebecca eyed the effect of that confession on Lester. The stocky beast smiled and licked his lips hungrily. He relaxed and drank his whiskey, feeling he would soon be busy.

Wanting to end this as quickly as she could, she anxiously suggested they lay down and get comfortable. Instead, Jess's hand slipped into her dark triangle as his mouth locked on her breast again. He teased the nipples with his tongue and teeth. His forefinger wiggled back and forth across the peak between her legs. Clearly Jess wasn't as naive as she had believed. From the way he used his hands and lips, he knew how to satisfy a woman and seemed set on arousing and pleasuring her! She knew she was right when he murmured huskily, "I been taught a woman gives good as she gits. Martha showed me all about girls and what they likes. She learned me all the tricks and let me practice on her all the time. Martha said it was important to make a woman crazy with yore hands and mouth. Then she'd do anything fur him and wouldn't never cast eyes on another man."

Rebecca felt ill at his incestuous confessions. He bragged, "I knows a woman's body better'n the trails around 'ere. You just relax and enjoy ole Jess's tricks. Lester's big and mean down there and hurts most women; that's why I wanted you first. By the time I git 'em after him, they's no good. I can't even make 'em crazy for me."

When Jess's slobbery mouth began to slip down her flat stomach, Rebecca was alarmed. She had to halt his ravishment. "My legs are cramping, Jess. I'm nervous about this. May I lay down?" she entreated.

"Go on. I'll shuck these pants and boots," he told her. "Then I'll make you relax and feel real good," he promised with a sly laugh.

Rebecca lay upon the sleeping mat which reeked of his foul scent. She spread her long, thick hair around her head on the rough material. Her hand secretly eased into the bushes and withdrew a heavy rock. She knew that the only way she could silence his shriek when she struck his head was by using her mouth. The thought of kissing Jess nauseated her, but it had to be done. She waited stiff and silent, the rock hidden beneath her flowing mane of auburn hair. Her timing had to be perfect. If she missed or didn't strike him hard enough . . .

The naked Jess sat down near her waist, content to stare at her for a few moments. "What's yore name?"

"Rebecca," she replied just above a whisper, watching him carefully and intently. "You won't hurt me, will you, Jess?" she pleaded as if frightened and shy.

"Yore beautiful, Rebecca. I wish I could takes you with me, but I ain't got no home. Since Ma and Pa died, Martha lives in a saloon. I just travels with Lester. I'm sorry Lester's gonna hurt you, but I'll take care of you after he finishes."

Rebecca stared at this crazy man. He wouldn't defend her or prevent Lester's assault, but he would doctor her later! What an odd sense of loyalty. Rebecca quelled her repulsion and smiled at him. "I'm lucky you came with him, Jess. Thank you." Rebecca decided she could muffle his outcry better if his mouth was filled with a breast and she was making passionate sounds. Her vision would also be clear for her attack. Lester would think she was only trying to stimulate Jess into a quick release! She summoned her courage and denied all pride. "You really know how to make a woman feel good, Jess. Would you . . . would you do it some more?" she encouraged.

As Jess began to feast ravenously upon her breasts and to labor skillfully at her womanhood with his deft hand, she writhed and moaned. She could hear Lester's chuckles over her sounds of passion. Jess was grunting and lapping noisily, believing he was inflaming her body and mind. When he shifted to enter her, Rebecca pleaded for a little more pleasure first. Rebecca's left hand went to the back of his head and crushed it against her firm mound as if mutely instructing him to work more swiftly and roughly. Jess was so involved in his actions that he didn't notice when she lifted her hand with the heavy rock. As she slammed the rock against his head, she sent forth a moan of ecstasy and said loudly, "Oh, Jess, you're so-o-o-o good. More . . . faster . . . yes . . ." Thankfully, he had gone limp without a sound. As she bound Jess with his shirt, she let her voice trail off to little moans and enticing words and finally to silence. Little did Lester know she was gasping with fear and moaning over the abominations she had undergone with Jess. She grabbed her dress and slipped into the woods behind her. She had to hurry.

Just as Rebecca reached the other side of the cabin and was sneaking down its side to await a chance to bolt toward the door and safety, Lester called out, "You two 'bout finished over there?"

Silence came back to him, and he called out once more. Rebecca was poised and ready to run the moment Lester stepped into the trees to check on them.

Realizing it wasn't sex that was keeping Jess silent, he lifted his gun and cautiously entered the dark shadows. Rebecca was inside the cabin with the door bolted and barred before Lester found Jess bound and unconscious, bleeding heavily. She hastily checked the windows to make certain they were barred securely. Then she took the gun and waited for Lester's reaction.

Recalling the axe which Bright Arrow used for

chopping wood, she quickly looked toward the corner, relieved to find it resting there. Hopefully Lester and Jess wouldn't have an axe with them, an axe which could chop through a door or window. Rebecca was trembling; she was terrified. She knew what Lester would do to her if he got his hands on her. Worse, she imagined what he might do to her children.

Suddenly she realized that she was naked and her body was moist. She shivered uncontrollably. Hastily she filled a basin and scrubbed off Jess's saliva and her perspiration. She pulled on a thin cotton chemise and bloomers, then covered them with an old, worn, faded calico dress. She listened and waited but nothing happened. She wondered if Jess was injured badly, then decided she didn't care, for his survival gave her two enemies rather than one. She hated those two men, and she despised what she had been forced to endure for the privilege of living past this fateful night. She was only grateful that the children were sleeping peacefully, unaware of the danger.

By midnight, Rebecca didn't know what her two attackers were doing or plotting. She shuddered at her harrowing experience, one she feared wasn't over yet . . .

Chapter Two

Hours drifted by slowly as Rebecca sat huddled in a chair at the small table, a gun before her. Her tawny gaze flickered from one barred window to the next, then over to the cabin door. She prayed there was no way those devils could get to her and her children, and she tried to force memories of their lecherous pawing from her mind. Every so often, a shudder raced over her stress-dampened body. Although her respiration came in short, jerky gasps, she was too frightened and numbed to cry. She glanced over at her girls sleeping on wooden bunks, relieved they had not awakened during the commotion.

She wondered why Lester had failed to react to her escape, as only silence greeted her strained ears. She knew that Lester must be furious, for she had sensed the evil and cruelty in him. And why Bright Arrow hadn't returned still remained a mystery. Had he unsuspectingly come across Lester and Jess lying in wait for him? Something must be terribly wrong, she suspected, or he would be home where he was needed.

One lantern cast its soft glow in the warm cabin. Fortunately, during her misadventure the open door had allowed some of the cabin's heat to be exchanged for cooler night air. There was no light coming down the chimney or through any tiny cracks around the windows, and she prayed for morning, hoping those men would be afraid to perform their satanic evil in God's light. She prayed also that they could not get inside and harm her family, and for her love's safety and return. She hoped that Lester and Jess had regretted their hasty actions and had left. But what if they were lurking outside, waiting to pounce on her the moment she rashly opened the door or a window? She realized she dare not move until her husband returned.

At dawn, Rebecca jumped when she heard a light tapping on the cabin door. Gun in hand, she hurried over and pressed her ear to it. Lester spoke calmly, "Rebecky, open this door and take yore medicine. If'n you kilt Jess acause he wuz hurting you, I'll be of a mind to let it pass. You done set this fire in me groin and you gots to put it out afore I kin forgive you fur trickin' me. We best finish our business afore your man returns and I hafta kill him. Them younguns needs theys papa and mama. You best pay me fur his life and yorn, then I'll be on my way. You got me word I won't hurt you none," he declared, his voice slurred from heavy drinking.

Rebecca listened without replying, her silence increasing his fury. "You hear me in there, squaw? I'll not leave afore you pays me my due. I'm gonna have you, woman, all I wants. Did ole Jess git his afore you kilt him? You cain't stay locked up fur long. You best do right by me afore I gits madder. I'll leave yore chillens be if you open this door pronto. Speak up, Rebecky," he demanded fiercely.

Lester gave her five minutes to think. When she failed to respond, he issued more threats and warnings, then gave her another five minutes to reconsider her position. Still, Rebecca remained speechless. She wasn't going to bargain for her life with a malicious drunk. She recalled how he had crudely fondled her womanly parts, and fury consumed her as she remembered having to endure his repulsive handling. He had the nerve and stupidity to think she would open this door and subject herself to more humiliation. If she were alone, she knew she would bravely open the door and kill the villainous bastard!

Lester banged on the cabin door, cursing her and describing horrible tortures she would undergo when she became his captive. He vowed to remain there until he had administered his particular brand of justice; he promised to slay her husband if he showed his face; he warned her of the consequences of no food, water, and air. Suddenly, she was all too aware of her sorry state.

The loud hammering of balled fists on the door aroused the children. They were confused, then frightened. Little Feet and Moon Eyes were old enough to realize that some evil force was trying to break into their home. They cried for their father, and Rebecca was unable to console them. Their fears mounted when Lester began a routine of beating on the door and windows every hour and shouting dire threats.

Lester knew he was terrifying the children, and he enjoyed their cries and screams. He realized the best way to get to Rebecca was through her children. He concluded that she would be forced to open the door when the cabin air became suffocating, or when they needed water for survival. For certain, he surmised, she couldn't remain inside for a week. He had enough supplies to outwait that sneaky bitch. Not that he cared so much about the attack on Jess, but she had tempted him and played him for a fool. He couldn't get her feel and smell out of his mind. She had become an obsession to him, one he resolved to conquer.

By nightfall, Lester was as hot and as frustrated as Rebecca. She had made no response to Lester and had tried to calm her girls by playing hand games with them. She had used the last of her firewood to cook a soup consisting of dried meat and vegetables. The cabin was insufferably hot once more, yet she dared not bathe the children's sweaty bodies or flushed faces to cool them, for her water was very low and had to be conserved for drinking. She had no idea how long Lester would continue his malicious siege, and she was growing weary of telling her girls, "He'll be home soon," each time they asked about their missing father. She feared her thoughts about Bright Arrow and his reason for delay. No matter how he felt, she couldn't believe he would ever desert them this way.

At last, the girls were so fatigued from the heat and crying that they fell asleep, and Rebecca suddenly realized that Lester had not pounded on her door for over two hours. It was past eleven.

Rebecca resumed her position at the eating table, as if standing guard could prevent future peril. Exhausted, she closed her burning eyes and dozed for several hours. When she awoke, she wondered why she was sitting in a chair with her head resting on the table. Slowly, the ghastly memories returned. She stood up and stretched her stiff body. Without a view of the moon, she couldn't determine what hour it was, but she knew it was still night and assumed Lester was still outside. She walked over to check on her children. Little Feet was awake, lying rigid and wide eyed, Moon Eyes was tossing restlessly, and Tashina was serenely asleep.

Rebecca smiled at her oldest daughter and reached for her. Before she could collect the child in her arms, Lester began to walk around the cabin, beating on the door and windows with a heavy wooden club. Little Feet squealed in panic and hid beneath the cover. The combined noises awoke the other two girls, and all burst into tears and shrieks. Nothing she could say or do would calm them.

Rebecca silently cursed Lester. She raced toward the window he was striking and yelled at him to stop. Lester laughed coldly and loudly, increasing the force of his blows. Distressed over her children's panic, Rebecca raced from one barred surface to the next, pleading with Lester to cease his cruelty and to leave them in peace.

Lester replied, "I ain't stopping or leaving 'til you pays me." This time his tone was stony and sober.

"I owe you nothing, you beast! Go away! When Br— Clay returns, he'll kill you for this!" She wished she had the courage to inform Lester that her husband was a fierce Sioux warrior and that his father was none other than the awesome and feared Chief Gray Eagle. But she knew she couldn't allow anyone to learn their true identity for future safety.

"Yore man ain't coming home. Jess and me done waylaid him. He won't be home 'til them wounds heal. That tale of gold was just a trick to git you to bed us," Lester lied, though Rebecca sensed his deceit. "How much food and water you got left for them younguns, woman? Ain't it gittin' mighty hot in there? Theys sounds mighty hungry and sceered to me. Why don't we end this showdown?"

"You're a thief and a liar, Lester! I know what you'll do the minute I open this door. If necessary, my girls and I will stay here until we're nothing but bones. I promise you'll pay at Clay's hands if you harm any of us!" Rebecca tried to retain a clear head and use words which wouldn't overly alarm her girls, but it was hard to think when she was so fatigued and frightened.

"Me temper is wearin' out, woman. If'n this door ain't open soon, you'll all be dead. I gives my word you'll be alive when I leaves."

Rebecca refused to carry on any kind of conversation with the black-hearted demon, and that day and the next passed in a similar pattern. Lester continued with his imposing threats and actions. The heat in the cabin increased, the tepid water was depleted, what little food that she had left was inedible without cooking, and she had no wood. She had broken up a chair, but it would not burn, and she knew the beds and table would be no different. She needed brush or kindling. Even if she burned all of their clothes, there wasn't enough to keep a fire going long enough to ignite the wood or to cook a meal. It seemed hopeless.

The children fretted until they were weak from heat and the lack of food and liquid. Drenched in perspiration, they lay quiet and listless on their beds. Rebecca was worried about them, for she hadn't honestly believed Lester would remain outside this long. She attempted to rethink her position, but her mind was groggy and her stomach was pleading for nourishment. She even lacked the body moisture to cry.

Three days and nights had passed; they were wearily entering a fourth night of terror. The sealed cabin was like a brick oven, the inner heat of which increased each day. Her children were suffering and possibly dying. Rebecca didn't know what to do next. She was so exhausted that she couldn't even remain furious. One way or another, the situation would be fatal. It simply remained to be seen for whom.

Lester knocked on one of the side windows. "Rebecky, you wants some fresh water?" he taunted, then tossed the life-sustaining fluid on the cabin wall. A few drops entered cracks and rolled down the inside surface. Helplessly, she witnessed the vindictive sight. She heard

Lester smacking his lips as he described his meal of fried salt pork, corn pones, and black coffee, all of which she could smell, though her mouth was too dry to form saliva.

Rebecca decided that Lester must be tired, for he was quiet throughout the night. With certainty, she realized he would not give up his evil quest until he won or they were dead. She was tempted to open one window for fresh air and to sneak out for water, but she rejected her plan. Lester could be anticipating such an act by a mother desperate to save her children. If only she could be positive that Lester wouldn't hurt her girls. . . .

By morning of the fourth day, the children couldn't talk or cry with their dry throats and parched lips. Rebecca couldn't even tell them everything would be all right, for she was filled with doubt. All three girls were steadily weakening, and it ripped at her heart. She was assailed by dry sobs when she thought of her alternatives—to have the children die in their sleep or to have them watch their mother raped, tortured, and possibly murdered.

Could she allow her children to suffer and die? Could she trust Lester to spare them if she yielded to his savage desires? Clearly Bright Arrow was dead, or else he would have returned by now. Could she live without him, with the blood of her girls on her hands? No matter what she did, she was doomed.

The next time Lester banged on the door, she called out to him in a cracked voice. "Lester! Do you promise to leave my girls unharmed if I come out?"

Lester halted his patrol around the cabin and lowered his club. Leaning against the door, he grinned wickedly. "You giving up, Rebecky?" he asked playfully, astonished by her surrender.

"If you'll give my children some water and food and promise not to harm them, I'll . . . unlock the door and come out."

Lester glanced toward the woods and opened his mouth to speak, then fell silent with a deceitful smile. "Yep. I'll fetch some water and put it by the door. You open up and gits some fresh air inside. I'll hafta be taking me pleasure afore you cooks 'em food. I hasta make sure you don't cross me again. While I rest, you kin feed 'em."

"They need food now, Lester. They're very weak. Please," she hoarsely beseeched him. "I promise, no tricks."

"I don't hold to hurting little ones. I'll fetch food and water. You gives 'em some air. Then me and you gonna have some fun. You try anything crazy and I'll wring ever'body's necks."

Rebecca listened cautiously, but she couldn't hear anything. She walked over to the bunks where her girls were dozing. None of them stirred as she kissed each forehead lightly. Returning to the cabin door, she summoned her lagging courage and strength, lifted the bar, and slid it aside. She inhaled deeply, then slowly released the used air. She picked up a sharp hunting knife and concealed it at her side in the folds of her dress. Placing her hand on the bolt, she closed her eyes and prayed one last time.

When the bolt was released, she waited to see if Lester would rush inside and attack her. He didn't. She slowly, reluctantly opened the door. Gripping the knife handle tightly, she looked outside but saw nothing unusual. She stepped into the sunlight, catching a glimpse of Lester to her right from the corner of her eye. She whirled and stabbed him in the chest before he could seize her. Shock registered on his plump face as he glanced down at the painful gash pulsing blood. Before he could react, she stabbed him again. He staggered and swayed, still finding her daring attack incredible.

"You sneaking whore," he sneered faintly. As his hand reached out toward her, she clenched her teeth and drove the blade deep into his heart. Lester grabbed her wrist as he fell, carrying her to the hard ground with him. Almost instantly he went limp. He was dead.

Rebecca pushed herself to her knees and gaped at the grisly sight. Three wounds were bleeding profusely. It was difficult for her to believe she had slain two men. As she wiped her bloody hands on her dress, she swallowed with difficulty, fearing she'd be sick. Dazedly she struggled to her feet and looked toward the cabin. Lester hadn't brought food or water, the vicious lying beast! she angrily concluded.

Rebecca knew she had to get nourishing broth and water for her girls, and in a hurry. Her own strength was vanishing rapidly. She went inside for a bucket, then headed for the nearby stream, stumbling and falling several times in her weakened condition. She ignored her scratched knees and hands, the buzzing in her ears, and her clammy skin. When she reached the stream, she splashed water on her face, neck, and arms to revive herself, then lifted her brimming bucket and headed for the cabin, commanding her feet to move steadily and her head to unfog. She refused to look in the direction of Lester's body. If anyone deserved death, it was Lester Paul!

Upon entering the cabin, she placed the bucket on the floor, then worked feverishly and desperately to unbar and open all the windows. Although it was hot outside, the heat inside the cabin needed to escape and be replaced with fresh air. She decided she would take the girls to the stream as soon as they were fed and would submerge their fiery bodies in the water to refresh them.

Needing wood, she went to the rear of the cabin where Bright Arrow had stacked it on either side of the rock chimney. She encouraged herself to work more swiftly, but she was so tired and weak. She knew she had to complete her tasks before she fainted from hunger and weakness. With arms loaded, she headed around the side and halted abruptly, dropping the wood. She gaped at the man who had stepped around the corner of the cabin and was blocking her path. He was supposed to be dead! He should be dead! He must be dead!

Petrified, she couldn't move or scream as her startled gaze fused with Jess Thomas's icy glare. His head was bandaged. His shirt was stained with his blood—blood for which she was responsible. White faced and shaking, she began to back away from the intimidating figure.

Jess's eyes narrowed and stared, but he remained motionless. "You done killed my friend whilst I was sleeping. Lester said you wouldn't come out if'n I was knowed I was alive. Why'd you try to kills me? Yore a bad woman, Rebecca. You ain't planning on leavin' yore babies in my gentle, sweet hands, is you?" he taunted.

Rebecca swayed against the wooden surface. She was trapped once more. Tears flowed down her pale face as she asked, "Why are you doing this to us, Jess? We've never harmed anyone. I agreed to open the door and let him do whatever he wished. Lester tried to kill me. He told me you were dead. He was going to get rid of you after he got the gold. He told me to trick you. I'm begging you to go away and leave us alone. My girls are weak and sick. They're dying, Jess. I need to take care of them. Please," she urged pitifully.

The man's expression never changed. "I'm gonna

punish you. I was real good to you, and you played me wrong. Come here, bitch," he ordered ominously. "If'n you don't, I'm heading inside that cabin."

There was no one to rescue them. There was nothing she could do to save herself or her children. If she tried to use one of the logs as a weapon, Jess would rush into the cabin and carry out his threat. By dusk, her family would be dead. Mentally and physically exhausted, she lost all hope and spirit and courage. She felt it was futile to resist.

Rebecca inhaled raggedly, then sluggishly walked toward Jess. She sensed he was going to kill her, murder her without ravishing her. She knew it would serve no purpose to apologize to him, to plead for mercy and understanding. Her heart lurched as she noticed what he was holding in his left hand at his side—the bloody knife with which she had slain his friend Lester. Her eyes returned to his and silently begged for the mercy which her words could not obtain.

She stepped before Jess. Roughly he placed his hand at her throat and pinned her against the wall. For a time he was satisfied to observe her beauty and her terror and, as he did, Rebecca cursed Bright Arrow's tribe, for their banishment had lead to this. She cursed Bright Arrow for deserting his family, and she prayed for the survival of her children. Anxiously, she waited for her death.

Jess raised his arm ominously. The bloodied knife glistened in the sunlight. Jess howled like a frenzied wolf, then put his nose to hers and disclosed, "When I finish you off, squaw, I'm gonna put yore body in that cabin and burn all you red nits to ashes. All we wanted wuz gold to build a home. Lester wuz gonna marry my sister. We wuz gonna be a family. You done spoiled ever'thing. You gotta pay fur killing him. 'Sides, Lester was gonna burn all you-ins anyway after he had his go atcha."

Jess's hand tightened on her throat, cutting off her air. Her vision blurred as she recalled seeing brush dropped around the cabin. She had been too distracted then for its meaning to sink into her dazed mind. As dry as the weather and cabin were, a fire would burn quickly and easily. Her babies burned alive . . . ! Instinctively her hands clawed at his as she discovered her new strength and courage from deep within. But he was too strong and she was too weak. His chilling laughter was the last thing Rebecca heard as blackness surrounded and claimed her.

Chapter Three

Just before leaving the covering of dense trees, the bronze-skinned figure halted to tie the reins of his newly purchased horse to a bush near the stream where the animal could graze and drink after their long ride. Each new journey fatigued him more than the last one, he mused. He had been unhappy for a long time and had become lazy and indifferent. He faced the fact that he had changed greatly, changed for the worse. He grimaced in annoyance as his fingers seized the fat around his waist and squeezed it. Years ago, he had ridden for days without trouble; now, two hours on a horse and he was sore and stiff! He could flex his body and hardly raise a muscle to attention! He was as weak as a woman or an old man.

As he considered his mental and physical condition, Bright Arrow's brow furrowed in shame. What had stolen his keen mind? When had his body turned traitor on him? When had he lost his strength, his vigor, his virility? He winced at that last thought.

Stepping into the clearing, his dark eyes clouded with confusion and shock. A white man was strangling his wife! And where were his children? Because his sharp brain had dulled, he stood spellbound for an instant. Why was he watching this battle and doing nothing? Suddenly, his mind blazed with fury as it took in his inability to act swiftly and vengefully. With quivering fingers, he fumbled for an arrow. When it was withdrawn from its sheath, he fired it into the back of the attacking white-eye. The man was dead the instant the arrow slammed into his heart. Jess lurched forward, then sank to the ground. His hold on Rebecca's throat weakened, and her slim body sank limply to the dry earth.

Bright Arrow surged forward to examine his beautiful love. At first he couldn't detect a heartbeat and he panicked. He shook her and called her name. There was no response. Finally he discerned an erratic beat and, hastily lifting her, he carried her into the cabin, anxious to see what he would discover there. His fury mounted when he saw the condition of his children. He ran to each of the girls, checking to see if they still breathed. Relieved that his family still lived, he hurried outside to make certain no other foe was lurking there. He quickly scanned the clearing. It was obvious to him from the bloodstains on Rebecca's dress that she had slain one man and had tried to battle the other one.

Blaming and cursing himself, Bright Arrow rushed back to the cabin and tried to arouse his wife. When he sprinkled water on her ashen face, her golden brown eyes opened briefly, and she pleaded for him to forget her and see to their children. Before she could explain matters or ask questions, she once again slipped into unconsciousness. Assuming she was overly fatigued from her recent battles, he felt sleep was best for her. Only later would Bright Arrow learn that she had denied herself food and water for days in order to have more for their children. But now time was precious, and he hastily set about saving his family.

He had witnessed the treatment for heat exhaustion many times and knew how to help his loved ones. He retrieved the packs of supplies from where he had dropped them during his wife's rescue. During the next two hours, the exiled warrior made a nourishing broth from the rabbit which he had slain just before reaching home and carefully fed each child, beginning with the youngest and weakest. He forced water into their dry mouths between trips to the stream to fetch water for the metal tub, which had been a surprise for Rebecca two years past. He stripped Tashina first and washed her thoroughly, then went on to revive Little Feet and Moon Eyes.

The fresh air and loving care revitalized the girls who had been sluggish and confused upon his arrival. Once fed and treated, they recovered quickly. They were ecstatic to see their father, hugging and kissing him and jumping on him. Despite his worry, Bright Arrow could not suppress his smiles and nervous chuckles at their playful and innocent antics. Clearly the children did not comprehend the severity of the situation they had recently endured.

"Why is Mama sleeping?" Little Feet questioned curiously when her mother failed to respond and join in their merriment.

"I will wake her," Moon Eyes offered eagerly, heading for the bed where her mother lay limp and silent.

Bright Arrow halted her. "Mama is sick, little ones. She must have rest and care in order to recover," he explained, trying not to remind them of their recently vanquished fears.

"Did the bad man hurt Mama?" Little Feet inquired gravely for such a small child. "He locked us inside, Papa, and we didn't have food or water." The painful words tumbled forth from quivering lips. "We were so hot and thirsty. Mama cried and screamed at him."

"Mama is not hurt, little one. Do not fear. She is tired

71

from watching over her children for many days. The bad men are gone. They will not harm my little ones again," he vowed.

"Will Mama be sick a long time?" Moon Eyes asked, wrinkling her forehead in bewilderment as she gazed into her father's eyes.

He smiled encouragingly and shook his head. "No, Moon Eyes, Mama will heal quickly. But we must be quiet and let her sleep. Come, I must put my little ones to bed so they can awake strong on the new sun."

The two older girls recounted the drama of the last few days, which now seemed like a bad dream to them. While answering their questions, reassuring them about their mother's condition, and dispelling the evil aura of Jess and Lester, Bright Arrow hurried the girls into bed so he could tend his wife and have time and silence to think about this and many other crucial matters. Finally at peace after making their frightening revelations, the girls obeyed their father's words and were soon slumbering. As the sunset lit up the horizon with lovely colors then began to fade to a rosy blue, Bright Arrow was able to focus his attention on Rebecca.

Bright Arrow was worried over her condition. He hadn't realized she was actually weaker than the children. He had been forcing water between her lips while he cared for the girls, but he had had trouble making her drink the soup, for swallowing had been difficult for her. He fretted over her lack of response. As he worked he scolded himself for wishing that Mind-Who-Roams, the Oglala medicine chief, were here to care for his cherished woman. He mopped her face and body with a cool, wet cloth, but she didn't awaken. He checked her again for injuries, finding only the bruises at her throat and minor scratches here and there.

While he observed and tended her, his tormented mind took in the dark smudges beneath her lovely eyes, which indicated she had had little sleep in the past days. Her flesh had an unnatural feel to it, and she was as limp as a freshly skinned pelt. There had been one bucket of water inside the cabin, untouched and newly obtained. He had found no edible food or firewood, yet the girls had responded to his care.

Suddenly he realized why his wife was in worse condition. He gathered her into his arms and covered her face with kisses. She had been brave and unselfish, as always. He knew how close he had come to losing his family, his true love. Memories of another such time flooded his mind, as he recalled the day he had rescued her from the fort. She had come to save him but had been trapped after doing so. The soldiers had been cruel to her, and she had nearly died after proving her worth and love.

He had fully realized then the depth of their love, and he had known for certain he could never part with her. He had defied the council and chosen Rebecca. But after that he had been rejected as if repugnant to his tribe.

He gingerly placed Rebecca on their bed. His fists clenched in rage as he accepted the blame for this new peril his family had had to endure. He went to sit cross-legged upon the floor in front of Rebecca. Every so often, he would arise to force more liquid down her throat. Now that he was home to protect his family, he left the windows and doors open for cooler air. He checked on the girls; they were sleeping soundly. He inhaled deeply and returned to his vigil over his wife. His heart thudded heavily as his eyes roamed over her.

He had sacrificed all he was to have this woman, and he wouldn't lose her now! Finally he saw himself—really saw himself and their life—for the first time in ages. He realized his many mistakes during these past two years, and he was displeased and angered by what he understood at last.

How had he been so cruel to the woman he loved and needed? How had she endured his moods and weaknesses for so long? Why had he tried to destroy himself and his beautiful love? As he watched over his beloved wife, he sought the reasons for his gradual loss of pride.

Besides the French and Spanish who had entered the Indian territories to explore, to trade, and to trap, there had been another band of white-eyes surging into their forests and over their plains who called themselves Americans. At first they had begun like a tiny trickle of rain; now they poured into these lands like a raging storm. Those dead men outside his home were Americans! Unlike the first whites, these Americans did not mingle with the Indians unless for some wicked or selfish purpose; they remained apart or murdered any Indian in their paths. He recalled too many times when the whites had tried to wipe out entire bands or murder leaders to disperse powerful tribes. Those dead foes outside had come to his home for greedy and evil reasons, and he wished he could slowly torture them for the suffering they had caused his family.

Most Indians felt as Bright Arrow did; American soldiers and settlers were the most dangerous and deceitful of the whites. They were as aggressive and sly as a crazed wolf. He had battled and slain these types of white foes at his father's side. How could he ever have believed he could live as his enemies lived, as Clay Rivera, who was said to be half-Spanish and half-Crow? The Crow were the most hated adversaries of the Sioux! He had chosen that tribe to prevent any suspicion of ties to his people. If anyone ever guessed he was *Wanhinkpe*

Wiyakpa, son of Gray Eagle . . .

For such reasons, Bright Arrow always traded with the French or Spanish at their posts or where they made their regular stops. Other times, he went to the Cheyenne camp or to the British trading post at Lake Traverse. Except for his wife and a few others, he detested and mistrusted the whites. He longed to drive them from his homeland, from his sacred grounds. But as a banished brave, this was impossible.

Bright Arrow was plagued by his thoughts. How could he endanger his family? How could he be so cowardly? He had done nothing wrong, nothing but lose hope and ruin himself! True, he had demanded to keep the woman he loved. But he had also agreed to surrender the chief's bonnet, to live and ride as just another warrior. All he wanted was Rebecca in his life-circle. How could that be evil and defiant? How could his parents and tribe turn their backs on him? And why had he taken his rage, bitterness, and anguish out on himself and on his beloved Rebecca? He had been terribly wrong!

This life of nothing in a white man's dwelling was not for him. He was a warrior! He should be guarding his lands and people from Indian and white foes. He should be with his family, at his father's side! He had been spiritless and resentful for too long. He had suffered and sacrificed enough for his one defiant deed. His instincts and skills had been dulled by years in the white man's world, in this stifling box of wood. He hungered for freedom, for adventure, for honor. He yearned to be the man he once had been so long ago. Was it too late?

And what of his family? They were in peril in this wilderness. He did not want his girls to go the way of the whites, to marry them and be taunted as half-breed squaws. He wanted his girls to know their heritage, to be

75

influenced and taught by Gray Eagle and Shalee. Indian families were very close, something that his girls were missing. Indian children had large families, which took part in their training and care. At birth, they were given second fathers and mothers to prevent their real parents from spoiling or overly protecting them. How he longed to see White Arrow and Wandering Doe, his second parents.

Indian children knew where they belonged, but he feared his girls would think themselves white! Against Indian custom, he had been present during the births of his children, had been compelled to assist with those births. He had not taught his children the Oglala tongue and customs, fearing they might innocently reveal such things to a foe. *Fear.* What a sour tasting word! It was wrong that his girls did not know who and what their father was, or had been.

And there was his beautiful and gentle Rebecca to consider. He wanted his love to smile and be happy once more. Her recent silence and dejection had not escaped him, and he had to admit he was to blame for that, too. This life had been lonely and harsh for her, yet she had shown such courage and determination. She had been patient, loving, and understanding, never taunting or nagging him. She had loved him enough to endure captivity and scorn at his side in the Oglala camp. When his pride demanded he resist his tribe's command to keep her only as a slave, she had followed his lead into the wilderness. She was a rare and special creature, one too precious to be harmed in any way. She had not asked or pleaded for them to leave; defiance and departure had been his choices. Would he make those same choices and mistakes again? Had he handled everything wrong?

Would patience and persistence have won his battle eventually?

He would have to do something to regain his honor, to regain his former life. He wanted to see his parents; he wanted to see his brother, Sun Cloud. He yearned to ride with the other warriors, and his soul needed to experience the singing and dancing at the ceremonies. He hungered to sit in council, to speak with the elders, to share adventures and victories. He needed to breathe the air of the Great Spirit in his prayer pipe. His body needed to be cleansed in the sweat lodge; it needed to be honed to its previous hard and agile state. He had been destroying himself, and that was wrong! He had been feeling sorry for himself, and pity was a weakness he could no longer tolerate. Had the Great Spirit also turned his back on them? It was not right for a warrior to be cut off from his people and their ways. He was tired of feeling useless, miserable, and helpless!

Bright Arrow glanced at his buckskin pants and cotton shirt. He ran his fingers through black hair which failed to touch his shoulders. His clothes and appearance screamed at him, *"Hanke-wasicun, Sunka-ska:* Half-breed! White-dog!" His ebony eyes surveyed the wooden structure. But for the bow and quiver of arrows, there was nothing there to suggest he was Indian or even part Indian; there was nothing present to reveal that his blood was Sioux and his past rank was that of a fierce warrior and future Oglala chief. His surroundings shouted, *"Ista-ska:* White-eyes!"

Yet hidden beneath the floor boards were objects which many Indians and whites would kill to obtain: Bright Arrow's Shooting Star shield, his headband, prayer pipe, medicine bag, armbands, a necklace of grizzly and eagle claws, a silver arrow *wanapin*, his garments, a *coup* stick, and many other items of past glory. Both ends of the lance which had been broken by the leader of the council when he had been forced from the Warrior Society were concealed there. No one knew of the secret place except Bright Arrow and his love. He would never have traded any of those valuable objects; they were as sacred to him as his life.

It was past time for action. It was past time for understanding and forgiveness. It was past time to replace all he had lost. He had been too proud and stubborn. Yet he realized that for all his resolve and determination, his tribe did not have to listen or to accept their return. Six winters had passed, and Bright Arrow longed to go home, to be a man once more.

He experienced a shiver of apprehension. He had never been a coward until after their exile. He didn't like his emotions and actions of these past six years. Even though he had sent his Cheyenne friend Windrider to guard his family, danger had befallen them. Their lives and happiness were his responsibility, and he had failed them. He was plagued by anguish, for Windrider was the one friend with whom he had not lost contact. Surely Windrider had been attacked and killed on his way here, as his body was nowhere near the cabin. His wife and children had been tormented for days by those white dogs, thinking he had deserted and betrayed them. Could his wife forgive him and understand?

When Rebecca recovered, he would explain his absence. He would explain how he had been several hours upriver hunting when he had met his Cheyenne friend heading to their cabin. Windrider had told him of Jean Truteau's early trip up the river for trading. There hadn't been time to return home and Windrider had agreed to guard his family while he sought Truteau. If they hadn't been so dangerously low on supplies, this situation would not have occurred. He was a hunter; yet his family had gone hungry! He was a warrior; yet his family had nearly been slain by enemies! He was the head of this family; yet they could not depend on him! How could he forgive himself for leaving his family unprotected, without food or water for days? He vowed to find a new life for them.

A Sioux warrior should not be forced to live in a world of enemies and pretend to be what he was not, nor should he exist alone and without purpose. If his people did not accept their return to the Oglala camp, he would take his family to live with either the Blackfeet or Cheyenne. Indians were known for their generosity and friendship to others. But would anyone accept them now? Banishment was usually the punishment for murder! Would he be able to make others understand that he had been exiled for a defiant love?

Bitterness threatened to engulf him once again. He wanted to blame his tribe for his lost heritage. Yet, was anyone responsible? If it had been another warrior involved, how would he have felt and voted? Never in his life had he imagined meeting and falling in love with a white girl. But he had not been able to change his feelings or their results, just as the council members had not changed theirs. Each had done as he felt best or necessary. But so many were being hurt by those decisions.

Bright Arrow stood up and stretched his stiff body. Soon it would be morning. He urged the drowsy Rebecca to take more broth and water. He noted that her flesh was sleek and soft once more, the dark patches beneath her eyes were fading, and her respiration came more easily and steadily. With rest and care, she would be fine. He prayed this staggering episode would not be a fatal blow, killing her love and patience.

Watching her, his heart beat faster with love and his body warmed with desire. He had been so entrapped in his dark world that he hadn't wanted to touch something so pure and beautiful as she. In all honesty, he had to admit that perhaps he had formed unbidden resentment toward the agent of his banishment. Perhaps he had felt undeserving and inadequate. Sex had become a forbidden and difficult stranger to him, and he wasn't certain why. Surely his wintry treatment had hurt her. He had been shown just how much he loved and needed her and, whatever their destiny, he would never be sorry for taking her as his woman.

A wonderful sensation filled his mind and body. He hadn't felt this confident in many moons. He was ready and eager to make changes in their life and in himself. He had done a great deal of soul-searching, thinking, and planning, and now he was eager to share this news with her. A sense of peace and joy flooded him as he made a decision too long delayed. It was time to return to the Indian way of life, and he had to convince Rebecca that all would be fine.

Bright Arrow reclined beside Rebecca, encircling her with his arms. His heart soared when she murmured his name and snuggled against him. He lay with his eyes open as bittersweet memories flickered through his restless mind.

Seven times the period which the white man called May had passed since he had met Rebecca. She had been traveling with a band of bluecoats and a black-hearted kinsman. When his band of warriors joined with a band of Cheyenne warriors to attack the small wagon train, he had sighted the white girl being attacked by one of the soldiers. As he watched her, a warm and strange emotion filled him. He had slain the soldier and taken her captive. Yet his claim had been challenged by Standing Bear, a fierce rival who hated and envied him. They had battled over Rebecca, and Standing Bear had been slain. Later, Standing Bear's friend White Elk had come to the Oglala camp to demand Rebecca's life in exchange for his friend's. Once more he had fought a challenge for his love. Two Cheyenne deaths over the possession of Rebecca had caused much anger and resentment, but only in his camp, for the Cheyenne had known the two challenges had been issued because of personal grudges. Many maidens of the Oglala camp had despised her and tried to cause trouble between them, and he had been mocked and taunted. Yet he had stood firm in his love for the white captive.

When he had been ambushed and taken prisoner by the bluecoats, Rebecca had risked her life and safety to help him escape. Her clever plan had worked, and he had gone free. Later, many tribes had attacked the fort to conquer it; he had freed his love that day, and for months afterward he had tried to persuade the council to allow them to wed. How could he force his love to live as his white whore? How could he wed an Indian girl and allow her to mistreat his true love? They had given him no choice but to rebel and leave. Still, he truly believed their refusal had been meant as a bluff.

Rebecca was like magical sunshine that warmed his soul, gave joy to his heart and vitality to his spirit. She possessed as much beauty inside as she did outside. Beneath the sun, her hair was like dark flames of fire. Her sun-browned skin was taut and smooth. He recalled how her gaze sent messages of burning passion when she looked at him. Her kisses and caresses could drive him wild with desire, could remove thoughts of all else but her. Her eyes of brown with flecks of gold could penetrate his soul and ensnare him. How could anyone scorn such a vital and loving creature?

Was that why he had been pushing her away—because she held such power over him? Had he unconsciously resented the fact that he had lost—no, sacrificed—everything for her? Had he unwittingly tried to force some of his torment into her to lighten his burden? He could not be sure.

Until now, he hadn't been ready or willing to confront himself, to admit his weaknesses. He hadn't wanted to place the blame where it belonged, solely on his own shoulders. Utterly fatigued yet somehow encouraged, Bright Arrow arose and barred the windows and doors. With Rebecca cuddled securely against him, he slept for several hours.

Rebecca's eyes fluttered and opened. For a time, the setting seemed natural. Then she realized she was nude and clasped snugly in her husband's arms! He hadn't held her in ages! She lay motionless, observing his face. Without warning, flashes from the last few days entered her mind. She no longer felt weak. Hunger pangs did not gnaw at her stomach. Dizziness and pain did not wrack her head. She observed her sleeping husband with curiosity. She wondered when he had arrived, for her last memory was of Jess strangling her and threatening to burn down their cabin. She bolted to a sitting position and glanced around, breathing rapidly. She was confused. All appeared normal. Had it been a horrible nightmare?

Bright Arrow sat up and tried to embrace her. "They are dead and will harm no one," he said softly. "You are safe, my heart." He watched her intently.

He had not called her that special name or used that tender tone in months; even so, it failed to move her this morning. She locked her probing gaze on his veiled one. At times like this, she hated his Indian ability to conceal emotions or secrets. It was one skill he had not dulled by lack of use! "Where were you?" she asked simply, drilling her gaze into his in an attempt to penetrate its barrier.

"Your body has recovered from your battle. Who were those men, Rebecca? What did they do to my family?" he inquired cautiously. It would require time, patience, and care to tear down the emotional wall he had erected over so many moons. He had to be gentle. Now it seemed that Rebecca wasn't ready or willing to change.

Rebecca's gaze was stony. "Why didn't you come home for days?" she demanded, keeping her voice low. "Why bother to return when it's almost too late? We could have died," she accused.

"I went to trade for food and supplies," he responded, pointing to the goods still lying on the table. "Where is Windrider? I sent him to protect my family while I was gone. I did not find his body outside. Were there more than two enemies? Did they steal Windrider's body?"

Rebecca did not know that Bright Arrow was asking for facts which he already possessed. She did not realize he was attempting to let her expose the truth of why he had been absent. He noted the astonishment and confusion upon her face. "Tell me what happened while I was away," he urged. "When I met Windrider in the forest, I decided it was best to hurry to Truteau's camp before he left. Windrider gave me gold to trade, and he was to come here and remain. What happened to him? Do you know?" he probed.

"I haven't seen Windrider for months. If those two

83

men ambushed him, they didn't say so," Rebecca began, then continued until she had shared the grueling tale with her distressed mate. Wisely, she did not disclose the extent of the sexual contact between the men and herself, for she knew how such news would affect her husband's pride. Some things were best left unsaid. As she concluded the account, she declared with tears in her eyes, "You left us alone and in danger. This is a bad place."

Bright Arrow explained, "I killed the white dog who tried to harm you. The Great Spirit guided my feet home before I lost my family to foes."

"If *Wakantanka* cares so much about us, we wouldn't be here," she snapped coldly and gestured to the cabin. "We can't continue to live this way, Bright Arrow. It's lonely and dangerous. What about our children? What if something happened to us?" she asked. It was time to leave this horrid place, she decided, with or without her love.

"You are right, my heart," he stated clearly, shocking her. "If we are still unwelcome in my father's camp, I will seek a home for us with the Blackfeet or Cheyenne. We were not born to walk the path of the white man. Our hearts have been heavy for too many winters. It is the moon for Bright Arrow to remember his name and to regain his honor. I have not been a man for many moons. I ask your forgiveness. Will you go with me to seek a new life after I discover the fate of Windrider?" he entreated in a tone which moved her deeply.

"You're serious?" she murmured skeptically.

Bright Arrow's bronzed hand caressed her smooth cheek. His igneous gaze fused with her doubtful one. "You are my heart, and I must be a man once more for you. I have lived as a child and a coward for many winters. I have permitted us to suffer. Love is not evil,

84

Rebecca. I cannot punish us for what others say is wrong. If this were true, the Great Spirit would have seized you from my life-circle. If our children of two bloods were evil, He would have let the white dogs take their lives. We will travel to the Cheyenne camp to learn of Windrider's fate. Then we will ride to the Blackfeet camp. I will leave you and our children in the camp of my mother's people, and I will seek out the Oglala council's decision. Do you agree?" he inquired anxiously, wondering what he would do if she didn't concur. He smiled at her.

He had spoken the words her heart yearned to hear. His features reflected the sincerity and urgency of his appeal, and she could not resist. A radiant smile flickered over her face like a beautiful butterfly, touching first upon her lips and then her eyes. She felt exhilarated by the smell and feel of his intimate proximity, and desire suddenly invaded her mind and body. She softly replied, "Yes, my love. I will follow you, even to the end of the world."

Bright Arrow's gaze engulfed her. She was lovely beyond dreams. She was gentle, yet strong. Her amber eyes were compelling. Her voice was as tranquil as a peaceful stream. Strength and tenderness rushed through him, as he remembered his first impressions of Rebecca Kenny. She had been soft and enticing, small and helpless, and she had fit nicely and perfectly against him. A sensual smile claimed his lips as he recalled his first seduction. A delicate girl would be no threat to a powerful warrior, he had believed then. How untrue that thought had been! She had changed his entire life, altered his feelings and dreams.

His smile was beguiling and disarming. Rebecca was fascinated and enchanted by it and by the man beside her. His hand tenderly pushed some stray locks of damp auburn hair from her face, then his finger moved ever so lightly over her parted lips. Lazily his fiery eyes explored her face, his senses absorbing her responsive mood. When his mouth came down to claim hers, her response told him she was eager to join her body with his. Pleased and relieved, his next kiss deepened. She quivered as he placed feathery kisses on her eyes, neck, mouth, nose, and ears. His ardent seduction was persistent, intoxicating. She could not resist his stirring quest, and lay motionless for a time, allowing him free rein over her body.

Bright Arrow leaned away from her, his loving gaze intensely scrutinizing his woman, and his look caused her to tremble. It was the stare of a hungry wolf, one who was skillfully stalking his prey before attacking and devouring it. It had been so long since they had made love, and her ravenous body craved his. They had shared so many sweet and urgent unions, she recalled blissfully, and her husband was skilled upon the mats, allowing no restraint in her. His prowess and knowledge had always rewarded them with exquisite pleasures.

His probing, warming gaze started its leisurely journey at her chestnut hair. As sunlight entered the side window, its glow touched her head and brought her tresses to fiery life. His gaze moved past her tawny eyes to linger briefly upon her pert nose, her slightly parted lips, and her dainty chin. It took in her perfect features, which were a deep brown shade from so much time spent beneath the golden sun.

His smoldering eyes then roamed over her inviting frame, with its gently rounded hills and flat plains. His hand tenderly stroked her soft, firm flesh with a touch that was unsettling and pleasing to both of them. A glow brightened Rebecca's cheeks as fiery passion consumed her eager body. She quivered and tingled as his deft mouth came down upon hers like a masterful raider plundering virgin territory. She did not want to staunch the liquid fire that seemed to flow through her body. His kisses made her respond to him with total abandon. Rebecca's arms encircled his head and, burying her slender fingers into his ebony hair, she gave herself freely to him. Her mind spun with rapturous delight. She wondered if there was enough time to make love before their girls came fully awake. In the Indian camp, privacy had been easier to find, as there was always someone to play with or tend babies and children when couples needed to be alone. In the Indian camp . . . Quickly she dismissed her line of thought before it poisoned her new feelings.

Seeking, demanding, stirring nibbles tantalized her breasts. As his hands explored and teased her pliant flesh, she could not resist the callings of her body, cries which demanded he douse her consuming wildfire. For a time, they were totally oblivious to their surroundings.

She moaned in rapture as his teeth worked lightly at her taut breasts. Her desire for him was selfish and powerful. Time and reality deserted her, as her slender arms encircled his neck, then roved the muscles of his broad back. Her body and mind craved this joining which had once been forbidden, for only Bright Arrow could feed and sate the longing that filled her womanhood.

Bright Arrow had been skilled and experienced in love-making long before meeting Rebecca. He was well informed about the female body and how to please it. In their years together, he had taken her down many paths of pleasure. Yet, never had he experienced such delights, such intense hunger, and such contentment until Rebecca. She was stimulating, often encouraging him to make love to her several times in one night. She could heighten and enliven his senses as no other female had. He had made her a woman, and she had known no other man. She was like powerful magic, reaching and touching the very center of his being. She was his heart, and he must never forget or abuse that knowledge again.

The intensity between them built to an almost unbearable peak. He rolled to her side, giving himself more freedom over her body. Bright Arrow had shown her from the first that the touching before and after lovemaking was as important as the joining of two bodies. Once, Rebecca had been like sacred red stone. Bright Arrow had chipped, smoothed, and honed her into a passionate woman, a priceless trophy. He grinned at her, his dark eyes carrying a glow which she hadn't seen there in a long time.

Excitement and happiness surged through her. She returned his smile, her hand going up to roam over the finely chiseled lines in his handsome face. Her finger lovingly traced his high cheekbones, his straight nose, his squared jawline, and his cleft chin. She pulled his head down to glue their lips together, thriving on the sweet nectar of his mouth. A sob was torn from her throat as she murmured, "It hasn't been like this between us for a long time, Bright Arrow. You've finally come back to me. God, how I've loved you and missed you," she confessed raggedly.

He gathered her shaking body into his powerful and protective embrace. With his body half covering hers, he held her tightly and fiercely. "I know, my heart. I am shamed by this." New fires and needs coursed through him and quickly spread to her as he fervently vowed, "I will never hurt you again, my heart, for I love you beyond my life. We will be happy and free once more."

It had been so long since he had taken Rebecca that he feared his manhood would explode with tightly leashed passion. His loins throbbed savagely with need of her, and he knew he must stimulate her to a quick fulfillment, for he couldn't master himself for any length of time. He whispered into her ear, "Come, my heart, let us walk into the edge of the forest. If our children awaken, we will know before their eyes touch upon us. I have great need of you. My body burns with a fierce fire."

His husky voice and stimulating words shot through her body like a bolt of potent lightning. She nodded and arose. Grabbing a blanket, she wrapped it around her shapely frame and, holding hands, they left the cabin and entered the coolness of the trees. He halted, drawing her close to him. His eager mouth worked upon her lips and ears as his deft hands fondled and inflamed her eager body clad in the thin covering. He took the edges of the blanket from her grasp and held them apart to view her loveliness. When his moist mouth traveled down her neck to tease at its sweet hollow, she moaned with irrepressible desire.

"Ni-ye mitawa," he murmured against her ear in Sioux, stating his claim upon her, confident once more of his enthralling power over her body and heart. He smiled at her again, this time in triumph, for he had not lost her during his crazed time.

He had not spoken his tongue in years and, hearing his words, her eyes brightened with hope and joy. "Yes, my love, I am yours," she replied before dropping the blanket to the earth.

Bright Arrow hungrily admired her beauty. "I have not taken you in many moons, since before the snows left our lands. Perhaps I am no longer man enough to please you. Perhaps my body will betray me and take you too

89

swiftly and roughly," he confessed. His attention captured, he failed to notice a movement in the trees. "I have become as fat and lazy as a bear in winter. I have lost my manhood. Why have you not left me?" he wondered aloud.

Suddenly Bright Arrow's gaze went past her head before she could answer his anguished words. His expression warned of an intrusion. Taken by surprise, Bright Arrow gaped at the sight.

Alarmed, she impulsively whirled to trace his line of vision. Her eyes widened and her face grew pale as a figure covered with blood and scratches staggered from the trees. The man stepped forward in an appeal for Bright Arrow's assistance, then collapsed heavily against him.

This invasion of their haven was like icy water tossed upon Rebecca's smoldering body. Her passions froze; she couldn't move. She seized the discarded blanket to cover her nakedness, her face flushing with a bright red that sprinkled color down her neck and chest. The special moment had been lost forever.

Chapter Four

Rebecca quietly slipped over to the narrow beds to check on the children who were still sleeping this close to dawn. She smiled in relief as she thought of their stamina and survival. Fatigued from their ordeal, they would probably sleep for several more hours if the three adults were cautious. She flushed crimson as she recalled rushing to the cabin ahead of the men to yank on her clothes, but there had been little time for modesty or embarrassment then.

Rebecca returned to her husband's side. She handed Bright Arrow another wet cloth to cleanse the dirt and blood from Windrider's injuries, for it was not permissible for a white woman to tend a great warrior—and Windrider was a powerful and high-ranking warrior among his people, the Cheyenne. He always moved with such vivid self-assurance and fluid agility. He was a commanding figure, and she doubted he had ever shown fear or hesitation. His towering frame displayed sleek and well-developed muscles, as Bright Arrow's had long ago.

Yes, she silently mused, Windrider was a male animal to inflame a woman's blood, if she were unattached. Strange, she had not thought about him this way before, perhaps because he presented such a stark contrast to her mate in his present state. Or was it Windrider's piercing gaze, which felt as if it was utterly encompassing and dominating her?

She curiously observed the Cheyenne warrior who refused to show any sign of pain or anxiety during Bright Arrow's ministrations. She noticed the way his acute senses appeared to collect even the tiniest details surrounding him. He exuded an undeniable pride in himself and his race. She wondered if he could ever be brought low as her husband had been. They were so similar, yet so different. It seemed miraculous that he had survived and traveled to their cabin, for surely he had been wounded many days ago, preventing him from arriving in time to repel her two white demons. "What happened to him? Do you think he'll be all right?" she asked worriedly.

"Yes, Rebecca, he will live and heal," he replied without looking at her. "As soon as he is able to travel, we will take him to his camp. We must be ready to leave as quickly as possible."

Rebecca perceived an urgency in Bright Arrow's tone. "Why?" she inquired instantly, leaning forward to peer into his tension-lined face.

"Our cabin is no longer safe. Enemies are near," he answered, averting his face from her gaze. Unintentionally, his secretive, distant mood was surfacing again. He didn't like being questioned before another warrior, even a friend. He wondered if Windrider had overheard his humiliating confession in the woods. His friend had innocently stumbled onto a private, embarrassing, and frustrating scene. "We must go soon."

"But they're dead, Bright Arrow." She paused, then asked, "Did they attack Windrider thinking he was you?" Tremors swept her body as she imagined other dangers from friends of Jess and Lester, for she assumed her love was referring to them. She would never forget those devils and the fate they had intended for her family. Fury assailed her, fury because she had been so helpless against them. If they had invaded her body and sullied her soul . . .

The banished warrior slowly and carefully disclosed, "Windrider's wounds were not caused by the white dogs who attacked our home. This is a wound from a Pawnee club," he informed her, pointing to the worst injury. "At the club's end, there is a blade like a long, pointed bird's mouth, which makes a wound of this size and shape. The Pawnee are friends of the Crow, fiercest enemies of my people and our Cheyenne friends. The danger of the two men who attacked you is smaller than the danger of one Crow." Both men's faces revealed hatred and the thirst for revenge. "Windrider will heal in a few moons."

More dangerous than Jess and Lester? her mind screamed. Rebecca was astonished. "You think they'll track Windrider here? How many?" she asked aloud in rising fear. Warfare! Why must there be so much death and agony? she cried inwardly.

"No," he replied, relieving some of her tension. "Windrider killed his foes. Others will come to seek the fates of their brothers when they do not return home. The Crow and Pawnee know the name and face of Bright Arrow. We must be careful," he warned, then wished he hadn't reminded her of the value of his scalp.

"Why must we hurry? Surely there is time to conceal Windrider's trail to our cabin? Who would dare attack us with Windrider here to help us? How do you know he killed his enemies?" she asked, for the injured warrior had spoken little since regaining consciousness.

Bright Arrow took her compliment on Windrider's prowess as a double-edged statement. Rebecca had expressed pride in his friend, yet had insulted him because of his own lost skills. Bright Arrow explained,

"He has three fresh scalp locks on his waist. Only by the deaths of his foes could he have escaped with such wounds. He has earned an eagle feather with three beads, one for each kill. But he must wear the *coup* feather standing up to show he was wounded during this battle. Many will chant his victory over the Pawnee."

Rebecca grimaced as her eyes shifted to the prized locks, items which indicated the loss of three lives. Enemies or not, she feared she was going to be sick. She swallowed rapidly several times. "Why did they attack Windrider? He wasn't on a raid. What honor is won in three warriors challenging a lone fighter?" she questioned.

"Because he is Cheyenne," Bright Arrow stated simply.

"So much hatred and so much killing," she murmured. "Tribes war against each other and the white man. Soon there will be no braves left to fight. It's senseless. It was over for you, Bright Arrow. Will you become a warrior in our new camp?" Her emotions in a turmoil, she sent him a frosty stare without meaning to do so. She wondered if a grueling life in an Indian camp was facing her again, and she was apprehensive about his answer.

Bright Arrow was concerned over the direction of her talk. Did she doubt he could regain a warrior's skills? He tried to soothe her worries. "I will be safe. It is rare for one Indian tribe to war against another. Most Indian battles are small raids by small bands. Bands attack for war *coups* and horses, or for revenge of a past attack. A band on a raid should fight bravely, but not against too many for victory. If there are too many foes, it is wisest to return home without fighting. A warrior's life cannot be replaced; it is not given or taken lightly. Acts of bravery and cunning are more worthy of honor than the slaying of a foe. The band leader chooses the target, and those who wish to follow him do so. A band leader must never endanger the lives of the warriors who follow his lead. If warriors are slain from his foolishness, he is shamed. Many times I have ridden from camp with the four joined lines painted on my horse's rump," he stated, remembering those days when the painted square indicated he was the raid leader. Memories flooded his mind.

Bright Arrow envisioned the war horse that had shared glory with him. His steed had been swift and agile; he had been long on endurance and quick to obey. Three hand prints which told of an enemy killed in hand-to-hand battle had adorned that spotted beast. Along one side of his neck had been five *coup* lines, and on the other side were many hoof marks to reveal his successful exploits on horse raids. When he had gone into battle, enemies had chased him just to capture this prized animal whose value and owner's rank were exposed by the markings and trophies. Bright Arrow wondered if his father still owned Tasia, for a wilderness trapper had no use for such a magnificent war horse. Tasia had been so well trained, so intelligent, and so loyal that he had responded to a mere glance or touch. Often, Bright Arrow had felt their minds were linked.

Rebecca watched the array of emotions that came and went on her love's face. She didn't have to ask; she knew what path his mind was traveling. Such sadness and torment were present in his midnight eyes, until he caught himself and concealed such undesirable feelings. The instant he clouded his gaze and stiffened, she was provoked to say, "The most important thing in your life is being a warrior. You must return to it before you destroy us. We're not enough for you, Bright Arrow. You've changed since coming here. I don't look forward to returning to your tribe. I cannot forget their cruelties to me." She did not speak aloud the tender thoughts which suddenly assailed her. *But you are my husband, and I'll do as you say. If it is the will of the Great Spirit, you will return to your people soon.* She left to care for their children as they began to stir, both men watching her retreat and mulling over her words.

Five days drifted by as Bright Arrow tended Windrider's injuries. Then the Cheyenne warrior told him and Rebecca how he was attacked by three braves, three men out to gain *coups* and glory any way possible. Such evil pursuits blinded a man and slowed his reflexes. Although Windrider had been stabbed once and had received many scrapes and smaller cuts, he had indeed slain all three men. His medicine bag had been knocked into a river during the battle; that was why he had not been able to tend his own wounds successfully. He had made his way to the cabin on foot as quickly as his fading energy allowed.

When Bright Arrow translated the tale for Rebecca, she was stunned by the brutal slaying of Windrider's horse to prevent his escape. As he spoke, Rebecca furtively studied the magnetic warrior with keen interest. Because he had been in excellent health he was healing rapidly. For the first two nights, Bright Arrow had placed Windrider's sleeping mat inside the cabin. During the last three nights, the two men had slept beneath the stars near the cabin door. Windrider's presence and injuries had allowed no time for Rebecca and Bright Arrow to be alone at this time when they so desperately needed closeness and conversation. Her disquiet mounted with each new day, with each time Bright Arrow unwittingly avoided her, with each time she discovered Windrider's smoldering gaze on her.

To distract herself, she asked, "What about his medicine bundle? Doesn't that make him lose his power?" She knew that such a pouch not only contained medicinal herbs, but also held "magical" and ceremonial items. Yet Windrider seemed unaffected by its loss and, sometimes, when Windrider was talking with Bright Arrow in his Cheyenne tongue—one she couldn't understand—the man's dark eyes would dance with liveliness and vitality.

Bright Arrow smiled and spoke. "If a medicine bag is lost or stolen, it can be replaced. It is a great *coup* to steal a warrior's powerful bag. If a bag is taken, only the power of the medicine inside is lost. To lose his power, a warrior must give the bag away or trade it. A great warrior who is dying can pass his medicine bag to his son or a friend. When Windrider returns home, he will go on a vision quest and prepare a new medicine bundle of greater power and magic."

"I see," she muttered thoughtfully. Respect for Windrider's distinction glowed in her sherry-colored eyes. In her vulnerable state, it would have been better for Rebecca if Windrider had possessed less power. Yet she failed to recognize how open she was to this constant exposure to his provocative appeal and obvious prowess.

The Indians had so many beliefs, customs, and rituals that she did not understand. She realized that their strategies and considerations in warfare were the reasons for their difficulties in battling the white soldiers. While Indian warriors were more concerned with earning battle honors—touching a foe during battle and escaping or stealing his possessions—the white soldiers were merely concerned with killing enemies or annihilating entire tribes. To survive, the Indians would have to become as aggressive and lethal as the whites.

During the following day, Bright Arrow assisted his friend with testing his renewed strength. They wrestled genially; they raced around the cabin; they held target practice with arrows and knives. While the girls napped, Rebecca secretly watched their exercises from the window. With Bright Arrow losing each match and exposing his deteriorated condition, she didn't want to embarrass him by going outside. She lingered in the shadows, fascinated. Once, when Windrider was standing behind Bright Arrow as he took aim with his bow and arrow, she noticed how the Cheyenne warrior's gaze traveled over her mate. She was surprised when he shook his dark head in disappointment and annoyance. Shame and guilt filled her. With Windrider standing beside her mate, she realized he had declined further than she had thought. Worse, she found herself having daydreams about Windrider. She blamed such wanton thoughts and desires on Bright Arrow's withdrawal from her. She needed touching, holding, kissing, and caring!

When she lifted her head, Windrider was standing before the window and staring at her with his piercing jet eyes. Fearing he could read her mind, she felt her respiration quicken and she flushed. She hurriedly lowered her head to conceal her guilt and to master her emotions. When her head came up again, he was gone. Why was he making her so aware of him? Why did he have to be so tempting!

That night, Rebecca observed Bright Arrow and his friend as they sat cross-legged outdoors on either side of a small campfire. She watched them converse and plan. The aura surrounding Bright Arrow tonight was dismaying. His shoulders were bent as if loaded with shame and self-reproach. After the contests with Windrider, he had found that his condition was reprehensible and dishonorable. Even though his back was to the cabin door, she could perceive the determination in his rigid form. He would become a warrior again, even if in an ally's camp. As much as she hated facing scornful hostility and her love's return to a warrior's ominous life, she knew it was best for him. To survive, he must reclaim and walk his destined path.

Bright Arrow came to the cabin to fetch his Shooting Star shield, explaining that Windrider wished to see it. From the cabin's shadows, Rebecca casually watched Windrider as he filled Bright Arrow's pipe from his personal supply bag at his waist. How very kind and generous to share such a precious item as sacred tobacco. She walked to the doorway with her mate. He didn't kiss or embrace her and she felt lonely and denied. She was worried over this new withdrawal from her. When she noticed Windrider's intense gaze on her, she felt she was disturbing them. How she longed to join their conversation and to hear their exchange of news and tales. Soon she would have friends if all went as planned. She smiled to herself, then completed her chores. Noticing the juice Windrider had made from crushing wild cherries and adding honey, she lifted the container to her lips and drank the pleasant-tasting drink. She then went to lie on her bed, for she knew the men would remain beneath the stars on sleeping mats.

Time passed. The heat gradually vanished as the night air wafted through the cabin. She decided she must be awfully tired, for she felt giddy and her body seemed weightless. It was as if she were slowly sinking into a placid pond of warm liquid, yet she had no fear of drowning. Suddenly a torrid sun appeared to her, stretching out his scorching fingers to lift her from those watery depths and place her sweltering and glistening body on the lush bank beneath his fervid gaze. His searing eyes ignited her naked flesh to a white-hot glow. As adroit hands teased over her susceptible body, it responded of its own volition. But instead of her beloved's face, Windrider's smug visage dreamily wavered before her drowsy gaze.

For an instant, there was a haughty gleam in his eyes, and a leer curled up the left corner of his mouth. Then the baffling expression vanished as his keen gaze traveled over her lovely features, reflecting his immense satisfaction in bewitching her. It was as if he had the power to mesmerize her with those entrancing eyes, for she couldn't pull her gaze from his or think clearly. His forefinger brushed over her lips and slipped inside her mouth. He withdrew it, then his leisurely swirling tongue erotically savored the nectar he had taken from her mouth. As he suggestively wet his inviting lips, she was spellbound.

It seemed as if she were watching this lusty scene from a distant cloud. This delusion was nothing like her confrontation with Jess and Lester, nothing repulsive or frightening, nothing to produce guilt or rejection. Windrider's lips feverishly captured hers as his deft hands moved over her quivering frame. It was wildly and shockingly delightful to have the handsome and masterful warrior's hands and lips stimulating her. It had been so long since she had felt such blissful sensations. The last time Bright Arrow had stirred her blood to life, he had halted at the worst moment, leaving her tense and flustered. And he had coldly and selfishly left her in that state!

In her euphoria, Rebecca felt naughtily daring and free. Windrider's sexual prowess seemed so different from her lover's touch and talents. It was a dream, and dreams could not be controlled. Dreams could not harm a person, and this dream was wickedly delicious. Her arms went around the fanciful image's neck, crushing her lips and body against his and relishing his taste and smell. He was as skilled a lover as he was a warrior.

Her body had a mind of its own, and it demanded that her conscience not interfere; it demanded that she seize this moment and all it had to offer. At her uncontrollable responses, his kisses deepened and he ardently meshed his mouth with hers. The sensations were wonderful and tantalizing; she savored them and mutely invited more. Smiling, she watched him use his braid to titillate each nipple, then encircle each with his hot tongue. Soon his caresses grew bolder. Yet this dream image was content to kiss and to fondle her. Perhaps she refused to allow the dream to progress further, but she possessed no will or desire to halt his siege upon her pliant body. When she moaned and writhed upon the bed, he smiled at his success, smiled as if he had won some vital battle, smiled as if he had discovered some monumental secret. "Sleep. You will be mine soon," the illusion murmured, then disappeared while she was engulfed in flames of desire. Her head whirled wildly, then she lost reality. When she finally aroused herself, it was dawn and the dream was a vivid memory. She scolded herself for such a wanton fantasy, for she truly loved Bright Arrow, and she earnestly wanted to help him regain his soul.

Bright Arrow and Windrider were very busy for the next two days, hardly noticing her presence. That suited Rebecca, for she needed some privacy and distance from the two enigmatic men. They deftly constructed a travois to fit on the horse which Bright Arrow had purchased on this last trip. Rebecca wondered if her mate had planned to leave this area even before he learned of the attacks on their cabin and on his friend. Of late, he had been so secretive!

Windrider had recovered sufficiently to leave for his camp. It had been decided that he would walk behind the travois as a rear guard. The day before, he had sent Bright Arrow to recover his remaining weapons and belongings, which he had hidden along the trail on his way to their cabin. While Bright Arrow was away, Windrider had guarded his family with great care and caution. He had made no attempt to speak with Rebecca or to come near her, even when she had served his midday meal. He had spent time sharpening several knives and arrowheads, and he had replaced the string on a bow and checked the arrows' bindings. Abruptly she had realized whose weapons Windrider was repairing and sharpening—Bright Arrow's. Was this to save time, or was her mate incompetent in that area now too?

Early the next morning, the horse was loaded with supplies and the few possessions they would need. The two older girls were placed upon the travois in a sunken area for their protection and transportation. Bright Arrow had built a cradleboard in which Rebecca could carry Tashina during the journey. All appeared ready just after sunrise. Then her Sioux husband returned to the cabin for something. Time passed.

Today, Windrider was dressed in buckskin garments freshly washed by Rebecca. A war club and knife were strapped to his waist, and a bow and quiver of arrows were slung across his back. Gazing at him, Rebecca concluded he was every inch the elite and fearless warrior. She was glad to have Windrider at their backs; he had always been kind and respectful to her, and his prowess was immense in battle. He would be a good influence and helper for her beloved.

Bright Arrow called Rebecca into their cabin for a last time. She left the girls and Windrider to answer his summons. Upon entering, she halted abruptly and stared at him. Bright Arrow was also dressed in buckskins: leggings, moccasins, and breechcloth. He was wearing his weapons and *wanapin,* a talisman in the shape of a silver arrow. He could do nothing about his nape-length hair, but his headband was in place. Despite his physical decline, he was handsome and compelling.

He moved with renewed courage and assurance as he came toward her, observing the way she was gaping at him. He held out his arm bands and asked her to secure them around his biceps. She hesitated briefly as she absorbed the significance of his clothing and mood. With trembling fingers, she tied the arm bands in place. After completing the task, she slid her hands down the smooth lengths of his arms. Her inquisitive gaze came up to join with his ebony one. Her heart fluttered, for he still was irresistible. Once he had been such a mountain of masculinity and prowess, so superior to all other men. His resolute gaze declared he would become such a man again. She was warmed and touched to see him this way. In less than a week, their dying world had been reborn. He had regained his soul, his spirit, himself. It thrilled and enlivened her to see that her love was transforming himself into the unique male he once had been. Yes, things were going to be fine for them.

In a husky voice for her ears alone he murmured, "I am a man in heart once more. Soon I will be a man once more in body and skills. Never will Bright Arrow walk the earth in shame again. I will stand tall with my eyes open before me. I will cower before no man. I am *Wanhinkpe Wayakpa,* son of *Wanmdi Hota,* chief of the Oglala and greatest warrior to ride the face of Mother Earth. Stand at my side, and I will love and protect you as no other."

She noted the confidence and happiness beaming upon his coppery features, features lined with boldness and determination. Even if his moods had swung back and forth during these past days, she savored this one. "You are a man to stir a woman's heart and body to passion. You are a man to instill fear and hesitation in your foes. You are a man above others, my love. My heart flutters with joy and pride to be your woman. But this is not the time to tempt me with . . . wifely needs," she jested, playfully squeezing his arm.

Bright Arrow clasped her face gently between his powerful hands. He lowered his head and sealed their lips in a provocative and stimulating kiss. When the kiss ended, he stated honestly, "You have been my heart since the moon my eyes touched on you. You will be my heart until it is cut from my body by an enemy or until the Great Spirit calls my feet to walk with Him. Before we seek this new life, my heart, know my love for you is strong and true."

Tears moistened her eyes. "You have come home to me, Bright Arrow; at last, you are whole again. Do not worry, my love. When your people see you once more, they will be filled with joy and relief. We will make them understand our love. They will not reject you."

They embraced fiercely, then parted with smiles. He picked up his remaining possessions, and they left the cabin without bothering to close the door or windows. Bright Arrow placed the cradleboard with Tashina in it on Rebecca's back. He secured it in place, then took his position at the head of the little group. He seized the horse's bridle and began the trek to the Cheyenne camp. The older girls laughed and glanced all around as the exciting journey got underway. Tashina wiggled to gain sight of her noisy sisters. Rebecca looked back at Windrider, who nodded and smiled at her, a curious expression in his dark brown eyes. She ignored it. In one hand he gripped his bow, an arrow in place in readiness for danger. She absently wondered which of his two wives received more of his attention and affection.

She turned and walked beside the travois near the girls to make certain they remained seated. She couldn't explain the overpowering sensation that Windrider was staring into her back so hard that she could literally feel the force of his gaze. He had never been offensive or cold to her. Maybe it was her wild imagination at work again. She should be gratified and relieved to have another powerful man along this trail, just in case danger befell them.

Rebecca's erotic dream about Windrider haunted her mind. Why had she fantasized about him and why now? She had seen him many times before. She admired and respected him, and she liked him as a person. Why did that sensuous dream distress her? Because it had seemed so real? Because she had awakened nude? Because she felt that such a wanton dream was a betrayal of Bright Arrow? How had her mind created such variety in kisses and caresses? She had known only one male! Had she said or done something to expose her wanton imaginings to Windrider! She trembled as she comprehended what raw emotion she had read in his enticing gaze. She dreaded to think what might have happened had the illusory episode taken place in reality while Bright Arrow was suffering such a loss of confidence.

After hours of walking, the group stopped to eat and rest. They consumed dried meat, wild fruit, and cornpones. It was the Indian custom to rest and nap at this time of day during the heat. The girls were so excited by this new adventure that they played energetically at the edge of the shallow stream. But Rebecca's mind was elsewhere.

She had tried to force thoughts of Windrider from her mind, but they refused to leave. It was unjust to dwell on such ridiculous ideas, she scolded herself. Windrider was Bright Arrow's friend! He wasn't tempting her! A friend didn't lust after another's woman, nor plot to get her alone. Nothing had happened when Bright Arrow had gone to fetch Windrider's belongings. There was no way Windrider could have come into the cabin that night, not with Bright Arrow sleeping nearby. It had been only a dream. She had to forget it and quell these wild ideas.

What was wrong with her? Was this delusion about Windrider a way to forget what Jess and Lester had done to her? Was she mentally replacing a crude nightmare with a romantic dream, which would have been different had the seducer been Bright Arrow? Had it been a result of their lack of lovemaking and that recent frustrating experience? Had it been a spiteful dream, a way to punish her love for his indifference toward her? Did she truly have lustful cravings for Windrider?

Rebecca shook her head of flaming hair to dispel such foolish ramblings. It was wrong to imagine such things. Windrider would never harm the mate of his friend Bright Arrow! He would never try to seduce her. And she could never wantonly encourage him.

"Do you have some pain in your head?" Bright Arrow inquired, finally relaxing after hours of bone-jarring and muscle-punishing exercise.

Rebecca met his gaze and shook her head once more. "I was just remembering . . . those two men who tried to kill us. It was awful, my love. I've never known such terror or utter helplessness. If you hadn't returned at that moment . . ." Her voice trailed off as she wept softly, for she had never lied to him before. He wasn't a jealous man, but she couldn't expose her real concerns. He would watch and study each word and move between them!

Bright Arrow grasped her chin and raised it. He smiled into her teary eyes. "It is passed, Rebecca; let such an evil moon die," he patiently advised. "Rest. We will leave soon. Do not fear. You have Bright Arrow and Windrider to protect you."

Her tawny gaze shifted to where Windrider was playing with the girls near the stream. "Yes, we have Windrider," she concurred.

Bright Arrow observed her from the corner of his dark eyes. She was in a strange mood; her odd tone was inexplicable. He wondered if she disliked Windrider, or if she was angry because the Cheyenne warrior had failed, albeit against his will, to protect her during that grisly bout with the two white men. How could she doubt the prowess of a great warrior like Windrider? He suddenly fretted. Surely she was not comparing him with Windrider? But how could she avoid noticing what was so obvious? He glanced down at the roll of fat around his waist. He was winded from his morning's journey. His instincts were not as keen or swift as they once had been; his senses were not as acute. His body didn't respond as quickly and agilely as he desired. His muscles were sore; they had lost their previous strength. His braids were missing because he had tried to live the life of a white man. He should bow his head in shame before the Great Spirit, for he had allowed his body and mind to lose their prowess. He must and would regain his former rank and power!

In the camp of the Cheyenne, he would train as never before. He would ride and hunt with his friends and brothers. He could not enter the Oglala camp in such sorry condition. They would laugh at him and taunt him. Who would want to welcome a fat and dull-witted brave back into the Warrior Society! He had lived in the white man's way for so long that he looked and behaved as Clay Rivera. He would become the indomitable and matchless Bright Arrow once more. Soon he would be a noted warrior again. Soon no male would be comparable to him—in looks or skills! He smiled and leaned his head against a tree to rest for a brief spell. Sleep overtook him.

Rebecca studied her unfortunate lover. She hadn't wanted to accept such changes in him; she had denied them to herself as long as possible. Tears burned her eyes, for it would be a long and arduous trail back to the man he had been. Did he have the courage and stamina to win this difficult battle? Could he retain his hope and patience long enough to succeed? Did he realize the height of the mountain he was to climb? She prayed he would triumph in his new life, but it was going to be hard for all of them.

The girls had fallen asleep on mats laid out by Windrider, who was nowhere in sight. She inhaled wearily, then went to refresh herself in the stream. Have I changed, too? she mused, leaning over to check her image on the placid surface. Is there some reason why he's lost interest in me? Am I no longer desirable? Inexplicably angered, she slammed her hand down, agitating the water. As the moving water mastered itself, Windrider's face wavered in the rippling surface. The wanton fantasy flashed before her mind's eye and she flushed in embarrassment. She tensed and tried to break their locked gazes. He knelt beside her on the bank. It was silly to behave this way! she told herself. Rebecca sat back on the grass, trying to still her racing heart and appear calm. She pushed stray locks of damp hair from her face.

"Your eyes speak words of confusion and fear, Rebecca," the Cheyenne warrior murmured softly. "This troubles me."

Stunned, she gaped at him. When she found her tongue, she stated hoarsely, "I didn't know you could speak English. Why have you kept it a secret from us?" she inquired suspiciously. She apprehensively traced her words to make certain she hadn't said something misleading.

"I hear and speak the white tongue. Bright Arrow knows of this gift. There was no reason to tell his woman. I do not wish the white tongue in my mouth until danger strikes. It is a weapon to be used in secret against your people. You are sad this sun?" he asked knowingly.

"Why are you telling me today, Windrider?" she asked, wondering if there was some significance to his revelation. Why hadn't Bright Arrow told her? She could have joined their talks! She felt a sense of betrayal and deceit in this long-kept secret.

"There is no smile in your eyes or laughter in your voice. Are you afraid to enter my camp? Do you fear Bright Arrow cannot become a warrior again?" Windrider's gaze shifted to his friend, his emotions concealed. "There was a time when his name could strike fear into the hearts of his enemies, a moon when all respected and were in awe of him. It has saddened my heart to watch such destruction."

"You mean he was a great warrior before he met me?" she demanded angrily. Windrider didn't answer, nor did his impassive expression reveal his thoughts to her. "You blame me for his being banished, don't you?" she hotly challenged. "Why not? Everyone else does. If I could give him back all he's lost, Windrider, I would. Bright Arrow can be whatever he chooses if his people will allow it. They are the ones destroying him, not me or my white blood. He was a proud and stubborn man. He was hurt deeply by the council's decision. I have watched him suffer and change for years. I tried to help him, to prevent it. He shuts me out of his pain. He's become like a stranger to me," she confessed.

Her teary gaze also shifted to the sleeping Bright Arrow. "We never realized what our decision would cost him. We believed they would finally accept me one day." She laughed coldly and cynically. "Don't you understand? I didn't capture and enslave him. I didn't trick him or enchant him with some evil magic. I was his prisoner; I was obedient and respectful. I did all I could, Windrider, but his people hated me and rejected me. Bright Arrow is the one who chose to leave. No matter how cruel they were to me, I never begged him to leave his tribe. I never even suggested it or hinted at it."

"He did not choose to leave, Rebecca. He spoke his challenge and the council accepted it. Once spoken, he could not recall his rash words," he reminded her. "If you love him, send him home. His people need him. His family needs him. He is no man this way. It is wrong for a warrior to live as white. It is wrong to destroy him."

"And what of our children?" she questioned. "If there were no children, I would have forced him to leave me and return home long ago. I never wanted to shame or hurt Bright Arrow. I never wanted him to be like this. Why must I accept the blame?"

Windrider was pleased by Rebecca's confession but did not remark on it. The sly warrior informed her, "The children would be accepted by his family and people. In time their white mother would be forgotten. They would live and marry as Indian, as it should be. Hear my words, Rebecca. The Oglala customs and laws have not changed. Their hearts are still Indian and hard against the whites. They will not allow a white woman to live as the honored mate of Gray Eagle's son, the first son to breath the air of *Wakantanka*. If you return to the Oglala camp, it will be as before. You must live as his . . . I do not know the white word," he deviously hesitated.

"Whore, Windrider, the white word for a female living with a man who is not her husband is *whore*," she declared frostily, refusing to allow guilt and shame to viciously attack her.

"You lived this way many winters ago. Why do you and Bright Arrow fight what must be? The Oglalas will accept the return of Bright Arrow and his children, but they will never accept you as his wife. If you love your mate and children, why do you not want what is best for them? Which is more important, Rebecca, your honor or his?" he cunningly inquired as his eyes and voice softened.

"Why is my honor any less than his? Before, I was his captive. Now, I am his . . . woman. Why should I be shamed? I didn't ask for this kind of life, but I have done my best to make it work. You can't understand what they demand of me, Windrider. You don't know what it's like to live as a lowly slave. Why is it so wrong for an Indian to love and marry a white?" She pleaded for his explanation. "Why must the Indian law declare me the enemy? Why must it say I am evil and without merit? Why must it force me to live in shame and misery? Why is skin color so much more important than feelings and actions?"

111

Her words seemed to surprise him. He cleverly responded, "I do not know. It is different with the Cheyenne. I could marry a white woman and not face dishonor. I could marry her and not be banished. It is bad you were not taken captive by a Cheyenne warrior."

Rebecca promptly told Windrider of the Cheyenne warrior Standing Bear's challenge for her and of White Elk's demand for her life. "The Cheyenne would have treated me no differently," she disputed.

"You speak of two warriors with black hearts, whose faces were stained with dishonor. Do you not recall they were slain for their evil? My people will accept you, Rebecca. Bright Arrow must return to the path marked for him by the Great Spirit. If you cannot share that path, you must let him walk it alone, or with another female of his kind. I do not wish to see you sad or shamed. If you cannot return to the Oglala camp in honor and peace, you are welcome to live in my tepee, as my third wife," he offered, stunning her. His alert gaze devoured her astonished features. "You will see you cannot return to the Oglala camp unless you live as Bright Arrow's who—captive. Send him to his people. I will wait for you to come to me. I know the white man's way of taking one wife. If you say it must be that way for us, I will send the others away. I will take only you to my heart and body. You can become a Cheyenne. In my tepee, you will be the honored wife of a great warrior. This new trail will be easier for all to walk. If you come to me, Bright Arrow will free you; he will free himself." His hand reached out to caress her flushed cheek. "You are tired and confused. Think on my words. You will see I speak wisely and true. Sleep. You will soon be mine."

Those last words echoed through her dazed mind. She went pale. "It wasn't a dream, was it?" she asked faintly.

His fathomless dark eyes fused with her startled ones. "No, Rebecca, it was not a dream," he calmly replied. "Is it not true you hunger for me as I hunger for you? Is it not true Bright Arrow has not made you feel such things in many, many moons? Can you deny the fires which I sparked within you?" he challenged.

Chapter Five

Rebecca didn't know what to say or how to react to Windrider's incredible confession and proposal. She panicked. She wanted to flee, but there was nowhere to go. As his words tumbled over and over in her mind, she remained speechless and still. Her brain was spinning at his bold admission, and when he spoke again, he further increased her anxiety, confusion, and astonishment.

"You do not remember when our eyes first touched on each other?" he inquired but didn't allow her time to think or reply. He continued, "It was many winters past, and I have never forgotten you or that day. You were brave, but frightened like the hunted doe. I rode with Bright Arrow the sun he took you captive. If he had not taken Standing Bear's challenge for you, I would have battled to the death before allowing Standing Bear to have you. I rode to the Oglala camp when the challenge was made for your life. When the order was given to slay White Elk for his evil, I placed my arrow in his body. I did not wish to see you harmed. Bright Arrow has forgotten that I tried to buy you from him. I offered him many horses and furs. He said you pleased him, and he would not trade you. Each time I come to see him, I also come to see you. You have more beauty than Mother Earth. You are as strong and cunning as the she-wolf, but as gentle as the butterfly. You have shown great courage and value

115

before the Oglalas. My heart burned with anger to see them reject you. I was going to purchase you if Bright Arrow put you aside. His pride was great, and he did not. It is not wise to feel such anger toward friends of the Cheyenne. You will increase my fury if you permit them to toss you away once more as if you are worth nothing."

Windrider appeared to leash his ire, and his chilling tone warmed as he whispered, "I have dreamed of you for many winters. I came to your white tepee many times to see that you remained safe and happy. You did not. I curse the evil of the Pawnee who kept me from your side when you faced danger. When I return home, I will raid their camp in revenge for your suffering. I forced Bright Arrow to see that his family was not safe in the white tepee. I told him he could become my brother if he would bring his family to live in my camp. Bright Arrow has not been a man for many moons. He cannot protect you as Windrider can. He does not think clearly. He punishes you for being white, for taking him from his people, but you are innocent. When you return to the Oglala camp, he will choose his people over you when the demand is made. Do not fear, Rebecca. I will take you to my heart and my tepee."

Rebecca was too stunned to debate his charges against Bright Arrow. She had had no inkling that Windrider was in love with her, had been pining for her for years! "You must not say such things, Windrider," she rebuked him. "I am bound to another; it is wrong to speak this way." He had opened his heart to her, and she couldn't insult or forbid his feelings for her, even if they were wrong. At least he had waited until he felt the relationship between her and Bright Arrow was over before speaking his mind. Love was a relentless emotion, she knew, one not easy to understand or govern, one that was often cruel.

She smiled and added, "Thank you for your concern and friendship. But after so long, surely they will welcome him home."

"Not with you at his side," Windrider argued softly. "If you blind your eyes to the truth, you will be hurt. Bright Arrow was filled with dark pride. He did not believe the tribe would dare to punish the son of Gray Eagle. They stripped him of his rank and honor. They took away his spirit and manhood. He has suffered for many winters. Do not be blind; he will pay the price to return. He can find new happiness in his camp without you, but he cannot find happiness with only you in the wilderness. Is that not true?" he gently challenged. She had failed to proclaim love for Bright Arrow; that omission gave Windrider the boldness to continue with his scheme. "Once his feet touch his lands, will he again leave with you?"

Tears moistened her tawny eyes. "Why do you say such cruel things, Windrider? He loved me and chose me. He gave up everything for me," she stressed. "Why would he betray me and desert me now?"

"I say such words to uncloud your eyes. Forgive me if they cut deeply. You have given him many seasons. Does his spirit sing with joy? Does he hunger for each new sun? Do you fill his life and heart, Rebecca? A warrior has needs which no woman can feed. Bright Arrow was raised as a warrior; he can be nothing less and be happy. Can he live as no man? Can he live with you, the reason for his losses? He does not own you as his horse or shield. Wives are free to leave their mates, to return home, to remarry. Make it painless for you and Bright Arrow. Put him away. Send him home. Join to me. Free him, Rebecca, before your heart suffers more," he urged her.

"I can't believe you're saying such things, Windrider.

117

What would Bright Arrow say if he heard you? I'm his . . . wife; you're his best friend. You must not love me. You must not speak this way again," she ordered faintly. "We have children. You know his people have the right to them if I free him. Children belong to the father's tribe," she emphasized raggedly, though it was a fact he knew well.

"Your girls must live as Indian. They cannot if you live in the Oglala camp as Bright Arrow's white whore. If you live that way, others will not forget they are half-blooded. Is your love for them strong enough to give them the life they need? Join to me and I will give you more children to love. When many moons are passed and you are accepted as my wife, we will visit your children in the Oglala camp. They will not forget their mother."

"I can't believe you are speaking this madness," she murmured. "I can't do what you ask, Windrider. It's wrong for me. Please don't say anything more," she pleaded.

"I will hold my tongue until you see my words are true. That moon, you will come to me. I will love you and protect you until the moon no longer crosses the sky," he vowed. Suddenly his gaze became intimidating. "I warn you now; I will not allow you to live as Bright Arrow's white whore. It would be as evil as destroying the sunshine. If you dare to yield to such a demand, I will challenge for you."

"No, you can't do that," she gasped in alarm. "What would others think? Please don't act so rashly, Windrider," she entreated him. "I can't allow you and Bright Arrow to battle over me."

"They would see the truth; I love you and want you. Hear me, Rebecca. I will not permit them to shame you or hurt you," he warned. "Rest. We have much land to cover before dark." He stood up and walked to the horses. After checking them, he sat down near the tree where they were grazing, purposely placing his profile to her.

Rebecca lay on the blanket which Windrider had spread beside her. She recalled the juice that he had prepared for them, remembering how he had filled Bright Arrow's pipe from his parfleche. Had the drinks and tobacco contained drugging herbs, some sexual stimulant? Had Windrider used the "dream" to arouse wanton desires in her? If so, was it the first time? And would she have reacted the same without magical compulsion? Had it been a ploy to entrap her, to tempt her beyond control? She recalled Bright Arrow's words about Windrider giving him gold and the news of the trader's arrival. If Windrider had not been attacked by the Pawnee warriors, they would have been alone for many days, and nights . . . Would he have confessed his love and desire for her? Would she have fallen prey to his manly prowess? Had he schemed to allow Bright Arrow to catch them together? She wondered whose idea it had been for Windrider to come to their cabin to guard her and the children. For certain, she wasn't drugged today. His desire and determination for her were intimidating, yet stimulating as well . . .

Rebecca observed her sleeping mate. His flabby stomach rose and fell each time he snored. He was sprawled on the ground like a drunk. He wasn't sleeping with one eye and ear open as a well-trained, acutely sensed warrior did on the trail! She sighed wearily. Her plagued heart cried out, *What has become of you, my love? How could you have done this to yourself? To us? Will it ever be as it was so long ago when we defiantly and brazenly surrendered to forbidden ecstasy? Has savage fate intervened? Is*

119

it over for us, Bright Arrow? Will I lose you to your tribe?
How can I fight for you?

Her haunted gaze shifted to the masterful and virile
Windrider. His eyes were closed, but his body indicated
he was alert. He was everything Bright Arrow had been,
and she almost resented that reality. Actually, she
mused, she should be delighted to have him along for
protection. But how should she deal with his feelings? If
only his challenges were false!

She couldn't dwell on such forbidden emotions. She
had to forget what Windrider had told her; she had to
force him to ignore her. She reclined on her side, away
from the entrancing warrior. She closed her eyes and
allowed her mind to drift lazily for a time.

The rest period was over. Windrider awakened Bright
Arrow. Seeing how much time had passed while he had
been deep in slumber, Bright Arrow flashed Windrider a
sheepish grin. Windrider smiled in return and encouraged, "Soon you will regain a warrior's body and skills."

"It will be hard, Windrider," he replied, casting his
somber eyes on his sleeping girls. "Many will laugh and
joke when they see how low Bright Arrow has fallen.
Once, few men could match my cunning and daring.
Now, a young brave could best me. A great warrior like
Windrider should avoid those who reveal meager
courage or honor. As my friend and helper, many will
taunt you," he sadly warned the puissant warrior who
grinned nonchalantly at him.

Knowing Rebecca wasn't asleep, Windrider cleverly
asked, "What will you do with your woman if the Oglala
council does not change its vote? Will you force her to
live as your slave? They will accept you and the children,

but not her. Does she know this? Is it not the same to be a warrior of another tribe," he pointed out. "She is special, Bright Arrow. She has given you much and endured much. You must guard her feelings with care. Will you take her and return to the white man's world if she is rejected?"

Bright Arrow frowned. "Never," he answered with cold finality. "I know it is hard for a banished warrior to find peace and honor in another camp. My heart and head have no answers this sun. I must become a whole man before I enter my camp. I pray they do not give me a choice between my tribe and my wife."

Windrider refuted, "She is not your wife, Bright Arrow. You did not join with her by Indian law. You took her in the white man's custom as a man called Clay Rivera. You are not that man. He is not real. She is not your true wife under the white man's law. She lived with you, but not as your wife. Will she do this in your camp?"

"Rebecca will do as I command," he stated firmly, embarrassed by Windrider's truthful statements. He knew he could not bear losing her after all he'd given up to have her. "She knows she is not my wife by any man's law. She will obey me and go where I lead. If she can live with me in the white world without a true marriage, why can she not do so in my camp?" he reasoned.

"I have intruded on your thoughts and feelings, my friend. I ask forgiveness. I will not speak of such painful matters again. I wish to see you and your family safe and happy. You wake the children. I will call your woman from her sleep. We must go; the sky warns of rain."

Bright Arrow's attention was captured by the girls as he aroused them. They went running off toward the stream with their father, their loud giggles trailing

121

behind them. Windrider knelt beside Rebecca and gently shook her shoulder. She rolled to her back and locked her eyes on his. Her probing gaze asked if Windrider had intentionally pointed out the fact that she was not legally or morally wed to Bright Arrow; their children were wood's colts. It was only a charade. For what? For whom?

His gaze craftily altered from one of tenderness to one of surprise, then remorse. "You were not sleeping. I am sorry. I know you are not wed. He has no hold over you. I wished to know of Bright Arrow's true feelings for you. It is foolish for a warrior to seek a battle which is lost before the first blow is struck. I did not mean to insult or shame you with such words. I will say no more."

As he turned to rise, Rebecca caught his muscular arm and said, "Say no more . . . until I have had time to think on your words."

"It will be as you say," he agreed. He smiled at her and extended his hand to help her rise.

Rebecca accepted it. Despite the heat of the day, her hand was cold within his warm grasp. With his towering, robust frame blocking hers from the others, his fingers pressed against the throbbing pulse in her throat. He smiled and murmured, "Your heart races as swiftly as mine. Do not fear my love or possession, Rebecca."

"I have never been afraid of you, Windrider," she responded. "We must go," she stated nervously.

Smelling sweet victory, he grinned and nodded. They joined the others, and the steady march continued on until dusk.

The scenery slipped by without Rebecca noticing it or the passage of time. She had never before allowed herself to ponder her iniquitous relationship with Bright Arrow. Where had her purity, honor, and modesty gone? She had been raised with virtue and morals; when had they fled? She had transgressed the laws of God and man. Listing the facts, her situation sounded so sinful. Willingly, she had entered a life of disgraceful wickedness. They had made love the first day he had taken her captive. Perhaps it had been a clever seduction, but not rape. They had been strangers and enemies, controlled and charmed by physical attraction. They had yielded to carnal temptation. Did initial captivity excuse her brazen conduct?

Love had come later between them. But did love justify her ensuing behavior? For nearly a year she had existed as his slave, compelled to obey his every order and whim. Yet she knew beyond a glimmer of doubt that she would have resisted any other man to the death before submitting to his desires. In all honesty, she admitted to herself that she had craved Bright Arrow; she had permitted herself to excuse her actions by pretending she had no choice in the matter.

When she was free to choose her behavior, had she changed? No. Had she refused his lovemaking? No. She had continued her life of iniquity. As if to justify their living together, they had pretended to wed. They had stayed together for years; they had created three children. Yet they were not married in any degree, and that admission troubled her deeply. What would her beloved parents have said if they were still alive? She had lived in sin . . .

How could she rectify this predicament? The Sioux Indian Bright Arrow couldn't wed Rebecca Kenny under the white man's laws. The white captive Rebecca Kenny couldn't wed Bright Arrow under the Indian laws. Without a willing minister, they couldn't wed under God's laws. Were all laws and powers against a mixed union?

There was no answer to her dilemma. Either they must live in sin, or they must separate. Windrider had almost demanded, "Free him. Send him away." But there were three children born out of wedlock to consider. Now that she had confronted this distressing situation, how should she deal with it? Did any of it matter to her husband . . . lover? Could she ever make love to him again without feeling shame and guilt?

Yet, Windrider could become her husband under the laws of the Cheyenne and under the eyes of the Great Spirit. It wasn't fair! Why did the Sioux have to be so different, so hostile to whites? Knowing all about her, Windrider was pursuing her as a future bride. To win her, he was willing to discard his other wives and his friendship with Bright Arrow. She felt like an unfettered lass being courted—and she was! Windrider had made his feelings and intentions known to her. Bright Arrow had no marital, legal, or moral claim on her.

That conclusion was a stunning shock. She had never verbally pledged herself and her life to Bright Arrow. She had given her love freely and wildly but had promised him nothing more. The vows they had exchanged had been issued and pledged between Rebecca Kenny and the imaginary Clay Rivera. There had never been any agreements signed or spoken between them. Rebecca Rivera . . . She had never called herself or thought of herself by that name! She had been born—and still was—Alisha Rebecca Kenny.

How ironic that her first name was from Bright Arrow's mother, Alisha Williams, now Princess Shalee, friend to both her mother and father. Such a strange twist of fate, to fall in love with the son of the woman for whom she had been named twenty-five years before. If her parents were still alive, would that change her fate, her rejection by the Sioux?

She had been like a puppet, yanked this way and that, always performing in a play which was written by some-one else. The illustrious son of Gray Eagle had captured and enslaved her. She had done as she had been told to avoid physical and emotional torment. He hadn't asked her to marry him. He had demanded they be allowed to join or he would leave his people. Had it been some rash strategy on his part? The council had forbidden a mar-riage between them, and he had been warned that they would be banished if Bright Arrow didn't halt his foolish game. He had left his tribe and taken her with him, to await their surrender to his terms. Neither side had yielded in nearly seven years. The mock marriage had been his idea when he had learned she was expecting their first child. Had it been to soothe her conscience? Had it been to place some hold over her? Had the child sealed his part in this bargain? She had never thought about leaving or staying with him; it had just happened that way. First, his captivity; next, his banishment; finally, their children. The years had fled as he con-trolled her destiny and emotions. He had made all the decisions, and she had blindly obeyed them. But so much had changed, especially recently.

What would her life be like today if she had escaped from Bright Arrow before he had left his tribe? What if she had chosen to remain at the fort after rescuing Bright Arrow? What if there had been no children involved? What if she had returned to St. Louis after her first child's birth? What if she had allowed Bright Arrow and the baby to return to his people? What if she had demanded he leave them long ago when he had first begun to destroy himself? What if they had gone to live with another Indian tribe? *What if, what if, what if,* her warring mind taunted her. She had not been free since her parents died when whe was fifteen. After that monstrous day, her life had been in one turmoil after another. Besides, Bright Arrow was no longer the man to whom she had given her pledge of love and loyalty . . .

They journeyed for six days without trouble. Game and wild vegetables were plentiful along the way, so they enjoyed good and nourishing meals. Twice they encountered a few hunters with whom the men conversed and smoked pipes around a campfire, and she played the dutiful wife, serving them and keeping silent.

One meal had nearly erupted into a verbal battle between her and Bright Arrow. She had been exhausted. The braves had arrived while they were consuming their meal, and Rebecca had wanted the men to prepare their own supper while she turned in for the night. Bright Arrow had scowled at her, then insisted she behave as a proper Indian wife. It was the custom to offer food to visitors in one's camp, and he did not wish to be embarrassed before the Wahpeton warriors. Facing the alternatives of cooking and serving a meal or creating a wider rift between them by refusing, Rebecca fumed with resentment but carried out his wishes.

In the beginning, Windrider had kept his distance from Rebecca; she, in turn, had tried to keep her eyes and thoughts from him. Bright Arrow had seemed oblivious to everything except trudging along the tiresome trail. And he had neglected to thank Rebecca for her courtesy and work.

It was apparent to all by the second day that Rebecca was in better physical shape than Bright Arrow. He was winded after an hour's steady pace, and became more fatigued as the day progressed. At night he slept deeply. Sweat would glisten and drip off his flaccid body from his exertions and the heat. From the way he massaged himself at each rest stop and each night, his companions could tell that his body ached all over. It became a common occurrence to see a grimace or scowl upon his flushed face. Yet she knew his body would be forced to respond to this daily exercise, and she was grateful for the hardships.

By the seventh day, a routine pattern had been set. They ate a light meal at sunrise, then walked until noon. They halted for another light meal and a short rest or nap. They walked until sunset, then made camp for the night. It was Windrider who helped Rebecca gather wood and prepare their meals, except when visitors were present. Even though it was uncommon for a warrior to do such tasks, he explained that he realized she was as weary as the men. Still, his kind actions did not encourage Bright Arrow to help her. The two men took turns caring for the horse, and when they halted for the day, Rebecca suspected that Bright Arrow spent time playing with the girls just to conceal his excessive fatigue and to avoid helping her. In subtle ways, Windrider never missed an opportunity to reveal the dissimilarities between himself and Bright Arrow.

The children traveled exceedingly well, riding on the travois much of the time. Bursting with energy and excitement, the two older girls pleaded to be allowed to walk occasionally with their father or mother, which exhausted them so that they slept well and gave Bright Arrow the relief of a slower pace from time to time. When they camped near water, the girls splashed around with their father or hunted frogs along the bank.

Several times Windrider offered to carry Tashina for

Rebecca, but she would smile and decline, for Tashina was light in weight and a mellow child. Often Rebecca feared she showed favoritism toward Tashina. Even at such a young age, Tashina was a beautiful and sweet child who possessed a resemblance to Princess Shalee. Her flesh was a softer bronze than that of her two sisters. Her large and expressive eyes were sherry brown with green flecks, and her features were delicate, set in perfect balance. Tashina would be a stunning woman.

At night, the girls slept together on one large buffalo mat in the center of the group. The three adults were situated around their mat as if to form a protective triangle. One night, Rebecca almost laughed aloud as she surveyed their positions. She was between the men, with the children between all of them. To one side of her was the fascinating and valiant Windrider. To her other side was the snoring, devitalized Bright Arrow. She warned herself to stop making comparisons between the two men, but it was impossible. They made it impossible!

Bright Arrow had disallowed any time for intimacy. He had not shown any ardor before the others, nor even tried to steal a kiss or a hug. She had ceased her attempts at affection after the second day, for he had seemed annoyed by her tender overtures, as if he lacked passion. His entire demeanor seemed to convey a "don't bother me" attitude. He was so tired and distracted that he rarely smiled at her, almost behaving as if she didn't exist—or, worse yet, as if she were his white slave once more!

She couldn't understand his aloof behavior. The closer they moved to the Indian camp, the further he withdrew from her. Were his mind and emotions consumed by what he would face there? Was he so blatantly single-minded and inflexible? Not once had he attempted a romantic overture or suggested they sneak off to make love. The two times she had tried to knead his aching muscles, he had shrugged away from her relaxing massage. The night she had secretly hinted at an intimate meeting in the forest, he had frowned at her as if she had implied something forbidden!

Bright Arrow hardly spoke with her, except to give orders of some kind. It was time to go, or it was time to stop. It was time to eat, or time to sleep. It was time to put the children to bed, or time to wake them to leave. It was load the travois, or it was unpack it. It was gather more wood, or it was fetch more water. It was serve me more food, or it was put out the fire. It was—no matter how weary you are—wait on my friends. It was everything—everything but time and attention for them! It was infuriating and depressing! It was frustrating and damaging! And it was just what Windrider wanted and needed . . .

Had Bright Arrow gotten over his panic of almost losing her to death, Rebecca wondered, or over his guilt and shame at endangering his family? He had been about to make love to her that day before the injured Windrider had appeared. Was he reluctant to expose his ardent feelings before another man? He didn't have to flaunt his love and passion, but he certainly didn't have to treat her so coldly! she fumed. She would be content with a romantic walk or a sincere conversation, or just a light kiss or comforting embrace! In her bewildered and emotionally weakened state, Rebecca desperately needed a show of love and consideration.

Wasn't he aware of the ever-increasing distance between them, this estrangement which he had created and was feeding? she silently puzzled. Didn't he sense her confusion and anguish? What about that last morning in the cabin? He had been so provocative, so tender, so strong, so romantic? Once on the trail homeward, he had become . . . frigid—that was the most accurate description. Was he unknowingly preparing her for a show of indifference in the Indian camp, possibly a total break from him? Had he already decided to betray and desert her if he had to, and was he feeling guilty and defensive? It was mid-July, and he had not made love to her since early spring . . .

On the eighth day, they stopped to camp at dusk, as usual. The terrain had been rough and the weather humid. Rebecca was exhausted, her clothes damp from perspiration. Wisps of hair clung to her face and neck, her cheeks were flushed and her breathing ragged. Her body had depleted most of its energy, and all she wanted to do was cook the evening meal, put the girls to bed, splash off in the cool stream, and collapse on her sleeping mat. Devilish Fate would not allow it. Some mischievous force seemed determined to darken her love and respect for Bright Arrow and to increase her susceptibility to the intrepid Cheyenne warrior.

Ever wily and astute, Windrider was cognizant of her fatigued state and eager to take advantage of the situation. He quickly gathered wood while Bright Arrow and Rebecca unloaded the travois. Bright Arrow headed for the stream to tend the horse as Rebecca futilely attempted to settle the children so she could carry out her chores. Full of nervous energy, the girls raced here and there. Rebecca called them back to sit on the buffalo mat, but the moment she turned her back to collect some necessary items, they were running off once more. Rebecca couldn't watch the active children and concen-

trate on completing her other tasks. Seeking Bright
Arrow's assistance, she glanced around, only to find him
refreshing his hot and sore feet in the tepid stream.
When she noticed the fire which Windrider had prepared
and lit for her and saw him fetching fresh water from the
stream, fury assailed her.

She inhaled deeply to calm her agitated senses. She
called to Bright Arrow for help with their girls. He irritably told her to bring them over to play near him in the
stream. She nearly bit her tongue to keep from screaming
curses at him. When he declared his hunger and
suggested she hurry with the evening meal, she was
sorely tempted to throw every item in her quivering grip
at him!

The girls hopped on Bright Arrow like three small field
mice boldly pouncing on a tom cat. As he frolicked with
the children, he paid her no further attention. Her gaze
narrowed and her teeth clenched painfully as she glared
at Bright Arrow. Suddenly Windrider blocked her vision
with his manly physique. He handed her the water bag
and smiled sympathetically. When he said he would
prepare the sleeping mats so they might retire early, tears
of gratitude threatened to spill forth from her eyes.

She stood helplessly as her gaze appreciatively mapped
his features. It traveled to his full, inviting lips to absorb
his smile. It moved to the indentation in his chin, which
reminded her of a tiny ravine between two solid boulders.
It examined his prominent cheekbones and sturdy
jawline, and traced his straight nose. Then her gaze
slowly drifted along his brows and lashes, which were
thick and sooty. It danced over his ebony hair of shiny
braids. It seemed to her that his body could belong to a
copper-skinned god. He was irresistibly handsome, dangerously tempting. Her gaze fastened on his watchful one

and searched it for some explanation to her wanton feelings. "Whatever would I do without you?" she stated impulsively.

His strong hands covered hers on the water bag. It required all of his willpower to master his urgent desire for her, to prevent himself from losing sight of reality. That realization astonished and vexed him, for it was not in his scheme. He knew he must be very careful in his dealings with her. He must not offend or alarm her. He must not allow her to suspect his motive. And love was his motive—a love she could never understand, a love and respect for his life-long friend, Bright Arrow. He must make her feel guilty about ruining his friend. He must discourage her where Bright Arrow was concerned, and instead make her turn toward him. He knew he had to set his trap for her carefully in order to free Bright Arrow from this magic force in white skin. What better way than by proving betrayal and evil?

As surely as the snows blanketed the sacred Black Hills in winter, she was turning to him and away from Bright Arrow. By yielding to another man, she would dishonor herself and betray her husband. Once she was unmasked before Bright Arrow, her hold over him would be broken forever! He realized that his impending success was more Bright Arrow's fault than his own clever plotting; yet he had not expected her to affect him so powerfully! He would have to be cautious of her magic!

He wondered if she realized what her tantalizing gaze was doing to him, and instantly decided that she must know how she bewitched men. How could she appear so innocent, so pure, so honest, so trusting? As he battled to conceal her forbidden effect on him, he remarked, "Perhaps his mind is trapped by worry. He faces much hardship in a few moons. He fears the other warriors will mock him. He fears he will not find himself again. He fears to learn the choices which are ahead. Do not be touched by his cruel words and deeds. He does not see how he hurts you." Windrider excused Bright Arrow's behavior in a tone which implied he was being kind.

His touch was so reassuring, so comforting, so disturbing. She looked at the contact of their hands but didn't break it. She replied, "A real man should fear nothing. You're never afraid of anything or anyone. You're never too weary or distracted to be kind. He's selfish and mean, Windrider. There's no reason for him to act this way. He hasn't faced this exile alone. What if the others do tease him? Words can't kill a man. There are times I don't think I know him anymore, Windrider. He can be so cold and hateful. Sometimes I don't even like him!" she blurted out before thinking. Yet she didn't retract her words.

Their talk was edging onto precarious ground, for Windrider felt it was too soon to inspire a confrontation between Rebecca and Bright Arrow. He cautiously suggested, "We must finish the chores. You are weary and need rest."

She smiled, then laughed. "You're right. Thank you, Windrider." Slipping her hands from his, she knelt beside the fire to cook the meal.

Windrider went to retrieve the sleeping mats. His keen eyes widened at the perilous scene before him. The two older girls were nearly out of sight as they rambled along the bank. His sharp gaze sought Tashina, quickly locating her on the other side of the watery divider. "Little Feet! Moon Eyes! Come back! Tashina, no!" he shouted sternly in English. With a surge of energy, he bolted across the ankle-deep stream. His hasty movements and yells caught Rebecca's attention. He grabbed Tashina as she was about to reach for a coiled water snake. The viper struck just as Windrider snatched the inquisitive child from its range. He quickly carried her across the stream and handed her to her pale-faced mother. He seized his bow and an arrow, and put an end to the snake's ominous threat. Dropping his weapon, he went after the other two girls. With one in each arm, he returned to Rebecca's anxious side, highly perturbed by Bright Arrow's carelessness.

During the commotion, Bright Arrow awoke from his exhausted slumber. He observed his friend's swift action through drowsy senses. He came over to where Rebecca was crying and hugging the confused children. Windrider took command of the situation and her feelings once more as he stated softly, "I will play with them. You cook. When their stomachs are full, they will sleep quickly." He led the girls away to begin a game.

Rebecca focused her disbelieving eyes on Bright Arrow. "How could you do such a thing?" she hotly accused.

"They were sitting beside me. I closed my eyes for a short time. I was weary and sleep claimed me. I did not mean to rest so deeply," he explained guiltily.

"That's the trouble! You never mean anything anymore," she shot back. "We're just as tired as you are, in case you're too blind to notice! Get your lazy body up and help us," she gritted just above a whisper, for his hearing alone.

Bright Arrow was shocked by her vehement outburst. Humiliation and rage filled him. How dare his wife embarrass him before another warrior! How dare she make such ridiculous and insulting charges! It had been an accident. He warned angrily, "Your tongue is sharp and cruel this day. A wife does not speak so to her husband. You insult me before Windrider; you offend him with your surly tongue. Speak no more or I will punish you. Prepare the meal and obey me."

Rebecca felt a curious calm overtake her. A wry grin flashed across her face as she mentally scoffed, *Your wife? Obey you like a lowly slave? Punish me? Like Hell! If you dare lift a hand against me, I will* . . . She couldn't complete her thought. She observed the concerned way Bright Arrow was studying her. She could tell that he knew he had spoken too brazenly, but he would not apologize.

"At least you're speaking to me and noticing my presence once more. I was beginning to think I was growing invisible. Nothing would suit me better than to keep silent around you . . . if you will be so kind as to continue doing the same with me," she stated sarcastically, then turned her attention to her chore.

When the meal was ready, Rebecca called the girls and Windrider to come eat. She refused to speak with Bright Arrow, who steamed in silence. After the food was consumed, the girls were put to bed by their moody father. Rebecca cleared away the remains of their supper and put away her cooking supplies. She dared visitors to enter their camp tonight! After excusing herself for a few moments, she retired to her mat. Oddly, she was asleep shortly after her head touched the mat, despite her previous emotional upheaval.

It was Bright Arrow who couldn't sleep. His pensive gaze shifted over the sleeping group, lingering briefly on Tashina, then moving to Rebecca. He tried to understand why he was behaving in this foolish way, knowing he had to stop before he lost his woman. He couldn't forget the way she had looked at him after his unforgivable tirade. Panic gnawed at him. What was wrong with him? He rolled to his back and watched the stars until they disappeared from the sky.

When Rebecca awoke, Bright Arrow was rousing the girls, and Windrider was feeding small branches to a hungry fire. As she pushed herself to a sitting position, she discovered ten wildflowers lying on her mat. She smiled and warmed to the romantic gesture. She glanced at Bright Arrow whose back was to her. Her appreciative gaze went to Windrider's profile, and she sighed tranquilly as she arose, inhaling the fragrant flowers which had surely been left by her ardent admirer.

As she performed her morning tasks, Bright Arrow wondered if she was touched at all by his implied apology. Evidently she wasn't ready or willing to forgive him this soon, and he couldn't blame her. He had pushed her down a difficult trail for a long time. He was disappointed when she failed to smile at him or at least thank him for the flowers.

Chapter Six

Rebecca decided that two could play at Bright Arrow's selfish game, which could be exactly what he needed. He had no right to be so heartless! She was finished being the ground beneath his stumbling feet and she became just as remote and silent as he had been. She refused to meet his gaze or to acknowledge his presence. She performed her chores as if he were the invisible one. If he insisted on a response to a question, she would issue it briefly and crisply. If he made any curt remarks about her mood, she would frown or shrug. She made no attempts to be romantic and brushed off each of his. If she smiled, it was a tight smile. It was as if she had cut him out of her life.

After the way Bright Arrow had been behaving for months, she felt he deserved this lesson. She knew that Bright Arrow was painfully aware of her drastic change of heart and conduct. Suddenly he was trying to talk with her; he was trying to be loving and considerate, but she was too piqued to allow him an easy victory. If she did, he could very well become distant again. She debated the possibility of using Windrider to make him jealous, but concluded that such a ploy was too reckless. Bright Arrow's initial anger over her cold treatment had turned to worry and remorse. At first he had tried to feign ignorance of her dark mood. Then he had tried to tease her from her sullen pose. She smugly perceived the panic and guilt in his tone when in vain he tried to coax her from her silent world.

Cognizant of the brewing storm between Rebecca and his friend, Windrider gingerly held his comments to himself and was careful not to interfere. If all continued as it had been he reflected, perhaps Rebecca might loosen her hold on his friend with her foolish actions. She appeared to have become scornful and doubtful of her mate, and seemed discouraged with Bright Arrow. Perhaps she was readying herself for a final break from her husband.

Windrider wondered if the seeds he had planted could be bearing fruit so quickly. Had his trick to ensnare her worked? Was she ready and eager to accept him and his false promises? Would she truly discard the famed warrior Bright Arrow for him? He was puzzled. Was it him she desired, or any superior man? Once she made her choice of Windrider known, Bright Arrow would cast her aside for her traitorous betrayal! Bright Arrow would believe she had turned her evil magic on his friend. He would think she was being vengeful, trying to shame him or to torment him. No matter if it cost Windrider his friendship, he was resolved to see Bright Arrow reborn. Yet Windrider was becoming wary of his wicked plan to unmask her.

Was it possible to set up a trap in which Bright Arrow could discover his woman trying to seduce his friend, make her the instigator of this treachery? Windrider recalled that night in the cabin. Rebecca had been a female of great passion and hunger. Could he so tempt her starving senses that she would seek him out with boldness? Could he arouse her to the point where she couldn't keep her eyes and hands off him? Could he so entrance her that she would rashly reveal her lust before

Bright Arrow? Would Bright Arrow slay her for such a wanton display?

That possible reaction curiously distressed Windrider. It was not in his plan to see Rebecca injured or slain. He wanted Bright Arrow forced back into his old life; he wanted Rebecca banished to her white world where she belonged. He had been watching her closely, perhaps too closely! Her constant magic was much too powerful for any man to battle endlessly! He could understand why Bright Arrow was so enchanted by her. Since he could not free himself, it was up to his friend to do so. Yet he would have to be careful not to entangle himself while freeing his friend. He had expected this game to be simple!

The timing had to be perfect. She had to choose him over Bright Arrow in the Cheyenne camp. That way, Bright Arrow's honor would not allow him to slay her or to forgive her. If a wife desired to leave her husband for any reason, all she had to do was confess it and leave him. No honorable brave would beg a wife to stay or prevent her from leaving. Disillusioned, he would return to his people. And once Windrider revealed his cunning game to her, she would flee to her kind and begin a new life there. All would be as it had been long ago.

Windrider envisioned the culminating scene of his daring drama and rapidly dismissed it from his mind. He had no choice but to hurt her! He must not feel shame or anguish over her impending pain! He was doing what he had to do to save his friend! He must not allow her to pierce his heart and alter his plan! If only Rebecca weren't so beautiful, so gentle, so brave, so passionate! If only she weren't a rare creature who had truly suffered much these past winters! If only she were to blame for all this trouble! Windrider closed his mind to such tormenting problems, failing to comprehend that his pretended concern was gradually becoming a reality.

For three days Rebecca maintained her obstinate position. Regardless of her feigned ignorance of Bright Arrow, her emotional appetite had been whet. It seemed as if she had been carrying the burden of their relationship for ages; she had needed his support, his attention, his tenderness. Yet it was Windrider who offered her those things. She continually found herself analyzing every look and word from each man. Would it come to a choice between them?

Today Bright Arrow did not nap during their rest period. He took his bow and quiver of arrows and left to hunt fresh meat for their evening meal. Was he trying to appease her? Or was he feeling more like his old self? Some of the fat around his middle had vanished during their trip. He no longer showed signs of being winded or excessively sore. He no longer sweated profusely. It was apparent to her that his body was responding favorably to his demands on it. Still, a full recovery would take many weeks.

The girls were resting peacefully in the shade on their mats, and Windrider was leaning against a tree not far away. Rebecca was plagued by his odd reserve during these past two days. She approached him. "Windrider, are you angry with me?" she inquired.

He glanced down at her upturned face. Dappled sunlight shimmered over her fiery locks, and her tawny eyes revealed an entreating glow. His heart drummed wildly. "Why do you ask such a thing?" he replied hoarsely.

Rebecca was surprised by his husky tone. "You've been so distant since my argument with Bright Arrow.

Did I offend you with my outburst? I suppose I behaved badly, but I was so frightened. In truth, I was furious with Bright Arrow. You've hardly come near me or spoken to me since that day. Please tell me what I did wrong?" she beseeched him. She nervously moistened her dry lips, drawing his dark eyes to them.

An overwhelming urge surged through him to yank her into his arms and to imprison those lips beneath his. He shuddered and inhaled deeply. "There is much trouble and anger between you and Bright Arrow. I gave my word to you I would say no more until you wished me to do so. When the grass is dead and brown beneath the feet of Bright Arrow, the grass which is green and alive beneath mine is tempting. I do not wish to lure you from him while you are weak and sad in spirit. You must come to me free in heart and head, not to spite Bright Arrow."

She stared at him in astonishment. She had not expected this strange behavior or these baffling words. If he were trying to lure her away, why did he not take advantage of their estrangement. "Surely you don't think I would use you to hurt Bright Arrow? I'm not trying to make him jealous. I'm not trying to spite him. He deserves my anger and resentment," she retorted.

He pretended confusion and distress. "My white words do not match my thoughts. Help me to explain. I do not say you reject him for revenge. I do not say you seek to recall his eye by showing desire for me. I do not say you wish to punish him by showing more honor to me. I ask you to come to me when all has passed between you and Bright Arrow. I ask you to make it your choice, not because I invaded your mind and removed Bright Arrow from your thoughts. Do not come while there is anger and bitterness swaying your choice. You must not come

141

until it is only Windrider you desire. If this is true, you must free Bright Arrow without pain or dishonor. Do you see?"

She gingerly probed the meaning of his words, needing to make her sure that certain suspicions she had begun to have were accurate. "I understand. You don't want to interfere in my relationship with Bright Arrow. You love me, but you don't want to be the reason we end our life together. You'll claim me as your woman, but only after I am free of him," she said, recounting his statements. When he nodded, she smiled knowingly. It was time to be clever and bold, and perhaps the time to practice a little deceit of her own! She had to discover Windrider's true motives. "The only thing you've done is help me to realize how impossible he's making it for us to stay together. He's swaying my thoughts and feelings, Windrider, not you. Bright Arrow's had a very hard time since he left home. I've tried to be patient, and understanding, and true to him. Whatever I do, it never seems enough for him. He needs more than I can give him; and as long as we hold on to each other, he'll be trapped between me and his destiny. Perhaps I am bad for him," she suggested softly, but he didn't reply. She was confused by his restraint. This was the perfect time for seductive persuasion! Why was he silent?

She audaciously ventured, "For a long time I tried to shut my eyes to his torment. I tried to convince myself that he was strong and brave, that he could overcome any obstacle, that nothing and no one could harm him. I was mistaken. Maybe I'm not the one who can help him recover himself. Maybe it'll be worse for him if I don't force him to leave me. I don't know," she whispered sadly. Furtively, she observed the effect of her statements. "Maybe it's time to let him go. Maybe it's time for both of us to admit we made a mistake by trying to defy the laws of our peoples. Perhaps it's time to begin new lives. If only I knew the right answer. Ever since the day he captured me, I've been bound to him. I've never considered staying or leaving. It was like he owned me, and I did as he commanded."

Windrider didn't interrupt her.

"Please understand one thing," Rebecca continued. "I'm not a she-wolf on the prowl, trying to find a new mate to replace Bright Arrow. He's the only man I've ever known. I've never found another man desirable or irresistible until I met . . ." She flushed, wondering if she should finish her statement. "I'm sorry, Windrider; I shouldn't have said that. You're a most honorable man. It isn't right to include you in the middle of this trouble with Bright Arrow. I only wanted to tell you what I've decided. I do want him to become the man he was long ago. I want him to be happy and whole. But if his people won't allow us to marry, I won't live with him in their camp. I won't be his slave or whore. And we can't go back to living in the wilderness. Ever since we met, we have been facing one storm after another. Maybe we've used up all the emotions we have to give each other. He's miserable and I'm miserable. Unless the Oglalas say we can marry and live without shame, Bright Arrow will return to his tribe alone. If things are as you say, I'll be free to chose a man who stirs my heart and body, and I hope the Oglalas make that decision easy for me." With that stunning declaration, she turned and left him staring at her retreating back.

The puzzle was intricate. Rebecca had hoped to solve it with ingenuity and patience. If her suspicions were correct, Windrider's plot was cunning and harmful. As many new pieces appeared as those already assembled!

What if she called his bluff? Would he lie and implicate her? Would he accuse her of being the instigator? What and who would Bright Arrow believe? Could she risk calling his hand or rejecting him until she had more evidence? It seemed wisest to play along with Windrider until he exposed himself . . .

Afterward, Rebecca mellowed to the point of being polite and amiable to Bright Arrow, as if she were trying to learn if there was anything left to their life together, as if there was hope for a new start. Yet she made certain they were never alone. When he tried to embrace her or kiss her on the cheek, she would playfully shrug it off. When he asked her to take a walk that evening, she gently refused and went about her tasks. To make sure there were no misunderstandings, she didn't encourage Windrider in the least. As far as both men were concerned, she treated them as her brothers. Neither man quite knew what to make of the situation.

Because they were traveling on foot and with small children, the journey had taken longer than usual, and Rebecca was surprised and pleased when Windrider told her that they would arrive in his camp in three days. *Three short days*, she mused pensively. That wasn't much time to deliberate her course of action.

The next day passed uneventfully, but the following one did not. The Cheyenne camp lay south of the Black Hills. Windrider led them through the area between the sacred mountains and the area known as the "badlands." Skirting that harsh and uninviting region required additional traveling time. Huge rock formations and barren hills were visible from their trail. Bright Arrow told her it was the short and heavy rains and long days of drought which created such terrain. The peaks had eroded into eerily shaped cliffs, sharp ridges, naked hills, and

144

countless hidden canyons. Here and there, a rare valley boasted prairie grass and scrub trees and, in some places, bands of colors encircled the rocks like imprisoning rainbows. From a distance, the area looked ghostly and unreal. In the bright sunlight, the craggy mounds looked sandy in color, but at dusk, they assumed a deep gray shade. She certainly wouldn't want to get lost in there, she thought, especially after Windrider told her it was infested with rattlesnakes. He said that if a man wanted to disappear forever, he could do so there. Even the children were fascinated by the scenery.

The area where they journeyed consisted of rolling hills with occasional gullies and ravines. Ripened shortgrass concealed most of the ground, though flat, submerged rocks exposed their gray speckled surfaces along the way to break the golden covering. Every so often the land would swiftly decline until a towering cliff would block a path carelessly taken. It was obvious that both men knew this area well, and when a violent storm threatened to overtake them, Windrider directed the group to a cave at the base of one of the towering cliffs.

Noticing several thirsty scrub trees nearby, Windrider hurried to them. He used his powerful legs to break branches from them for a fire before they could be wet beyond use. Bright Arrow led the horse and travois inside. They had barely entered the darkened area when the storm unleashed its fury. Bright Arrow removed the cradleboard from Rebecca's back and placed Tashina with the other girls.

As Windrider built a fire and Bright Arrow unloaded the travois, Rebecca talked with the girls to calm their anxieties. She withdrew handmade dolls from a pack and encouraged the girls to play while she prepared a light meal. As she did so, the two men stood at the entrance watching the storm and speaking in low voices. When the meal was ready, they sat around the fire to eat. Rebecca carefully fed Tashina the mashed vegetables and finely cut meat, delighted that her nineteen-month-old daughter was weaned. Afterward, the girls played on a large buffalo mat until sleep overtook them.

The rumbling thunder and dazzling lightning had moved off into the distance, but a heavy rain continued. Bright Arrow announced he was going hunting for a deer, for he knew they frequently roamed the area. He said it would be a simple task, for the creatures would be seeking shelter from the storm. He gathered his weapons, smiled at her, then left quickly. Clearly, his spirits were recovering gradually as was his body!

Rebecca stood near the opening to watch his exit. When he was out of sight, she leaned against the rocky surface at her back, closed her eyes, and inhaled deeply. A hand went against her jawline as a thumb moved over her lips, then cupped her chin and lifted it. She opened her eyes just as Windrider's eager mouth claimed hers. She was drawn into his steely embrace and held possessively as the feverish kiss assailed her dizzy senses.

Windrider's hands imprisoned her head between them. His fingers vanished into her flaming hair as his mouth possessed hers urgently, almost savagely. When his aroused body pressed snugly against hers, she knew his passion was not false. Had she been wrong? She must know! Her arms slipped around his waist, and she clung to him, returning his kisses with fiery results. Another groan escaped her lips as his mouth softened on hers, but his grip tightened around her.

He murmured huskily into her ear, "I want you, Rebecca. I would give all my possessions to have you, to have no one between us. If it is not Windrider you love and desire, do not tempt me this way."

She wondered if he was inducing her to make a commitment to him. He had given his word not to press her. Why wasn't he willing to keep his distance until she had made a final decision about Bright Arrow? Did he suspect she was trying to rekindle her relationship with her husband? Was he afraid she might succeed? Was he demanding a promise from her? She had told him she must wait until she was positive there was no chance of marriage for her and Bright Arrow. He had said he didn't want her to come to him until she was free in heart and body, until it was over between her and Bright Arrow. He had said he didn't want to sway her, to lure her from his friend while she was confused and angered. She knew that love was his motive, but love for whom? Freedom was his desire, but whose freedom? Was she mistaken in believing he plotted against her? Or had Windrider carelessly ensnared himself in the trap he had set for her? Could she trust him? Believe him?

"Why do you not answer?" he inquired apprehensively, his gaze trying to penetrate her obscure one. "Why do you cloud my mind?"

"I'm not sure what to say, Windrider," she replied, stalling for more time to think. "The ending of something precious is hard. If we did not share children, the answer would be simple. Many times I have felt Bright Arrow should leave me and return to his people. It has pained me to watch him grow soft in body and weak in spirit. If I said anything to make him feel he must stay with me, I feared he would become restless and bitter. He would feel trapped. Yet, I couldn't bring myself to demand he leave. I didn't know which would hurt the most. His spirit was dying. I didn't know how to stop it. I wondered if I was responsible for changing him from the man I met. I was as vulnerable as he was, Windrider. I was hurting too, but he could only see and feel his own pain. I tried to excuse my cowardice by saying that if I truly loved him, I would settle for less than perfection. I would forgive his weaknesses. I told myself to be patient and kind. I kept thinking he would awaken from his deep slumber. I couldn't force him to stay or leave. One person can't see inside another's heart or mind. One person cannot choose another's destiny. Only the Great Spirit has that power and right. It was wrong for me to interfere in his decisions. He must find the answer within himself, then seek the courage to make it happen. His past life created ghosts which lived in the cabin with us. They refused to grant him peace. They haunted him; they tormented him; they drew his mind to where he should be. His suffering came from resisting the truth."

As if dreading to hear her response, he asked tensely, "Do your words say you choose Bright Arrow?"

"My words say the decision has never been in my hands or power, Windrider. Bright Arrow chose to capture and enslave me. The council chose to banish him when he refused to cast me aside. He chose to defy their vote. He chose to ruin his own life and mine when he decided to punish himself and me for his losses. He chose to remain in the wilderness, just as now he chooses to return home. Now, he must choose his tribe or me, for the Oglalas will not allow him to have both. In his place, what would your choice be, Windrider? There is nothing I can do except wait for him to find himself. The decision will be hard for him. I will not try to sway his mind or heart, for perhaps our destinies were not meant to be joined. If it should as you said, when the moment comes, I will walk away without pleas or tears."

"Will you walk to me?" He pressed for an answer. He

captured her chilly hands and placed kisses over them, fixing his gaze on hers.

"Is it right to speak such words at this time?" she replied with a question, alarmed and shocked by his seemingly undeniable sincerity.

"Are words less important than actions? You will give me kisses and embraces, but you can offer me no hope, no promise? Will silence stop feelings?"

"Until the matter is settled with Bright Arrow, we should not speak or touch in this way, Windrider. What if Bright Arrow returned and saw us? We must not hurt him. When his choice is made, then I will speak my mind and heart to you," she promised. Whatever happened, she vowed inwardly, she would clarify matters with Windrider when the time came.

"You fear to accept the truth that stands before you?" he challenged her.

Rebecca fused her gaze to his and responded faintly, "Yes, Windrider, I fear to accept the truth before my eyes. I fear to speak the words in my heart and mind. This is not the time and place for such secrets to be shared. Whatever happens, I will reveal them to you."

"It will be as you say," he conceded, knowing he could not and would not keep his word. He was plagued by his own choices. Should he continue his dangerous game? Had he been wrong to start it, wrong about her? Should he expose it to her and ask for forgiveness? Should he bury it forever? Or should he make the game real . . .

Windrider's gaze traveled over her lovely features. There were so many possibilities. What if Bright Arrow cast her aside? What if she chose him over Bright Arrow? What if he won his victory? But other fears cried louder in his turbulent mind. What if the Oglalas accepted her into their tribe? What if she was lost to him forever?

149

"Will you let me hold and kiss you once more?" he entreated, wondering if it would be for the last time, and pained by the thought. When she nodded, he hungrily closed his arms around her and his lips over hers. He seemed pleased when she responded to him. Finally he released her, then quickly left the cave to master his warring emotions.

Rebecca observed him as she had Bright Arrow, while tears eased down her cheeks. "Oh, Windrider," she murmured sadly, "why are you doing this cruel thing to us? You were not with Bright Arrow when he captured me. You do not love me or want to marry me. Your honor would not allow you to seduce and steal the woman of your best friend. Why have you set this trap for me? Why do you seek to dishonor and destroy me? Do you love Bright Arrow this much? Do you want to plant seeds of fury in him, fury against me? Do you think I am that evil? How far will your deceit go?"

Yet her mind challenged, *But what if you're wrong? What if his feelings are real? What if there is no evil plot against you? What if he truly loves and desires you? What if Bright Arrow and his people reject you? What if you are freed? Will you reach out to Windrider?* She couldn't deny that he inflamed her senses and ignited her passions. She couldn't deny that if there were no Bright Arrow . . .

Chapter Seven

The next day was hectic for everyone. They traveled quickly to end their arduous journey, and the small group entered the Cheyenne camp just before dusk. When the Cheyenne people were alerted to their arrival, they surrounded Windrider and his friends. Little Feet and Moon Eyes clung tightly to their father's legs. At the same time, Tashina snuggled against her mother's chest, curiously peering at the commotion. Being encircled by many people was a new experience for the children, especially because they couldn't understand their words. At first, they were shy and fearful. Rebecca knew it would take a while for them to relax and adjust.

As Windrider greeted his people, Rebecca scanned her new surroundings. This camp looked much like the Oglala camp where Bright Arrow had lived. The largest and most colorful tepees were in the center circle. With an ever-widening band, the circle of tepees increased to make an encampment of over two hundred dwellings which indicated a warrior society of approximately three hundred. From Windrider's reception, it was evident he was highly respected and loved. She wondered if a man of such valiance and distinction could be guilty of plotting against her.

Many warriors gathered around to question Windrider and to gape at Bright Arrow. Never had they expected to see the illustrious Sioux warrior in this condition. In fact, they had not expected to see him ever again. His banishment was no secret to them, nor was Windrider's continued friendship and concern. Dark eyes roved Bright Arrow's body, and keen senses perceived the drastic changes. Their reactions were varied. Some were sad and sympathetic; some were angered; some were amused or pleased; and some were repulsed. Bright Arrow had to force himself not to show his embarrassment.

The two wives of Windrider stepped forward to take charge of the feminine group. Rebecca was apprehensive about staying with the two women whom Windrider had offered to discard for her—if he were being honest. She asked herself how he would behave now that he was home. She couldn't forget what it had been like to be in his arms. Perhaps it would be best if they weren't allowed any privacy. Fearful of exposing her emotion and doubts, she dared not look at Windrider or Bright Arrow as the two wives led Rebecca and the children into their tepee.

The two men stayed behind to talk, to share the news of Windrider's new *coups* and to announce Bright Arrow's return to his lands. Only the last fact brought looks of surprise to several faces. "Our brother has returned to us," Windrider stated in a clear and confident voice. "We must help him regain his skills and hone his instincts. He will be reborn in our camp. When the moon comes, he will seek forgiveness and understanding from his people. Bright Arrow wishes to return home. He wishes to return to the life of a warrior. The Great Spirit sent me to his wooden tepee to bring him home. The Cheyenne will know great joy and victory in helping him."

"Come," Chief Yellow Robe invited. "We will sit and

speak. We will smoke the pipe of Grandfather. We will listen to His words."

In Windrider's tepee, the genial Sucoora offered Rebecca and her girls nourishment. Fortunately, Sucoora could speak broken English, and Kajihah was Oglala and spoke the Sioux tongue. Between the two languages, Rebecca had no trouble conversing with the two females, who occasionally broke into rapid Cheyenne and laughter. Rebecca was told that Kajihah and Windrider had two girls and one boy. Sucoora tended the boy more like he was her son than Kajihah's. When the children had been fed and put to bed on thick buffalo mats, the women talked while Sucoora and Kajihah did beading on new garments for their family.

Rebecca learned that Kajihah's girls were five and seven, and the boy was three. She had been a gift to Windrider eight years before, given by her father after Windrider had saved his life. Sucoora's son had taken ill and died at age four, and her expression and tone hinted that she could not bear more children. Rebecca realized that Windrider did not have a child less than three years old, and she wondered why. She remembered what he had said about giving her more children, children to replace the ones she might lose to Bright Arrow's tribe. As his wives worked and talked, Rebecca considered each in turn.

If Kajihah had been with Windrider for eight years, that meant she had left the Oglala camp the same year Rebecca had been captured and enslaved. She wondered if it had been before or after her humiliating experience. Kajihah did not say, and Rebecca did not ask. Appearing to be in her mid-twenties, Kajihah's skin was dark brown, as were her hair and eyes. If first impressions could be trusted, Kajihah's gaze and mood alerted Rebecca to the

woman's vanity and coldness. She was a slightly plump
creature with an aloof and secretive air. Although she
wasn't verbally bossy, there was a dominating aura about
her, one which implied that Kajihah gave the orders and
was obeyed. So far, the other woman had done nearly all
of the work, though, from the beading in Kajihah's
hands, Rebecca could see she was talented in that area.
Somehow Rebecca couldn't imagine Windrider making
passionate love to this arrogant woman.

Sucoora had given her age at twenty-nine winters old,
two years older than Windrider. Her expressions
indicated she was a serious person, but a kind and gentle
one. Her skin was lighter than Kajihah's, with a much
redder tint, and her eyes were like two large brown balls
with smiles painted on them. Her sleek, black hair was
braided almost to her waist. She had been joined to
Windrider's brother, but, when he was slain, Windrider
had taken her into his tepee. Without children of her
own, she helped with Kajihah's and took on many of the
chores. She had been learning English from Windrider's
brother before he was killed by the Crow and was
delighted to have Rebecca there to teach her more
English. She said it would help her when dealing with the
white traders; naturally Rebecca agreed to help her and
warmed to her infectious smile. Windrider's two wives
seemed direct opposites in mood and personality. As
Rebecca watched Sucoora string the tiny beads, she tried
to envision Windrider kissing and embracing this woman
as he had her; she could not.

Neither wife had Rebecca's height or slimness, though
Rebecca knew she was considered tall for a female. Both
wives were plump, indicating that Windrider was a good
provider—and they were voracious eaters. Rebecca
reflected that she was glad she would have still fit into the

dresses she had worn at eighteen, had she still owned them. The only place her figure had increased was at her bosom; that had happened after her pregnancies and breast-feeding. Neither wife was beautiful, she observed, but both were pretty. Sucoora had a softer appearance and manner about her, and Rebecca promptly decided that she liked Sucoora, reserving her decision about Kajihah until she got to know her better. She wondered if she should feel guilty about her wanton behavior with their husband, though she didn't.

The hour grew late. Sucoora prepared two sleeping mats for the men near the tepee entrance, which seemed to be the only difference in the regular sleeping arrangements. Kajihah went to sleep with her two girls, and Sucoora lay down with the small boy. Rebecca's children shared another mat, while she was directed to a mat near those of the two men. Soon all were sleeping soundly except Rebecca.

When the two braves entered the tepee just before midnight, Bright Arrow took the mat nearest the opening. Having smoked pipes laced with strong herbs, Bright Arrow fell asleep a few minutes after his head touched the mat. As the moon shifted, its light fell over Rebecca's face. She blinked, then looked out over the reclining males, gazing up into the clear night sky. A hand reached across the short distance between the two mats and grasped hers. Windrider squeezed her quivering hand, holding it until she was deep in slumber.

Rebecca could hear dogs barking and horses neighing. Voices filtered into the quiet tepee, telling her it was nearing time to arise. Her eyes fluttered and opened and, glancing over at the women and children, she saw that no one was stirring yet. Turning her head toward the entrance, she found Windrider's intense stare focused on her. Her pulse and respiration quickened, though she was relieved when he did not try to touch her. This siege on her emotions had to be kept secret between them! Abruptly he smiled, then sat up. When he yawned loudly to arouse the others, she hastily shut her eyes and pretended to be asleep.

The men went hunting that day, and Rebecca was delighted by the reprieve from Windrider's covert attentions. If he were not truly serious, she mused, why would he risk discovery? Surely she was mistaken about his motives. But whatever his plan, she wished the situation were easier to control.

Rebecca spent her day with his two wives, their children, and her girls. The older girls made friends incredibly quickly and easily. Despite the language barrier, they spent much of their day playing and watching the Cheyenne children. The two wives went about their chores, with Kajihah laboring at an exceptionally slow pace. Rebecca offered her assistance, and it was instantly accepted. Kajihah seemed eager to care for Tashina while Rebecca helped Sucoora with the tasks, a sly way for Kajihah to avoid work. The four older girls were under the supervision of an adolescent named Prairie Flower, daughter of Shooting Star and White Bird.

Sucoora was pleased with Rebecca's skills and friendliness. During the morning, they gathered wild vegetables, fruits, and berries, then cooked the midday meal. Later, they gathered wood and fetched water. While caring for the two smallest children, Kajihah kept busy with her sewing and beading—and with her gossip.

After the rest period, the children sat beside the tepee and shared their handmade toys. Kajihah began work on several parfleches for storage of winter pemmican. She sat near the children with other women who were performing similar tasks, and in the presence of others, she appeared to work diligently and deftly.

It was a peaceful camp. Everyone seemed occupied with his or her chore. Rebecca helped Sucoora with the two hides she was tanning. They had been stretched taut on frames built by Windrider, and the fat and hair had been scraped from them. Only the smoothing with a fleshing tool was left. Rebecca took one hide and Sucoora the other, and they talked as they labored. Sucoora halted at one point to tell Rebecca in a low tone that she was happy to have her help and company. She smiled and confided that Kajihah did very little work, which was no secret to the astute and observant Rebecca. There was sadness in her brown eyes when the Indian woman told Rebecca that Windrider favored Kajihah because she had borne him a son who still lived. Rebecca got the impression that Sucoora neither liked nor trusted the other woman.

When she asked why Kajihah had not borne him more children in the past three years, Sucoora grinned mischievously and told her that Windrider did not find Kajihah pleasing on the sleeping mat. Since he had three children, he had not felt the need to try for more! Rebecca bit her tongue to keep from asking if Windrider found Sucoora pleasing in that carnal way. Then she realized something she hadn't noticed before; the two females put on their best faces before their guests and their husband. Surreptitiously, they were bitter rivals!

Rebecca sighed heavily. At this point, she certainly didn't need to be trapped between two jealous and competitive wives! Perhaps that explained why Windrider was eager to find another woman, why he was susceptible to temptation. Perhaps he would be glad to rid himself of these two bickering creatures. Clearly he didn't desire Kajihah, and Sucoora seemed more a sister than a wife. After all, children belonged to the father's people, so he wouldn't lose them. Neither female was provocative or exciting company for such a virile man. Rebecca could see why Windrider would find her desirable in many ways. Rebecca was not a vain woman, but she was aware of her beauty and appeal. She could understand how a passionate and vigorous brave like Windrider would want and need more than either of his wives could give him. In a curious way, that saddened her.

At the evening meal, the two wives carefully concealed their enmity, but Rebecca was certain Windrider was cognizant of their rivalry and pretense. As was the custom, the men ate first, then the children and women. The main course of their meal was a deer stew, the one slain by Windrider that morning. Unaware of how their words affected Windrider, the two wives highly praised Rebecca for her skills and labors. The devious Kajihah did so to encourage a longer stay from the helpful, hardworking white woman. Sucoora added compliments on Rebecca's geniality and kindness. Windrider smiled at Rebecca, then boldly complimented Bright Arrow on his choice of a woman. He surprised her and his wives by giving Rebecca the lovely deerskin to make a garment for her new life among the Indians.

Rebecca smiled demurely and thanked Windrider for his kindness and generosity, as it would have been improper and insulting to refuse a gift. The Indians were known for their charity and brotherhood. When a warrior was ill or away, other warriors provided his family with meat and protection. At a warrior's death, his property was given away or placed on his scaffold. If a warrior accumulated wealth, it suggested he was stingy, selfish, and cowardly. A respected warrior owned nothing but his weapons, horse, clothing, his children, and his sacred objects. The wife owned everything else.

As Rebecca uttered her words of thanks to Windrider, she sought hidden meanings in his compliments and generous gesture. She had noticed that Windrider had called her Bright Arrow's "woman," not "wife." Her husband had smiled and thanked him, but what would he have done if he had known the truth! And what exactly was the truth? She wondered.

The sleeping arrangements were the same that night. Rebecca lay tense and rigid, praying that Windrider would not reach out to her again. Fearing someone might notice the interaction between them, she cautiously placed her back to the entrance. Windrider was alert and careful, for he did not make contact with her until all were asleep. Dozing lightly, she rolled to her side toward the incoming breeze. Sleepily she felt a finger caressing her lips, and she caught herself just before jumping up and squealing. Her eyes flew open and she sent Windrider a warning glare. He smiled engagingly, then brazenly passed a kiss along his forefinger to her lips. She stared at him in disbelief, unable to comprehend why he was being so rash, and she was greatly relieved when he crossed his muscular arms over his brawny chest and closed his enticing eyes.

This was the disquieting pattern Windrider set for many days. Her emotions were in an ever-increasing turmoil. The handsome Cheyenne warrior cleverly and covertly elicited wanton feelings within her, sensations which chewed hungrily at her body, sensations which she could not feed and which brought her discomfort and frustration. She tried to hide her tension and needs, desperately wishing Bright Arrow would request a private walk with her. But this constant smoldering fire of unrequited passion burned destructively within her mind and body without relief, for Bright Arrow was too distracted by his own problems and feelings to perceive hers.

It seemed that things were not going well for Bright Arrow with some of the Cheyenne warriors.

Rebecca and Sucoora had just finished filling the water bags at the river, when Sucoora enlightened her about Bright Arrow's situation. Rebecca hadn't known about the treatment her man was receiving and enduring. Many of the warriors were using every occasion to tease and best Bright Arrow. Whenever there was a hunt, it exposed how blunted his skills and instincts were. Whatever the contest, Bright Arrow always came in last. Any warrior could pin him to the hard ground in wrestling, and any brave could outshoot him with arrows or outthrow him with the lance. He hadn't been successful in a single hunt, sport, or raid.

Rebecca listened as she was told of his many problems. He had difficulty keeping up with the well-trained, well-toned bodies of the Cheyenne warriors. Sucoora hinted that he was getting depressed and discouraged. He had even accused his allies of appearing more interested in embarrassing and mocking him than in helping him.

Rebecca couldn't believe her ears when Sucoora told her that he had passed out in the sweat lodge. During a foot race, he had been carried back to camp on a young brave's horse after collapsing with pains in his side. He had been wheezing violently, hardly able to breathe. Rebecca claimed it was the heat, but Sucoora shook her head. On a raid, White Antelope had saved his life after he had been knocked from his horse by a Pawnee warrior, a gift of life Bright Arrow would someday have to repay. He had wanted to seek a vision quest, but Windrider and the medicine chief, Running Elk, had refused to allow it. They told him he lacked the stamina to survive.

Rebecca grimaced in dismay. Bright Arrow couldn't seem to do anything right. He had lost himself in the wilderness with her. Yet he had been raised a warrior. Surely those skills were merely dulled; they couldn't just vanish forever! she told herself. Maybe he wasn't trying hard enough, or maybe too hard. Rebecca asked Sucoora why they were being so cruel to him. Sucoora grinned and vowed it was best for him. She claimed that Bright Arrow needed fury, fury which would inspire courage and determination to prove the others wrong.

"You mean it's all a trick?" Rebecca cried in astonishment.

"He does not try with all heart, Becca," Sucoora responded, calling her the shortened name she had chosen for her. "He gain strength and bravery from taunts and laughter. He must push. He will fall many times but must push more. He wishes them easy on him. No can be that way. Bad for Bright Arrow. Blood must burn to be one," she stated, holding up one finger to indicate first place. "When blood burn, victory is captured. He must try more. He must prove he be big man. Little man no good for people."

"But he needs encouragement, Sucoora. He needs kindness and help. He probably thinks they're laughing at him. No man likes to be a fool. Maybe I should talk to him," she murmured pensively.

"Must not!" the woman declared. "He no fight; he no win his battle. If he learns trick, he no try hard. He no have fury to give guts," she asserted, punching her stomach for emphasis. "If you no hold tongue silent, he no become man. You good woman, Becca. Not right for

Bright Arrow. You best be Cheyenne wife. Sioux strange. They no take back white woman. Bright Arrow join Oglala woman. You stay here. Sucoora speak to Windrider. He bring you to his tepee like Sucoora. Sucoora and Becca be sisters. We make good fight for Kajihah. You live here, Windrider no have use for Kajihah. She bad. He send away. Windrider good man. He need woman like Becca. You beautiful; you strong; you smart. You good woman."

Rebecca was staggered by her unexpected words. Had Windrider instilled such thoughts in her mind? Had he sought this woman's help in obtaining her? Did Windrider want her to replace Kajihah or both wives? The puzzle was becoming more and more complex.

Rebecca asked, "Why would you say such things, Sucoora? I belong to Bright Arrow. Windrider has two wives. He doesn't need me."

"Windrider need good woman; Becca good woman. Windrider deserve beautiful woman; Becca beautiful. You live in Windrider tepee; you be happy. Windrider best Cheyenne warrior. He make Becca good husband. I see no love in Bright Arrow. He no smile or touch Becca. He no make Becca smile, happy. He no give Becca good moon on mat. He sees only warrior's life. He selfish, not good. Man who love woman touch her plenty, smile at her. Hands and eyes no stay off her. Not true with Bright Arrow. Windrider make Becca good man."

Rebecca shook her head and admonished the woman, trying to hush her, "How can you entice me to marry your own husband? Don't you love him? How can you bear to share him with another woman? I couldn't live that way," she confessed hastily.

"I love Windrider's brother. He gone to Great Spirit.

162

No place to go. I stay with Windrider. He kind. Be good to woman. Windrider best warrior, good man," she stressed. "Windrider need woman to love. Windrider no love Sucoora, no love Kajihah. If Becca smile, she steal Windrider's eye, set fire in heart and body. Send Bright Arrow to Oglala; they help him. You stay. No share Windrider with others," she boldly promised the shocked woman whose spirit was greatly troubled.

"You must not say such things, Sucoora. If Kajihah heard you, she would be angry. I'm sure Windrider wouldn't want you to speak such words to me. I belong to Bright Arrow. He's having trouble, and he needs me. I don't want to hurt him. Let's forget about this talk, all right?" she entreated anxiously.

"I pray each night for Great Spirit to guide Becca to Windrider's heart and tepee. You no be sorry. You no be sad. You be good mates. I shut mouth. I take water to tepee. I come back, help with wood." With that, Sucoora lumbered away toward camp, leaving Rebecca with her disjointed thoughts.

"I pray for the same thing, Becca," a masculine voice stated playfully behind her. "What fills your prayers each sun and moon?"

Rebecca whirled to find Windrider lazing against a tree. A broad and beguiling grin tugged at the corners of his mouth and brightened his obsidian eyes. "I . . . didn't . . . see you," she stammered. "Where's . . . Bright Arrow?" she asked, wondering how much he had heard.

"He went hunting with White Antelope. He will not return until the sun is high again," he responded.

"You mean tomorrow?" she queried nervously, aware of their isolation and his dangerous proximity. She wished Sucoora would hurry. Anxious, and alert to his probing scrutiny, she flushed under his discerning gaze.

"White Antelope will train him in secret. It will go good for Bright Arrow to move without the eyes of many laughing warriors on him. Mistakes are smaller when no one sees them. Soon he will be ready to train hard and fast. He will be a warrior before the snows fall. His body obeys him more each sun. When that moon comes, Windrider will no longer shine brighter than his friend. Do you fear to be alone with Windrider?" he challenged, coming to stand before her.

"Did you ask Sucoora to say those things to me?" she inquired, watching his expression closely. She hadn't known he was around and was embarrassed and dismayed to realize he had overheard their talk.

"I did not. But she speaks wisely and true," he added. He chuckled when she blushed and lowered her lashes for a brief time.

"What if she repeats them to Kajihah or others?" she fretted, bravely meeting his gaze.

"She will hold her tongue. She is loyal to me," he asserted confidently. "There is no love or passion between Windrider and Sucoora. We are friends and helpers. Will you think on her words?" he coaxed.

"You can't keep pressing me like this," she pleaded.

"Because you fear you will surrender to me?" he asked as he trapped her between the tree and his stalwart frame. "Have you forgotten what it was like between us that moon in your wooden tepee? Have you forgotten how we touched in the cave? You must be mine," he declared forcefully, urgently, as his lips brushed against hers. He stroked her cheek with his smooth one.

Rebecca tried to push him away, but his body refused to move. "Please, Windrider, you must not do this," she pleaded in alarm. "Sucoora will return at any moment. She must not see us like this."

A surge of daring shot through him, and he boldly declared, "I care not who sees or learns I want you as I have never wanted or desired another female. While you are near, I must pursue you for my wife. We do nothing wrong; you are a free woman. I will not stop my battle for you until you marry Bright Arrow."

"But everyone thinks we're joined," she argued. "Bright Arrow would challenge you to a fight if he learned about us. You know how proud and possessive he is. He thinks I belong to him. One of you could be slain. This isn't the time for me to make a choice between you. Bright Arrow needs me, Windrider. He's so miserable."

"I need you more," Windrider retorted. "Bright Arrow knows the Indian customs and ways. He does not own you. He will not battle for a woman who chooses another man," he stated smugly. He seized her chin and restrained her movements, commanding, "Say no man lives in your heart and mind but Bright Arrow. Say his hands and eyes cannot stay off of you. Say he fills your needs. Say you are happy. Say you do not want me. Say I do not make you tremble with desire. Tell me such words and I will walk from you."

Rebecca paled, then flushed. She licked her dry lips as her eyes darted about aimlessly, nervously. She tried to shift in his embrace, to free her chin from his confining grasp. "You're his friend. You can't hurt him and end that friendship over me," she argued.

"Yes," he replied, the decision already made in the back of his mind. Still, it surprised him as he heard himself speak it aloud. Once he had done so, he repeated, "Yes, I would steal you at any price."

165

Sheer terror washed over her, for she knew he was telling the truth. "But what about Bright Arrow?" she inquired faintly.

Windrider remained deep in thought for a time. Then he suggested, "I will send Bright Arrow into the mountains with White Antelope to hone his body and skills. Once he has regained himself and his rank, your loss will not pain him as deeply. I will take you to the Oglala camp to speak with Gray Eagle and Shalee. You will learn if they will accept you in his life and tepee. If they say yes, I will allow you to choose which man you love and desire. If they say no, you will free Bright Arrow on his return. When he leaves my camp, you will join to Windrider. Is that not fair?" He watched her contemplate his words.

"I'll go to see Gray Eagle and Shalee. I'll explain everything to them. If they reject me, I'll return here with you. But Bright Arrow must have a chance to speak with them before I free him. They could tell me no, but they might give him a different answer. I'll send him home for one full moon," she decided, setting a time limit of almost a month. "If he cannot convince them to allow us to marry, then I'll free him." She waited for Windrider to protest her decision, but he did not.

"Will you join to me the sun you speak such words to him? Will you give me your promise?" he persisted.

"If he decides he doesn't want me to return home with him . . . or if his people still reject me after a month, I'll marry you that day." She delivered the shocking words in a low and quivering tone.

"We will leave when Bright Arrow is gone. He must not learn of our visit; he would try to stop us. I will hunt for a beautiful hide to make a joining dress. You will be mine before two full moons cross the night sky," he vowed with self-assurance.

"There is one demand, Windrider," she stated clearly and distinctly. Her next words brought a disarming smile of amusement and pleasure to his lips. "I will share you with no other woman. And I will share our tepee with no other—slave or wife. I will fill your heart and life completely, or I will not come to your tepee. If you do not agree that I will be enough for you, speak now."

He cupped her face between his hands, allowing his admiring gaze to travel over her features. The promise came easily and tenderly. "I will share you with no other man, and you will share me with no other woman. We will be perfect mates. Your demand is fair. I accept it. It is hard to keep my eyes and thoughts from you. My heart and body burn for you. Our joining day cannot come too soon."

Before he could kiss her, they heard Sucoora returning. He sent her a mischievous grin and wink, then vanished into the trees. Rebecca returned to her task of gathering wood. If Sucoora observed that she hadn't collected much in the length of time she had been gone, she didn't say anything. The older female hummed merrily as she worked.

Rebecca was ensnared by her thoughts. Was it wicked to love and desire two men at the same time? Had she really told Windrider she would marry him if things didn't work out with Bright Arrow and his people? How could she behave so wantonly when she was bound to another man? She truly loved Bright Arrow, but she was enchanted by Windrider. He and his offer were so tempting, so encouraging, so timely. And Bright Arrow was making no attempt to hold on to her. She hadn't shared his life in far too long. Was it so wrong to plan for the

167

inevitable? She knew now that Windrider was sincere about his amorous feelings. Her doubts and suspicions had been wrong.

Neither woman noticed the Sioux warrior who had witnessed the romantic scene between Windrider and Rebecca. He stealthily slipped into the trees. He had much work and planning to do . . .

Chapter Eight

A few days later, the camp was preparing for a great feast to be held that night. Chief Yellow Robe's son, Little Crow, had returned from his vision quest. A few days earlier, he had entered the sweat lodge to purify himself and, afterward, he had rubbed his body with sage leaves. Wearing only his breechclout and moccasins, he had gone to a secluded hilltop to pray and fast for days, until his quest succeeded. The medicine chief had gone with him, to call on the spirits and to watch over the boy from a distance. This was Little Crow's initiation into manhood. The fifteen-year-old brave had already proven himself as a hunter. It was time for him to begin his training as a warrior.

After three days of praying and fasting, Little Crow had returned this morning. He had eaten a light meal to refresh himself, then he had bathed in the river and donned his father's finest robe for the ceremony tonight. Many warriors had hunted to supply game for Chief Yellow Robe on this momentous occasion. Many women had worked hard and long to prepare food to offer to their chief. It was the custom for the father of the boy involved to give presents to chosen warriors. That afternoon, he made his rounds doing just that. Chief Yellow Robe gave Windrider an exquisitely carved prayer pipe, and his last gesture was to give Bright Arrow a swift and agile pinto.

169

The feast began at dusk. Food and drink were abundant. Wine had been made from buffalo berries and chokecherries. There were pones dotted with bits of dried fruit and berries, and a wide selection of meat and vegetables. The men sat in circles around a large campfire in the center of the village. They talked and ate, then passed around a ceremonial pipe. The women and children ate their meals, then the women cleared away the remains of the feast. Small children were put to bed, with older girls watching over the babies. The women stood behind the men, observing the ritual.

Music from kettle drums, eagle-bone whistles, and gord rattlers filled the night air. There was dancing by warriors, then women, then the men and women simultaneously. Prayers were sent skyward to the Great Spirit. Since this was Little Crow's special night, no other warrior's *coups* were chanted.

Little Crow claimed the center of the ring and told of his experiences on the lonely hilltop. He said he would no longer be called Little Crow; that child's name would be discarded. He said the Great Mystery had appeared to him as a large, black bird. The bird had told him that he was a man now; he was a little crow who had become a big crow. He was told the crow could move as secretly as the night, sounding warnings when danger was near. The crow had no fear of birds larger than himself; he could chase and pester eagles and hawks until they flew away. The crow was difficult to discourage or to trick. He said that Grandfather wished him to take the name Big Crow. With that announcement, the ceremony ended.

Rebecca was bewildered when Bright Arrow approached her, insisting they take a walk alone. When she mentioned the children, he told her Kajihah had agreed to look after them until they returned. There was something in his expression and tone which piqued her curiosity. She detected a quiet seriousness emanating from him tonight that was neither fatigue nor a loss of spirit. It was grave determination.

He had to be feeling better about himself. She knew he had slain an elk for the feast tonight, and he had not come in last during the footrace this morning! During practice yesterday, she had secretly observed the warriors. Bright Arrow's lance had struck near its mark almost every time, and his arrows had come amazingly close to the heart of the target on nearly every unleashing. In wrestling, it had required longer for the Cheyenne warrior to best him. Just as evident to her was the fact that his waist had narrowed and hardened considerably since they had left their cabin. She knew that he spent hours in the clearing lifting and tossing heavy rocks to increase his strength and to firm his arm and shoulder muscles. She knew he had been leaving camp at dusk to run around the entire camp several times to build up his lung power and to tone his leg muscles. And she had learned of the trick taught him by White Antelope; he would chase a rabbit who was trapped in a small canyon. The creature's rapid changes in speed and direction sharpened and honed Bright Arrow's agility, alertness, vision, and quickness.

They hadn't been alone in weeks, and she wondered why he was demanding privacy tonight. Maybe he was just being considerate of Windrider, attempting to give him time alone with his two wives.

The thought of him made her shiver. She already feared she had given Windrider her promise of marriage because she had been afraid of facing the unknown. She actually believed the Sioux would not allow her to marry Bright Arrow or to live with him. He had to return home, even if it meant without her. She feared she was losing everything. She had reached out to Windrider to have something real and stable to hold on to during her turmoil and, though she did find him attractive and compelling, she did not love him. He did inspire passion in her, but there were good reasons. She was vulnerable, lonely, miserable, afraid, and had been untouched for months. Those were the things which made her susceptible to Windrider, those and Bright Arrow's romantic indifference.

It was time she was honest with herself. How could Windrider or any other man ever take Bright Arrow's place in her heart and life? It wasn't Windrider she wanted—it was Bright Arrow as he had been long ago. Did it matter if they weren't wed? Only a little. In her heart and mind, she was married to him. She loved him and she needed him. Why did he continue to hold her at such a distance? Was he also afraid of his tribe's imminent demands on him? Was he torn apart by the choice that would soon face him? They could have so little time left together. Why was he wasting it? Why wasn't she making it special? If the demand to sacrifice her was issued, he would be forced to accept it. Otherwise, he would destroy himself, their love, their dreams, and their peace. Didn't he see how much she needed his love, his touch, his solace, this last time with him?

They had walked quite a distance in the refreshing forest, in total silence. When Bright Arrow halted in a small clearing, the thought-entranced Rebecca kept moving. He called her name and reached for her arm to stop her. As she turned and looked up at him, brilliant moonlight illuminated his bronze frame. It danced off the silver arrow on his necklace. It gleamed on his ebony hair and glimmered in his midnight eyes as he glanced up at it. Rebecca's gaze followed his, to stare at the intimidating full moon.

His voice was deep and rich as he spoke. *"Hunwi's* face is as bold this night as the first night we joined. Perhaps she seeks to remind us of that night and many others which have passed between us."

Her heart lurched madly at those stirring words. No matter how skilled Windrider was with kisses and caresses, he did not hold a spark to the blazing power of Bright Arrow's words or nearness. She was crushed when he instantly changed the subject. His tone and gaze were mellow as he reminisced. As he leaned against an oblong rock that came to his waist, she listened intently to his words, for he seemed to have a great need to release his tormenting ghosts.

"I remember the feast my father gave when I became a man. When I was small, he would take me into the forest to practice with my bow and arrow. I would shoot at pinecones and large leaves. He would mark a place on a tree, and I would fire until I hit it. When I could strike the target on each try, he taught me how to track small game. It was many winters before I could bring down large deer or swiftly moving creatures. He showed me the animals' markings on trees and on the earth. I could find the territory of bears or deer by reading their marks. Now, my father teaches his second son such things."

There was sadness, but no jealousy, in his voice. He went on. "When I was fourteen winters old, I was this tall," he remarked, placing his hand across his nose to indicate almost six feet. "I was strong and swift. No Oglala brave could best me in fighting or shooting. No animal could hide from my keen eyes and skills. I went into the sweat lodge. I sat naked before Grandfather, inhaling his breath in the white clouds. All fear and evil

173

left my body. I dried myself with sweet sage. I went into the hills with Mind-Who-Roams, our medicine chief. Many say he is a powerful man who can see into the new sun and moon. Mind-Who-Roams called on the Great Mystery to visit me."

He inhaled deeply, then released the breath. "I could not eat or sleep for many days. I sat on a white buffalo mat with my legs crossed and my back straight. I faced the direction where the sun awakens, blowing on my eagle-bone whistle to let Grandfather know where to find me in the dark. Mind-Who-Roams put four cottonwood sticks into Mother Earth. He joined them with rawhide. He hung sacred grasses and herbs on the rawhide. I was not to step outside those boundaries until my quest was over. Mind-Who-Roams went down the hill to wait for me. A seeker of visions must be alone," he explained, and Rebecca did not interrupt.

"I sat for many passings of the sun and moon. I was afraid. I did not fear dying or suffering; I feared I was unworthy of Grandfather's words and signs. I knew when I left that hill, I would become a warrior. I would train to be the new chief of my people. I tried to clear my mind to allow only Grandfather's voice to be there. Many thoughts came to me. I tried to imagine my father sitting on a hill long ago, seeking his first vision and new name. I tried to envision my grandfather, Running Wolf, battling hunger and doubts. I prayed for *Wakantanka* to show me how to become a great man as were Gray Eagle and Running Wolf. On my last night on the hill, a strange thing happened. I was dizzy from lack of food and sleep. I was thirsty. The moon was full that night," he stated, as if revealing some vital secret.

"As I watched *Hunwi's* face, it became a large arrowhead. It was so shiny that my eyes hurt and burned to stare at it. Even so, I could not look away. The bright arrow held great magic and power. I heard a voice speak inside my head. It said the arrow would protect my people. It said an arrow was straight and true; it was swift and accurate; it could slay enemies. It said the arrow could point the way to peace for my people. It said the brightness of the silver arrow could light a path for my people during days of darkness. It said I was the arrow, and greatness for my people was my target. Then the arrow was gone and *Hunwi's* face was there once more. I called to Mind-Who-Roams and told him of the vision. He said I should take the name Bright Arrow. He said the moon and night powers would give me prowess to defeat enemies. We returned to my village. I told the council of my vision. My father was happy. He gave a great feast to celebrate my new name and manhood. I became a warrior in less moons than my father or grandfather. Why did the vision lie, Rebecca? Why did *Wakantanka* desert me when I needed his help and guidance? I have no great power and magic. I am not the light to guide my people."

Rebecca refuted softly, "You do have great power and magic, Bright Arrow. The Great Spirit didn't betray you or desert you; you walked away from your destiny. You listened to what you wanted, not to what He was telling you. You never asked Him to guide your decision about me, did you?" His guilty look spoke louder than any words could. "Your vision didn't lie to you; you did become a great warrior. Many followed your lead. You could chant numberless *coups*. Have you forgotten you earned enough feathers to make a war bonnet? Look inside your parfleche; it is filled with feathers with notches and painted spots to tell of your many deeds. What enemy didn't fear and envy you? What friend didn't respect and love you? What white man or blue-

coat hasn't heard and trembled at the name of Bright
Arrow? The vision told you what to do; you didn't follow
its direction. You found me, and I changed your life. I
ruined it, Bright Arrow. If you hadn't met me, you would
be with your people. You would be wed to an Indian girl.
You would become the new chief. My magic was evil; it
weakened you. I made you as much my slave as I was
yours. It's my fault. I stole you from your fate. I never
meant to harm you. I'm truly sorry, Bright Arrow," she
whispered hoarsely.

When he started to speak, she pressed her hand over
his lips. In a strained voice, she told him, "Your life isn't
over, Bright Arrow. It isn't too late to follow your vision
and the will of the Great Spirit. Each day I see you
becoming the way you were long ago. Soon, all will know
that Bright Arrow has returned to his lands and people.
Again they will fear and envy you because of your great
prowess. No one will dare to challenge you or laugh at
you. No woman will turn away her head when you pass.
Your tribe will forgive you; they'll forget your defiance.
Perhaps I was given to you as a test, a way to strike you to
the earth on your knees, to force you to rise taller and
stronger than before. You have learned many lessons
from me; it is time for your teacher to release you. It's
time for the vision to become real, Bright Arrow. You
must return to your people, to your rightful destiny.
You must prove you are the light and power to guide
them. You must prove that only you can lead them. Can't
you feel the Great Spirit tugging at your heart with the
truth? Can't you feel Him drawing your feet to your lands?
Long ago, you defied your fate and chose me; we've had
many years together. It's time you obey your vision and
choose your people over me. Don't you see, Bright
Arrow? You can't have both. There's an invisible bar-

rier between our peoples; we've tried to ignore it, to demolish it. It's too strong and evil. If I do not send you home, I will lose you anyway. We cannot avoid your destiny. We cannot share a life-circle and be happy," she admitted painfully. She had witnessed his downfall, then his rebirth. She couldn't help but feel she was bad for him. Wasn't it her duty to free him, to save him from her cruel love?

Bright Arrow pulled her into his arms, pressing her cheek against his thudding heart. "To make such sacrifices, your love is as large and strong as a mountain. As long as there is breath in our bodies, there is hope for us, Rebecca. With all my heart, I believe the Great Spirit sent you to me. I do not understand why my people cannot see this truth. They cannot resist it forever. There is a reason why I was banished. Just as there is a reason why I must return." His voice softened as he said, "You are not evil. You did not change my life; you changed my heart. You taught me love and sharing and tenderness. I do not hear the Great Spirit telling me to toss you aside. If I had you all my life, it would not be enough time. I cannot choose between my love and my destiny, for surely they are one. Each night I pray the Great Spirit has opened their eyes."

"And if He has not? If He never will? What if you are wrong, Bright Arrow? What if it is you who resists the truth?" she debated dejectedly. Her arms went under his and looped around his shoulders as she snuggled against him.

"How does a man choose between sunlight and moonlight? How does he choose between living and existing? How does he choose between his heart and his head? How does he choose between good and good, between right and right?" he asked.

177

"You did years ago, Bright Arrow, and look what it did to you, to us. As long as I stand between you and your fate, it does not matter what we think or feel. It's time we admit that to ourselves and each other. I love you and I need you. But more, I need you to be whole again. I need you to be happy. I need you to stand tall and proud." She lifted her head to look up at him as she said, "I need you to return to your life-circle, even if I must lose you."

Bright Arrow gazed down at her. He had known she would make such a sacrifice for him. He didn't want to think about such things tonight. "This moon, all I need is you," he murmured in a heavy voice.

"I need you, too," she responded. "It's been terrible without you. We could have so little time left together."

Lifting her in his arms, he carried her to an expanse of thick grass and, kneeling, he gently placed her on the soft covering. For a time, he was content to visually explore her face in the moonlight. Then slowly he came forward until his body was touching hers. Reaching out his hand, he fondled her cheek, then ran his fingers through her silky hair. The distance between them disappeared as his mouth closed over hers.

Bright Arrow's lips deftly and hungrily captured Rebecca's. It had been so long since they had touched with passion searing their flesh. The last time, both had been left frustrated and despondent. In this heady moment, nothing and no one else existed. It was a time for total possession, for complete giving and taking and sharing. Their hearts pleaded and their desires soared.

The Sioux warrior covered her face with kisses, then rained them down her throat. Her eager fingers untied the fastenings of her dress and slid it from her shoulders to expose her satiny flesh to his greedy senses. His mouth explored the twin peaks he uncovered, teasing and stimu-

178

lating each one. She groaned as he kindled and fanned her smoldering passions and didn't stop him when he removed her clothes; instead, she shifted to assist him. Quickly, his buckskin pants and his moccasins joined the pile of clothing beside them. Hungrily he drew her into his possessive embrace, and they became lost in their private haven. Lying upon the earth, their bodies entwined, they were oblivious to its dewy surface and their surroundings.

His experienced hands tantalized her quivering flesh, mutely demanding her response to his loving assault. Slowly one hand drifted over her flat stomach, causing it to tighten momentarily. It sought another peak to caress, driving her mindless with achingly sweet sensations. Their passionate needs too great to be restrained any longer, he eased between her parted thighs, slipping smoothly and gently into her moist paradise to explore, conquer, and claim it once again. When he entered her, she arched upward, willingly accepting his full length. His skillful movements within her created blissful sensations she had long been denied.

As he advanced and retreated several times, he feared he would lose control over his manhood and cost her their mutual victory. He tried to master his torrid shaft, to use its power to carry her over the mountain that she was rapidly climbing. Briefly ceasing his stimulating movements to cool his fiery ardor, he began tasting love's sweetness from her lips. He teased her breasts, inspiring her to writhe beneath him. When she feverishly ground her auburn forest against his dark one, he knew he could not wait much longer to have her completely.

He whispered words of caution into her ear, but she was too entranced with desire to hear or to heed them. He gingerly began to move within her once more, his

179

manhood teasing the tense nerves along her dark, damp passage. The moment he realized she was approaching the summit of ecstasy, he increased his rapturous thrusts. The intensity between them was stunning, and he worked until she was driven over the crest of rapture, to go spinning and falling into a peaceful valley. His pace set, Bright Arrow could not have prevented his own release if his life had depended on it. Tossing all cares to the wind, he surged after her, joining her in that serene place of total joy and satisfaction. Rebecca went limp in his embrace, sighing in contentment and pleasure.

When all emotions were spent, he rolled aside, and Rebecca curled against his moist body. His arm encircled her and drew her close. When his labored breathing slowed and eventually returned to normal, he moved to press a kiss on her damp forehead. His fingers lazily stroked her back and arm and she cuddled against him. They lay thus for a lengthy time.

Later, he began to press light kisses on her hair, his fingers trailing up and down her spine. He inhaled her special aroma, as she inhaled his. They were utterly relaxed; yet their desires were growing anew. Bright Arrow's hands gently cupped Rebecca's firm buttocks and pulled her hips snugly against his. One hand drifted up her side to capture and tantalize her brown nubs, running a finger round and round them. Then he rolled her to her back, replacing his hand with his lips.

Rebecca closed her eyes and savored the stimulation of her unbridled senses. He stirred and tempted her until she reached down for his head and drew his mouth to hers. Ravenously she meshed her lips to his. Her hands roved his body from head to thigh and, when one hand captured his rigid manroot, she stroked its warm, smooth surface. Bright Arrow groaned and twisted his hips to give her more freedom to pleasure him. They kissed and caressed each other until their desires burned uncontrollably.

Again they joined with a blissfully savage intensity. Raging passions overcame them, passions that could not be governed. They raced over Bright Arrow and Rebecca like wild mustangs galloping across the open Plains, reveling in their freedom and excitement. Their bodies came together in an overwhelming union which devoured their energies and all their past sufferings. As he erupted deep within her, Bright Arrow mentally vowed to begin their new life this very moon. Wonderful emotions washed over them, cleansing and revitalizing them, and their eyes fused in understanding and renewed commitment. Their estrangement was ended.

"Just as our life began under a full moon, it is being reborn under one. You could never betray or desert me," he whispered.

Rebecca fused her gaze to his. "The choice is not in our hands, my love," she reminded him.

"It is in mine," he debated tenderly with new self-assurance.

"No, Bright Arrow, it is not. In all the time we lived in the cabin, didn't you learn that? Whichever path you take, it is marked by the order of your council. Do not blind yourself to that fact," she urged. "I will give you time to convince them of our love, to persuade them to allow us to marry. If they reject me again, I will not block your path of return. Neither can I return to live as your white whore. Please don't ask me to exist in such a degrading way. If I cannot be your wife, I cannot return with you. If that is their vote, you must return alone. Promise you'll do this for me—for us?"

"I give you my word," he replied after a long silence.

"Come, let us bathe in the stream. The night grows old, and I have much to do on the new sun. Promise you will not leave me until I have the council's final vote."

"I promise," she murmured, a tightness in her chest and throat. There was so much she wanted to ask him and tell him, but this was not the time. Within a month or two, either they would be wed and with his tribe, or they would be parted forever.

They headed for the river, hand in hand. Bathing quickly, they moved toward the camp. When they entered the tepee, they saw that Windrider was not there and the others had fallen asleep. Bright Arrow took the mat closest to hers. Three hours before dawn, Windrider returned and took the mat nearest the entrance.

Chapter Nine

Bright Arrow left the Cheyenne camp two mornings later, riding out on his new pinto in the company of White Antelope. He didn't tell Rebecca how long he would be away, only that he must be gone for a while and would train hard and swiftly when he returned to camp. When Rebecca asked if he were going to see his parents, Bright Arrow grimaced and told her he was not yet ready to enter the Oglala camp. Then, removing his silver arrow and handing it to her, he instructed her to keep it until he returned. He didn't tell her why, but she guessed. It would be perilous for him if anyone saw that particular *wanapin*. After she thanked White Antelope for his help and friendship, the two men rode away.

Windrider was behind her when she turned to enter the tepee. "We will seek your answers from Gray Eagle," he reminded her.

Rebecca wanted to ask him where he had been the other night, for he didn't seem to know about her passionate evening with Bright Arrow. If he had, surely he would have ceased his overtures toward her. Since her life with Bright Arrow was at stake, she felt that perhaps it would be best to test the emotional waters with Shalee and Gray Eagle before she and Bright Arrow appeared together in their camp. She wanted to explain matters to them, perhaps to convince them to help Bright Arrow if the council voted against her once more. She needed to see if there had been any changes in the Sioux camp, changes that might affect the tribe's attitude toward her.

"We can't leave yet, Windrider. Kajihah is . . . in the . . . woman's tepee," she murmured modestly. Rebecca knew that there were certain rituals Kajihah and Sucoora performed during their monthly flows. She had been told that it was a Cheyenne custom to have a celebration when a girl had her first menses. The village was told of the fact, allowing all to know she was entering womanhood. For most Indian girls, this happened around the ages of fourteen to sixteen. It was a proud and exciting time, for the Cheyenne held their women in high esteem. After a special ceremony, the girl was sent to a separate hut for women undergoing their menses. There she received instructions on becoming a woman, a future wife, and a mother. Each time she had her monthly flow, she was to seclude herself in that special lodge, for if she did not, anything she touched became a carrier of evil and danger. If she touched any weapons during that time, they would lose their powers of protection. "There are too many children and chores for Sucoora to tend alone." Rebecca continued. "We will leave when Kajihah returns to your tepee."

"I will give Shooting Star's daughter two pelts to help Sucoora. We must go quickly. I do not know when Bright Arrow returns. The Oglala camp is four moons from my camp. We must leave with the rising sun or risk discovery. Do you agree?"

"Yes, Windrider, I agree. Will others talk if we go alone?" she worried aloud, praying she could control this persistent warrior.

"We will not ride alone. Cloud Chaser will ride with us. He came to speak with Chief Yellow Robe. I asked him to stay another moon. I did not wish others to think badly of you. It would not be wise for us to ride alone; my hunger for you is too great to trust."

Sometimes Windrider was too honest! she thought, flushing a deep scarlet. He chuckled, then walked away. Rebecca entered the tepee, quickly learning that Sucoora knew all about her plans. The woman was glad Rebecca was taking matters into her own hands and reminded Rebecca that she could live here if the Oglalas spurned her.

That night, Windrider was in a genial mood. He played with the children and talked with the two women. The tepee was very obviously more peaceful with Kajihah gone. When Rebecca inquired about Cloud Chaser's absence, she was told he was sleeping in Yellow Robe's tepee. He grinned and confided that the Sioux warrior was studying Yellow Robe's daughter. Medicine Girl was a lovely creature who was skilled in healing and herbs. Cloud Chaser couldn't decide if he wanted to ask for her hand or that of a girl from his own tribe.

Sucoora laughed and jested, "A warrior must take best woman as first wife. Beautiful woman. Smart woman. Woman he love and desire. Then, he take second woman to help his true wife and love. Becca a first woman, even if she become second wife to warrior."

Rebecca blushed once more. Windrider laughed heartily, guessing the jolly Sucoora's meaning. The two women put the children to bed. Tashina was restless; new teeth were trying to push through her gums. Rebecca held her and sang to her, and as she did she could feel Windrider's potent gaze on her. The scene was uncomfortably cozy for Rebecca.

Sucoora retrieved a parfleche which contained a packet of medicine for Tashina's problem. She had taken wild prickly lettuce and cut off the stem tops. The milky liquid had been collected and dried. She had mixed the white powder with finely crushed bark from the prickly ash and wild plum. Sucoora knew the mixture would relieve the gum pain and help Tashina sleep. The potion worked, and Tashina ceased her whimpering and fell asleep in her mother's arms.

It was shortly after dawn when Windrider nudged Rebecca and told her it was time to dress and leave. Rebecca moved sluggishly, dreading the impending confrontation. She had to go to Shalee and Gray Eagle and beg forgiveness for taking Bright Arrow from his destiny's path. She had to persuade them to compel the Oglalas to allow Bright Arrow to come home where he belonged. Suspense and doubt chewed at her nervous stomach this morning, and she prepared herself for the worst.

Mounting the horse Windrider had loaned her, she respectfully followed the two warriors from camp. Windrider reined his mount and informed her she was to ride between them for protection, and Rebecca urged her horse into position. They rode away at a steady but leisurely pace. Windrider knew that Rebecca was a rider but that she hadn't been on a horse in a long time. He set their pace to prevent excessive discomfort until her body had again familiarized itself with such exercise. Furtively he observed her along each mile they traveled.

The small group rode all day with only two stops. They halted at noon to eat a light meal and to rest. At midafternoon, they stopped again to rest and water the horses. As it neared dusk, they reined in near a copse by a shallow stream. To prevent discovery, they did not build a campfire. The horses were hobbled near the stream to drink and graze, then Windrider unpacked their supplies and passed out each one's portion. They consumed a cold meal of dried prickly pear and yucca seeds with small chunks of dried venison. With that mixture, they enjoyed dried camas bulbs which were sweet on the tongue.

Again for protection, Rebecca was told to sleep on a mat placed between the two men. Knowing she shouldn't debate their instructions, she reluctantly obeyed. Clearly Windrider had noticed that it was a habit of hers to sleep on her left side, for it was on that side that he placed his mat. She tried to lie on her back but was too uncomfortable to relax or sleep. She tried reclining on her right side, but had the same problems. She twisted to her stomach and allowed her hair to fall over her face, sighing loudly without meaning to do so.

Windrider inquired, "Do you have pain from the long ride? Do you fear the end of your journey? Do you wish a herb to help you sleep? You do not rest, and we must ride with the waking sun."

Rebecca shoved her auburn waves aside and looked over at Windrider. She was going to be exhausted and tense if she didn't get some rest and sleep. "Yes, please," she said, accepting his offer.

Windrider fetched his *pezuta wopahte,* his new medicine bundle, and withdrew a small leather pouch. From it he took a pinch of white powder, which Windrider told her was the dried, milky juice from wild lettuce. He mixed it with water and handed it to her. Without hesitation, she drank it. He told her to lie down and relax.

She reclined on her left side and smiled at him. "Thanks," she murmured, then closed her eyes. Whether the result of the herb or her fatigue, she was soon slumbering peacefully.

Windrider watched her for a time, then closed his eyes to shut out the haunting picture before him. He had to have her . . .

The next day, their schedule was the same. They passed within easy range of several deer, but neither man would shoot one, saying it would be wasteful only to use a small portion for their evening meal. Without proper care, the meat would not last in the hot August sun. That night, they hungrily devoured raw breadroot, leeks, and more dried venison. How Rebecca longed for a hot, delicious meal—that, and a soft bed made of feathers.

That night, without her asking or his suggesting, Windrider mixed the white powder with water and handed it to Rebecca. After swallowing it, she reclined on her left side, too tired to worry about facing him. And she felt as if she had just closed her eyes when, many hours later, Windrider nudged her to rise for a new day.

She was careful not to complain or sulk or lag behind. She didn't want them doubting her mettle and stamina. As with the first two days, the third passed similarly until midday. After their rest stop, the pace increased steadily and noticeably every few miles. Rebecca didn't remark on the swift gallop, and she managed to keep up with the two men. The mount she was riding was strong and nimble and, as her soreness vanished, her excitement grew. The wind raced through her hair and over her flesh. It was an exhilarating sensation.

Just before the sun kissed the far horizon, they slowed their pace to unwind the horses. At a leisurely walk, they entered the area where they would camp. It was obvious to her that both men knew this territory by heart, for each campsight had been near water and grass. After the horses were unloaded, the men walked them into the edge of the river and splashed the animals with tepid water to cool them, then hobbled them nearby.

Their meal was no different that night. Rebecca ate it at a snailish pace, wishing she could survive and function without it. There was only one camas bulb left, and Windrider grinned as he handed it to her, telling her to take small bites between her other food. She hadn't meant to make her dislike of the repetitious food noticeable, and she grinned ruefully.

"On the new sun when we camp, we will have fresh meat and greens," he promised, extracting a smile and sigh of relief from her.

Cloud Chaser had been quiet for most of their journey. He spoke rarely, and then only to Windrider. He did not frown or scowl, but neither did he smile. His mood was private, and his expression stoic. She wondered what he thought about her quest. After all, he was an Oglala Sioux warrior from Bright Arrow's tribe. She wanted to ask if he were on the council but decided he was too young. She wanted to ask what he thought their decision would be. She couldn't.

Cloud Chaser excused himself to go upriver to bathe and swim in a spot secluded by tall bushes and twisted cottonwoods. Rebecca sat on her mat, hugging her knees to her chest. Windrider asked if she would like to bathe and change clothes after Cloud Chaser's return. She beamed and nodded hastily. He laughed. When he said he would go along to guard her, her smile faded instantly. She gazed at him indecisively, uneasily.

A playful grin flashed over his face, then he laughed aloud. "I will guard you, Rebecca. I will not gaze at you. I dare not," he declared humorously. "You must not face danger, but you will have privacy. I give my word I will not let my eyes touch you this moon. But soon they will grow fat from feasting on you," he teased.

Rebecca felt ridiculous for doubting his integrity. Of course a woman couldn't be allowed to leave camp alone, she mused, especially not to strip and bathe. She was confident he would keep his word until she made her choice known to him and Bright Arrow. How she wished that choice did not exist, as she knew it would hurt one of them.

She glanced over at Windrider. He was observing her strangely. "Something troubles you?" he questioned astutely.

Without exposing the amorous details, she revealed the highlights of her talk with Bright Arrow following Little Crow's feast. Windrider had been semi-reclined on his back, his shoulders propped up by his elbows. He immediately straightened and came to his knees beside her. "What did he say when you spoke such words?" he probed anxiously.

"He tried to tell me his problem wasn't my fault, but we both know it is. It wasn't intentional; it just happened. He gave me his word to obey the council's demands. He knows I cannot and will not return to his camp as . . . without marriage. And he promised to return home without me if he must. He asked me not to leave him until he had the council's final vote." She waited for this last statement to have its effect on Windrider.

"What did you tell him?" Windrider pressed in rising tension.

"I promised to make no decision until the vote. After that, we would either be joined or we would part," she answered in a shaky voice.

"You are very brave, Rebecca. It is best to prepare him for losing you. Cloud Chaser told me of two other warriors banished for taking white slaves over Oglala maidens. They have not changed in heart or mind, Rebecca. Do not hope it will be different for you. Cloud Chaser says the Oglalas refuse to allow any white to enter their village. He says we must camp while he rides there. You must have permission to visit their leader. If you enter without it or against it, you will be scorned and rejected. Cloud Chaser fears they may punish you if you defy their orders. If that happens, it will ruin all for Bright Arrow's return. He would be angry and bitter over your treatment. You must do as Cloud Chaser commands. Do you understand?"

"Yes, I understand, Windrider. I'll do as you say," she agreed. Her heart thudded heavily at his news. It sounded utterly hopeless. All she could count on was the hope that Bright Arrow's identity and past rank would have a favorable effect on them. How could they hate and spurn a man who had done so much for them, the man who was the son of their chief? She was terribly aware that it wasn't Bright Arrow they rejected. God help them if he was compelled to return to his home alone . . .

Windrider placed his balled fist under Rebecca's chin and lifted it. "Do not be sad or afraid. Bright Arrow will understand and accept your words. He cannot move a mountain. He made his bed of cactus spines when he captured, enslaved, and demanded to keep you. Now he must destroy it and heal his injuries. When many moons pass, he will seek another woman to take your place in his heart and tepee. When many moons pass, Windrider will be the warrior who fills your heart and head."

"Will you give your word and promise to obey the council's vote?" she asked unexpectedly, her gaze never leaving his eyes.

"You have my promise I will accept the words Cloud Chaser speaks to us on the next moon," he responded gingerly. "If the Oglalas say you can return to them as Bright Arrow's wife, I will not fight a lost battle. I will not accept you as his slave. If you join to Bright Arrow, I will free you. If you do not, I will claim you. When the choosing moon comes, if you desire Windrider more than Bright Arrow, I will reach for you. You must follow the command of the Oglala council; Windrider must follow his heart."

Clearly this Cheyenne warrior was not going to make her decision easy, Rebecca mused just as Cloud Chaser returned to camp with damp skin and wet hair. Windrider told him he was going to guard Rebecca while she bathed. Rebecca left them to seek a change of clothes, soap, and a drying blanket, missing the exchange between the two men.

In Cheyenne, Cloud Chaser warned, "Be careful, my friend. I saw you in the woods with her many moons past. I did not understand your white words, but I could not miss the looks which passed between you. Have you forgotten we joined forces to free Bright Arrow from her? Do you fall into her evil trap, Windrider?" he queried gravely.

"She falls into mine, Cloud Chaser, and pulls me in with her," he confessed readily. "It will go as we planned. We will free our friend. But I will not cast her aside when victory is ours. She is not evil. She is good and special. The Cheyenne will accept her as my wife."

"What will Bright Arrow do when he learns you have taken his woman to your heart and mat?" the Sioux warrior asked.

"When he casts her aside to return home, she will be free to become my wife. He will be glad she is safe and happy," he alleged.

"We will see," Cloud Chaser muttered skeptically.

Rebecca walked behind the Cheyenne warrior as they left Cloud Chaser smoking his pipe. Windrider halted behind the thick line of bushes, telling her to call out at the first hint of danger.

She left him there and threaded her way along a narrow path made by deer and other creatures. There was a small grassy area on the riverbank where she laid her garments and disrobed. The moon had passed its fullness, but there was enough light for Rebecca to see. She slipped into the water and swam for a short time. Then she retrieved the soap and lathered herself from head to foot in the shallow edge. Afterward, she walked into the deeper water to rinse off, relishing being able to remove the dirt, body oil, and perspiration.

She dried off and put on fresh garments, then rolled the others into a tight ball. She would wash them when they camped tomorrow. When she rejoined Windrider, he scanned her features thoroughly. "I ask for one kiss before you return to camp," he stated in a muffled voice.

"I . . . we . . ." she stuttered in surprise and dismay.

Windrider closed his arms around her and kissed her tenderly, then turned her around and guided her to within sight of their camp and Cloud Chaser. "I will bathe and return soon," he told her.

He vanished into the shadows. She walked toward her mat and sat down. She put away her things, then vigorously rubbed her hair once more and brushed it. Soon it was nearly dry. Rebecca lay down and was fast asleep before Windrider's return.

They broke camp later than usual the next day and rode until early afternoon before stopping. Cloud Chaser had selected an area with tall rock formations. Boulders sat precariously on top of other boulders, forming artistic shapes. There was one grouping that was a semi-circle of assorted rocks. Near the base at the center of the area was an underground spring. It was the perfect place to camp, for they would be out of sight. From atop one of the formations, a guard could see the surrounding area in all directions. There was water for everyone, and plenty of grass for the horses. Scattered trees nearby would supply firewood for a hot meal, Rebecca noted, if the men allowed one.

Windrider vanished for a time while Rebecca and Cloud Chaser unloaded their horses and ate more dried venison. Then Cloud Chaser relaxed on his mat to take a short rest—or, she suspected, to avoid her company. There was one scrawny tree inside the partially enclosed area, and Rebecca leaned against it and closed her eyes to rest them briefly. Gradually she was overcome by sleep. She eased to the mat that Windrider had placed to her left side.

Nearly two hours had passed when Rebecca's mouth began watering from the delicious aromas attacking her nostrils. The dream was so stimulating that she hated to open her eyes and end it. Yet she did and was astonished to discover it was no dream. She didn't see Cloud Chaser anywhere, but Windrider was hunkered down near a small fire over which a rabbit and vegetables were slowly roasting. Her eyes widened and laughter spilled forth from her lips.

She hurried forward, dropping to her knees across from Windrider. "A rabbit and breadroot!" she shrieked in delight. Her eager gaze shifted to where wild carrots and leeks lay on a flat rock. "Wherever did you find breadroot this late? You've been busy. I must be lazy to sleep so long while you hunted and worked."

He chuckled at the animation in her eyes and movements. "I found two stubborn bushes while I hunted. We have no pot to cook the other vegetables in; we must eat them raw. There is one camas left; I hid it for you." He removed it from his bag and placed it on the rock.

Bubbly laughter came forth once again, and she protested his generosity. "No, we'll share it. Where's Cloud Chaser?" she asked, glancing around to find that his horse was missing.

Windrider concentrated on turning the rabbit and breadroot as he casually responded, "He has gone to the Oglala camp. He will return with the new sun. I must gather more wood. Tend the fire and food," he instructed.

Rebecca had stiffened unconsciously at that news. Noting her hesitation, he dropped to his knees before her. "You must learn to trust me, Rebecca. You have no reason to fear being alone with me. My body burns for you, but I will not make love to you until you are my wife. If I took you this moon, I would never allow you to return to Bright Arrow. I gave my word to honor the council's vote."

"I'm sorry, Windrider. I do you an injustice. Forgive me," she beseeched him.

"There is nothing to forgive. You know the power of burning bodies, and you fear they cannot be controlled. I am strong. I will not allow the fires to consume us before you say it is time." His lips brushed over hers, then he stood and left.

She scolded herself for being so foolish and untrusting. She wasn't a young girl or a virgin. He would never ravish her, and he would never take her unless she willed it. Then what was it? Was she afraid to trust herself with him? In spite of her love for Bright Arrow, there was an undeniable spark Windrider ignited within her. She had to make certain nothing happened between them! He was just so appealing in looks and masculinity. He possessed the skills to drive a female wild with hunger and passion, skills she could recall too vividly.

After a delectable meal was appreciatively devoured, Windrider allowed the fire to burn out. He placed two mats beneath the tree, close together, for he wanted Rebecca near at hand in case of danger. As they lay on their backs, she asked him about his family and his name.

Windrider placed his hands under his head. "My father had three sons. One brother was slain by the Pawnee. One brother was killed battling many Crow. My father sought revenge on both tribes. He died from wounds, but many Crow and Pawnee scalps decorated his war lance. My mother was taken to wife by Kajihah's father. She lives in the Oglala camp. When one brother died, White Antelope took his wife and two sons into his tepee. All children except Little Turtle have joined to others. When another died, I took Sucoora to my tepee as my brother had asked of me. Only Windrider and his son carry the warrior's blood of Thunder-In-His-Mouth. When my father spoke, all listened."

He shifted slightly before going on with his tale. "I named my first son Little Thunder, to follow his grandfather's path. He did so in death two winters past. Eight winters past I saved the life of Standing Rock of the Oglalas. He offered me his daughter as a reward. Kajihah was a pretty female. I had eyes and hunger for no woman. I needed my own tepee and sons. I took her to wife. Two moons after our joining, I accepted the death wish of my brother and took his wife Sucoora to my tepee. When Kajihah gave birth to a daughter, Sucoora was unhappy. I had not taken her to my mat. To please her and to keep my tepee happy, I did so. We had one child; he is the son who died. Kajihah had another girl. Sucoora pleaded for

196

another child, but the Great Spirit did not will it so. Kajihah gave me another son. He was five moons old when Little Thunder became ill and died. The medicine chief and Medicine Girl could do nothing. I have not taken either wife to my mat since Kajihah learned she carried my son. There is no love or pleasure with them," he admitted honestly.

He stared at the heavens above their heads. "With other females, my heart does not beat swiftly and my body does not burn as with you, Rebecca. My lips do not hunger to taste theirs. My hands do not plead to caress their bodies. My eyes find no joy in looking at them. I do not wish to pass words with them or walk in the forest with either at my side. My mind does not think of them while they are far or near. You are different. You do such things to me. Only you, Rebecca. No other woman has caused such feelings to grow within me."

Windrider had not turned toward her or looked at her, but he could detect her erratic breathing at his passionate confession. She was alarmed by the desire smoldering between them. To calm her, he went on with his story. "In my vision at the opening to manhood, I was given the name Windrider. I saw a warrior with many *coup* feathers racing across the night sky. His face was in darkness. His horse had many markings of victory. The warrior rode as swiftly as the wind. He moved as secretly as the mild breeze. His enemies saw his actions, but they could not see him. He could blow gently or hard, and could move things with his powerful breath. No enemy could catch his fast mount. The winds protected him from all harm; they guided his path. He rode with courage and daring. When he turned and the moon revealed his face, it was mine. I am a wind rider. No one can reach my height but you. You have shown me love

197

and gentleness. I have not known such feelings and desires before your coming. I do not wish to lose you and what could be between us. I envy Bright Arrow his winters with you. Forgive me, but I cannot feel pain for his coming loss of you, for, with it, I will have you. I feel only anger at the suffering and shame he has brought to your life. Perhaps it is wrong, but I pray they will reject you as they do all whites. Sleep now. The new sun will be long and hard." He rolled to his side, away from her.

Rebecca turned her head to gaze at him. She was touched by his story and doubted he had ever revealed such feelings to anyone else. She remembered what Bright Arrow had said to her one night: "You taught me love . . . and tenderness." Isn't that what Windrider had just told her? Was it so wrong to elicit such emotions in another? It didn't matter what either man prayed for, as powers greater than all of them would decide her fate. Now she was even more confused and unsettled than before but she wasn't puzzled about one thing—she would marry him if she could not have Bright Arrow.

Deeply ensnared by slumber, Rebecca instinctively curled against Windrider. He lifted his right arm and put it under her head. She lay her arm over his chest and rested her palm near his heart. When his embrace welcomed her, she nestled even closer. His free hand captured a lock of her hair and held it to his nose. It smelled of flowers. He was baffled, then realized she must have put flowers in the soap she had used the night before. The fragrance assailed his senses, and his lips pressed to her temple. He rolled to his side, his lips nibbling at her right ear.

Rebecca sighed in her sleep. A serene smile dreamily touched her mouth. He moved his lips over her face, tasting each area. She moaned, seeking his lips instinctively and unknowingly. Greedily she savored his mouth as she meshed her body against his. For a brief and maddening moment, Windrider permitted her to inflame his senses. When her hand caressed his hardened manhood and she murmured, "I want you," he realized he would soon lose all control of his mind and body. This was perilous; he had to stop. Otherwise she would believe he had taken advantage of her during her slumber. He had to be patient and do nothing to lose her trust and affection. As much as he craved her, he moved out of her reach and endured the aching in his loins.

Rebecca was restless for a time. Gradually she quieted and became lost in a land of dreams where she was pursuing the elusive Bright Arrow through a hot forest. Why did he tease her and tempt her, then flee and hide? she wondered.

When she stirred the next morning, she was tense and stiff. The ridges beneath her tawny eyes were dark. She had not slept well. She glanced around for Windrider, and his expression told a similar tale.

Rebecca went to the spring and washed her face and hands, then took her brush and worked the tangles from her hair. She walked to where Windrider was sitting. "Good morning," she ventured when he remained rigid and silent.

As if he hadn't been aware of her presence, he shook his head and looked over at her. "You did not sleep well," he remarked.

Her gaze traveled over his weary features. "I kept you awake?" she asked. "I'm sorry, Windrider. Dreams plagued me all through the night."

He smiled. "You did not trouble me. Dreams also danced in my head, dreams of you, dreams of our life together." He thought it best not to expose what had happened, or had nearly happened. And he knew it would be best not to question the subject of her dreams.

"What do we have to eat?" she asked to break the strain.

"Dried venison," he jested.

Her brow furrowed and she wailed in distress, "Please tell me you're teasing. If I eat more venison, I will begin to look like a deer!"

They both laughed. "What if we cook *this?*" he inquired playfully, pulling a fat bird with brightly colored feathers from his hunting bag. "We have three breadroots and one carrot. Will that fill the stomach of one lazy and hungry female?" he teased.

"I am not," she debated between giggles. "To prove it, I'll gather the wood and build the fire. I'll even clean the bird," she added.

"You do not need to prove your skills and value to me. We will work together," he stated, exhibiting unusual behavior for an Indian male.

"You don't fool me, Windrider," she taunted mischievously. "You don't trust me out of your sight. You fear I'll get into trouble. But if you insist, come along."

They gathered the wood, and Windrider built the fire while Rebecca plucked and cleaned the pheasant. She removed the longest feathers carefully, knowing their value as decorations. She cleaned their tips and handed them to Windrider. As he examined them, he smiled.

The fowl took over an hour to roast. She warmed the breadroots and halved the wild carrot. When all was ready, they sat side by side and consumed the meal. She told him it was the best food she had ever eaten. He chuckled and replied it was only because she was weary of dried venison. As they waited for Cloud Chaser's return, Windrider related tales of his *coups* and of tribal rivalries.

Just as he began entreating her to reveal her life story, Cloud Chaser rode into the semi-enclosed area and dismounted. He had brought supplies with him, insuring them of better meals on their return trip. Rebecca watched him curiously. She was eager yet reluctant to hear his news. The Sioux warrior glanced at her, then spoke to Windrider in Cheyenne.

"Cloud Chaser said you should sit on the buffalo mat. He must tend his horse. He will come and give you the words of his people," Windrider told her gently, curious about Cloud Chaser's odd mood.

Rebecca walked to the shade tree and stood there a moment with her back to the men. She fretted over her state of mind. Was she prepared to hear Cloud Chaser's words? Had this been a terrible mistake? It was too late to turn back now. She sat and waited.

Windrider placed the supplies near the smoldering campfire. He asked in dread, "What did the council say? Did you speak with Gray Eagle and Shalee? Will they meet and talk with her?"

Cloud Chaser stated in a voice inaudible to her, "There is no need for us to trick her, Windrider. There is no need to guide her to the false trail we marked. You need not trap her to free Bright Arrow."

"I do not understand. Have they agreed to let her return as his wife?" Windrider questioned, two worry lines marking his forehead.

"No," the Sioux warrior replied calmly. "We joined as friends to end her hold over him. You were to make her choose you over him. If she did not, you were to dishonor her in his eyes. That game is over."

"You muddy my head. Did the council speak against her?" Windrider asked. Now that the awesome moment had arrived, he wanted to be certain he was doing the right thing for everyone involved.

"They have since banished two other warriors who also chose white females. My people hate the whites, all whites. Why should we blind our eyes and cool our angry hearts for Bright Arrow and for no other warrior? He chose to love a white slave; he chose to leave with her. He can return, but not with her. The whites hate no Indian more than the Sioux."

"You are sure they reject her?" Windrider pressed before making his irrevocable decision.

Windrider was not aware that Cloud Chaser was playing his own spiteful game. He did not know that the Sioux warrior had ulterior motives for his actions, black and evil motives. He did not know that Cloud Chaser was betraying their bargain, that he had spoken to no one about Rebecca Kenny or Bright Arrow. He would never have guessed that the Sioux warrior wanted Bright Arrow to return home, but without the strength and joy of Rebecca's love and courage. He would never have suspected that the fierce, envious Sioux warrior wanted to destroy Bright Arrow and his memory.

Without a flicker of guilt or remorse, Cloud Chaser lied convincingly, "Upon my life and honor, she will not be allowed to return or to join with him. They refuse to see her. They say she is the enemy of the Oglala. They say she cast evil magic on the son of our chief. It is best for all if she does not ever enter the camp. Her coming has stirred bitter memories to life. If Bright Arrow is a man and a warrior, he will do what he must. Come, I have no need to use the plan we made on the moon of Little Crow's feast. My people's demand will free Bright Arrow, not our trick."

Cloud Chaser had observed the strong attraction between Windrider and Rebecca. He cursed the white girl for entrapping another mighty warrior. He hadn't expected Windrider to actually fall in love with the woman. Yet his quarrel was with Bright Arrow. He should have known his rival would return one day. As long as he lived, he was a threat. To destroy him for all time, he had to get within reach. He had to be stealthy and careful. He could not trust Windrider to carry out their malicious plan. A man enslaved by passion would not hurt the woman he loved and desired. Once he spoke his crafty lies, Rebecca would seek out the Cheyenne warrior—and Bright Arrow would be devastated by their betrayals.

"Do you hate her, Cloud Chaser?" the Cheyenne warrior asked. He did not want the Sioux warrior to be cruel when he spoke to her.

"I do not hate her. I am angry because it is Bright Arrow's doing, not hers. My words will be as the icy snow falling on her ears and heart. She might resist them, but she cannot enter the village when it is forbidden. If you desire her, help her. She must choose you over him. You must not allow her to sway him with pleas and tears. Pull her from his life. She will not harm you. You are strong. You know her great magic. Your people will accept her," he deviously explained.

The horse was watered and hobbled by that time, and the two men walked to where Rebecca sat. Cloud Chaser spoke in Cheyenne; Windrider translated his words. The astounding, vengeful tale poured forth.

Cloud Chaser began his charade. "Bright Arrow is my friend, my brother. I spoke for his return. The council has agreed." He halted as Windrider spoke words that brought a sunny smile to her lips.

"I told the council of his love and need for you. I told them of three children you share. I told them Bright

203

Arrow wants to come home. I said he wishes to join with you by our laws. I told them of his many sufferings. I spoke until my lips and throat were dry."

Windrider translated those words for Rebecca. When Cloud Chaser did not continue, she asked, "What did the council say?"

"The council said Bright Arrow can return home. Bright Arrow can bring his children to his camp. He can take his place of honor at his father's side. He will be accepted into the Warrior Society. He can have such things returned . . . if he meets their demand."

Rebecca held her breath as Windrider spoke those words. The Sioux warrior had not mentioned her, and she sensed what was coming. "What is their demand?" she inquired in a deceptively calm tone.

"To prove his loyalty and love for his people, he must join with an Oglala female, or a female of a tribe who is our ally. Rebecca cannot be his mate. No white female can share his life. Tell her of the two warriors who have been banished for this same deed. Tell her the other words I spoke to you."

Windrider grimaced inwardly as he interpreted those agonizing words. "Ask Cloud Chaser if they might change their minds," she instructed him, maintaining her control over her tears and nerves.

"Two members of the council spoke for another punishment. They said Bright Arrow should be allowed to keep you as his slave. Others argued, saying he would not touch his Indian wife while you shared their tepee. They have forbidden you to enter the camp. They do not wish to look into the face of Bright Arrow's shame. They say you must free him of your evil magic. They say you blind his eyes to his customs and laws. They say you steal his love for his people. They say you make him weak like a baby. They say he cannot be a man or a warrior until your bonds on him are cut. They say you must go to your lands. Sun Cloud is but seven winters old. It will be many winters before he is ready to follow Gray Eagle's path. Bright Arrow must return and prove his honor and courage. If our chief is slain in battle, the council will vote that Bright Arrow take his place. Will you deny him such happiness and honor? Prove your love is true and unselfish," he boldly and vindictively challenged, the trace of a smile on his face.

Rebecca listened to those words. Anguish and suspense filled her. When she asked if they would make these same demands of Bright Arrow when he came home, Cloud Chaser told her yes. When Cloud Chaser added something, Windrider bristled in anger and shook his head, refusing to reveal those infuriating words. They argued loudly.

Rebecca insisted he tell her what the warrior had said. He grit his teeth and declared forcefully, "They say the choice is Bright Arrow's, as before. Cloud Chaser said Bright Arrow might persuade them to let you live in his tepee as his . . . white whore. If so, there will be more demands. If he does not father a child by his Indian wife within one span of seasons, you will be sold to another tribe. You cannot agree, Rebecca. You know his wife would be cruel and cold to you. What if she is like Sucoora? What if she can bear no children? You must not agree." His dark eyes blazed with fury.

"If he goes back home without me, his life will be as it was before he met me?" she questioned gravely.

Windrider spoke with Cloud Chaser, and they both nodded to her. Cloud Chaser spoke again. Windrider explained, "He says Bright Arrow will die if he returns to the wilderness with you. He says Bright Arrow will never be happy with another tribe. He says Bright Arrow can never become the warrior he was with another tribe. He says Bright Arrow will become bitter and angry. He says he will become careless. He says Bright Arrow must fulfill his life-circle in the Oglala camp."

"What do you say, Windrider?" she entreated sadly.

"Do not ask me. I have the same prize to lose as Bright Arrow. I am selfish. I cannot trust my words to be true," he replied.

Cloud Chaser spoke to Windrider a last time. "The council said it was wrong for her to come in Bright Arrow's place. A woman should not interfere in a warrior's affairs. It is worse because she is not Indian; she is not his wife. They fear Bright Arrow will be angry over her visit and their words. They say she should hold silent to him. They fear his pride will prevent his return. They fear he will rebel once more."

When Windrider passed those words along to her, Rebecca frowned in dismay. It had been a mistake for her to come here. All she had accomplished was refreshing their resentment toward her. She should have let Bright Arrow handle this distressing and critical matter. He would be angry. He despised compromise, and he would never grovel before them. She knew he would be embittered and disquieted, and she didn't want to create new problems and hard feelings. They were right; silence was best. "Is that all?" she inquired distantly.

Windrider smiled encouragingly. "You must decide what to do after Bright Arrow makes his choice."

Rebecca's solemn gaze fused with Windrider's concerned look. "How can we refuse their demands? We've proven we can't live alone in the wilderness. You saw what it did to Bright Arrow. We're helpless, Windrider. Whether they're right or wrong, we must all obey his people's demands. Bright Arrow is to return home alone, and I am to take a separate path. The council has made the choices for us."

"There is one choice left for you to make," Windrider tenderly reminded her. "You can fight a daring battle for Bright Arrow, or you can release him quickly with less pain . . . and marry me."

Chapter Ten

Windrider had not expected the extent of the Sioux tribe's hostility toward Rebecca. He had realized there was a chance the council could swing in either direction, yet he was stunned by the venomous reaction to her that Cloud Chaser had related. He almost wished he hadn't brought her here to face such animosity and rejection. Windrider was torn between relief and empathy, and he wished there were an easier, less painful, way to win her. He told himself he should not feel guilty. If Bright Arrow couldn't have her, why shouldn't he? He shouldn't feel he was betraying his friend. She needed to know of his love and desire before she was crushed by her losses. She needed to know that someone loved her and wanted her, that she wouldn't be alone and needn't be afraid.

Windrider's ire against the Oglalas returned. They were being unjust. Did they possess no mercy? The evil and prejudice were in their hearts and minds, not Rebecca's! It was understandable that Bright Arrow had taken her away from such coldness and cruelty. How could he have expected the woman he loved to live in such a demeaning way? The Cheyenne warrior felt that the least they could have done was to see her and talk with her! Nevertheless, Windrider was glad he wouldn't have to use his previous ploy to free Bright Arrow and win Rebecca. The council had spoken and they would not change their minds, even for the son of Gray Eagle. It would be wrong and destructive for her to force her way into the camp, and he hoped she would not try.

Rebecca looked at Windrider. Her gaze was unreadable, but her words reflected his thoughts. "Yes, I have to make up my mind soon. This not knowing what to do or say is destroying my happiness. But we must keep our promises, Windrider. Bright Arrow must be given the chance to work things out for himself and for us. I know we're not joined by any man's law, but I did commit myself to him long ago. I can't be unfaithful to him or myself. How could you ever trust me, knowing I turned to you while . . . committed to him? You would always doubt my honesty and loyalty."

There was a faraway look in her golden brown eyes. "It seems as if we've shared a lifetime in only a few years. I helped to tear his life apart, and I must help him to rebuild it. Losing him, I'll also lose my children. I love my girls, and I want to raise them. Don't you see? I must wait until I'm certain our life together is over. I owe him that much. Can you understand what I'm saying and feeling?"

A smile of admiration filled his eyes and softened his features. "You are a special woman, Rebecca. Your heart is good and pure. I will do as you ask. I will go with Bright Arrow to see his people when the time is right. I will try to ease his pain when he hears their demand. I did not wish to see you hurt. I will help ease your suffering. Will you tell him of your pleas to his people this sun?"

"No. It would only hurt and confuse him. I don't want him to be filled with new bitterness. Cloud Chaser said the council would not tell him of my visit. It's best that he doesn't know just yet. If there's one thing I've learned, Windrider, it's that you cannot go against the council's orders and votes. It can do no harm for Bright Arrow to hope for a while longer. This way, I'll be ready for his departing words."

"I will leave you to think," Windrider offered kindly. He returned to where Cloud Chaser was sitting.

The demands seemed harsh and cruel to her, and Rebecca could not accept them—any of them. She had no hatred or prejudice, and she knew she could live peaceably with the Sioux in the Indian world if they would allow it. Yet Bright Arrow could not live contentedly with her kind in the white world. Nor could they live between the two worlds, as they had tried to do for so long. Bright Arrow could not live or work as white, and he could not survive without his people, his ways, his customs, his warrior rank. He needed the rituals, the ceremonies, the excitement, the danger, the glory, the honor. For such a complicated problem, there was only one answer. If only she could accept it and end this torment.

That night, Rebecca slept under the dying tree, while the two men slept near the campfire. Windrider had offered her more of the sleeping potion, and she had accepted it quickly. Tonight she hadn't wanted to think or dream. She hadn't wanted to cry before the two men, exposing her anguish. She only wanted black nothingness to fill her mind and to halt the agony deep within her soul.

They rode for two days without mishap. The return trip was similar to their ride out, except that the food was better. They resumed the same riding and camping schedule as before, camping in the same places. But Rebecca wasn't the same. She kept as much to herself as possible. Sensing her attempts to come to terms with herself and her news, Windrider respected her privacy and feelings.

The following night, two Blackfeet hunters ate and camped with them. Rebecca wished she were wearing a buckskin garment instead of the faded cotton dress, for the visiting braves stared and leered at her as if she were a lowly white slave. She barely restrained her anger. How could they justify their double standard? A white woman was good enough for them to bed but not wed! How she loathed this hostility and scorn! Why couldn't people live in peace and harmony? she wondered. Why was there so much hatred and killing? Why couldn't some powerful person plant seeds of joy and peace instead of seeds of fury and aggression?

The last morning on the trail, Cloud Chaser rode out with the Blackfeet braves, and Windrider and Rebecca completed their journey alone. When they reentered the Cheyenne camp, nine days had passed, and it was past dusk.

When Sucoora learned of Rebecca's defeat, she was not surprised by it. She smiled and offered words of encouragement and sympathy as she quickly prepared the leftover food for the weary travelers. After eating, Windrider headed for the ceremonial lodge to discover what had occurred during his absence.

Kajihah's reaction was very different. She had returned to the tepee from the menses hut to find her husband and their beautiful female guest missing. She made no attempt to conceal her resentment and suspicion of the time Rebecca and Windrider had spent alone together. Kajihah glared at Rebecca, refusing to speak with her. She strode about, inhaling and exhaling in scornful puffs and huffs and, when Sucoora warned her to behave, Kajihah sneered at her and spouted Cheyenne curses at both women.

"She is jealous. Do not look at her or speak to her. She is bad. I pray Windrider sends her home to her father. She fears Windrider's eyes are for no female but Becca. I pray it is true," Sucoora chatted freely and openly, delighted by Kajihah's envy and sullenness.

Rebecca neither agreed or argued with the gregarious woman. Moving to sit with her girls, she began playing and talking with them. Later, she sang several songs for them. Moon Eyes and Little Feet fell asleep during the story she was telling. When Rebecca lay on her mat, Tashina crawled over and snuggled up with her, as if sensing that her mother needed her love and closeness. Rebecca embraced the child, and both fell asleep.

Five days passed before Bright Arrow and White Antelope returned to camp. Windrider was on a hunting expedition, Sucoora and Rebecca were washing clothes at the river, and Kajihah was the one to greet the Sioux warrior. Once Rebecca had returned to the tepee, Kajihah's jealousy and hatred had mounted with each new sunrise and sunset. She feared that Windrider would soon compare her with the hard-working and beautiful woman of Bright Arrow. Worse, she feared Rebecca would be irresistibly drawn to her powerful and virile husband, for her man seemed much less desirable. Determining to see the white creature gone, she spitefully revealed Rebecca's secret journey to Bright Arrow.

Kajihah smiled warmly and deceptively at the Sioux warrior. "You have changed much since you rode from our camp, son of Gray Eagle," she began the malicious conversation. "It is good to see you become a man once

213

more. Your woman's eyes and thoughts will now return to you and leave her foolish ways behind," she hinted cleverly.

When Bright Arrow appeared to ignore her statements, she added, "I hope your anger at her behavior does not darken your reunion. I begged her not to ride to your father's camp and speak in your place. I told her others would laugh at you. She is white and does not understand our ways. She is stubborn and grows weary of exile. She would not listen to Kajihah's words. She asked my husband to ride at her side. They were gone many days . . . and many nights. When she looks upon you, her eyes and feelings will return where they belong. The men of our camp regard her beauty highly. Perhaps you should not leave her side again," she remarked suggestively.

"What silly words run from your lips?" Bright Arrow inquired impatiently, knowing there was some sinister point to this talk. "Rebecca would not ride into my camp without my permission," he argued stiffly.

"If you did not speak it, then she rode without it," she declared, then revealed only the details which she knew about the trip. She guilefully pressed the point of the solitude shared by Rebecca and Windrider along the trail and belabored Rebecca's daring behavior.

Bright Arrow listened to this tale told with deceitfully innocent eyes and a honeyed voice. He was astounded by this incredible discovery. Rebecca had dared to ride to his camp and confront his people! It was not her place to intercede for him. He was the man! He was the warrior! He was the Indian! She had no right to interfere!

His turbulent mind was besieged with questions. Why had she wanted to spoil things? Why hadn't she waited for him to approach his tribe and the council first? Why had she been so disloyal? He should have been the one to explain matters to his tribe. He should have been the one to arrange their return. He agonized over the crushing points that Kajihah had voiced aloud. Had she revealed his self-destruction? Had she revealed his return to life? What had she told them? Why had she gone?

Bright Arrow asked where Rebecca was. When Kajihah told him, he stormed out of the tepee and headed for the river. When he called her name from behind her, his voice was cold and stern. Startled, she dropped what she was doing and whirled around. Her eyes widened in amazement. She couldn't believe the changes in him in such a few weeks. Her eyes helplessly roamed up and down his sleek bronze frame. The extra weight was gone! His toned muscles were firm and prominent. His stance was self-assured, and his expression was confident. There was a glow of pride in his dark eyes, while his body exuded control and prowess. The midnight hair that barely grazed his shoulders was braided; several feathers and tufts attached to the ends made it appear longer. His headband was in place, and he wore snug-fitting, sienna-colored leggings and breechclout. His chest and shoulder muscles seemed to flex and bulge with each breath, and his stomach was flat and taut. It was as if she were staring at an image of the warrior she had fallen in love with years ago!

Rebecca's heart drummed wildly. Her breath caught in her throat, and her mouth went suddenly dry. Her blood raced hot and swiftly through her veins. She couldn't make herself move or respond but merely stared at him as if he were a ghost.

He absently noticed his effect on her, but his mind was distracted by another matter. He roughly seized her arm and yanked her forward. "Come, we must talk," he growled impatiently and angrily between tightly clenched teeth. He walked rapidly toward the privacy of the forest, tugging the stunned and speechless Rebecca along with him.

She wondered why he was in such a hurry to speak with her. There was undeniable urgency in his behavior. Was he ready to go home? When they reached a secluded area, he halted and released her. Instantly she tried to fling herself into those powerful and tempting arms. "I've missed you so much," she murmured, her hands seeking to pull his head lower so she could reach his lips.

He prevented her kiss and contact by turning away to lean against a tree with his shoulders and one foot. "You have worked hard. You did not have time to miss me," he casually retorted.

"Never," she rebutted. "I've been helping Sucoora and Kajihah with their chores. I wish we had our own tepee. We need privacy, my love. It's so lonely here without you," she added softly.

"You have not had enough to keep your hands and mind busy?" he inquired nonchalantly, his raised knee keeping her from getting too close while he delved for the truth.

"I would rather you keep me busy," she replied provocatively, smiling at him. He did not return the smile. Her starving senses ravenously feasted on his body and face. She was simultaneously aware of his manly odor, his arresting appeal, and his sensuality. "We sleep on different mats. When will this separation be over?" she asked.

"When do my people say it will end?" He delivered the stunning question without a noticeable change in his expression or tone.

"What?" she murmured shakily, paling slightly

beneath her glowing tan. She deliberated whether his words were an accusation or a rhetorical query. She didn't know what to reply and waited silently for his next move.

When he felt she was not going to expose her treacherous actions, his eyes narrowed and flamed. Straightening and resting his hands on his hipbones, he stated, "The sun I ride away to recover myself, you play the fox behind my back. Then you seek to lie and hide your black deed. You dared to go to my village and beg mercy for me! You dared to ask and hear their demands without me! How dare the council meet with a female! It was not your place to speak! It was not your place to make choices! No doubt my people and the Cheyenne laugh at us. No doubt they say Bright Arrow cannot control his woman! What did my people say? Do they think I am too weak or cowardly to handle my troubles? Why did you embarrass and shame me this way? Why did Windrider allow you to do such an insulting, unforgivable thing?"

Rebecca didn't want him blaming Windrider for her rash behavior. "He rode with me to protect me. He said you would be angry and hurt. That's why I didn't want you to know about the journey," she blurted out. "I was only trying to help. I didn't lie to you!"

"Holding silent is the same!" he shouted back at her. "If you are to live as an Indian, you must behave as one. An Indian wife would never take her husband's place in any matter. My people have punishments for wrong deeds. A thief must return what he has taken; he must give the injured person many gifts to prove he is sorry. If he lies, he must bestow gifts upon the person he lies to and the person he had darkened with his false tale. If he murders another, he must be banished. How shall I punish you for your evil deed?" he snarled in fury.

"You have punished me greatly in these last years!" she flung back at him. "I only wanted to spare you more shame and torment. Can I do nothing right for you?" she cried breathlessly.

"Right?" he scoffed. "You know nothing of right if you can betray and deceive me! I sacrificed all I owned and was to take you as my woman. I tried to live with your ways, but I could not. Now I try to find my path home, and you toss branches across my trail. Was this some trick? Do you seek to prevent my return home? You are cruel and selfish, Rebecca Kenny!" he charged.

He had cause to be angry, she knew, but did he have to attack her so viciously? "You're not the only one who's suffered! I didn't ask you to enslave me! I didn't ask you to leave your people! I didn't place your feet on the path of self-destruction! I didn't ask you to give up anything for me! Those were your choices—your decisions!"

"Perhaps those choices were wrong for me! I was a crazed lover! I should not have captured you. It was foolish and cost me too much. I am returning home. I will lose nothing more—for you or anyone!" he declared rashly, not meaning the words he spoke in anger. Her mischief and intrusion had riled him beyond caution and control.

"Then go home where you belong!" Rebecca retorted, no longer able to bear his accusations. "You haven't been a man since you left! I have no more patience or understanding for you! I'm tired of living this way! My God, we haven't been happy in years. I wanted to spare you more anguish. I wanted to know if the council was still determined to keep us apart. If so, I could prepare you to lose me. I didn't want you to face that same cruel demand when you returned home. If they said nothing had changed, I was going to free you. Don't you think I know what you've endured because of me? How long are you going to blame me and punish me for your mistakes? How can I help being white? It's me they're rejecting, not you or the children. We're not married, so you're free to go home, Bright Arrow. Go home and be happy again. Go home before we tear each other to shreds with this forbidden love."

Tears were streaming down her cheeks. Slowly her anger subsided, and she realized they could not end their stormy love affair this way. She took the only door left open to her. "I didn't go to your village," she admitted. "Windrider and I camped a half-day's ride from it. I was going to visit your parents the next day, to see if they would influence the council in my favor. I wanted to learn if there was even the smallest hope they would allow me to return with you. I never rode to their village. I never spoke with your parents or the council. We stayed one night, then returned here. Windrider rode along to protect me. I have not been to the Oglala camp or seen your parents since we left years ago." She told the truth subtly, leaving out Cloud Chaser and his part in the drama. There was no need to damage that friendship, she thought, no need to inspire more bitterness in her haunted husband.

She summoned her sagging courage in order to sever their bond. "It's over between us, Bright Arrow. Isn't it time we face that reality and accept it? Isn't it time we stop hurting and blaming each other for our problems? We tried to cross the barrier between our two peoples; your tribe will not allow it. You tried to live in my world, and it didn't work. We've got to end it now, before we destroy all that was good and beautiful between us. I will not cause you any more suffering and humiliation. Take the children and go home tomorrow. There's no hope for us," she asserted painfully.

"You would give up your children?" he asked incredulously. His rage had faded during her confession, and her anguish gnawed at him.

"Even if children did not belong to their father and his people, their faces are Indian," Rebecca said. "In my world, they would be taunted and abused as half-breeds. I cannot protect them and care for them alone. If I must choose the world in which they will live, I wish it to be yours. They need friends and family. They need loving grandparents. They need a happy and safe home. You're a man once more; you're their father. Your tribe will accept you and your children but not me. You must find a good woman to marry, one who will love our girls as I do. You must leave and seek your destiny alone, Bright Arrow. Please, do this for us," she entreated.

"I will not free you," he vowed stubbornly, reaching out to draw her into his arms. She dodged his grasp. He yearned to comfort her, for though she had done wrong, it had been only to help him. He had not realized how she had suffered. He had to find a way to keep her!

"You must let go, Bright Arrow. Many years past, you chose me over your family, your people, your destiny. Remember what it did to you? Soon that same decision will confront you again. If we part now, they won't have to order you to make a choice. They can't force you into another corner. If a command is spoken, we both know what it will be—just as we know what your answer must be. I will leave in the morning," she announced impulsively.

"You cannot!" Bright Arrow shouted in astonishment and dismay.

"If I do not, I might be tempted to fight for you," she replied. "You have told me many times that it is foolish to inspire a battle that is lost before the first blow is struck. Besides, there's trouble in Windrider's tepee. We've stayed too long. Kajihah hates me. I know she's the one who told you about my journey," she stated matter-of-factly. "Sucoora is siding with me; we've become friends. If I don't leave, Windrider's tepee will be filled with bickering. We should not do this to a friend. Take the girls and ride to your camp in the morning. Forget me, Bright Arrow. Forget me and all the pain I've brought into your life."

She started to leave him standing there. He seized her shoulders and whirled her around to face him. What if she were right? What if the council issued the same heartless edict once more? This time, there could be no choice; Bright Arrow had to return to his people or cease to exist. "I love you and I need you," he declared earnestly, fearfully.

Rebecca's teary gaze fused with his entreating one. "You need your destiny more," she replied simply. "Do not make it harder for us," she pleaded. "You claim I'm strong and smart. I'll be fine."

Bright Arrow grasped his temples as if he were in great agony. A bellow of rage and frustration roared from his muscular chest. "Why can I not have you *and* my destiny?" he thundered in torment.

"Because we are of two warring worlds, Bright Arrow. No matter how much we love or accept each other, it changes nothing around us. We have been prisoners trapped between those two worlds. We must have freedom. We must have joy and peace. Do not resist what you know is true. It makes the pain and bitterness worse," she informed him sadly while he continued to shake his head in resistance. She stormed at him, "Damn you, I am white! I am your enemy! You must hate me and reject me," she commanded.

"I cannot," he protested obstinately.

"You must. The choice is not yours. You can't have everything you want! Ask the Great Spirit to guide you, to ease the pain. I can say no more. I must be alone." She raced into the woods and vanished from sight.

Bright Arrow started to pursue her, then changed his mind. Rebecca needed time to think, time to realize he could not sacrifice her. He would find some way to keep her. How could he live without her? She was his heart, his breath, his spirit. Recalling her words about Kajihah, he headed for camp. He had to make other arrangements. He would not allow that malicious woman to torment his love. Yet he also realized it was too soon to ride to the Oglala camp. He needed more practice and training.

Windrider was in camp speaking with two other warriors when Bright Arrow left the forest and strode toward his tepee. Each sighted the other simultaneously. Windrider perceived some inner turmoil in the Sioux warrior and left his friends to meet Bright Arrow.

When Bright Arrow revealed his problem, Windrider's anger flared. "Kajihah will be punished for her loose tongue and disobedience," the Cheyenne warrior vowed. "She seeks to cause trouble. She has never been a good wife. I was a fool to take a wife as a gift! A man should choose his woman carefully. Kajihah is lazy. She refuses her share of the tasks and treats Sucoora as a slave. She mocks and teases her when she thinks I do not hear. Her wit is dull, and her tongue is annoying. She sickens me on the sleeping mat, and I have not touched her since I planted the seed for my son within her. I have been too lenient and kind. I can take no more of her spite and interference. Sucoora can tend my children, and I will seek another wife. I will send Kajihah back to her father," he concluded.

"Come, let us walk and speak of another matter," Bright Arrow requested. The two men walked along the riverbank for privacy.

Windrider spoke first. "You are angry because I rode with Rebecca to speak with your people?" he asked.

"No. I am pleased you did not allow her to ride alone. Sometimes she does not understand the Indian ways, and she innocently defies our customs. She did not wish to harm me with her action, yet I am glad she did not enter the camp. I am relieved she exchanged no words with them."

His last statement caught Windrider by surprise. He had assumed Rebecca had confessed everything when Bright Arrow had confronted her. Apparently she had told him very little! Bright Arrow had dropped to a cross-legged position near the river's edge and, in doing so, he had missed Windrider's reaction to his words.

"What did she tell you of her journey?" Windrider offhandedly inquired, taking the same position nearby. After Bright Arrow related the highlights of their conversation, Windrider sighed heavily. He didn't know if he should tell Bright Arrow about Cloud Chaser's part in her quest and wondered if it would be best to let the matter drop.

Bright Arrow was distressed and dejected. He needed to discuss his predicament with someone who would listen and understand, someone who had proven love and friendship. He had endured many hardships and difficulties, but nothing like the ones facing him on this sun and those to come. Perhaps Windrider could offer some advice, he mused.

As he and his friend sat facing each other on the riverbank, Bright Arrow exposed the remainder of his earlier talk with Rebecca. He disclosed his warring thoughts and emotions and divulged his fears, his hopes, his dreams, his worries, his speculations.

Windrider didn't want to hear such words and feelings. Yet he listened intently and sympathetically. They had been close friends since childhood, when their fathers had shared the warpath and ridden together on buffalo hunts. Later, they too had ridden together on raids and hunts. Windrider had begun this matter with sincerity and honesty, but things had changed along the way. All had not been as he had believed. He knew he shouldn't feel guilty; the separation wasn't his fault. Bright Arrow was a Sioux; he should understand his own people. Windrider could hardly believe Rebecca had told Bright Arrow it was over between them. She was freeing his friend, just as he had encouraged her to do so many times on the trail. Would Bright Arrow accept his freedom, or would he battle to keep her?

As had Rebecca, Windrider selected his words cleverly and cautiously in order to speak the truth without exposing too much. "She did not tell you why she returned here without visiting your camp? She is being unselfish and kind, my friend. She wishes to shut out the words she was told. She is trying to save you from such hurt as she feels. She knows the council will reject her. She knows you must push her from your life. She seeks to make this ending less painful for both of you."

Suddenly, Bright Arrow realized there was more to the story than Rebecca had told him. He probed, "You hint at words or deeds my woman did not reveal to me. Speak. Windrider. My heart beats swiftly at your concern, but I must know the truth."

"While we camped, Cloud Chaser came to us. We talked. He told us of two Sioux warriors who chose white slaves as their women after you left. They too were shamed and banished. Your father forbids any white—good or evil—to enter his camp. Cloud Chaser told us that your people's hatred of whites has grown since you were exiled. He says they vote against all who side with whites. Any Oglala who takes one to heart is rejected. No white—slave or free—is allowed to live in your father's camp. Cloud Chaser told Rebecca it was not her place to seek forgiveness for you. He said your people would be angry and resentful if she rode into his camp. He said it is your place to speak to the council when you return. He said there is no hope they will allow her to return with you. If they do, it would be as your white whore. You cannot show her such cruelty," he stated quietly.

"There is no hope?" Bright Arrow questioned hoarsely.

"I can only tell you of Cloud Chaser's words. I do know he speaks true of your father's actions. No white enters his camp; no white lives there. White prisoners are sold when they are captured; they cannot be brought to camp even for one moon. The council believes their white blood is evil, and all agree no white should mate with an Oglala. You must return to your people, Bright Arrow; you must free Rebecca. Braves who hunt near your wooden tepee or trade where you trade have told them of your sufferings in the white man's territory. They blame Rebecca for dishonoring and weakening you. Cloud Chaser said your people wish you to return, to ride with your father, to take his place if he is slain before Sun Cloud is a warrior. Many mourn you as dead. They despise Rebecca for stealing your heart and body from them. They say she is killing your spirit. They say she is evil." He paused. "It is true that they do not know her or understand your love. Yet you must obey your laws."

"I cannot free her! Where would she go? Who would

protect her? Who could care for her? I took her into my life and tepee. I am responsible for her. What about my honor? How can I endure the guilt and shame of tossing her away? She is the mother of my children. She has trust in me. She never deserted me during my suffering and exile. What warrior shows no mercy to one so helpless and gentle? It is wrong to cast her aside. I must make them understand. I must make them accept her in my life-circle," he declared.

"If they cannot accept white women in the hearts and tepees of braves, how can they allow one to live with the son of their leader? How can they allow one to live with a warrior who could become their next chief? They think she is bad for you. They will not change their minds. There is too much hatred and bitterness toward her. If you force their hand, it will be worse than before. You must return alone to your camp. There is danger if you take Rebecca with you to speak to your council. Men with hatred and anger in their hearts commit rash acts. An arrow could find its way into her heart to free you," Windrider suggested. "When the time is right, go to your people, my friend. Stay with them one full moon. Earn their love and respect. If they will not accept Rebecca as your woman, then free her as she asks. Do not make her your slave or whore. There can be no bond between a white girl and a Sioux warrior. Have you not learned this by now?"

"I cannot choose between them," Bright Arrow stated defiantly.

"You did many seasons past," Windrider reminded him. "You do not wish to face this trouble again, but you must. You cannot have both. Seek the prize that you cannot live without, then release the other forever."

"I cannot survive as a white man. I will die slowly and

painfully in his wooden tepee and in the lands that he has stolen from my people. I am a hunter and a warrior. I can be nothing less," he explained wearily. The more Bright Arrow mulled over his problem, the more he tried to find hope that there was a way out.

Windrider sighted his opening and daringly took it. "Then your choice is clear. Accept it and stop this torment of two friends." He inhaled deeply to steady his nerves before boldly saying, "Your heart is heavy over her safety and happiness. Your mind swirls as rapidly as a muddy river after a fierce storm. Take heart, Bright Arrow; she can live in my tepee. I will protect her. I will hunt hides for her to make her garments. I will hunt game to feed her. I will let no one harm her. She will find peace and safety in Windrider's tepee."

Bright Arrow turned and looked at Windrider. "You would do this for me?" he inquired in astonishment and pleasure.

"I would do this for my friend Bright Arrow, for the gentle Rebecca, and for Windrider. When I send Kajihah away, I will have need of another woman in my tepee. There are many tasks and children for Sucoora. They are friends. It will be a happy tepee. My people will accept her. I will accept her. Does this lighten your spirit?"

Bright Arrow sighed gravely. If he could not win his battle with his council, Windrider had offered him the perfect solution. She would be safe in the Cheyenne camp, and she would be near for visits. His spirits soared, and he smiled in relief. Yes, she could live within his reach. If the council voted differently one day, he would come and claim her. If not, he could sneak here to be with her as often as possible. He placed his right hand on Windrider's shoulder and squeezed it in affection and appreciation. "It will be as you say, my friend," he agreed without revealing his secret plans. After all, Windrider had said "woman," not wife. The thought of his friend marrying Rebecca had never entered his mind.

Windrider was too shocked to reply. Could his dreams be coming true? Rebecca had agreed to become his wife if the vote was against her. Cloud Chaser had vowed she would be rejected. Bright Arrow had given him permission to take her when that order was given. Once Kajihah was gone and Rebecca was in his arms and tepee, he would surely know ecstasy and serenity, he reflected. Windrider's body and mind became inflamed with visions of taking her to his mats each moon. And the best prize was not having to trick either his friend or his love!

"I must seek Rebecca and give her this good news," Bright Arrow stated, relieved. "She will see it is best for all concerned if she lives in Windrider's tepee." The two warriors clasped hands tightly and smiled at each other as Bright Arrow added, "My heart is glad I call Windrider friend."

Chapter Eleven

Bright Arrow returned to the area where he and Rebecca had spoken earlier. He looked around for her and called her name, but she did not answer or appear. He dropped to the ground on one knee and sought evidence of her trail. Finding it, he followed the markings to where she sat beside a thick bush near a tree. A tremor of concern and indecision raced over him, as he feared she wouldn't agree to his plan.

He observed her. Her knees were hugged to her chest, and her forehead rested on them. From the shallow rise and fall of her respiration, it seemed she hardly breathed. He stepped in front of her and spoke her name. "Rebecca." When she did not respond, he hunkered down and said, "We must talk."

Without lifting her head, she replied in a muffled voice, "There is nothing more to say. Your tribe will never accept me. It is over. I must find another life and home."

Rebecca had reached the point of numbness. She couldn't cry, and her mind didn't want to think. Her tongue refused to speak. It was hopeless, she thought. She had battled his predicament so long that she was mentally exhausted. Her warring emotions had drained her of energy and stamina. At last she had admitted defeat. She wasn't sure she even cared anymore, except

229

about her children.

"Do not fear. If the vote is against us, I have made plans for you. You cannot live alone and in danger. Windrider will take you to live in his tepee. He will keep you safe. He will provide for your needs. He is sending Kajihah home to her father; she is a bad woman. You will be Sucoora's sister. I will bring the children to visit you. It will be good for all," he asserted eagerly, forgetting to explain his underlying meaning. "If the moon comes when my tribe will allow you to join me, I promise I will come for you," he added, unintentionally withholding the words that would make his intentions and feelings clear.

As Rebecca raised her head, her chestnut locks fell over her slumped shoulders. Her tawny eyes observed his relaxed manner and enthusiastic gaze. She noted his sunny smile. Was he serious? Was he actually giving her to another man? He even looked cheerful over his decision! Why not? she thought angrily. It would solve his problems nicely and neatly! And if he thought for one minute she would sob and plead, he was wrong.

"If that is what you wish, Bright Arrow, then I will remain here in Windrider's camp and tepee," she concurred, her response so quick that he was baffled. "I have no people and no place else to go. When will you ride to your camp?" she questioned, her expression blank.

"I will be ready in ten days," he replied, using the white man's time description. "I must have more training. I must visit the sweat lodge and seek a vision. Then I will ride to the Oglala camp and speak with my father. If the council allows, I will remain there. I will ask permission to have you. If they say no, we will be patient until they change their minds."

Rebecca's obscure expression never changed, though she was very much aware that Bright Arrow's mood and voice were light. He was casually planning her fate as he wished it to be! And she was to be *patient?* she angrily reflected to herself, despising the offending word he had probably used just to appease her. With her tossed into Windrider's lap without a fuss, his problems would be over. "You have given this situation much thought," she said aloud, "and your decisions are clever. The hour grows late. We must return for the evening meal." As she spoke the words, she wondered if he expected or desired her to protest.

When she started to rise, his hands captured her shoulders. "Do not go. I wish to be alone with you. Come, we will make love beneath *Wakantanka's* stars," he huskily entreated, his hand slipping down to cup her breast. "Soon we will part. We must spend our remaining moments together." His fingertips teased the nipple.

Rebecca pushed herself to a standing position, causing him to fall to his seat. She was rankled by his mood and suggestion. *He offers me to another man, then wants to enjoy me one last time!* she inwardly fumed. Then she tightly announced, "We cannot touch again. You are to leave soon, and I am to stay. I do not wish to burden Windrider and Sucoora with a pregnant female. I would be of little use to either one. I would cause Sucoora more work. I cannot allow your seed to enter my body and grow there," she stated with finality.

"But I have need of you. You are my woman," he argued, his manhood taut and fiery. "What does it matter if you bear another child of mine?" he reasoned in bewilderment.

"Until the council agrees, I am not your woman. We have three children who can be called bastards; we are not wed. We have never been wed. I do not wish to live here heavy with your child. If you have needs, visit the prisoner's tepee," she suggested indifferently.

"There is no prisoner's tepee in my camp! My father does not allow any white to come there, free or slave, friend or foe!"

"I am sure there will be plenty of Oglala maidens eager to please the glorious son of Gray Eagle, on your mats or in the cool forest. While you are still a free man, seek the pleasures of many females. You might enjoy a variety for a change," she spat at him.

"Why do you speak such vulgar words?" he scolded her.

"Men have needs. You do not have a wife. What is the harm in filling those needs with willing women?" she debated, angry and bitter that he was throwing her at another man. His calm acceptance of that fact ranked her greatly. Did he truly understand the implications of his shocking decision?

"You wish me to make love to other women?" he asked in disbelief.

"I wish you to be happy, whatever that requires," she replied, shrugging her shoulders. "Some woman must feed your hungers, for I cannot. Tell me, has your appetite for the mats come back with the return of your prowess?" she asked sarcastically.

"Did I not feed you a few weeks past?" he taunted angrily.

"What is one meal in many, many months?" she cruelly retorted. "Now that your hunger has returned with your manhood, you must feast elsewhere. Or do without, as I did for many months while you ignored me. I will not bear your next child until we are joined."

"What if you already carry my child?" he challenged.

"That cannot be helped. But taking more risks can. I do not do this to anger you or hurt you, Bright Arrow. Don't you see how difficult it would be for me?" she asked, trying another strategy to cool his passion. "My carrying a child under these conditions would be difficult for everyone."

Bright Arrow quelled further insults or rebukes. She was right, he realized. If his manhood ached too fiercely, he would find some female to ease its suffering while she was lost to him. "We will do as you say," he reluctantly and sullenly acquiesced.

When they entered the outskirts of the camp, Bright Arrow announced he was going to visit the medicine chief for a short time. He told her he needed to make plans for his vision quest. Rebecca went to Windrider's tepee. Only Sucoora and the children were present. The children were playing outside while waiting for the evening meal, so fascinated by Kajihah's daughter Tansia's play tepee, travois, and handmade dolls that the girls didn't notice their mother's arrival. A youthful Cheyenne girl was teaching them about tepees, travel, camps, and families—the women's concerns in Indian society. Rebecca recognized her as the daughter of Windrider's deceased brother, the one whose mother had wed White Antelope. Even Tashina sucked on her forefinger and sat in entranced silence as Little Turtle spoke with knowledge and authority.

Sucoora was busy completing her chores. She had suspended a buffalo paunch from four stakes. Inside it was their venison stew. Sucoora took hot rocks and dropped them into the mixture to make it boil. She would continue this procedure until the meat and vegetables were done. Bread pones slowly cooked on flat rocks nearby. They were made of dried berries and corn purchased from another tribe.

As Rebecca walked over to her, Sucoora ceased her task to hug her, laughing merrily. At Rebecca's baffled expression, Sucoora shrieked in glee, "Windrider sent Kajihah to her father, Becca. He says you will live here if the council refuses your joining with Bright Arrow. Kajihah will speak many lies to them. She will say you took her place. Their hate will grow as the Prairie grass. Do not fear. Sucoora and Windrider will love and protect you. We will be sisters," she babbled excitedly.

Rebecca frowned. It seemed she was the last one to learn her own fate, a fate planned by others! Doubtlessly Kajihah would kill any minuscule chance of her joining with Bright Arrow! "Why did he send her away?" she asked solemnly. "She is the mother of his children. It is cruel to separate them," she fretted, praying she wasn't to blame for this deed. She worried that Windrider had done this intentionally, to end all chances of the council accepting her and to rid himself of one wife.

Sucoora sensed Rebecca's anxiety and self-recriminations, and she resolved to make certain Rebecca didn't blame herself or Windrider. She hated Kajihah; she was glad that lazy creature was gone. And she knew Windrider would find Rebecca pleasing on his mats. She didn't care about more children; she loved Kajihah's as her own. Also, she had never enjoyed the mats with any man except her beloved husband, Windrider's brother. If Rebecca lived with them, she would fill Windrider's every need and dream. She was not a blind fool; she had noticed the way Windrider secretly watched Rebecca. She understood that hungry gleam in his eyes. She had seen his buckskin pants tighten while his eyes watched the white girl who was beautiful and gentle. She had noticed how Rebecca had tried to hold her feelings under tight guard; now she could free them. No one would be hurt, for Bright Arrow had given his permission for them to become mates.

"Now I will speak of matters that must not pass beyond Sucoora and Becca," Sucoora began in a conspiratorial tone. She glanced around to make certain no one could overhear her words. "Kajihah is evil. She placed the death camas in my son's mouth. She did not gather the camas with blue flowers; she picked those with cloud colors. She wished Windrider to have no son but hers. She hated my son and feared Windrider loved him more than all her children."

"You cannot mean she poisoned a small child?" Rebecca argued in horror.

"Yes. When she was sick on her mat, I tended her. Her fever brought many words from her mouth. I could not tell Windrider. He would think me crazy over my son's death. I have watched her many years. I feared she would poison me. That is why I gather the food and cook all meals," the woman revealed earnestly.

"But she is lazy. She loved having you do the chores."

"If I were dead, no one could uncover her evil. She could find another slave to do her work. I have watched her since you came. She knew Windrider dreamed of you. I feared her hatred and envy would slay you. She is sly; she pretends to sew and tend the children. She has not pleased Windrider since she took his seed for their son. It is good she was sent away. She burned with hatred, for she could not entrap her husband. She wished to hurt him, to make his spirit weak, to bring him under her power. She is evil and dangerous, Becca."

"Did you tell Windrider your suspicions?" Rebecca inquired.

"I told him I feared her jealousy would bring harm to

235

you. I told him she was bad and lazy. Come, I will show you what I found," she entreated. She pulled Rebecca by the arm.

They entered the tepee. Sucoora retrieved a parfleche from beside Kajihah's sleeping mat. She withdrew a small branch; from its damaged stems, Rebecca could tell it had been plucked hurriedly. Rebecca gazed at the purple flowers and two scarlet fruits, each the size of a hen's egg. She didn't have to be told that it was wahoo, or that it was poisonous. "She hides *wanhu*. She seeks to poison another. I do not say it is Becca. Kajihah hated Sucoora. Now she is gone. She can cause no danger or evil in Windrider's tepee. Come, I must cook." Sucoora left her alone.

Rebecca went into the forest. After digging a hole with a buffalo horn, she buried the offensive and deadly *wanhu* where the children could not find it. She returned as hastily as possible to help Sucoora. Soon the meal was ready. Since the men were gone, the children and women ate inside the tepee. On questioning Sucoora, Rebecca learned that Windrider was not going all the way to the Oglala camp with Kajihah; he was to return in two days. Friends of his were to escort Kajihah to her father's tepee.

When Bright Arrow finally came to sit on his mat, Sucoora served him. Then she rolled Kajihah's mat and stored it, putting Rebecca's in its place, out of reach of both warriors.

Two days passed and Windrider was still away. Rebecca knew that if he had decided to escort Kajihah home, his journey might require eight days or less, depending on how swiftly he rode home. She couldn't be sure that Sucoora's words were true, but she did know that Kajihah had no reason to have a dangerous plant in her possession. One of the children might have found it and consumed it! She could only assume that Kajihah had intended to harm someone. But whom?

Three more days passed, and still Windrider did not appear. Bright Arrow continued his exercises with White Antelope and other warriors. His skills improved and his instincts sharpened. Now he won more contests than he lost. There was no doubt he was working hard. After three more days passed, only a few elite warriors could challenge him and win. Each time he went hunting, he always returned with some kind of game. Each time they went on a raid, he returned with a prize from a defeated enemy. When two more days passed, the Cheyenne medicine chief said Bright Arrow was ready to enter the sweat lodge to purify himself to seek his vision. It was time; the waiting was over. Ten days had passed and Windrider had not returned.

Early the next morning, Bright Arrow approached her. "It is time to begin my journey home. I will enter the sweat lodge and purify myself. I will go to the hilltop for many nights to seek guidance from Grandfather. When I return, I must leave. Do you have words to speak?"

"If the council says no, send word to me. I will wait for one full moon for you to change their minds. Then I will agree to live in Windrider's tepee. Go, and be happy, Bright Arrow," she encouraged him.

Her implication was lost on him. "I will pray for Grandfather to give me answers," Bright Arrow said. "I will pray for him to show me the right path." He kissed her on the forehead, then left her side.

Near the edge of camp stood a ceremonial lodge that reminded Rebecca of a large beehive sliced in half. The

237

small hut was constructed of supple cottonwood saplings covered snuggly with buffalo hides to shut out light and to trap the steam. The purification ceremony that warriors underwent there was the first step in a lengthy, possibly dangerous, ritual; it was the next step in Bright Arrow's quest for rebirth into his old life.

She walked to the last circle of tepees and watched Bright Arrow and the shaman bend to enter the sweat lodge. The medicine chief came out with Bright Arrow's moccasins and breechclout, leaving him naked to face his ordeal. The shaman went to a campfire where rocks were heating, and he carefully examined them. Then he checked his supply of water bags and sweet grasses. When all was ready, he left to call Bright Arrow's helper.

Rebecca's eyes widened as she saw Windrider return with the medicine chief and White Antelope. Just before he entered the sweat lodge, Windrider saw her standing there. He nodded a greeting, then vanished inside to join Bright Arrow. The two Cheyenne warriors' garments were passed outside to the shaman. He folded them and placed them next to Bright Arrow's beside the entrance. Rebecca was bewildered. She wanted to know when Windrider had returned home, where he had been, and why he hadn't made his presence known.

The Shaman passed several rocks into the hut as he sang a special chant. He handed White Antelope, the helper, a bag of water, then closed the flap, sealing the three men in near darkness. Rebecca could hear melodious voices singing and praying inside the hut. She watched the shaman as he tended the fire and prepared to pass more hot rocks to White Antelope as they were needed to keep the hut filled with steam. The men would remain there until midday. She fretted over this ceremony. From past experiences, she knew how weak a body could get from excessive sweating and a loss of precious body fluids. Then to go into the hills to sit for days without food and water was even more perilous. No wonder a man needed great stamina and strength to survive! She turned her back on the hut and slowly walked away.

Inside the lodge, White Antelope had stacked the rocks in a pile in the center. He poured water over them, creating steam which surrounded the three men. They inhaled the cloudy breath of the Great Spirit as they swayed to and fro chanting and praying to be worthy of this rite. The ceremony continued, with the shaman passing fiery rocks and water to White Antelope when necessary.

No words could be exchanged among them once the ceremony had begun. But upon his entrance, Windrider had made one statement. He had told Bright Arrow, "We started this search for peace and new life together, and I must remain at your side until you have found them."

As the day grew warmer, the August sun beat down on the small structure with its full strength; the heat and humidity inside the dark hut would have been unbearable for weaker men. Steam mixed with sweat on their naked bodies and trickled down them in tiny rivulets. The furry mats upon which they sat cross-legged were soaked. Wet hair clung to necks, faces, shoulders, and backs. Faces were flushed, and breathing was labored. Still they sat and chanted as if nothing was sapping their energy.

Around noon, Rebecca slipped into the forest and made her way toward the sweat lodge. She concealed herself to observe the action. Although women did not perform this ritual or enter the sweat lodge, it was not a crime to observe a male between the stages of his rite.

There was no secrecy about this practice, but it was carried out in a reverent manner. However, due to her modesty and desire for privacy, Rebecca didn't want to be seen observing this break in the ritual, as two other naked males would be present with her love. She wanted to know if her love had survived the demanding ritual with enough endurance to take the next step of his spiritual journey and if Windrider was going with Bright Arrow on the vision quest.

The shaman removed the buffalo hides from the side away from the camp. The men emerged, naked and soaked. They stretched and flexed powerful bronze frames, then dried themselves with the aid of the hot sun and sweet grasses mixed with sage. Rebecca scolded herself for spying on the naked men, but her mind was absorbed by thoughts of things other than their powerful and manly bodies. Even so, Rebecca did not remove her intrigued gaze from that meaningful sight. Her attention was held by her love and the stamina he visibly displayed.

The men dressed in moccasins and breechclouts. White Antelope moved toward his tepee, his part in this ritual complete. The shaman, Bright Arrow, and Windrider mounted horses and rode from camp. She wished she could follow them and observe their vision quest, as it also affected her destiny. Once those men were under the spell of the quest and were weakened from lack of food, sleep, and water, there was no guessing what they would experience; there was no speculating on what they would think the Great Spirit was saying to them! Even if it were only an illusion produced by self-induced behavior and a drug, they would believe and accept their fanciful delusions; they would act on them—no matter what.

As Rebecca returned to her chores, she realized she had almost ignored Windrider's presence at the sweat lodge. How was that possible when he had been totally naked! She recalled the many days and nights they had been thrown together, times when she had been powerfully and helplessly attracted to the Cheyenne warrior. Somewhere in the back of her mind she had noticed him today. When she closed her eyes, she could view both men in a mental image. She had to admit there was no stark contrast between them any longer, though Windrider possessed a coppery body of beauty and strength that could draw any female's eyes to it. Was it so wrong to admire such special appeal? Besides, it was Bright Arrow who stirred her passions to uncontrollable flames. She warmed inwardly as she envisioned him flexing his muscular body outside the lodge.

The two warriors and the shaman rode toward a lofty hill miles away from camp. Leaving their horses at its base, the two vision seekers climbed the rocky slope and looked around them, pleased with the shaman's choice. For the Great Spirit to see the warrior who was seeking his vision, he had to be in full view on the top of a secluded hill. They had ridden nearly two hours to find this perfect spot. Because both had been deeply ensnared by thoughts of this mental and spiritual quest, they had not spoken along the journey. Now, as they realized the sun had reached its height three hours past, they knew it was time to begin the second leg of their journey toward truth, courage, and honor.

The shaman placed four stakes in the ground, one for each direction of the sacred medicine wheel. He secured a rawhide rope to one, then ran it to the next one, continuing until the rope formed a square large enough to contain two men in sitting positions. He placed two animals skins on the dry earth and hung sweet grass, sage, magic charms, and bits of cloth on the rope. He instructed Windrider and Bright Arrow to step inside the enclosure and be seated, facing eastward. When they complied, he handed each an eagle-bone whistle. He placed a dried cactus button on the edge of each sitting mat, then covered it with the corner. The peyote could not be eaten until the body was ready to receive it. The shaman prayed, calling on *Wakantanka* and other spirits to protect and guide these warriors along their journey to a vision quest. He left them to tend the horses, then made camp at the foot of the hill and waited patiently.

It was dusk. Windrider and Bright Arrow blew on the whistles to guide the Great Spirit to their location. The sun set behind them, creating a glow on the horizon that slowly faded into night. They chanted and prayed, waiting for a sign from the Great Spirit. Night passed into morning, and with it came the blazing ordeal of the summer sun. Sweat glistened on their coppery frames and ran down to soak into the thirsty earth. Their lips and throats were dry. No soothing breeze stirred all day. Their bodies were rigid and muscles were taut. Still they did not move. *Hunwi* revealed her glowing visage once more; she had passed her fullness and was seeking a half-moon shape. Slowly she moved across the night sky.

The sun once again appeared to lighten the face of Mother Earth. He gradually climbed beyond snowy clouds to stand high in the blue heaven overhead. Reddish brown flesh was wet; hair was soaked. Lips and throats pleaded for water that could not be consumed. Eyes burned and teared from the heat and brilliance of the sun and the sandy-colored earth. Salty sweat rolled into the corners of two sets of dark eyes; sooty lashes blinked rapidly to combat the stinging sensations. Hairless chests and faces glistened with moisture. Bodies were stiff; muscles were cramped. They had kept their vow of silence; they had not looked at each other. Their trial by the elements continued into the night.

The radiant ball of light appeared once more before heavy eyes. Their self-inflicted agonies would continue a third day and a fourth night. The men did not sweat as much this day, for their bodies had lost much life-sustaining fluid. They were exhausted. Hunger had given way to a dull ache just above the waist. Both men swayed in the heat from weakness. The sun burned hotter and fiercer today, but, at last, twilight fell over them. Their dazed minds began to wander. By midnight, it was time to use the peyote.

As if by some mystical signal, both men placed the peyote buttons in their mouths at the same time. Soon this ritual would succeed or fail. By morning, both men would have had their visions, or they would return to camp to seek the reason for their failure. A short time passed. Colorful lights and fuzzy images flickered across both minds. The peyote was strong and quick. From the mental merging of their deepest dreams, darkest desires, countless experiences, varied thoughts, and warring emotions, hallucinations formed. The illusions came and went as the men helplessly endured the power of the drug. Hours passed as they were assailed by sights and sounds that lived and labored both men's turbulent minds. Despite their helpless states, no enemy dared to attack a warrior who was visiting the world of the Great Spirit. The only danger to Windrider and Bright Arrow lay in death from within themselves.

Windrider's peyote wore off first. He watched and listened to Bright Arrow as he remained ensnared by the sacred button. He knew it was forbidden to interfere, to make suggestions. Yet, he thought, perhaps Grandfather awoke him first to be His helper. He knew a man most remembered the last images and sounds in his vision. Should he say words that would command Bright Arrow down the path that would be most advantageous to himself? . . .

By dawn, both men were free of their drug-induced states. The shaman returned. He asked if either man needed his vision interpreted. Bright Arrow and Windrider looked at each other, then shook their heads. The shaman gave them water and dried jerky. He told them to rest and refresh themselves before the journey home.

Bright Arrow glanced over at his weary friend. He said, "I must tell you of my vision, but the words will come later. I am tired and thirsty. Grandfather has told me how to reclaim my destiny."

Windrider didn't have to ask any questions. Bright Arrow's tone and expression answered all of them. "I must tell Bright Arrow of my vision," he stated. "You will not wish to hear such words. Rebecca is no longer part of your destiny; she belongs in my life-circle," he stated tensely.

Bright Arrow nodded in comprehension and acceptance. "I saw many times and places in my vision. She was not with me. Danger approaches our lands; I must leave for many days to prevent it. When I return, I will tell her of Grandfather's message." His voice was strained as he entreated painfully, "While I follow the commands of Grandfather, seek to pull her into your life and tepee. It is clear why Grandfather sent you to recall my feet to my lands. My rebirth and quest must be shared by you. My woman must be given to you."

Bright Arrow, Windrider, and the medicine chief returned to the Cheyenne camp at mid-afternoon. They had eaten the meat prepared by the shaman, then had bathed in the waters which soothed their fiery flesh. They had consumed the necessary fluids to replace those lost during their ordeal and had rested and restored their energy and strength. It was time to ask for a council meeting so they could relate their visions. They approached Chief Yellow Robe's tepee and asked permission to enter.

Yellow Robe listened to their words, then sent for the ceremonial chief. He instructed him to call the council together after dusk and the evening meal. The shaman left to prepare himself for his part in the ritual, and the two warriors headed for Windrider's tepee.

Sucoora greeted them with a broad smile and told the men Rebecca was fetching water from the river. Bright Arrow and Windrider exchanged expressions which piqued Sucoora's curiosity. Windrider told his wife they were going to speak with White Antelope and Shooting Star. They would return at the evening meal. He informed her of the council meeting later that night. During this exchange, Bright Arrow remained pensive and silent.

As they were departing, Windrider instructed, "On the new sun, prepare food for a long journey. Bright Arrow and Windrider must leave for many moons. You will care for the children and Rebecca. Shooting Star and White Antelope will bring game to my tepee and protect all who live in it. Ask no questions; this is for the minds of men."

When Rebecca entered the tepee, Sucoora hurriedly revealed the bewildering news. *Long journey?* Rebecca's mind echoed. The Oglala Sioux camp was only four days' ride from the Cheyenne camp; that wasn't considered a long trip in these parts. "They didn't tell you where they're going or why?'' she inquired. When Sucoora shook her head, Rebecca frowned in dismay. What was the big secret? Why hadn't Bright Arrow looked for her?

At the evening meal, both men seemed preoccupied. Rebecca was nettled by their silence and seeming unconcern. Neither offered a single clue about their impending plans or a single fact about their vision quests. She was provoked by their aloof manner. It seemed neither one dared to meet her probing gaze, as if fearing she might read a secret message written there! Yet her pride stubbornly refused to allow her to press them for information. She could behave just as indifferently. How she wished she were not dependent on either man! If she lived somewhere besides this perilous wilderness, she wouldn't be!

Sometimes it was so difficult to be a woman, she mused inwardly. Women were expected to do their chores without question or hesitation. Women were told little of men's affairs. Women couldn't fend for themselves. Women had no say about where they lived or how they existed. Women had no say about laws; they couldn't even attend meetings.

A woman alone was a death sentence or a sentence to a life of whorish degradation for survival. A man could come and go as he pleased, without explanations or judgments. A single woman could not partake of the pleasures of the flesh without soiling her name; yet a single man could enjoy as many women as he desired! A woman alone was a bright target for men to aim at and attack. She could go nowhere and do nothing unless a man went along or gave permission. A single woman was the property of her father, brother, or male kin until she became the property of a husband or owner.

A married woman was invisibly chained to her home,

husband, and children. She was little more than a wedded slave! She had no rights or freedom. She had no adventures or excitement. Life for her was one endless series of labors, or one unceasing task of putting others before herself. Was it so wrong to be selfish from time to time? she wondered.

Rebecca was trapped between two valiant warriors who wanted her. One believed he possessed a claim to her, but he did not. One wanted to stake a claim on her, seemingly with her mate's permission. Both were leaving in one day; yet neither felt he owed her an explanation! She was expected to sit and wait for her life to be settled by other forces and people, sit patiently and calmly! Neither man had a right to her without her consent. She might just shock both of them by departing alone! she decided. Then she recalled how helpless she had been when Bright Arrow had captured her and again when Lester and Jess had attacked her cabin. She admitted angrily that she was no match for any man, unless she killed him. Even if she escaped to a white settlement, what kind of existence would she face there? She irritably scoffed to herself, *If warriors can have more than one wife, why can't I have more than one lover?* Yet invading thoughts of Bright Arrow and the rapture she had found in his arms belied her angry musings.

After telling the children a story and singing them a song, Rebecca put the girls on their sleeping mats. She glanced over at Sucoora who was doing the same with Kajihah's children. A pang of anguish and doubt chewed at her. The children hadn't asked for their mother, hadn't seemed to care that she was gone forever! Had Kajihah meant so little to them? Did Sucoora feel as much their mother as Kajihah? She recalled Bright Arrow telling her that a child was reared by many people, including an adopted set of parents, to avoid spoiling the child or to prevent excessive anguish if the real parents were slain or died. He had told her it helped the child feel more a part of the whole tribe, which was vital for loyalty and unselfishness. She wondered if this would happen with her girls when Bright Arrow took them away.

In the ceremonial lodge, the council was meeting to hear the news from Windrider and Bright Arrow. The council and warriors made a circle around the campfire, sitting cross-legged on small mats a few feet from it. The medicine chief sang and danced around the fire as he shook a gourd rattle. Another warrior beat on a skin-covered drum with a thick-ended stick, as Indians never touched the drum with their hands. The shaman offered prayers of supplication and gratitude to the Great Spirit, then tossed sweet grasses and "magical" powders into the small blaze. It burst into radiance for a brief moment, then settled down to a soft glow. Gray smoke swirled upward, vanishing out the air flap. The ceremonial pipe was stuffed with sacred tobacco, passed around, and smoked twice by each man present. All were careful not to drop it to the earth.

It was the custom for a close friend to chant the *coups* of the warrior or warriors involved in this special ceremony. White Antelope arose to relate the valiant deeds of Windrider. He added those obtained during Windrider's battle with the Pawnee warriors, then took his seat. Many were astonished, even displeased, when Windrider arose and chanted his friend's past deeds of glory. Many felt that since Bright Arrow had fallen into disgrace, only those *coups* earned since his rebirth should be chanted. Windrider added the *coups* Bright Arrow had earned since coming to the Cheyenne camp, then took his position at his friend's side.

Windrider was given permission to relate his vision first. Again the Cheyenne warrior arose. "Grandfather says the Spirits of the sky will send a new woman to the tepee of Windrider. The stars, sun, and clouds will send signs to reveal her to me. She will show much courage. She will accept my people and help them in times of great pain and sadness. She will be guided to me by an act of great sacrifice to her. Grandfather says He has chosen her to be my mate." He sat down without exposing her name or more information, for he believed the faceless vision of his next wife was Rebecca.

Bright Arrow stood up and mentally prepared himself to speak. "Grandfather sends ominous words to me. He says strange white men have entered our lands from where *Wi* awakens each day. He says they bring many soldiers and a strange black spirit with them. They carry many weapons. He says these white-eyes enter camps of our brothers; they give many presents to fool our brothers and friends. He says these men come to draw pictures of our lands; he says they call these pictures maps. He says they will mark where all tribes live; he says they will tell where hunting and sacred grounds are located, where rivers flow and mountains climb into the sky. He says these maps will be taken to the White Father, the leader who sends bluecoats to build wooden fences and tepees. He says they will tell all Indian secrets to whites far away. He says those whites will come and steal what is ours. He says the white-eyes claim this territory as theirs. He says bluecoats will use the evil maps to war against the Indian. He says I must dress as a white man and travel with them; He says I must watch them. He says I must destroy their maps and tell my people of their plans. He says I must leave in two moons. I must not return until I conquer these new enemies.

When I return with news of their evil plans, my people will rejoice; they will allow me to return home in full honor. This is the command of my vision."

Many inquisitive faces turned upward to stare at Bright Arrow. "Where do these white-eyes stay? How did they invade our lands?" asked Chief Yellow Robe, fully alert and straining to hear.

"Grandfather says they are in the camp of the Yankton, our Nakota brothers. There is a white man called Pierre Dorion, who lives with the Yankton. He is what the whites call French. He joined with a Yankton maiden many winters ago before their evil was known to us. He lives in their camp. I have traded with him. I will seek him as Clay Rivera, a half-white trader. He will take me to the whites called Lewis and Clark. I will join them as scout. I will steal their secrets and bring them home. They travel in big canoes on the muddy river that runs through our lands. They have many weapons."

"Does this French white-eyes know you are the son of Gray Eagle?" White Antelope asked worriedly.

"The white-eyes do not know of my shame; only the Indian know of my banishment. They will not see a Sioux warrior in a man with short hair and white garments. A white-eyes named Joseph Garreau, who lives with the Arikara, called me half-Spanish, half-Crow. Long ago, I took the life and name of a Spanish trapper. I speak their tongue and know their ways. All whites are fooled by this mask. I will find no danger, my friend," he assured White Antelope.

"What will Bright Arrow do if he is captured?" another asked.

He sat straight and proud, vowing without hesitation, "I will hold my tongue silent. I will die as a Sioux warrior."

"Will you take your white woman to help on this mission?" an older warrior inquired.

Bright Arrow never faltered before replying, "No. My family will remain in Windrider's tepee. He will protect them and supply their needs. I cannot travel as scout with a family. The soldiers bring no women on their journey."

Shooting Star queried, "What of this black spirit? Will he not guess your plans? Is he of great power and magic?"

"Grandfather says I will not fear him. Grandfather says I am stronger and braver. He is trapped in a man's body with black skin. He behaves as one wild in the head. His magic will not harm me. Grandfather says to be careful of the white leader with flaming hair."

The shaman probed, "Do you fear the power of these whites?"

"No, I fear no white-eyes," Bright Arrow stated confidently. "I only fear what harm they bring to my people and brothers. I must follow Grandfather's message. I am not afraid to battle many enemies. I am not afraid to give my life for my people."

When no more questions were asked, Yellow Robe said, "If you do not return, my people will chant your courage and honor. Go with our prayers for your safety and victory."

The rest of the council nodded agreement with their chief's words. Windrider declared, "I will ride with you many moons. When you are near the place Grandfather revealed in your quest, I will return to my people. I will protect your family with my life."

Windrider and Bright Arrow exchanged looks which intimated some secret between them. The council meeting ended; all returned to their own tepees. The hour was late, and most were asleep. When the two warriors returned to Windrider's tepee, they immediately noticed that Rebecca was not on her sleeping mat. A drowsy Sucoora informed them she was walking to relieve her tension.

Bright Arrow glanced at Windrider and sighed heavily. He couldn't face her with his dismaying news. He asked Windrider to go find her. It was dangerous for her to be out alone in the dark; enemies had been known to sneak into camps and steal possessions or take captives. The Sioux warrior went to his mat and lay down, placing one arm over his stinging eyes. He couldn't believe he was going to lose her and wondered how he would ever accept that agonizing fact. Far worse than losing her was imagining her in the arms and life of another man. He wished he could close out such images, but he could not. When he had left the wilds, he had known there was a possibility of exchanging her for his return. Yet he had never really believed it would happen. He almost wished they were back in the cabin, with him trying harder to live in her world. There was a tightness in his chest and a burning in his eyes as he raged at why he could not have both his love and his destiny. He was torn between wanting her to accept this decision and wanting her to resist it with all her might.

Bright Arrow's mind raced up and down many paths, finding each one covered with obstacles that inflicted wounds. He pondered his love's recent actions and behavior. Perhaps Rebecca had glimpsed the future in some magical dream. Perhaps that was why she had ridden to his camp, to anger him into pushing her aside. She had pointed out their freedom, their lack of marriage bonds. She had refused to make love to him; she had tried to turn him to the mats of other women. Even though they had lived together for years without marriage, she had refused to continue in that way in his camp; she had said marriage or nothing. Why wasn't she willing to have him in any way possible? And she had not refused or resisted the idea of Windrider taking his place! She had traveled with his friend for days. They had shared many times together while he was busy training. Did she desire Windrider more than him? Had he lost her even before the vision quest? Had she somehow sensed what Grandfather would say and been planning her new life and love? Did she merely want him to be the one to sever their union? Had she been giving him reasons to force their separation before he experienced more suffering, before Grandfather and his tribe ordered him to discard her? Even if such things were true, he couldn't blame her. After all, he agreed with her choice of a new mate, since that staggering reality could no longer be avoided. The signs and messages were all there, and he had to accept them. He had prayed for guidance and answers, but not these . . . no, not these.

Windrider observed Bright Arrow, comprehending his anguish and the demands that had been placed on his friend. He prayed that his part in all of this was justified. As he left the tepee to seek Rebecca, he asked himself just how much he should reveal to her. He was glad he had not mentioned Rebecca in the words he had spoken during Bright Arrow's vision quest, and he was relieved that he had nothing to do with Bright Arrow's belief that she did not belong in his life-circle anymore. His friend had actually encouraged him to pursue Rebecca! His vision about a new life was true, and the faceless woman was surely Rebecca. It had to be true for he had not influenced Bright Arrow against his woman, though he had been sorely tempted . . .

Chapter Twelve

Bright Arrow's defensive attitude and secretive behavior were driving the bewildered and vulnerable Rebecca into Windrider's eager arms. It seemed to her that Bright Arrow had already admitted defeat in the battle to keep her, for it was as if he were attempting to force her from his heart and arms to spare himself the ordeal of publicly discarding her. He made it appear that she was no longer a part of his life, that she had nothing further to do with his affairs. He had cruelly shut the door between them, without explaining his motives or timing. Did he want it ended so simply, so quickly, so thoroughly? He certainly couldn't have made his rejection any clearer. What more did he want—for *her* to end their union, to save him the trouble and guilt?

Rebecca strolled along the riverbank, the moonlight glowing on her chestnut curls. Dejection and concern marked her golden brown eyes. If Bright Arrow loved her, she wondered, why wouldn't he fight for her? If he loved her, how could he casually hand her over to another man? If he loved her, why wasn't he agonizing over her loss? If he loved her, why was he leaving when they had so little time left together? If he loved her, why was he keeping it a secret? Couldn't he share his vision quest and his decisions and his plans? It wasn't fair that she was suffering alone in this cold and empty world of silence.

If he had ever loved her, how could he end their relationship in this brutal manner? How could he so easily betray and spurn her? Could he truly ride away without saying farewell? If he had ever loved her, why—

Windrider severed her torturous line of thought. "Why do you stand alone in the dark, Rebecca?" he asked.

"I needed some fresh air. I needed to think," she responded, turning to face him. Who was this complex and tempting man who had been thrust into her life? Why was Bright Arrow being taken from her? How could she stop this mad whirl?

"What thoughts cause such sadness in your eyes and heart?" he inquired, raising her chin to peer into her haunted tawny gaze.

"Why do you and Bright Arrow refuse to tell me of your vision quests? Why have you two behaved so strangely since returning? You two treat me as if I don't exist. You plan to leave, and you will not say why or where," she complained.

"While you are his woman, it is not right for me to reveal Bright Arrow's vision. Until you are my woman, I must not reveal mine. It is our way. Do not be sad or afraid," he replied tenderly.

"As far as he's concerned, I'm no longer his woman!" Rebecca declared fiercely. "Don't you understand, Windrider? It's my life, too. Surely I have the right to know what's happening to change it? If you love me, why can't you trust me?" she challenged. In rising frustration, she scoffed, "Must I also seek a vision to learn which path I should take? Perhaps Grandfather will end everybody's trouble by striking me dead for such an offense!" she declared sarcastically.

Windrider seized her and roughly shook her. "Do not speak such dangerous words!" he ordered sternly. "Hear me with your head, not your heart, my love. You cannot change Grandfather's commands. We must obey them. Do not interfere," he admonished. "Bright Arrow must go away for many suns. When he returns, he will speak his heart and mind to you. He will take the children and return to his people."

Rebecca wondered how much Bright Arrow had confided in this man. To entice information from him she said, "He speaks his heart and mind each day, Windrider. I'm not a hunter, but I can follow a marked trail and such bold clues. In his heart and mind, he has already rejected me. Soon his words will match his thoughts and feelings. I don't know why he hesitates to confess the truth. It would be simpler and kinder for all concerned if he made his feelings and intentions known."

She sighed loudly, weary and depressed. "Bright Arrow will ask permission to keep me, but I can tell he thinks it's useless. He knows how his people feel about me, about all whites; he knows how the council will vote. He's admitted it to himself and accepted the inevitable, so why does he continue to pretend with us? He said if the council refuses my presence and our joining, he wants me to live in the Cheyenne camp . . . in your tepee."

Rebecca looked up at the attentive warrior who had such warmth and tenderness displayed on his handsome face. Tears dampened her eyes. She wished she did love Windrider; she wished he had been the one to take her captive, preventing her from ever knowing Bright Arrow and the anguish he was causing her. She wished this tormenting triangle didn't exist. In a strained voice, she confessed, "He no longer speaks of love or desire. He only speaks of returning home. It's all that matters to him. He doesn't seek my presence. He doesn't wish to talk with me. He avoids me as much as he can. Are those the actions of a man who loves me and needs me, who suffers over my loss? No," she answered herself in a near whisper.

Throwing restraint to the winds, she disclosed brazenly, "He hasn't made love to me but once since Mother Earth renewed her face. You have touched me more times than he has. You have spoken more words of love and desire. You have been kinder to me. You've shared words with me. You make me laugh and smile. You make me feel worthy. You make me feel loved and desired. You have taken the stinging pain from his betrayal and rejection. I know what words he will speak when he returns. He will say it is over between us; he will say our life-circles can no longer touch. If you do not change your mind or feelings, when those words leave his mouth, I will come to you as your woman."

Windrider's heart drummed swiftly, for he sensed sweet victory within his powerful grasp. How he wished this waiting were ended! "I will ride with Bright Arrow for many suns. Then I will leave his side and return home. He must ride for many more suns and seek his quest alone. I will return and make you sing and smile. Soon only Windrider will live in your heart and mind. You will fill my heart and life with joy. I have loved no woman but Rebecca," he vowed in honesty.

Windrider gingerly reached for her, fearing Rebecca would resist his touch. She did not, for she needed his comfort and protection. She needed him to remove Bright Arrow's crushing presence from her mind. In light of Bright Arrow's withdrawal and rejection, she needed Windrider's closeness and commitment. She felt so alone, so vulnerable, so out of control, so dispensable.

His arms closed around her protectively, and he rested his cheek on the top of her head. He hungered for her lips and her body, but more, he hungered for her pain to cease. Her face was smooth and warm against his chest, and her hot teardrops burned his flesh as they slid down his muscled torso to his waist and were absorbed by his garment.

"It is hard to slay love and sever bonds to another," he remarked knowingly, with a sensitivity that touched her. "The pain will flee on a new sun. You will forget Bright Arrow. Windrider will be patient and gentle. He will wait for you to come to him. Windrider's love is strong and true; it will never betray you. It will never bring tears to your eyes or pain to your heart. This Windrider promises Rebecca."

Rebecca shifted demurely, breaking his hold. She looked up at him. How she wished those words and emotions were coming from the sensual lips and passionate heart of Bright Arrow. Despite their problems and the dangers, she wished she and Bright Arrow were still in the wilderness cabin. How she longed for one more chance to free him of his haunting past and to make their defiant love work. As much as it hurt to think it, such words and feelings probably would never come from Bright Arrow again. Her heartache was stifling, strangling. She needed to be held tightly and possessively. She needed love and consideration. She needed to be kissed hungrily and passionately. She needed reviving emotions to erase her suffering, to fill her thoughts, to rekindle her spirit. She needed new hope, new life, new vitality. Windrider was offering all these things that Bright Arrow had taken from her, things that he denied her at a time when she needed them most.

Rebecca's hands clasped Windrider's neck and pulled

his face downward. She wanted to show her appreciation and affection, her gratitude. She feared she might lose him too if she weren't cautious. In order that he await her choice and her freedom, he also needed hope and consideration. He needed to know that he wasn't fighting a losing battle. She raised herself on her tiptoes and fused her lips to his. Windrider's arms encircled her back as his mouth urgently responded to hers. They stood entwined beneath the moonlight, savoring sweet kisses and embraces, each offering encouragement and blissful pleasure to the other. Windrider shuddered, but tightly leashed his potent desires.

Neither saw the Sioux warrior who abruptly halted his approach, then stared at the plaguing scene before his stunned senses. Bright Arrow had begun to suffer guilt and shame for directing Windrider to seek his woman, but, until a few moments before, he had not been able to summon the courage to do so himself. But now only fury and jealousy raged through his body. He wanted to race forward and yank them apart—yet the soft aura surrounding them prevented him. He could say or do nothing, for he had encouraged each to seek the other. But must they respond so hastily and fiercely? he asked inwardly. He told himself he should feel relief that his racking problem over Rebecca was solved, and he should feel joy that his beloved and his friend had discovered and helped each other. He did not. He could not even allow his mind to dwell on a union that could torment him so. He had compelled them into each other's arms, and it appeared too late to alter the situation. Hanging his head in anguish and sadness, he soundlessly returned to Windrider's tepee. He gathered the seeds of fury that had escaped his loose grasp, for he could not allow them to take root and grow. He wasn't perfect! He was only a man—a man who could make mistakes, a man who could take a wrong trail. He was not all-knowing and all-powerful like the Great Spirit. Now he would pay for his recklessness and weakness, for his flaws and mistakes.

Rebecca and Windrider parted and exchanged smiles. "Come, we must return to camp," he advised cautiously, his breathing ragged. "I must not take you until you are my woman," he vowed with difficulty. Hand in hand, they walked to his tepee. Before entering, he squeezed her hand, then released his grip on it.

Bright Arrow glanced up at them. Hope surged through him, for he knew there had not been enough time for them to have made love. He should have known they would not betray him behind his back. He realized both were waiting for him to relinquish his hold over Rebecca before Windrider claimed her. He prayed there was reason to hope and dream. He could not free her until there was absolutely no other choice. If they loved each other, why couldn't she live here in her own tepee, waiting for his visits, waiting for Grandfather to find a path to send her home to him? He could supply all of her needs; he could make gifts to Windrider and others for her protection. He smiled to himself confidently, now doubting he would ever release her.

Early the next morning, Windrider and many others went hunting. Bright Arrow remained in camp to prepare himself for his journey and mission. Sucoora was occupied with the children and with preparing food for the men's trip, while Rebecca spent her time doing the chores—gathering wood, fetching water, collecting vegetables, and washing garments. She told Sucoora she was riding over to a secluded area not far away to gather elm

261

caps, spider lilies, and leeks for their evening meal. She said she also needed to collect yellow pond lilies for the men's medicine bundles; the plants were used to stop bleeding. Bright Arrow announced that he would put aside his own tasks to accompany her.

She gaped at him in astonishment. "You want to go with me? Why?" she asked skeptically. As if mesmerized, she remained immobile, her eyes wide and her lips parted.

With joy, Bright Arrow observed her reaction. His gaze went to those soft lips that Windrider had tasted the night before, lips he longed to taste for perhaps the last time. "I ride away on the new sun. Do you not wish my company and last words?" he inquired, a lump in his throat making it difficult for him to utter the torturous question.

With honesty shining in her eyes, she responded, "You have not sought or desired my company or words in many suns and moons. Is there some reason why you do so today?" she ventured in dread. Did he plan to sever their relationship before he left? If so, how could she stall Windrider until Bright Arrow's return, when she could fight for him and for their life together? Was he going to end her final hope?

Bright Arrow noted her hesitation, which seemed to be laced with fear and torment. "Do you reject my presence?" he probed anxiously.

"It is you who have rejected mine," she accused softly. "If you think to protect me from enemies, I'm not afraid to go alone. A warrior does not ride with a woman when she does her chores. Is there something you wish to say before you leave?" she queried nervously.

"There is much danger and great honor in obeying Grandfather's commands. If I do not return, there are

262

things I wish you to know from my lips. If I do return in honor, my deed could win great favor with my people. It will earn my return to them. It could influence their vote for you," he added.

Shock registered on her face. Was he leaving to attempt some perilous deed in order to keep her? She was confused; his current behavior didn't match his past words. "I don't understand, Bright Arrow. Are you saying you haven't given up hope for us?"

Her tone and expression said that she believed he had. He suspected that it was the reason she was turning to Windrider. He quickly reflected on his recent behavior and realized why she was bewildered and doubtful. In his turmoil, he had been sending her false signals. Even if he were ordered to sacrifice her, that didn't mean he agreed with such a decision or accepted it. It didn't mean that he was relieved to have Windrider take his place. She doubted his love and loyalty! She felt betrayed and rejected! How foolish and rash he had been. He had to clarify these matters before he departed.

"If you believe such words, then we must talk," he stated gravely. "I have clouded your mind and injured your heart. I will ride with you, and we will clear this haze between us." He took her arm, leading her to the horses, and together they rode from the camp.

Rebecca gathered the leeks and stored them in a parfleche. She mounted again and rode to another location. There she collected the lilies, one for greens and one for medicine. Then she guided the horse to a grove of elms to collect the mushroom caps. When all of her tasks were completed, she turned and observed Bright Arrow. He had followed her moves without speaking or interfering. She wondered if he had changed his mind. "I'm ready to return to camp," she informed him.

"I am not," he casually replied. "Do you still love me?" he asked, stunning her, his dark eyes drilling into her startled gaze.

"I don't follow your meaning," she stammered.

He stepped to within inches of her, watching her gaze roam over his features and body. He noted with pleasure the sudden flush on her cheeks. Clearly she was disturbed by his nearness. "I love you, and I need you, Rebecca. I want you and no other woman. I will battle to keep you. I will not free you until I am certain there is no hope for our life-circles to join. Do not ever doubt such feelings," he implored her.

Rebecca turned her back to him. She wondered why he was doing this to her. How could he tempt her this way, then leave? *Damn!* she raged inwardly. He knew he was going to choose his people and rank over her, so why was he tempting her with a prize she could not win? Did those words and emotions mean so little to him? He was ready and willing to end it, so why did he play with her in this brutal way? He couldn't have her, but he couldn't stand for another man to do so! What did he expect from her— to be bound in heart if not in life?

Bright Arrow's pulse quickened. Was it too late? he wondered in silence. Had she given up on him, on them? Had he hurt her too deeply for her to forgive him? Was she afraid to respond to him, to reach out to him? Did she fear she had lost him? Did she wish to punish him, to hurt him as she was hurting? The cold knife of fear entered his gut and twisted painfully. Was she in love with Windrider? Was she afraid she would lose Windrider if she revealed any love or desire for him? Was she trying to protect herself, her new future, by withdrawing from him?

Bright Arrow gently captured her shoulders and

We've got your authors!

If you seek out the latest historical romances by today's bestselling authors, our new reader's service, KENSINGTON CHOICE, is the club for you.

KENSINGTON CHOICE is the only club where you can find authors like Janelle Taylor, Shannon Drake, Rosanne Bittner, Sylvie Sommerfield, Penelope Neri and Phoebe Conn all in one place…

…and the only service that will deliver their romances direct to your home as soon as they are published—even before they reach the bookstores.

KENSINGTON CHOICE is also the only service that will give you a substantial guaranteed discount off the publisher's prices on every one of those romances.

That's right: Every month, the Editors at Zebra and Pinnacle select four of the newest novels by our bestselling authors and rush them straight to you, usually *before they reach the bookstores*. The publisher's prices for these romances range from $4.99 to $5.99—but they are always yours for the guaranteed low price of just *$3.95!*

That means you'll always save over $1.00…often as much as *$2.00*…off the publisher's prices on every new novel you get from KENSINGTON CHOICE!

All books are sent on a 10-day free examination basis, and there is no minimum number of books to buy. (A postage and handling charge of $1.50 is added to each shipment.)

As your introduction to the convenience and value of this new service, we invite you to accept

4 BOOKS FREE

The 4 books, worth up to $23.96, are our welcoming gift. You pay only $1 to help cover postage and handling.

To start your subscription to KENSINGTON CHOICE and receive your introductory package of 4 FREE romances, detach and mail the postpaid card at right *today*.

We have 4 FREE BOOKS for you as your introduction to KENSINGTON CHOICE

To get your FREE BOOKS, worth up to $23.96, mail the card below.

FREE BOOK CERTIFICATE

As my introduction to your new KENSINGTON CHOICE reader's service, please send me 4 FREE historical romances (worth up to $23.96), billing me just $1 to help cover postage and handling. As a KENSINGTON CHOICE subscriber, I will then receive 4 brand-new romances to preview each month for 10 days FREE. I can return any books I decide not to keep and owe nothing. The publisher's prices for the KENSINGTON CHOICE romances range from $4.99 to $5.99, but as a subscriber I will be entitled to get them for just $3.95 per book or $15.80 for all four titles. There is no minimum number of books to buy, and I can cancel my subscription at any time. A $1.50 postage and handling charge is added to each shipment.

Name _____

Address _____ Apt. _____

City _____ State _____ Zip _____

Telephone ( ) _____

Signature _____

(If under 18, parent or guardian must sign)

Subscription subject to acceptance. Terms and prices subject to change.

KC1194

We have
4
FREE
Historical
Romances
for you!

(worth up
to $23.96!)

Details inside!

turned her to face him. "I have hurt you deeply these last moons. I am unworthy of you. You sacrifice all for me; yet I seek my honor above all else. How do I explain I am not a man without my honor? How do I explain I cannot survive without my destiny? What good is half a man to you? I am only a lowly man. I have a man's flaws. Do not expect me to be perfect, to be strong and wise at all times. It is impossible. Two voices cry out to me, and I cannot answer and follow both. How do I make you understand that I wish you to be part of both? It is easy to say I can release you, but the doing brings pain beyond endurance. Even the sun dance does not hurt as much as losing you. How can I free you and return home? How can I return home if I do not? Is there no end to this torment? I love you, Rebecca Kenny."

Bright Arrow meshed his mouth to hers in almost savage desperation, as if the urgent kiss and embrace would stress his feelings and thoughts. She was dazed by the potency of his unleashed desires and clung to him ardently, matching his eager kisses. His arms tightened so much that she lost the air in her lungs. His lips eagerly plundered hers. He feared he would be consumed by the fires that raged within his body. He knew he could easily rip the garments from her body and make fierce love to her. As he tried to master his searing passion, he leaned away from her and longingly memorized her face.

It was a look she had not seen in a long time, but one she recognized. Her heart sang joyfully as she saw that the exercises, practices, hunts, raids, and Indian surroundings had been extremely good for him. He radiated such tremendous strength, such dauntless courage, such utter masculinity. She marveled at his arresting appeal, his undeniable prowess, his stimulating virility. Once again their passions kindled as they had when first they had met; he was a potent magnet that her iron will could not resist. He was a copper-skinned male animal with bold onyx eyes and a predator's skills and instincts. She acutely sensed and smelled his heady proximity, and overwhelming desire invaded her body and mind. He was beguiling, disarming. He was masterful and magnificent; he was the legendary Bright Arrow once more. Tremors of anticipation passed over her tingling flesh.

Bright Arrow observed her just as intensely. Was it her beauty, her compelling aura, or some other force which irresistibly drew him to her? She was breathtaking and vital. She was fragile, yet she was strong. Her amber eyes were compelling, caressing, adoring. Her voice was as soft as the petals on a flower, as was her sun-kissed flesh. Tenderness and desire filled his body. He fondled a flaming curl, then grinned as it clung to his finger. Skillfully he enticed her with his deft hands, his stimulating lips, his alluring smile.

"How I do love you and want you," he repeated seductively.

"As I love you, Bright Arrow." The words helplessly slipped from her lips as she flung herself into his arms. "I will love you until the day I cease to breathe," she murmured against his flesh before spreading kisses over it and swirling her tongue around the two brown peaks on his chest. It thrilled and tantalized her when he shuddered and groaned. She could feel the straining hardness of his manhood against her and knew that he was as deeply aroused as she.

When his hands wandered over her quivering body, she whispered raggedly, "If you do not make love to me, I shall surely die from need."

Without inhibition or care, Rebecca responded to him with a fever that spread its fiery warmth to Bright Arrow.

He unfastened her dress and removed it, tossing it over a fallen limb. Her bloomers quickly followed, and his garments were cast aside with a matching swiftness. They sank into the grass and wildflowers, clinging fervently and urgently. The time was right for them to declare their love and share their passion.

His mouth greedily sought the points on her breasts, encompassing and stimulating each one in turn. She closed her eyes and enjoyed this long-denied pleasure, these blissful sensations that sensually attacked her body. As if he wanted to sample every inch of her delectable body, his exploring tongue roamed the willing territory that his hands traveled. She was like the newborn fawn, and he, the attentive doe. His mouth roved her silky skin until it glistened with his loving moisture. Every so often his lips would find a special place, causing her to writhe and moan in exquisite pleasure. He would linger there to tantalize her until she pleaded for mercy.

To give such rapture was intoxicating. It inspired a heady feeling of power in him. Suddenly she joined his tempting game. Hundreds of tiny kisses flickered over his bronze frame, stirring his senses to a higher level of arousal. His respiration became labored and uneven. Through passion-glazed eyes Bright Arrow watched Rebecca ecstatically torment his throbbing shaft. The tension mounted until he squirmed in the grass. Undeniably, her hands and lips were as skilled at giving pleasure as his!

He pushed her to her back and lifted her legs. Gluing his ravenous attention to an enticing sight that threatened to steal his control, he delivered several more kisses to her inner thighs, then locked his lips to a quivering peak that pleaded for relief. His experienced tongue circled the tiny mound, then nibbled teasingly at it.

"Please," she whimpered in great need to end this sweet agony.

He smiled, then drove into her moist and receptive body. As he set a regular pattern, he watched the erotic and titillating vision. Her body was greedy for his. Each time he entered, her womanhood locked around him, almost refusing to release him for another blissful plunge. From her reactions and dampness, he knew it was time to increase his speed and carry out his intent. Pressing his weight to her breast, his mouth fused to hers, he pounded his groin against hers. He worked swiftly and deliberately, guiding her over the point of no return, then quickly followed. Their spasms blended together as each reveled in the staggering explosion of passion.

Bright Arrow mastered his breathing, then propped an elbow on either side of her neck. "No matter what power says otherwise, you are mine. No matter where our bodies are, our hearts will beat as one. Whatever the future holds for us, my true heart, there can never be another love as powerful, as perfect, or as passionate as ours," he murmured tenderly.

"Where are you going, my love? What did the vision tell you?" she inquired apprehensively, believing she could now ask these questions and receive the truth. Her fingers playfully teased the toned muscles on his back. She looked up into his yearning gaze, which altered rapidly at her queries. Instantly she realized he did not want to discuss those crucial subjects, for tiny lines of resistance had furrowed his brow.

Despite his obstinate expression, there was almost a note of pleading in his voice when he said, "Do not ask. I must keep this mission secret from all. If it slips past any mouth, I will be in grave danger. I have told no one but the council and Windrider. Remain here and wait for my return. If all goes as planned, my people will be unable to reject either of us."

"What if something happens to you? I won't know where you are or why you went away," she protested. "If the Cheyenne can know of your mission, why can't I? Am I not closer to you than all of the Cheyenne combined? I will not try to sway you from this quest," she promised, thinking that this might be the reason for his reluctance.

"My life depends on secrecy," he insisted refusing to explain further.

"I would tell no one!" she declared angrily. "Do you no longer trust me? Besides, who would I see to tell such a secret?"

"You must trust me, Rebecca. I cannot speak of the quest until it is over," he replied, firmly standing his ground.

"But you told others," she argued. "When will you return?" she delved, trying another approach to this vexing quandary.

"I do not know," he replied. He rolled to his broad back and placed his hands beneath his head. Though it appeared he stared at the leaves above him, his thoughts were far away in Yankton, where the two white-eyes whose exposure could expedite his freedom from this life of nothingness were camping. If he had not been living as half a man in the white tepee of logs, Grandfather might have sent him this message sooner! The white dogs would have been stopped before they entered the Sioux territory. It riled him to know how the whites were deceiving his Yankton brothers and many other tribes with their false words and blinding gifts. He was glad Grandfather had waited until he had recovered himself before sending this critical vision to another warrior. Surely there was

269

some vital reason why Grandfather had chosen him! Surely this meant Grandfather wanted him returned to his people—and in great honor. Yet, Rebecca had not been in his vision; or if she had, he could not recall it. Perhaps Grandfather would send a message about her later, after this victory had been won . . . for Bright Arrow could not envision defeat or failure.

Rebecca rolled to her side and observed him. He was tightly ensnared by his tangled thoughts. Now that he was sated, she realized, he had returned to his remote world where she was not permitted entrance. She should have questioned him while he was trapped in the throes of wild desire! But she had been too distracted by her own urgent passion to think about anything but him and her needs. It was too late to provoke information now that his wits and will had returned. "Where do you ride tomorrow?" she asked.

He inhaled deeply, then flexed his agile body. "Wherever the quest leads me," he responded distractedly, closing his eyes as if to take a nap, or to sink deeper into his private domain.

Rebecca shook him to gain his attention. She was tired of being left out of everything! She had a right to know where her husband was going and why! Her husband . . . He wasn't and might never be her lawful mate. Yet, for all the years and emotions and hardships they had shared, he owed her an explanation; he owed her some consideration and loyalty! "If you loved me, Bright Arrow, you would trust me," she challenged frostily. "No doubt you can hardly wait to be gone from me and your troubles! Go then!" she shrieked. "But don't give me another thought, for I might not be around when you return. I might be tired of waiting in the dark alone," she warned. "If you truly loved me and wanted me, there wouldn't be this wall between us." She pushed him aside and sat up to retrieve her garments.

"That is not so, little heart," he replied, sitting up quickly.

Tears stung her amber eyes, and she sniffled to control them. She reminded him as she yanked on her clothing, "There was a time when we shared anything and everything. That day is lost forever, and it pains me deeply. Your enemies know more of you and your plans than I do. You are forcing me from your life as surely as if the council had already voted against me. Go if you must, but torment me no more."

Rebecca raced for her horse and mounted while Bright Arrow was still struggling to dress. Without glancing back, she galloped to the pond where she had collected the lilies. Sliding from the horse's back and tying her reins to a small bush, she brazenly yanked off her clothes and cast them aside. Then she flung herself into the pond and splashed around, needing to wash off the clinging feel of Bright Arrow and their passion. As she rubbed her hands over her body, she inwardly cursed her weaknesses and his obstinate pride.

A rider topped a nearby hill, then reined his horse before he was spotted. He retraced his last few steps and dismounted quickly, dropping his reins to the ground, certain his well-trained beast would remain still and silent while he grazed and awaited his master's return. Stealthily the man made his way to the top of the hill and lay flat against the grassy earth to conceal his presence. Lifting stolen field glasses, he secretly observed the curious scene at the pond.

Bright Arrow pulled off his garments and dove into the soothing water. With smooth, powerful strokes, he swam to Rebecca and tried to reason with her, but she refused to listen or to discuss the matter further. She shouted at him to leave her alone as she furiously splashed water into his face. Using all of her skills and strength, she hurriedly swam to the nearest bank and pulled herself from the water. Bright Arrow followed her and seized her arm. As she struggled to break his oak-hard grip, she berated him and beat on his chest with her other hand. She wiggled and stamped at his bare feet, forcing him into an erratic dance to avoid the blows. Though she ignored his orders to stop her outburst, he was finally able to capture her other flailing hand and pinned them both behind her water-beaded back. He demanded she listen to his words. When she refused, he attempted a different approach to reach her—seduction.

At that distance, the furtive interloper could not hear the words that passed between the bronzed-skinned man and the white woman, but he knew they were quarreling violently. He carefully observed the expressions and actions of each, but it was the nude white woman with whom he became captivated. His starving senses feasted on her naked body, glistening with drops of water. Her legs were long and slim, her waist narrow, and her stomach flat. Each buttock was a tempting handful of taut flesh. Her skin looked as smooth as the surface of a tranquil pond. Wet curls, the color of the reddish-brown mountains not far away, hung luxuriously down her back. Her face, with its upturned nose and naturally pink lips, was too beautiful to be real. With eyes exposing angry flames of golden brown, she seemed more entrancing than the loveliest sunset or the most delicate flower.

The observer's gaze drifted down her throat and halted. He noted that her breasts were ample and firm, and the enticing vision had a stimulating effect on him.

His pulse raced wildly with his heartbeat and respiration, and he grimaced at the throbbing in his erect manhood, which was pinned between his body and the hard ground. He shifted his position to ease his discomfort, only to clench his fists in frustration when the Indian fastened his mouth on those entreating mounds, then swirled his tongue around each peak to arouse them. The woman squirmed and tried to stop his assault. He watched as the Indian imprisoned both her hands within one of his, the other hand skillfully roving her body and attempting to inflame it with the same fiery passion that was vividly exposed by the Indian's hardened shaft. The Indian's mouth covered hers, cutting off her protests. It was clear the Indian had the upper hand physically, and the tortured witness wondered if he should interfere. It was just as obvious that the girl wanted nothing to do with the persistent man. When his lips moved down her throat, her resistance was voiced loudly.

She closed her eyes and clenched her teeth as if summoning all her strength to spurn him. Shaking her head, she screamed, "No! Let go of me, you snake!"

Bright Arrow fused his gaze with hers. "I want you, Rebecca. Soon I will be gone. Does this not prove my love and desire?" he asked hoarsely, wrapping her hand around his rigid maleness.

"Lust does not prove love," she argued, breathless from her previous exertions. "Truth, honesty, sharing—they prove love and faith. You offer me nothing but a joining of bodies, when I need a joining of hearts and spirits. Until you are willing to grant what I need, do not come near me again."

Bright Arrow could tell she was serious. Still, he knew a vision could be shared only with the council until it was fulfilled. If he broke that law, it might prevent his success; and his success might be the only path to saving their love. As much as he wished he could explain, he dared not. He had to believe her love would outweigh her anger. He dropped his hands to his sides. "I will explain all when I return. If you love me and trust me, you will wait for my words and my return."

Rebecca quivered with pent-up frustration and anger. Needing release, she instinctively brought up her hand and was about to slap him, but comprehending her imminent action, she balled her fist and cursed him instead. "Damn you, Bright Arrow! You've ruined my life and happiness. Do you get pleasure from hurting me? Don't you see what you're doing to me? You're trying to destroy me. Be merciful and end it here and now. We both know there's no hope left for us. Free me from the madness that drives us apart."

Bright Arrow shocked her with his response. "Free you so you can flee into the arms and tepee of my friend Windrider?" he sneered in jealousy. "I have done nothing to harm us. I do all within my power to find a way to keep you. Am I not a man once more? Do I not capture your eyes and desires more than he does? You cannot have him until I free you, and that sun will never show its face! You are mine!" he declared forcefully. "You know the laws; you know I cannot speak of my vision until the time is right. You seek ways to build this wall between us that you spoke of; I do not. You will wait for my return and release. If you do not, I will slay both of you!" His onyx eyes blazed with gravity and fury.

"How dare you threaten me!" she panted in astonishment. "Aren't you forgetting I'm not your lowly slave anymore? And I'm not your wife! You don't own me. I'm free to come and go as I please, just as you do. You're the one who chose Windrider to take your place. You're constantly prodding us toward each other. You've done everything to push us together . . . except stake me to his sleeping mat! If you don't want me, I'm perfectly capable of selecting a new mate. I certainly don't need or want your help to replace you!"

She pounded her fists on his strong chest. "You bloody fool, there's no way you can blame me for this estrangement between us. You created it long before we came to the Cheyenne camp; it has only grown larger here. You deny me for weeks and months, then seek me out when your lust burns out of control. How dare you accuse me of betrayal; no man has ever taken me except you!" Her eyes narrowed and chilled as she accused, "Now I understand why you followed me here. Never before have you loved in such a vile and punishing way. What's the matter, my love? Are you afraid Windrider won't take me off your hands? Is this little tirade supposed to finish your unpleasant task of getting rid of me? If it hurts so much to lose me as you claimed, then why are you so relaxed, so cheerful, so resigned to the matter? You hold my fate and happiness within your hands, but you won't share yourself with me. Don't you see that the vision quest also affects me? What has happened to the man I met so long ago, the man I loved above my own life and pride?"

"He nearly destroyed himself trying to prove his love," came the unexpected answer. "I have never wanted to be rid of you. Why do you say such a wicked thing? I will never free you to go to Windrider or any other man. Marriage or not, you are mine. Can you deny I am the only man you love and desire?"

They stared at each other. "Can you deny our life together is almost over? Can you deny we both know what answer lies in your head and mouth, ready to come forth when your council asks, 'Do you choose this white woman or your people and destiny?' I say such things because you imply them each day. Love that demands proof is not strong and pure."

He held himself silent as her words invaded his mind.

The observer on the hill wondered what was being said between the furious warrior and the riled white woman. Whatever it was, the warrior's passions had cooled and his temper had kindled. She spoke to him again, then he merely stared at her as if unable to reply. The onlooker watched the woman pull on her clothes, concealing her body from his hungry eyes. She whirled and said something more to the man, then mounted and rode away. He remained where he was until the warrior had dressed and ridden off in the same direction, toward the Cheyenne camp. If there was one thing he knew for certain, it was that he fiercely craved that white woman, and he was going to have her . . .

Chapter Thirteen

Rebecca returned to camp in a state of agitation and inner turmoil. She couldn't understand why Bright Arrow would push her toward his friend, then be angry and insulting when his selfish plan worked. Had he made love to her to prove his lingering hold over her? Prove it to whom—to her or to himself or to both? Had it been a vain show of power, possession, and masculinity? Did he honestly think she and Windrider were carrying on an affair? If so, was he so jealous or vindictive that he wanted to destroy any budding relationship between her and his friend? How could he impel them toward a union, then threaten them for seeking one?

Or had she misread his meaning? She reflected on the words he had spoken in the forest. He had said Windrider would take her to live in his tepee, and he would keep her safe, an he would provide for her needs. He had never actually said she was to live in Windrider's tepee as his wife or his woman! She anxiously recalled his words and expressions once more. Bright Arrow had not come right out and said such words as "marriage" or "joining." But he had implied them, hadn't he? No, she determined, she couldn't be wrong about his meaning. Too, there was Windrider's behavior and conversations to prove she was not mistaken. Her beloved had spoken with Windrider many times, and the Cheyenne warrior had gotten the same impression—if Bright Arrow couldn't keep her, he wanted them to become mates. If Bright Arrow hadn't been referring to marriage, then what? Surely he didn't mean for her to live here as a servant or slave!

Rebecca pondered Bright Arrow's passion and fury. Could it be he was simply jealous of Windrider? Could it be he was angered by the idea of losing her to another man? The old Bright Arrow had not been one to accept defeat or rejection, weakness or dishonor. To willingly sacrifice his woman could seem cowardly to him. To lose her over another's orders could appear a choking defeat, his humiliating failure to defend her from harm. If he were aware of Windrider's desire for her and if he suspected her impending acceptance of Windrider in his place, he could see these developments as betrayal and rejection. What did he expect from her? Did he expect her never to love again or marry? He was the one walking away from their relationship! He was the one suggesting she go to his friend!

Was it merely his singed pride? To accept orders was one thing, but to have others rule his life was quite another. Perhaps rebellion and stubbornness still flowed in his veins. Perhaps he was furious for losing control of his life. He didn't want to make the choices before him; yet he couldn't avoid them. Perhaps he had just realized the consequences of sending her to another man. As he had insinuated before, saying it and doing it were vastly different. Perhaps he had suggested that union at a time he had seen no hope for them. And now he had changed his mind, seeing the possibility that he had spoken too soon and caused an unwanted rift. Perhaps he had wanted to enjoy these last days with her on his mats.

Suddenly she recalled something he had murmured in her ear while they were making such savagely sweet love.

She had been so enchanted by his immense prowess and sensual assault that his words had drifted past her. He had mentioned something about being glad she would be within his reach while he was trying to sway the council in her favor. There was something about visits . . . What had been his exact words? She closed her eyes and mentally tried to slip backward in time to withdraw the vital clue that could explain his stormy outburst. She could not recall. Who could recall words mumbled huskily from a mouth that was blissfully tormenting her senses? Who could have heard muffled words when love's moaning music and her drumming pulse filled her ears? She trembled at the stirring memories.

She tried to reason out his meaning. Surely he had meant "within reach" until the council voted no. Surely the visits were for the children as he had promised once before. Why would he visit her once she was the wife of another man? Even though Windrider was his friend, he could never be a guest in their tepee! It was true that Bright Arrow was being pressed into a corner, but he couldn't expect her to meet him secretly after she belonged to another! Once he rejected her, it would be over between them forever . . .

Turning her mind from her confusing reverie, Rebecca began helping Sucoora with the men's traveling supplies, suddenly eager to have both men out of her sight for a while. When Bright Arrow finally returned, he completed his packing for the journey, ignoring Rebecca completely.

Suddenly, Windrider entered the tepee, dragging with him a prisoner. She was a lovely, though dirty, white girl with bound hands. He pushed the girl to a mat and turned to relate his adventure. When the frightened creature lurched toward the entrance, Windrider raised his fist in warning and shouted for her to halt. The girl did not understand his Cheyenne words, but she grasped the meaning of his threat. She backed away from the handsome, intrepid warrior.

When Windrider said he was going to trade the girl to another warrior, Rebecca quickly spoke up in the girl's defense. "Please let her remain here for a while, Windrider, at least until you return. She's scared and she's hurt," she fretted, noticing an injury on the girl's arm. "She's too young and lovely to be abused by a rough owner. Please, may I keep her? I'll trade whatever I have of value, and I'll share my meals with her," she offered.

Windrider stared at Rebecca in confusion. "You wish her to be your slave?" he asked, deliberating the matter quickly but thoroughly.

"Yes," she answered. "I'll see what I have to offer for her," she stated hopefully, then turned to check her parfleches.

Windrider caught her arm, halting her movement. "If you wish to have the white girl as a slave, she is yours as a gift," he said calmly, realizing Rebecca would need help when he sent Sucoora away.

Bright Arrow silently observed his interaction but did not interfere. He knew why Rebecca wanted to help the girl, and he also suspected why Windrider allowed her this request. If he weren't careful, Bright Arrow thought, he wouldn't have to argue for Rebecca's return before his council! In his apprehension and jealousy, he had ruined a special day, a beautiful farewell. She was right; it did appear he was driving her into the arms and tepee of his friend! She truly believed he had chosen Windrider to take his place! In her eyes, their blissful moments this afternoon had been a punishment, a cruel display of power. But she was mistaken! Windrider was mistaken!

Suddenly he recalled what he had said to Windrider after his vision while his mind was still groggy. He hadn't meant for Rebecca and his friend to share love, sex, or marriage! He reflected on the verbal exchange that had taken place that fateful day. In his dazed state, he hadn't truly conprehended what he had said or recalled the words until now. "Seek to pull her into your life and tepee." His misleading words echoed across his brain. Yes, he had to take the blame for their misconceptions. He had to find the privacy to apologize and explain. He dared not leave for a lengthy trip with such bitterness and suspicion between them.

Bright Arrow's gaze slipped over the striking captive, then he witnessed the exchange between Rebecca and Windrider. Standing before the kneeling prisoner, he blocked her view of the people who were deciding her fate. When she lifted her head, Bright Arrow's heart skipped several beats. He stared at her intently before she lowered her head to weep over her terrifying predicament. Then he smiled mysteriously.

The two men left for a final word with the Cheyenne council. Rebecca approached the girl whose face was covered by her scratched hands as she softly wept. Rebecca watched her for a moment. Recalling the demands of captivity, she felt her heart going out to this fragile girl who was clearly younger than she was. She couldn't bear the thought of this delicate creature being abused by some harsh master. "What's your name?" Rebecca inquired pleasantly, touching her shoulder.

The girl looked up at the sound of English words from a feminine voice. The woman kneeling before her had tawny eyes, lightly tanned skin, and flaming chestnut locks. She was white! Her voice was soft and soothing, her expression friendly and encouraging. "Are you a captive, too?" she asked nervously, almost joyfully.

Rebecca smiled genially to relax her. She swiftly noted the girl's features and colorings and decided she was very attractive, despite her dirty clothes and tangled hair. She had the bluest eyes Rebecca had ever seen, the shade of a peaceful sky, and they sparkled as if containing tiny stars—or was it merely glimmers from the moisture of unshed tears? Her hair was mostly a honey hue with streaks of gold and silver, as if some force had captured rays of the sun and beams of the moon and lightly stirred them into a pot of honey and dyed her hair with the magical mixture. Her skin was as creamy and white as fresh milk or puffy white summer clouds.

Distracted, Rebecca replied before thinking, "I was long ago, but now I'm joined to a Sioux warrior. My name is Rebecca Kenny. Sucoora calls me Becca." Suddenly she wished she could take back her words. After all, they would both be living here with Windrider, not her Sioux warrior. What would this girl think of her when she learned the truth? The girl appeared to settle down; she wiped away her tears and came to full alert. "What's your name and how did Windrider capture you?" Rebecca asked as she cut the girl's bonds and handed her a wet cloth to soothe the rawhide burns.

She cleared her throat and replied, "I'm Bonnie Thorne. I was traveling with my father and some soldiers when those savages attacked us. They killed everyone but me."

Though Rebecca was unaware of it, Bonnie had not understood the meaning of the Indian word "joined;" she had assumed the beautiful woman was using a polite word for mistress. Also, she didn't know the difference between Cheyenne and Sioux; to her, all Indians were the same. She had been terrified by this horrible experience, for she had never seen a wild Indian before this trip. She wondered if she would be viewed and treated as the black slaves of the South. She was afraid to attempt escape and petrified not to try, and she was delighted to have found a white woman who could help and advise her.

Despite her first impression that Bonnie was delicate and fragile, Rebecca sensed a keen intelligence and courage in this girl. On closer inspection, she seemed quite strong willed. Bonnie made no attempt to snatch the knife or to race from the tepee. Honesty would help Bonnie the most. "Please don't call them savages, Bonnie. It isn't true, and it could get you into trouble. There's so much you don't understand about them. If whites would stay out of their territory, they wouldn't be killing so many to drive us away. You don't know how many soldiers and settlers steal things from their burial grounds and how many Indians they murder. They didn't start this war, Bonnie; our people did. The sooner you realize we're the intruders and enemies, the better off you'll be. I've seen and learned so much since I was captured. It's tragic that people like you and me get caught in the middle. We have to pay for others' greed and cruelties."

"My father wasn't greedy or mean," she protested too quickly. "He was a doctor. He came here to help people, and they murdered him!"

"War parties don't usually attack without just cause. I'm from the Missouri Territory, near St. Louis. My capture was much like yours. Believe me, Bright Arrow and his band had plenty of good reasons to attack our group. I was a sole survivor. What happened to your group?" she probed. The only way to help Bonnie accept her captivity was to help her understand the reasons for it, to help her realize the Indians weren't the savages she believed them to be. Defiance, disobedience, and resentment would only bring her suffering. When Bonnie remained silent, Rebecca asked, "How old are you?"

"I'm nineteen," Bonnie replied almost sullenly, trying to ignore the shameful and tormenting truth in Rebecca's words.

"Were you married?" Rebecca asked curiously.

"No. Papa needed my help with his work, so he turned down every man's offer. I was sort of his nurse. I helped with surgery and doctoring. I gathered plants and herbs and made medicines. Truth is, I'm a better doctor than Papa was." She laughed at that disclosure. "People don't trust female doctors, so I was Papa's assistant. He promised he would find me a husband after we settled here." Suddenly she changed the subject. "How can you stand being an Indian slave?" she wailed. She hadn't wanted to confess that her father had been mean and selfish, that he would have kept her around like a slave for as long as he could!

"Did you see the two men who were in this tepee?" When Bonnie nodded, Rebecca challenged, "Have you ever seen any white men as handsome, or as strong, or as brave?"

"What does that have to do with accepting captivity?" she gasped. She eyed Rebecca intently, piqued at her attitude and words.

"I just wanted to point out that they are not very different in appearance from white males, and they have many good qualities other than their looks. I'd be willing to bet Windrider didn't cause that injury, that he never harmed you at all," she declared confidently. Bonnie's expression answered for her. "He's not a savage, Bonnie; he's a kind man. And he's one of the most famous warriors in this area. If you obey him, he'll take care of you and won't allow anyone to harm you. If you foolishly display your hatred and hostility, these people never accept you. Don't prove you're an enemy, and don't constantly remind them you're a spiteful captive. If you do, he could trade you to another warrior who isn't so kind, or handsome, or gentle. Please, give yourself time to see things from their point of view. Don't fight this thing, Bonnie; you'll be the one to suffer, and you've suffered enough. I'll do everything I can to help you adjust. But the choice to make it easy or difficult or even impossible is yours. I can protect you only so far. Please help me to help you," she urged the attentive girl.

"Do you . . . sleep with him?" the panicky girl questioned.

Rebecca grinned, for she was able to answer, "No. The other woman is his wife. I help her do the chores. Her name's Sucoora. You'll like her. I'm teaching her English and she's teaching me Cheyenne. I can also speak Sioux. I belonged to the other warrior who was here when you entered. They're close friends, so I've moved into this tepee. He's returning to his people, and . . . they won't allow him to keep a white slave. They've ordered all whites from their camp. Bright Arrow is Sioux; Windrider is Cheyenne," she explained.

"Is it too bold to ask if you love him?" the perceptive girl queried. She had noticed a sad expression cross those tawny eyes.

"I've been with him for many years. He loves me, but the Sioux won't allow him to keep me. He's the son of a chief, the fiercest enemy of the whites. When you've been here a while and witnessed a few white massacres, you'll understand why the Indians hate the whites and resist their intrusion. I know that's hard for you to believe at this time, but the day will come when you can no longer ignore the truth. You might even be ashamed to be white. Bright Arrow's a very special man. I wish there were time for you to get to know him. He's been very good to me over the years. I guess I can't blame his people for despising and rejecting all whites. Soldiers have tried to kill both Gray Eagle and Bright Arrow countless times. They've attacked their camp and slaughtered innocent children, women, and old people. How I wish a lasting peace or truce could be made!"

"Will you be this Windrider's woman now?" Bonnie probed.

Rebecca replied honestly, "Bright Arrow will try to change his council's mind about me. If not, then I'm to . . . become Windrider's wife."

"His wife!" Bonnie shrieked. "But he's a savage!"

"Just because his skin is another color doesn't make him a savage. You'll probably be as dark as he is by the end of the summer. Will that make you a savage?" she teased to lighten the heavy gloom. "The difference between us is simple. It's like the difference between Americans and French or Spanish or any other country where people vary in looks and language. It's the same with the Indians. They have different tribes and nations. Some are allies and some are enemies."

"But you said they reject whites," Bonnie reasoned.

"The Sioux reject whites; the Cheyenne do not. They're friends, but they have different laws and customs. I'm not a slave, Bonnie. I'm free to leave if I wish. I don't have any family or any place to go. Windrider is very kind and generous to take me in and take care of me. He doesn't view me as an enemy; we're friends. He was going to trade you to another warrior," Rebecca began to disclose.

"I don't want to go!" she cried out in alarm, interrupting her.

"I begged him to let you remain here, and he agreed for now. If you do as I suggested, he'll keep you. If not . . ." She left her implied warning hanging in air for emphasis.

"Will I have to . . . do everything he says?" she inquired, her face glowing red. Her insinuation was clear and disturbing.

Rebecca selected her words carefully and spoke them lightly. "I can almost promise you he will not take you to his sleeping mat. I think the sun would turn as blue as your eyes first. He has Sucoora and might soon have me. I doubt he needs three women," she jested. She impulsively added, "But if Bright Arrow returns for me in a few months, your fate and safety will be in your own hands, Bonnie. They won't allow you to go with me to the Sioux camp. Besides, you'll be happier and safer here with the Cheyenne. If that day comes, you'll know enough to be fine here with Windrider and Sucoora."

Suddenly this situation didn't seem so dark or ominous. Bonnie curled her legs behind her, then leaned forward. There was an odd feeling of suspense and excitement filling her. As if at home already, she smiled and chatted freely and easily. "Do you think Windrider is tempting? Is that why you'll become his . . . woman?" Bonnie asked boldly, recalling the warrior vividly in her mind. For some inexplicable reason, her fear and antagonism were vanishing. She was an intelligent girl who realized how lucky she was to be a prisoner in this particular tepee. Now that her panic and ignorance were subsiding, she began viewing this situation and her handsome captor in another light.

Rebecca blushed, then responded, "Truthfully?" When Bonnie nodded eagerly, Rebecca grinned and admitted, "Yes, but not as much as Bright Arrow. I would never look at another man as long as I can have him. If I can't, Windrider is the perfect replacement. When you've been here a while, you'll see what I mean." Rebecca curiously observed the dreamy look filling Bonnie's eyes. Could it be possible that this white captive was enchanted by Windrider? How would Windrider react to Bonnie if Rebecca remained here—or if she did not? Crazy thoughts and images flashed through Rebecca's mind, but she quickly dismissed them. If Bright Arrow discarded her, then Windrider was hers! She decided this silly girl-talk was foolish and immodest. She didn't know what had gotten into her, acting like an adolescent discussing swains! She should not be discussing such personal and intimate things with a stranger, even a white stranger!

"Come, I'll show you where to bathe and wash your dress. Then we'll see to your wound and finish the chores. The men are leaving on a trip tomorrow. If you escape from here, Bonnie, you'll face worse dangers alone," she added in warning, then rose.

Bonnie stood up to follow her. They passed Sucoora, and Rebecca told her their plans. The two white women walked to the river and found a secluded spot. Rebecca told Bonnie to strip and bathe. After a brief hesitation, she complied. Rebecca scrubbed her dress and lay it over a rock to dry in the heat and sunshine, while Bonnie washed her hair and body with the soap and rag Rebecca had supplied. When she was finished, she sat on the bank clad in a blanket, allowing Rebecca to tend her wound and bind it.

Bonnie explained timidly, "I was trying to get away and ran into a tree stump. It tore the flesh, but it doesn't seem too bad," she remarked, eyeing the injury and treatment. "Thanks, Rebecca."

Rebecca smiled at her, then handed her a highly prized brush to untangle her cornsilk and honey hair. While Bonnie worked with her long hair, Rebecca gathered wood nearby. By the time she was finished with her task, Bonnie's dress and hair were nearly dry. The girl slipped into the sun-dulled paisley garment, then braided her hair for coolness. She helped Rebecca carry the wood back to camp.

To Sucoora's surprise and Rebecca's pleasure, Bonnie did not rebel at a single order given her that day. She seemed only too glad to obey quickly and efficiently. Her tone was respectful and her expression was amiable. By the time the two men returned, all of the chores were completed and the evening meal was ready. Between tasks, Rebecca had explained many customs to Bonnie to prevent insults or mistakes.

When the children hurried over from their games, Bonnie appeared astonished to learn three of the girls belonged to Rebecca and Bright Arrow. But she was horrified to learn the children would leave with the father and Rebecca might never see them again. She did not understand this cruel custom. How could anyone reject a woman as beautiful and gentle as Rebecca Kenny? Bonnie watched and remembered each action and expression from the people in her new world. With each passing hour and kindness, she surrendered more readily to this inevitable fate. Yet she knew she had Rebecca to thank for her position and treatment. She observed the way the Sioux warrior gazed longingly at the flame-haired woman he was losing to Fate, and she noticed the way Rebecca would sneak similar looks at him. Bonnie admitted to herself that Bright Arrow was a handsome and manly creature, a man to turn a woman's head and flutter her heart, but not like the other male.

Bonnie Thorne was particularly intrigued by Windrider. Each time she looked at him, she experienced funny sensations in her chest and lower, in the region of her womanhood. In fact, she found it difficult not to stare at him! His face and body were like magnets to her eyes! It wasn't hard to see that he held little affection for or interest in Sucoora, but he seemed quite taken with Rebecca. She didn't know why that annoyed her, but it did.

When the men finished their meals, the children and women ate. Windrider and Bright Arrow sat in the center of the tepee, reclining against backrests made of slender, supple branches lashed together with rawhide thongs. They smoked their pipes and discussed their impending journey in Cheyenne, as only Sucoora knew that language and she was out visiting friends. Rebecca and Bonnie played with the children at one side of the tepee. After a short time Little Feet and Moon Eyes were put to bed on one mat; Bonnie had been told to sleep with Tashina on another one close by. Rebecca put Windrider's children on their assigned mats.

Bright Arrow stood up and stretched, then asked to speak with Rebecca outside. Anxiety lined her forehead, but she obeyed to avoid a scene. Windrider said he was going to speak with White Antelope and Shooting Star one last time. He wanted to follow them to make sure Bright Arrow didn't coerce her as he had seen him do at the pond, but he didn't. He stood, flexed his body, and left. Rebecca told Bonnie to watch over the children and that she would return soon. Bonnie nodded and lay down with the smallest child. The idea of escape did not enter her mind as she drifted off to sleep on this exhausting and monumental day.

Rebecca and Bright Arrow strolled in silence until they had left the last circle of tepees. "I have given your words and our quarrel much thought. There is much to explain," he murmured in dread, then went on to reveal his love and desire, his fears and his hopes, his mistakes and his plans for them. He tried to clarify the misconceptions he had unconsciously planted in her and Windrider. He made it known he had not given up on their relationship and wouldn't until he died. He made certain his meanings were clear to her. For all time she was his woman, he told her, his love.

"I don't understand, Bright Arrow. You say one thing, then behave another way. Are you saying you don't want me to live in Windrider's tepee?" she questioned in mounting confusion.

"Live there, yes; but marry him, no. I meant live there as his friend, his sister. I would not give my woman—my one love—to another. If my words meant such to you, then I spoke them poorly or you heard them incorrectly. I wish you to remain safe and near until I can come for you. I do not know how many moons it will take to earn the council's approval, but I must find a way. You are my heart, my life, and I cannot live without you. I beg you, Rebecca, do not turn to Windrider while there is still love and hope between us. I fear the look in his eyes and the pain in your heart. If Grandfather shows me victory on this quest, my people will deny me nothing," he vowed confidently. "I spoke in haste and jealousy. I ask your forgiveness and patience. Many times I have been cold and selfish. I have pushed you from my arms and warmth when you needed them. In my heart, I was not a man. I was afraid, and I was ashamed. I could not bear for you to touch me in such dishonor. When I became a man once more, I feared my love for you would weaken my

291

purpose. You do not know the powerful hold you have on me," he confessed. "If I yield myself to you, I will be unable to meet this awesome challenge before me."

When her gaze continued to hold that expression of puzzlement, he mumbled sadly, "I cannot find the words to explain my feelings. I love you and I cannot lose you. Please stand at my side," he urged.

"How can I when your people won't allow it?" she replied. "Must we retrace this same painful ground? There is no path to happiness for us. Didn't your vision tell you that?"

He grinned, then laughed. "It is not our way, but I will share my vision with you to prove my love and trust. There were things in my vision that I did not understand until this sun. I feared the words that were missing from my vision. Now I understand all, and my heart sings with joy and relief. The same is true of Windrider's vision quest. I feared what I did not understand and did not want to accept. Words were spoken before my mind cleared of the peyote, words that misled Windrider and you, my love. His vision has come to pass this day, but he does not realize it. You must speak of this to no one," he cautioned gravely.

Rebecca locked her inquisitive gaze on Bright Arrow's arresting face. "I swear to you I will tell no one of your words or direction."

He led her to a place far from camp where a rock formation hid them from view. He leaned against it, then pulled her close to him. She stood between his spread legs with her palms resting on his shoulders, and his interlocked hands were looped around her waist, causing their bodies to come into intimate contact. His breath was warm and fragrant as he spoke, and their gazes fused as she listened intently.

After he revealed his vision and imminent quest, Rebecca said nothing. She knew how important visions were to the Indian. She knew they followed them without question and accepted their guidance. There was no way Bright Arrow could have obtained such facts about an expedition, so it must have been a dream or drug-induced illusion. As soon as he tired of seeking these white men who did not exist, he would return and work on their problem. She would never say anything to discourage him or to deny the power of his visions. Instead, she smiled complacently.

"I must go," he stressed. "When I return in great honor, my people will be forced to accept my demand to keep you."

Rebecca was touched by his wishful plans. What was the harm in letting him dream and hope a while longer? The trip would be good for him. It would finish toning his body and sharpening his instincts and skills. Surely he would find some evil whites to punish—using his victory to prove his daring and honor—for many invaded his lands each day! It would be good for him to be alone with his thoughts and dependent on his prowess. And it would give her the time and opportunity to see what her life would be like without him; it would allow her to see what her existence with Windrider would be like. It was time she discovered if she could live without him if it became necessary. Yes, the journey was critical for all concerned. At last, he was trying to communicate and share with her, and his mood and words warmed her heart and body.

Rebecca's hand went up to caress his smooth jawline. "Yes, my love, you must seek this quest that will determine our fates. Until the council's vote after your return, you will be the only man in my life." She smiled at him as she tickled his lips with a fiery curl.

Bright Arrow wished she had added "and my heart." He was worried over this attraction between her and Windrider. He prayed it wasn't too late to prevent them from falling in love. Yet he knew why they had been kissing and embracing that night. Windrider believed she was the answer to his quest and no doubt had told her about his vision and their talks. "Tell me of the white captive Windrider gave to you," he coaxed disarmingly.

Rebecca related all she had told Bonnie and her impressions of the white girl. "Are you angry because Windrider gave her to me?"

"No. It was the will of Grandfather that she remain in his tepee," he stated mysteriously, then told her of Windrider's vision. "He believed Grandfather meant you, just as he believes I have given my permission for him to have you. I saw her and knew it was not so."

"You think Windrider will marry Bonnie Thorne?" she asked in disbelief. "He was going to sell her. Does that sound as if he has love and desire flowing in his body for her? I didn't notice any magical attraction between them. He hardly looked at her."

"Grandfather used you to halt the trade. When the time is right, He will open Windrider's eyes to the truth of his vision. The Spirits of the sky have touched her body and painted their signs there: sky, moon, sun, stars, and clouds. Bonnie will accept the Cheyenne and Windrider. Grandfather has chosen her and sent her to Windrider, just as He chose you and sent you to me. My people will not part us, Rebecca; it is not the will of *Wakantanka*," he asserted confidently.

"But what of the vision's words about her sacrifice and her help to them?" Rebecca reasoned, balking at what she thought were foolish conclusions.

"Losing her father, her people, her home, and her possessions to find Windrider were great sacrifices. Grandfather will find a way for her to win favor in the eyes of the Cheyenne. Hear my words, Rebecca. She will help the Cheyenne in a time of great pain and sadness. When that moon arrives, you will know I speak the truth. You are not to be the new woman in Windrider's tepee; you are to remain in my life-circle."

As she considered his wild claims, Rebecca frowned at the blinding and misleading effects of his customs and beliefs. How could she tell him he was wrong! How could he possibly believe Windrider would fall in love with and marry Bonnie, a captive he had barely noticed! Was it wishful dreaming? Didn't he realize Windrider was in love with her? Didn't he realize Windrider would marry her at a moment's notice! Were his words merely a clever ruse to keep them apart until his return?

"Does this news make you angry and sad?" he inquired.

"If it is true, I will do nothing to prevent their union. If it is not, I don't want Bonnie hurt," she told him in dismay.

"How would she be harmed?" he probed in confusion.

"If you and Windrider believe she is the answer to his quest, would you force her to comply with the demands of his vision? What if you're wrong? What if Bonnie doesn't love him or want him? What if she resists being the answer to his quest? What if she falls in love with him, and he decides she isn't the one Grandfather sent to him? She's so young and vulnerable, Bright Arrow. Love can be painful sometimes. What does Windrider think?" she asked.

"I saw this truth when he brought her to his tepee. He has not seen it. His eyes and mind are blinded by you. The vision will come to pass. No one can prevent it. Just as I

295

was sent here to reclaim myself, you were sent to help Bonnie. Do not be hurt when he does not chose you as his wife. That love and desire will fade when the truth enters his heart and mind. Do not fall in love with him, Rebecca."

Vexed by his words, she protested, "How can I fall in love with him when I'm in love with you, you foolish man! Don't you know I love you and desire you? You're the one who's chilled our closeness all these months. Let Windrider have Bonnie and Bonnie have Windrider—I don't care," she snapped. "If I had my wish, we would still be in our cabin and it would be five years ago when we were happy and free," she blurted out, revealing her secret desires.

He seized her shoulders when she tried to move away from him. Lifting her quivering chin, he looked deeply into her misty eyes. "If I had my wish, it would match yours. Then I would have another chance to make our life work in your world before I faced such agonizing choices in mine," he disclosed in an emotion-laced tone.

Rebecca dropped her face to his brawny chest and sobbed. His embrace tightened around her, but he said nothing. Both knew she needed to release the pain of many months, many quarrels, and the many demands that had been made on her. She had tried so hard to be strong and patient. Now she desperately wanted to beg him to take her and run away, but she could not. There were too many ghosts between them. He was a warrior, and his destiny was calling to him. She could not destroy him. She knew he could not become a white man under any circumstances. It would be cruel and selfish of her to demand such destructive changes.

When she brought her tears under control, she vowed against his thundering heart, "I love you and I need you,

Bright Arrow. Please return safely from this quest." She lifted her tear-stained face and pleaded earnestly, "Please convince them to let us remain together. No man could ever bring me the happiness and fulfillment you do. You must believe that I love you with all my heart and soul. No matter what they say, you are my destiny, my very reason for living."

Bright Arrow imprisoned her face between his hands and lowered his mouth to sear hers. Her arms embraced him fiercely as she feverishly responded to his kisses. Both were very much aware that this could be their last night together for a long time. They knew that they would have to battle to remain together. If Fate tried to separate them, they would have to find a way to outwit it. Slowly they sank to the earth and there made passionate love, oblivious to the hard ground beneath them. This night their love was at first savage and urgent, then gentle and leisurely. Bright Arrow now had the answers and encouragement he needed to carry out his vital mission. And Rebecca had received answers and encouragement in return.

Chapter Fourteen

Minutes after dawn lightened the sky, Bright Arrow and Windrider mounted their horses and rode away. As if nothing unusual were taking place, Sucoora began her morning tasks without paying any attention to the departing warriors. Rebecca observed them until they were out of sight, then turned to find Bonnie standing just behind her. Her bright blue eyes had shifted from the backs of the men to Rebecca's curious gaze.

"How long will they be away?" Bonnie asked casually, rubbing her sleepy eyes and stretching languidly. She was shorter than Rebecca, and she was forced to lift her chin to see the other-woman's face. Wisps of silver and blond hair had escaped her braid during the night; now they moved gently in an early morning breeze that was rare for this time of year. Rebecca noted that her mussed state made her even more appealing.

She recalled Bright Arrow's claim that this white captive was the answer to Windrider's sacred dream. She didn't laugh or smile, but wondered silently, what if there were some mystical truth to visions? Surely this coincidence was eerie and thought provoking. If Windrider did choose Bonnie over her, it didn't necessarily mean she was fated to remain in Bright Arrow's life-circle, as he had confidently alleged. If such things came to pass, where would she be? What would happen to her?

She panicked. Without Bright Arrow and her children, Windrider was her only hope. Could she allow Bonnie to replace her—even if a powerful spirit desired it and had arranged it? Perhaps mischievous, envious spirits interfered too much in the lives and fates of mortals!

Nevertheless, Rebecca couldn't shut out memories of the passionate hours and tender words she had shared with Bright Arrow under the stars and moon the night before. She loved him and needed him desperately, and she despised the differences and animosity that were forcing them apart. He had just ridden off, and she was already lonely and afraid. Windrider was handsome and virile, displaying immense prowess on the battlefield and in passion. But could he ever take Bright Arrow's place in her heart and life? She raged at her inability to influence or change the harsh demands on them, and she prayed her love would be given the opportunity to win the favor and power he was seeking.

Bonnie shook her arm and inquired anxiously, "Rebecca, are you all right? Is something wrong? Is he riding into danger?"

Rebecca met her worried gaze and smiled faintly. "What did you say, Bonnie? I was thinking about something else. Come, let's freshen up and collect firewood." She headed for the forest, knowing the rest of the camp wouldn't be astir for a while longer.

"Is he coming back?" Bonnie ventured as she hurried to tag along. She had witnessed Rebecca's haunted gaze and visible trembling.

"Which one?" Rebecca asked, using the time to master her turbulent emotions and to furtively study this oddly cheerful prisoner.

"Your love," Bonnie replied. "Are you worried about him?" She pushed aside the wisps that were dancing in her eyes.

Rebecca sighed heavily, then replied, "Yes, my love will return. But only the Great Spirit knows what the future will hold for us."

Bonnie observed her unpredictable friend as she splashed cool water on her face. She realized that Rebecca could have been speaking of either man. "Rebecca, will you marry Windrider if things don't work out for you and Bright Arrow?" she boldly questioned, unable to keep the distressing words from spilling forth.

Rebecca stared at her. "Can I ask you a question just as private?" She continued before Bonnie could give or refuse permission, "Does it matter to you this soon after your arrival?"

Bonnie flushed a bright red, and Rebecca grinned and teased, "Is that a blush of modesty, or guilt?"

Bonnie stammered, "I . . . I don't know . . . what . . . to say."

"The truth between us will be fine," Rebecca responded directly. Having brought along a drying blanket, Rebecca decided to ease her tension with a stimulating swim and proceeded to strip off her garments and drop them to the grassy bank. Then she continued, "After all, I did tell you all sorts of things about me and my life. I take it you're fascinated by Windrider? You won't mind being his slave?"

Bonnie's blush darkened, and her respiration quickened. She lowered her head to think. Suddenly Rebecca recalled the first time she had met Bright Arrow. She had been drawn to him instantly; she had been unable to resist him, for he had mesmerized and bewitched her. And she had been his lowly and helpless captive! The attraction between them had been so powerful and magical that it had overcome all of her fears and all of their differences. Love at first glance was a definite reality. She had not meant to doubt or to make fun of Bonnie's feelings.

"You shouldn't be embarrassed, Bonnie," Rebecca consoled her. "The first time I saw Bright Arrow I wanted him beyond all thoughts of freedom or pride. When our eyes met, nothing existed but him and me. It's crazy and wild, but some feelings can't be prevented, or explained. If Windrider affects you that same way there's nothing wrong with loving him and wanting him. And don't tell yourself it can't happen this quickly or against your will," she laughingly warned as she dove into the water.

As Bonnie gave those astonishing words careful contemplation, a conflicting thought came to Rebecca's mind. The attraction had been mutual between her and Bright Arrow. She shouldn't encourage Bonnie to have false dreams and hopes about Windrider. Love was a two-way path, or else it was an agonizing trail. She fretted over Windrider's amorous feelings, for she didn't want him to make a painful journey. It wasn't fair to give him false hopes and dreams either. If he truly loved her as Bright Arrow did, one or the other of them was eventually going to be hurt by her loss. Should she discourage his pursuit? Should she aid Bonnie's love quest? Was it wicked to help cultivate seeds of desire for Bonnie in Windrider's body and mind? What if her daring ruse worked, and then she lost Bright Arrow? Fate was a dangerous Muse to trick. She decided it would be best to allow Fate to chose its own path.

Bonnie watched the graceful Rebecca until she swam near the bank. Holding on to a grass clump with most of her body submerged, she swayed back and forth deep in thought. "But Windrider's pursuing you," Bonnie argued to obtain her attention, as if Rebecca had already advised her to chase the stalwart warrior.

Rebecca looked up into Bonnie's concerned expression. She inhaled deeply and tried to get out of this difficult situation. "Windrider needs another wife, and I might be available soon. We've known each other for years. We're close friends. And Bright Arrow is worried over my safety and happiness if his tribe continues to reject me. It's a very complicated problem. Fate can be sly, Bonnie, even cruel. Who's to say which of us will make Windrider the better wife? Perhaps Windrider's feelings for me are controlled by friendship, or loneliness, or physical attraction. In time, anything can happen."

Bonnie sighed heavily. "You're right about one thing; this matter is wild and crazy and complex!" she declared tensely. "I don't understand what I'm feeling or why. I'm a prisoner here! My people were slain! Yet . . ." She stopped and inhaled deeply once more.

"Yet what?" Rebecca probed inquisitively as she left the water.

"I don't feel like a prisoner whose life or chastity is in danger! It's strange, but I feel safe here. I'm perfectly calm and relaxed, and I'm happy! It's because of you, Rebecca. I can't imagine what would have happened if you hadn't been here to help me, to be my friend and teacher. I wasn't happy with my father," she confessed. "He was mean and brutal. Many times he beat me for what he called disobedience, or for glancing at some man. I was more his slave than I am Windrider's. I had to wait on him hand and foot. He wouldn't let me have friends or be alone with any man. He said he would kill me if I did that, and he would have! Sometimes I hated him. I used to dream of running away, but I didn't have any money or any place to go. It's so peaceful here. I don't see these Indians as my enemies." Her expression was one of consternation.

"What happened on the raid?" Rebecca questioned gingerly, drying her body and hair as the younger woman spoke.

"You were right again. Three Indians came to our camp to trade. The soldiers gave them whiskey and got them drunk. When they passed out, they tied them up and stole all their possessions. They said the Indians would have trailed us and attacked while we were sleeping. They said we would all have been murdered and scalped. They took the Indians into the woods, telling us they were going to tie them up and leave them there until we were out of their reach. But I suspected they killed them, for two of the soldiers had blood on their clothes when they returned. That next night, Windrider and his men attacked us and killed everyone but me. They burned the wagons and captured the horses. I was hiding under a wagon behind some supplies. When it started to burn, I raced for the woods. That's when I fell and hurt my arm. Windrider rescued me and brought me to his camp. Here, let me brush and braid your hair," she offered, needing to be busy.

Rebecca wrapped the blanket around her wet form. She had astutely noted that Bonnie had used the word "rescued" instead of "captured." She smiled as she presented the brush and her back to Bonnie. "You almost sound as if you're repeating my experience, Bonnie. Except . . . except one of the soldiers had dragged me into the woods and was trying to rape me when Bright Arrow killed him and claimed me as his war prize. You're lucky Windrider's Cheyennne. I was taken to the Sioux camp, and they hate whites. Their chief and council have ordered all whites from their camp; they don't want our blood to mingle with theirs. Bright Arrow's trying to get them to change their vote against me, but it's a losing battle." She closed her eyes tightly against her anguish.

"But you have children. You must have been his . . . woman a long time," she protested as she briefly halted her work.

"We met in June of 1796. He was banished for refusing to trade me or send me away. We lived as trappers in the wilderness, but it didn't work. You can't make a white trapper out of a Sioux warrior. He wants to go home; he needs to return to his old life. It's a difficult choice, Bonnie—me or his destiny. I'm supposed to stay here until we're certain there's no hope for us. Our children will go home with Bright Arrow. Under Indian law, children belong to the father and his tribe. Besides, I couldn't take care of them alone." Rebecca thanked Bonnie and rose to don her garments, feeling slightly refreshed.

"Wouldn't Windrider take them?" Bonnie asked softly, touched by this bittersweet love story. She began to brush and braid her own hair.

"He can't. It would cause conflict between the Oglalas and the Cheyenne. If I lose Bright Arrow, I also lose my children. Damnit!" she exploded in rage. "It isn't fair! I've never done anything to them! Why must they ruin my life and happiness? At least with Windrider, there won't be any problems or demands," she unwittingly blurted.

"How can you marry him when you love Bright Arrow?"

"Don't you mean, how can I marry him knowing you love him and want him?" she retorted in unnatural spite.

"No, Rebecca, that isn't what I meant," she replied sadly.

Tears filled Rebecca's eyes. "I'm sorry, Bonnie. I didn't mean that. It's just so hard to understand and accept losing him. I will promise you one thing—I won't marry Windrider if he doesn't love me."

"What about your feelings?" Bonnie sympathetically entreated.

"My feelings?" Rebecca echoed dreamily. "Sometimes feelings have to come second to survival or peace of mind. Windrider is a handsome and virile man. He's kind and gentle, and he's a good provider. He makes me laugh and forget my pain for a time. He's been there when I needed a shoulder to cry on or someone strong to lean on. He's honest and dependable. He's helped me and Bright Arrow many times. He's brave, and he's a very famous warrior. Truthfully, I find him desirable. In time, perhaps I could learn to love him." Rebecca paused. "We need wood for a breakfast fire."

The two women began their task at a leisurely pace. "Is love a lesson to be learned?" Bonnie inquired softly, tossing a limb on the pile.

Rebecca laughed. "And you claimed to be a novice with men and such emotions?" she jested. "You sound as if you know more than I do, and I'm supposed to be the experienced one."

"I can see more clearly than you right now. You're too involved in this situation. I won't get in your way, Rebecca," she promised.

To Bonnie's surprise, Rebecca responded merrily, "And I won't get in yours. We'll let Fate decide for us, agreed?"

Bonnie smiled. "I think I'm going to like it here," she concluded aloud. "I've never had a friend like you before. Thanks, Rebecca." Enjoying this quiet time, they gathered far more wood than they needed.

"Maybe that's why we took an instant liking to each other, why we can trust each other." Rebecca mused aloud. "I've never had a friend like you before either. I lived in the wilderness with my parents until I was fifteen. My mother was mute, so we couldn't talk like regular folks. We had to use sign language. When they died of a fever, I was taken to St. Louis to live with my mother's uncle. He was an evil, mean devil. Your father sounds like him! I worked in his roadhouse for free, like a slave. The few women working there weren't the types to make friends, and the ladies didn't even notice me. When my guardian decided to move into a new area, he forced me to go along. Like you, I had no choice. Oh, how I dreamed of escaping from his clutches! Some nights, I even plotted how to kill him and run away to where the law could never find me," she disclosed, her face flushing with unforgotten hatred.

Rebecca's voice chilled as she continued her shocking tale. "Along the way, some of the soldiers started making offers for . . . my company and . . . attentions. Uncle Jamie was greedy and evil; he had actually planned to deal with them, and then the Indian attack came. The captain in charge of the wagon train had wanted to be first to have me! He was shouting all kinds of threats and trying to rip my clothes off when Bright Arrow appeared like magic. I'll never forget that lecherous snake! I'm glad he's dead; now he can't attack any more innocent victims. The worst part was being so helpless; not a single man would defend me against Uncle Jamie! I was rescued, Bonnie, not captured. The trouble was, Bright Arrow and I did the forbidden—we fell in love. And we haven't stopped paying for that innocent mistake since we met. And I always thought love would be so simple and easy," she murmured, slinging a heavy limb into the bushes to

307

vent her anger. She instantly retrieved it, for she knew it would burn a lengthy time.

"I'm so sorry, Rebecca. It must have been terrible for you. How long will they be away? Are they riding into danger?" Bonnie returned to the original questions with which she had begun their conversation.

"Any time an Indian rides into a white settlement, he faces danger. But with Bright Arrow, there is more. His father is the most wanted Indian on the soldiers' and whites' lists. Sometimes I think they would sell their souls to have Gray Eagle's scalp. He's untouchable. He's like magic, and no force can harm him. In spite of his fierce hatred for whites, he's a great man, Bonnie. I doubt a braver, more intelligent, or daring warrior has ever lived. Bright Arrow looks and fights like him, and he was to become the next chief; that's why it was so destructive for him to take me. How could an enemy become the wife of their glorious warrior and future chief? And since the soldiers and whites can't get to Gray Eagle, they'll settle for Bright Arrow. He'll never be safe alone. Someday someone will recognize him. He belongs with his people, at his father's side. He should become another legend, not some forgotten exile or white trophy. I don't know how long he'll be away; it could be weeks or months. Windrider is escorting him to the edge of the Yankton territory, and he should return in about two or three weeks. I'm not sure how far away it is or how fast they'll travel."

"If he's not returning to his people, where is he going, and why?"

"On a mission revealed in a vision quest, a mission that he hopes will sway his people's vote in my favor," she answered cryptically. Seeing how much wood had been gathered, Rebecca chuckled, then suggested they start hauling it to camp, as it would require many trips. When Bonnie asked about the mission and vision quest, Rebecca explained the ceremony and its meaning to her, but withheld the vision's message.

"What did this vision tell Bright Arrow to do?" she pressed.

"Until his quest is fulfilled, a warrior can't relate his vision to anyone but the council. Once it's carried out, the village is told and there's a celebration and feast. When Bright Arrow returns, he'll relate his message and adventures to everyone," she replied without lying.

"It must be hard to sit around and wait for some vision or another person to decide your fate," Bonnie remarked absently.

"Truer words were never spoken, Bonnie," she concurred. Then she looked at Bonnie and asked, "Do you know what day it is? I lost track of time out here. It feels like fall is just about here."

"September third," Bonnie informed her, confirming her thought that it was time for the winter buffalo hunt. They made another trip to the river for water, then built their morning fire as other faces appeared from many tepees to begin the new day.

The children awoke and came outside to see their mother. Rebecca knelt and hugged each one tightly, then told Bonnie it was time to prepare their meal, feed the children, and begin their other chores for the day. Both women took small hands and ducked to enter the large tepee decorated with colorful, artistic scenes of Windrider's *coups*.

Miles from the Cheyenne camp, Bright Arrow and Windrider rode swiftly in pensive silence. They covered a great distance before the sun vanished from sight behind them. When they halted to camp for the night, Windrider glanced over at his friend to check his stamina after the long, hard ride. From Bright Arrow's nimble movements, his even respiration, and his glittering eyes, Windrider could see that the exertion had not adversely affected him. The Sioux warrior didn't appear in the least fatigued or stiff. Windrider was glad, for his renewed condition would protect his friend's life during this perilous quest.

"The moon will pass over us ten and three times before we reach the camp of our Yankton brothers. I will count many *coups* when I defeat the white enemies of all our brothers," Bright Arrow declared confidently. He wondered if he should discuss Rebecca and Bonnie with his friend, but he decided it was best to allow the Great Spirit to reveal Windrider's vision. He didn't want the Cheyenne warrior to resist the message or the truth of his words by thinking it was only a jealous game.

"The Yankton camp lies ten and one moon passes from my camp," Windrider corrected him genially. "Do you wish to ride as a woman?" he teased. "You are strong once more; we can ride swiftly."

"Three camps of my Lakota Teton brothers stand between the Yankton camp and Cheyenne camp. We must visit. We must learn all news of these strange white-eyes. A man must gather all clues and signs before he rides into a dangerous battle. Defeat and death easily strike down a warrior with an empty head. I must speak with my brothers, the Itazipo, the Hunkpapa, and Minneconjou. I must learn of the whites' plans and travels. And I must be careful, for I am to pass as white when I reach the Yankton camp of our Nakota brothers. I must know all facts before I join the white band," he explained.

Windrider did not expose his inner anxiety as he reasoned, "It is the buffalo season on the Plains. Your Hunkpapa brothers will be hunting. The Minneconjou did not return to camp near the river with two tongues. They made camp many days up the big river, near the place where your father burned the bluecoats' fort many winters past. Winter comes, and we must hurry. I must return and hunt game for my family; you must seek the whites before they travel fast and far." Windrider did not tell Bright Arrow that the true reason he did not want his friend to enter the Sans Arc Itazipo camp was because he feared he would meet a brave called Weasel Tail there . . .

"You are right, my friend. We must hurry before the whites are hard to trail. Clues will be fresher as we near the Yankton camp," Bright Arrow agreed, his acute senses perceiving a reluctance in his friend to visit the Sans Arc camp. Perhaps, he mused, there was conflict between him and a Lakota warrior. Perhaps he had visited there before the vision quest, when he had been away from camp so long. Whatever his reason, Bright Arrow decided that the Sans Arc tribe was probably too far from the source of his challenge for them to be of any help.

There was a great deal of excitement in the Cheyenne camp the next day. During the rest period, an exhausted horse walked to the edge of camp and halted. A white trader was lying semi-conscious across his back. The limp man slid to the ground, landing roughly and painfully. He begged for assistance and mercy from those who gathered around the strange sight. The reins of a pack-mule were tied around his left hand and, as the man fell, the horse's head was jerked downward. The frightened animal reared and neighed. If a brave had not grabbed the bridle, he would have bolted and dragged the sick trader. The brave untied the reins, then claimed the mule and horse as his. Clearly the trader was dying; his belongings would go to those who could seize them the quickest. The brave scowled and wiped the sticky fluid from the trader's injured hands on his leggings.

Rebecca had been leaving the forest after a refreshing swim in the river. She observed the curious scene as a crowd gathered around the fallen man. A chill of fear and danger tingled over her body, and she shuddered at the eerie sensation. Rushing to Windrider's tepee, she entreated Sucoora to remain inside with the children while she examined the situation that had shot warnings through her. So intent was she that she didn't notice Bonnie racing after her.

She approached the group and moved close enough to witness the action. Many Cheyenne were stripping the pack-mule of possessions. Others were actually taking items from the man's horse and his aching body! The man was too ill and weak to stop them, and he continued to plead for water and help. Rebecca stared at the numerous blisters on the man's face, palms, arms, legs, and the soles of his feet. She could understand why he wasn't wearing his boots and why he couldn't place those tortured feet in his stirrups or grip the reins with his raw and blistered hands. There was a variety of sores on his body. Some were like tiny pimples; others were small blisters; and still others were raised sores with fiery heat and pus sacs. He was covered with them. From his exertions and contacts, some had burst; they oozed a sickly liquid.

The petite Bonnie wiggled close to sneak a look around Rebecca's arm. Her blue eyes widened in shock and fear.

Seizing Rebecca's arm, she shook her violently. "Get them away from him, Rebecca! It's smallpox! It's very contagious, and it kills! They have to burn everything, including him when he dies," she nervously blurted, her conclusions and advice startling Rebecca.

"Are you certain?" Rebecca murmured in rising panic, glancing down into Bonnie's ashen face and frantic eyes.

"Yes. Don't touch anything he's touched! Don't let anyone who's touched him touch you. We must get the children away from camp. It's too late for them," she remarked sadly, pointing to the ones tightly gripping the man's possessions. "You must convince them to burn everything, including their clothes. Everyone who's touched him or his belongings should leave camp before infecting others."

"If they get sick like this, who's going to take care of them?"

Bonnie replied in a rush, "They should make camp away from here. They'll have to take care of each other. The ones who die should be burned, and all possessions touched must be burned. It's the only way to prevent the spread of this horrible disease. No one should enter or leave camp; the illness must be contained here until it's run its course. Listen to me, Rebecca; unless this disease is handled carefully and sternly, everyone in this camp could die." Bonnie tugged on Rebecca's arms in her urgency, trying to convince her of the disease's danger.

"My God, you're serious," Rebecca mumbled faintly. "Are you sure it isn't chicken pox? Or some other illness?"

"I told you; I'm a better doctor than my father was. There's no medicine for this illness. Once they get it from him, there's nothing to do but make them comfortable, force them to eat and drink, and pray. The disease's evil is on anything he's touched. Until every dead body and infected item is burned, the disease will run rampant."

"Let's go; we must hurry," Rebecca stated apprehensively. They rushed to the tepee and warned Sucoora of the lethal evil that had invaded their camp. They told her not to allow anyone to enter or to give her anything. Rebecca ordered Bonnie to remain there and to keep the children inside while she and Sucoora went to speak with the chief, as she needed the Cheyenne woman to interpret for her. Then they rushed to Chief Yellow Robe's tepee with the dire news.

The man listened to Sucoora's words as she translated Rebecca's warnings and advice. He asked skeptically, "You say we must send those who touched the white man away for twelve moons? We must not leave our camp or allow our brothers to enter? You say we must burn bodies and possessions for an evil we cannot see?"

Rebecca grimaced. She tried over and over to persuade the chief of the danger they were facing. He shook his head and refused to believe her, or to believe the situation was so serious. "It is time for the buffalo hunt. You wish us to look like fools who follow the crazy words of two white women?" he scoffed sarcastically. "We do not make war with your kind. We have been your friends. Why do you wish to trick the Cheyenne?" he demanded.

When Sucoora interpreted those insulting words, Rebecca winced in emotional pain, then flushed red with anger. "Tell the old man to choke on his stubbornness and hostility! I've warned him. If he refuses to do anything to protect his people, then he must explain their deaths to the Great Spirit when he joins Him soon. Tell him Bonnie is a white medicine chief, and she knows of this evil. In twelve passes of the moon, those who touched the white man or touched his possessions will become ill; Death will battle fiercely for their lives. We wished to save the lives of our Cheyenne friends, but he sees us as sly enemies and foolish women. Tell him he cannot stop this evil; his medicine chief will be helpless to fight its power. Tell him not to ask for the help of two lowly white women when he and his people are suffering and dying. Once he has allowed the powerful illness to overrun his camp, we can do nothing to conquer it. We must fight it now while it is weak, or face bitter defeat later. Ask if it is not better to appear the fool for a few moons in order to save lives? Tell him I take my family and leave to prevent the evil from attacking us." With that, she haughtily turned and left before Sucoora could repeat her stunning words.

Sucoora boldly and bravely suggested that the chief should discuss this matter with the full council. If the white women's warnings proved true, Chief Yellow Robe would stand alone with the blame for an awful defeat on his shoulders. He nodded agreement, knowing the council would not heed such ridiculous claims. He left to view this dying white trader and the so-called enemy that lived on his body. Sucoora returned to her tepee to find Rebecca and Bonnie packing their belongings.

"Hurry, Sucoora," she instructed. "We must dismantle the tepee and move away from the camp. We must protect ourselves and the children. That foolish man will regret his decision. When Windrider returns, he'll agree with our action. Make sure you take only the things inside the tepee," she cautioned, then returned to her task.

Sucoora remained rigid and watchful. "We are women

and children. Who will protect us? Who will provide our game? We will be scorned and mocked. Our chief has spoken; we must obey. We must not leave camp and safety," the woman argued.

"What is a little laughter and a few insults in the face of such a deadly alternative? We'll defend ourselves; we have weapons. Besides, what enemy is going to come around to raid during the hunting season? I'm good with a gun and knife; I can even shoot an arrow and make traps. I will hunt and fish for us. We must not touch food they've touched, Sucoora. We must not let them come near us. We won't go far, just up the river a piece. We'll camp and wait for Windrider to return. We must stop him from entering the camp. He could take ill and die." When the woman remained unmoved, Rebecca snapped, "If we obey the chief, we won't live to see the winter! It is safer out there than here. Please help us; please come with us," she earnestly beseeched.

"We will not go far?" she pressed fearfully.

Rebecca smiled and replied, "We will put up the tepee within sight of camp. We need an empty distance across which the illness cannot travel. We cannot accept any food or contact with others for twelve moons. Then, we must not allow anyone ill to visit us. I promise everything will be fine if we do as Bonnie says."

Sucoora shifted her probing gaze from one woman to the other, then nodded agreement. "First, we must take the children to the safe place," Rebecca continued. "Bonnie can watch them while we take down the tepee. It's been a long time since I've helped do that chore, but I'm sure you can teach me again." They both laughed.

Fortunately most Cheyenne were in their tepees or still grouped around the dying trader and didn't notice the curious action taking place at Windrider's tepee.

Sucoora placed their belongings on the backs of two horses, then led the animals out of camp and headed along the riverbank. Rebecca carried Tashina in the cradleboard and held Little Feet's and Moon Eye's hands. She wanted them close enough to protect them from being approached by others. Bonnie carried Windrider's small son and held Pretty Rabbit's hand. Tansia was told to stay close to Bonnie. When the seven-year-old girl halted for a moment, Bonnie turned and called for her to hurry. They walked until they found a flat area without grass. Sucoora nervously glanced back at the camp, which was now a mile away and unobscured by trees. She sighed heavily; they were near, but a safe distance away.

The women unloaded the horses. Rebecca instructed her children to remain with Bonnie until she returned, and Sucoora told Windrider's children the same. Rebecca took the reins of one horse and Sucoora took the other; they headed back to camp to dismantle and fetch the tepee. Tansia sat down in a grassy spot to play with the bundle of red trade beads she had just picked up as she walked from the camp. When sticky liquid clung to her fingers, she rubbed them in the grass . . .

By nightfall, the women had their one-tepee camp in place. The children were fed and put on their sleeping mats. It was unusual for a foe to raid at night, but just in case one did, Rebecca suggested they take turns guarding the tepee and the horses that were hobbled outside. She took the first watch, too distressed to sleep. While the others surrendered to slumber, she stood outside with a gun in her hands. The night breeze was cool across her face and arms. As she glanced at the dark tepee points against the moonlit horizon, her heartbeat and respiration began to race. She dreaded to imagine what the next two weeks would bring.

Before dawn, the trader was dead, and the insidious disease had already begun its incubation period in many of the Cheyenne. Soon, the whole camp would know Rebecca and Bonnie had spoken the awesome truth, but it would be too late to change their courses of action. Many would believe that they would not survive unless they thwarted the evil, vengeful spells the two white women had cast . . .

Chapter Fifteen

According to Bonnie, it was the morning of September fifth. The three women silently watched the trader's body being hauled away from camp. Bright Arrow and Windrider had been gone for two days, and Rebecca was glad, for both men surely would have examined the trader and gotten the disease. She was grateful for Bonnie's arrival. If she had not been there, Rebecca would have felt compelled to doctor the white man and, in doing so, she would have condemned herself and her family to agonizing deaths. She reflected on Bright Arrow's statements about Bonnie and Windrider's vision. Indeed, Bonnie had tried to help the Cheyenne, but they had denied her the opportunity. If in some mysterious way the vision were true, what could be more painful or saddening than a smallpox epidemic?

Again, Bonnie warned both women to keep everyone in the camp away from them and the children. She added seriously, "If you want your families to survive, you had better shoot anyone who refuses to stay clear of this tepee or the children. Some of them are walking dead folks but don't know it," she commented dryly.

Later that day, Shooting Star tried to deliver half a slain deer to provide game as he had promised Bright Arrow and Windrider. Sucoora begged him not to approach their area or leave the meat. He protested what

319

he called the silly madness that had come over the entire tepee of Windrider. Finally he left, carrying the meat back to camp to share with another family in need. After all, promise or no promise, he couldn't force the women to accept the food or his protection.

Chief Yellow Robe had met with the council the night before and had related the white women's words of warning and advice. The men had laughed and dismissed their nonsense. The council had instructed everyone to leave the women alone until the madness left their minds and they returned to camp. If they needed help or food, all they had to do was cease their foolish behavior and ask.

Later that afternoon, Windrider's two girls and Rebecca's two older daughters were playing with Tansia's small tepee, travois, and dolls. Tashina and Silent Thunder were with Bonnie. Rebecca walked by the four girls on her way to fetch water and gather wood. It had been agreed that two women would remain nearby at all times to defend their camp and health.

Rebecca glanced at the girls and smiled as she passed them. Then suddenly something unfamiliar registered in her distracted mind. Abruptly she halted and whirled around, her heart drumming wildly. Racing back to them and dropping to her knees, she snatched the small pouch from Tansia's hand and shouted, "Where did you get this?"

Frightened and confused, Tansia stared at her sister, Pretty Rabbit. Rebecca had spoken in English, so the child did not know what she had done to incur this anger. Rebecca yelled for Sucoora to come over and question the seven-year-old. At Tansia's reply, Rebecca burst into sobs, and Bonnie came running over to question this odd behavior.

Rebecca brought her fury and tears under control,

feeling the weight of a terrible burden on her shoulders. Once again, she had failed to protect her children. Perhaps she didn't deserve them! "It was all for nothing, Bonnie. Look at this," she murmured dejectedly. "Somebody dropped them. Tansia picked them up while we were leaving camp. They're trade beads. His . . ." she groaned, the word explaining everything.

Bonnie hurriedly flooded her mind with all she knew about this vicious disease. She had to help these people she had grown to care for and respect. She had to use her skills and knowledge. Taking the pouch from Rebecca, she tossed it into the fire. "Make sure they don't have any beads hidden anywhere. Ask Tansia where she kept them, and burn whatever they've touched. We'll need to boil water and scrub all of the children. We've got to get rid of everything that's contaminated. Ask her if Silent Thunder or Tashina have played with the beads."

Rebecca and Sucoora rapidly questioned the four girls. When they gave Bonnie the answers, she sighed heavily. "After we handle all this, we need to keep these girls away from the other two children. If they haven't been exposed yet, the best time to take the illness is after the fever strikes and the rash appears. I'm safe, so I'll doctor any child who gets ill. Once you've had this illness and survived, you can't get it again," she informed the two women who were hanging on her every word and expression.

Rebecca stared at her. "You've had it? You can't get it again even if you touch it?" she probed curiously.

"When I was thirteen, my father treated a patient with it. My mother and I caught it. She died a few days before I started getting well. Sometimes it leaves terrible scars. I have a few small ones on my legs and arms, but I was lucky; my face wasn't marked."

The three women carried out Bonnie's instructions, using sticks to avoid touching anything unless absolutely necessary. "All we can do now is wait and pray," Bonnie announced wearily.

"You two take care of the children while I go set a few rabbit snares," Rebecca suggested, aware they needed food for the next day and wanting to be alone. "I'll fetch water and wood when I return." She smiled faintly at both women and thanked them for their help and friendship. Her misty gaze lingered briefly on her three girls, and she bit her lower lip to halt its quivering and to keep from weeping again. Then she strapped on the knife and gathered the items needed for her task.

As Bonnie and Sucoora watched her enter the forest and vanish from sight, they exchanged knowing glances. Without speaking, they began to prepare the last of their vegetables and dried strips of venison for the evening meal. No one came near their tepee that afternoon.

When the snares were set and her chores completed, Rebecca went to sit with her girls. She played hand games with them until the meal was ready. Afterward, they sang children's songs, which she had taught them.

Bonnie volunteered to take the first watch of the night, and Sucoora and Rebecca agreed. As they turned in for the night, Bonnie picked up the gun and sat on a mat before the entrance. In all of her wildest imaginings, she never had envisioned herself going through all this.

The next afternoon, White Antelope tried to bring the women several freshly slain birds. Again, the game was politely refused. The Cheyenne hunter told the women to send word when they were hungry, warning them of Windrider's inevitable displeasure with their absurd conduct. He even hinted at punishment. In turn, Rebecca warned him of the illness that was breeding in camp. When he frowned and shook his head skeptically, Rebecca asked him to recall her warnings and advice in nine more moons, then come and apologize for his disbelief and scorn. He scowled once more, then rode back to camp.

For the next three days, the women managed fine on the rabbits and fish that Rebecca caught and the vegetables and wild fruits she gathered. Sucoora and Bonnie smiled and complimented her on her skills and cunning. It was obvious the people of the village thought they were being ridiculous and allowed them time to get this foolishness out of their systems. No one approached their little camp. Even the Cheyenne women avoided this area when seeking wood and vegetables for their families. In the camp, the white women and Sucoora were the objects of many jokes and much laughter.

Two more days passed with nothing to eat but vegetables and a few fruits. Rebecca decided she would go hunting for a larger animal at dusk the next day, something that would offer more meat for a longer period of time. And she would collect plenty of wood, for, in the back of her mind, she feared she would become ill and helpless. She wanted to provide their tiny camp with enough food and wood to last for many days. To insure Rebecca's stamina for the hunt, Bonnie and Sucoora took the guard duties that night.

Rebecca spent her morning avidly gathering firewood and as many vegetables she could find. This late in the season, many of the wild vegetables, greens, fruits, and berries were gone. She bemoaned the fact that there was no maize, for it lent itself to a variety of nourishing dishes.

A pang of resentment toward Sucoora shot through her body. Why hadn't the woman been preparing winter supplies? Where were the dried meats and berries for pemmican? Where was the jerky? August through October were the months for doing this chore, which was vital for winter survival. Any game killed and prepared now could be contaminated if handled by infected hands. She raged over this horrible calamity. Strength, fame, and stamina would not guard anyone against smallpox. Then Rebecca realized where the extra food and time had gone—care and nourishment for Bright Arrow's family . . .

She considered riding to the Oglala camp and pleading for help and food for Bright Arrow's and Windrider's children. Knowing she might be carrying that malicious disease inside her body, she dismissed the idea. She couldn't risk spreading the disease to another camp, and certainly not the camp of Bright Arrow's family and friends. In a way, the Oglalas were responsible for her family being in this current danger, as well as for many perils in the past. So many critical events had hinged on Bright Arrow's exile because of her. Still, revenge and just punishment were not the same thing. She couldn't be responsible for condemning many innocent women and children to certain death.

Shortly after noon, Rebecca took the gun and entered the forest. To her waist she strapped a long, sharp hunting knife. She had even dared to borrow Bright Arrow's tomahawk. What did it matter that warriors believed it was bad luck for a woman to touch their weapons! If he thought it had lost its magic, he could make a new one! Heading into the white man's world, he had left behind his Indian weapons. She needed these weapons for hunting and defense, weapons she could use easily and quickly. If she didn't have any success with the gun and snares, she would dare to try his bow and arrows tomorrow!

She walked and searched for hours. What few tracks she found led nowhere. The two times she had seen game, it had been out of range. When Jess and Lester had had her imprisoned inside the cabin, she had sworn her children would never go hungry or be that frightened again. She was determined she would hunt until she found something edible to take home!

The squirrels in the trees seemed to mock her desperation. There was an abundance of game in this area, so where was it? To conceal her presence as much as possible, she had worn a brown dress the color of the tree trunks. She moved quietly and gingerly, careful not to snap twigs or rustle leaves and branches, and she kept traveling downwind, as Bright Arrow had taught her. But defeat seemed to be her unseen companion today.

Stealthily she moved away from the riverbank to walk near side streams, hoping to catch an unsuspecting animal drinking the cool water. She tried to recall which animals roamed in the day and which ones moved around at night. Since the weather was cooler, she felt they would not be avoiding the heat. She halted near a large tree to rest for a time.

Silently from the brush, a deer came to drink just beyond her. He visually checked each direction with his keen black eyes, but she was concealed from his view by leafy bushes growing in a thick cluster beside the tree. He sniffed the air, but her scent was carrying in the other direction. He twitched his tail, then he bent his head and drank leisurely, his ears twitching and cocking to detect the first sound of danger.

Excitement surged through her. Rebecca ordered herself to stand motionless and quiet. He was a beautiful, sturdy buck with six point antlers that were still in partial velvet. Where he had been rubbing them against trees, some of the furry covering over his antlers hung in ragged strips. He was a deep fawn shade, a majestic creature almost too lovely to kill. She hurriedly plotted her strategy. At this quartered angle, if she shot him half way up his rib cage, the ball should penetrate both lungs and guarantee her a kill. With a steady aim and luck, he shouldn't bolt more than fifty to a hundred yards. Bright Arrow usually aimed at the rib cage just above where the far leg was showing. She raised the loaded gun very slowly and cautiously to fire through the bush leaves and took aim on the deer's body.

To her astonishment, two arrows simultaneously thudded into her target area. As expected, the wounded buck took off as if nothing had happened, with the two arrows protruding from his side. Her startled gaze swiftly retraced their flight path. White Antelope and Shooting Star were heading after the injured animal!

She didn't realize she had issued a shriek of dismaying surprise that had alerted the hunters to her presence. Both men noticed her and they exchanged stares. "That was my deer!" she screamed at them.

White Antelope told her words to his friend. When he started to walk toward her to scold her for being alone in the forest, she backed away a few steps and shouted, "Don't come near me! You were both near that sick trader!" Rebecca hoped and prayed that after becoming ill the white man had not touched the trade beads that Tansia had found and shared with the other girls. She also prayed whoever stole them from him had not touched him or any soiled items. There was a slim chance that the children were not breeding the illness and, if so, she could not risk taking it home with her.

Vexed with Rebecca and her wild behavior, he shouted in return, "You are not a hunter! You are a woman! Return to camp and stop this silly game! What dark spirit plays in your head? You are a fool!"

"In five moons, if no one in the camp becomes ill like the trader, we will return. Not before!" she sharply insisted. "If nothing happens, I will gladly confess my stupidity before the entire camp."

White Antelope exhaled loudly between clenched teeth. "Then be a fool for five moons. If you do not return to camp in six moons, I will come and take the children. I will leave them with others who are not touched by an evil spirit in their heads! They must have food. I gave my word to Bright Arrow and Windrider to provide meat for their families. I will cut you a haunch from the deer," he offered angrily.

"No!" she shrieked. "Don't touch it! Your hands have touched the soiled belongings of the trader. We cannot eat the deer if you stain him with the illness. Stay back and I will cut the haunch myself." Rebecca knew that the arrows, if infected, were at the other end of the deer. If the hunters didn't touch it before her, it should be safe.

"He has fled and must be tracked!" White Antelope argued.

"I know how to track a wounded animal; Bright Arrow taught me. Let me trace his path and take our portion. Then you can claim him," she offered. Her voice and expression softened as she wheedled, "Please, White Antelope. I'm not crazy. Just do this kindness for me. In a few moons you'll understand."

"Then go. We will wait here until you call out and return to your tepee," he agreed, resigning himself to her madness and her plea.

Rebecca smiled and thanked him profusely. As the two Cheyenne hunters sat down to await her signal, she headed in the direction in which the buck had fled. He had bolted across the stream and darted into the woods. Lifting her skirt, she dashed across the water. Then she traced the blood spots and broken branches to where he lay on the earth about sixty yards from the stream. She approached him gingerly, knowing the damage those antlers could inflict if he weren't dead and he tossed them violently in her direction.

She nudged him in the rump a few times. He didn't react. Then she glanced at the two embedded arrows, their nocks and fletchings still visible and intact. Both arrows had entered his body accurately and deeply. Because they had pierced his lungs, he had choked on his own blood. She laid her gun aside and, carefully avoiding contact with either arrow, she withdrew her tomahawk and hunting knife. She swallowed several times with difficulty, praying she wouldn't be ill. Then she grit her teeth and hacked off the lower portion of his leg, which was inedible. Discarding this section would also reduce the weight of her precious burden on her return walk.

Taking the sharp knife in hand, she began to carve off as large a portion as she felt she could carry. She didn't want to be greedy, but she knew the men were excellent hunters and could find more game. If she left her long rifle hidden nearby, she realized, she could carry part of a second hindquarter or loin section. She quickly concealed the gun beside a fallen tree under dead leaves, deciding to return to fetch it later.

She cut a blanket in half and placed one hindquarter minus the lower leg on one section and wrapped it to protect it from insects and to keep her from getting bloody.

She worked to flip the deer over, hearing the snap of the arrow shafts. Again she performed this same task, glad that the meat was still warm and pliable. She wiped her weapons clean on the deer's hide, knowing it was ruined by her haphazard cuttings on its rump. She didn't know how to skin one, but she couldn't allow the men to handle the meat first. Wiping her bloody hands on her dress, she struggled to lift the two weights, groaning beneath them. She headed away from the deer, calling out to White Antelope that she was finished and leaving.

She halted and turned to shout her thanks once more. The two men were standing not far away, observing her intently. Shooting Star's expression was impassive, but an unmistakable gleam of amusement and respect for her shone in White Antelope's eyes. He actually smiled at her and nodded a compliment to her spirit and mettle. She smiled and remarked apologetically, "Sorry about his hide. Next I'll learn how to skin one. Thanks for the game, and thanks for the privacy," she added sincerely. She turned and headed for her small camp.

Rebecca labored under the loads she had thrown over each shoulder. Often when she weaved between trees or crossed narrow streams, she staggered and nearly fell. She had traveled a greater distance than she had realized, but she wasn't lost. The farther she walked, the heavier the two burdens became. Her back, shoulders, and arms ached, her legs trembled, her respiration was strained. Sweat poured off her face and soaked her garments. Blood had seeped through the blankets and saturated the bodice, back, and upper sleeves of her dress. The stench and stickiness of the fresh blood threatened to nauseate her, but she told herself she must keep going. She coaxed herself not to cast aside either of the heavy quarters, as some wild animal might find it before she could return for it. She knew she was pushing beyond her limits of strength and stamina, and still she ordered herself forward. She attempted to clear her mind of all matters except trudging onward to obtain victory.

She became so exhausted that she started to halt her journey and rest for a time. She warned herself not to do so. She might fall asleep, and the odor of freshly slain meat could attract trouble. She recalled she had left the rifle behind, and she was too fatigued to battle an enemy—two-legged or four-legged. Salt from her excessive perspiration stung her eyes, but she didn't have a free hand to wipe it away. She compelled herself to continue this vital trek for survival. She had no way of knowing that White Antelope was tailing her for safety. She determinedly pressed herself onward toward her goal.

Finally she came within sight of her camp. Using the last of her strength, she called out to Sucoora and Bonnie for help. The two women looked up at her faint call for assistance, then rushed to her side and lifted the prizes from her weary shoulders. They anxiously questioned her condition, and she managed to say she was fine but that she needed to rest a moment before going onward. She dropped to her knees to master her erratic breathing and weakness. Bonnie and Sucoora returned to the tepee to prepare a nourishing, much-needed meal.

From his concealed position, White Antelope observed this interaction. The white woman who belonged to Bright Arrow was strong and brave. She was smart and skilled. Qualms filled him. What if she were right about the illness? Even if she were mistaken, she was doing what she felt was best for her family. How could he mock such love and sacrifice? He slipped into the forest to return to Shooting Star's side to hunt more game for their families, but not before Rebecca had caught a glimpse of him from the corner of her eye.

She prayed for White Antelope's survival, for he was a kind and generous man. A chuckle vibrated her sore chest. He wanted to appear so aloof and masterful, but his heart was good and sympathetic. He had guarded her safety, yet he had honored her wishes by not approaching her. Someday she would find a way to show her appreciation. Little Feet and Moon Eyes ran over to her, one falling into her lap and the other hugging her fiercely. Seeing the blood on their mother's dress, they feared she was injured. She assured them she was fine, just tired. She laughed merrily and hugged them tightly. Then she pushed herself to her feet and clasped two small hands. The three joined the women and the other children, with the exceptions of Tashina and Silent Thunder, who were being segregated from those who had played with the trader's beads.

To the east of the Cheyenne village, Bright Arrow and Windrider spent their tenth night on the trail in the camp of the Hunkpapas. They shared a meal with the chief, who was full of intriguing tales about the strange white men who were visiting the camps of the Yankton and Minneconjou down the big river. They shared the pipe of friendship as the chief related stories of the courage and daring of the men named Lewis and Clark.

The one called Clark was said to have hair as fiery as *Wi* before he sank into the bosom of Mother Earth to allow *Hunwi* to lighten the lands during the night. The chief said both carried strange skins that they marked with pictures and white words and kept in parfleches strapped around their necks. He said they asked many questions about the Indians, the lands, and the creatures here. He said they gave away many presents to both tribes. He spoke of the fiery water called whiskey, which made grown men stagger as wounded and fall to the ground to sleep deeply. He said they captured many animals and collected many plants and herbs to send to the Great White Father far away.

The pipe was refilled and passed around once more. The chief told Bright Arrow and Windrider the white men offered peace. They met with councils and invited the chiefs to go far away with them to meet the Great White Father in his tepee. He said the Yanktons on the James River had been friendly to these men. But the Minneconjou had forced them to run the gauntlet to prove their courage and worth. He said the white men had three boats, one very large and two smaller ones. He said the two leaders, called captains, brought many white men with them and one with black skin. He revealed that the captains wore long knives called swords and carried long fire sticks.

Bright Arrow asked many questions which the chief eagerly answered. The chief told him the one called Lewis had given Chief Black Buffalo a medal with the Great White Father's picture; Lewis said it was an honor to earn or receive such a medal, like a *coup* feather. The chief said there was a man called Peter Cruzat with them who could call music from a piece of wood with strings and a long shaft. He said the white men were clever and dangerous. He said they marked the numbers of Indians in each camp and their locations. He said they marked where buffalo herds and bands of game roamed. He said they asked about winter camping grounds, sacred grounds, and the red stone quarry. He said they planned to ride the big river through all of their territory. They would visit all tribes, friend and foe to the Sioux. The

Hunkpapa chief was happy when Bright Arrow revealed his secret plan to join them, expose them, and defeat them.

That night was a long one for Bright Arrow. He could not sleep, for weird images and visions filled his mind. In two moons they would reach the big river. There, he and his friend would part company, and Windrider would return to his camp. Bright Arrow would continue on to the camps of the Minneconjou and Yankton, as a white man. The plan seemed so simple and cunning. Why did he have this overpowering feeling of doom? Why did thoughts of Rebecca haunt him all day? He closed his eyes, trying to force himself into slumber.

Far to the west, Rebecca also tossed and turned restlessly. For the first time since this deadly drama began, she realized she might have seen her love for the last time.

Chapter Sixteen

Two days later, on September fourteenth in late afternoon, Bright Arrow and Windrider reached the Missouri River to discover some nettling facts. Lewis and Clark had left the Yankton and Minneconjou camps in a large keelboat and two pirogues. Early that morning, they had passed this point where the big river curved northward. They were heading toward the Brule camp just below the Pierre settlement and Two Kettle village.

Black Buffalo, chief of the Minneconjou, and a few of his braves had journeyed upriver for a distance with the expedition. Bright Arrow and Windrider found the chief and his braves camped near the river where it angled southeastward. The Minneconjou were preparing to spend the night, planning to head home on the new sun, and Bright Arrow and Windrider were invited to share their food and camp. Many facts and feelings tumbled forth from the chief, who had clearly been impressed and deceived by this clever white scouting party.

Apparently, one renown Sioux Chief, The Partizan, had refused to come along, as he disliked and mistrusted the whites. According to Black Buffalo, The Partizan had not gotten along with the two white captains. From the chief's remarks, it was easy for the two arriving warriors to grasp that the Yanktons had also befriended the leaders of the expedition, but they had remained behind in their village. The white leaders had promised to pass this way again on their return journey and had offered the chiefs an exciting trip to see their white world and leader. Black Buffalo sounded as if he planned to accept the perilous invitation! Had he rashly forgotten that the whites were enemies of the Indian, especially the Sioux? Didn't he realize he would be surrounded by thousands?

Bright Arrow and Windrider camped with the Minneconjou that night, asking many questions about the white men and their plans. They listened intently, then talked later in private. It was decided that Windrider would head homeward the next day. With luck and good weather, he would arrive at his camp in ten to twelve days.

Bright Arrow would try to obtain a boat from Black Buffalo, as water travel would be faster than a horse. He would tell the chief that he was curious about these men, that he wanted to meet them and speak with them. If necessary, he would trade his horse. He needed and wanted to catch up with the expedition before it left the Brule camp. Yet the two warriors knew they could not break camp until the Minneconjou left, as they had to prepare Bright Arrow to appear white. He would need to change his hair and clothes, then let Windrider take his belongings and hopefully his horse back to camp with him. When the time came for escape from the expedition, he could steal a horse or a boat. Since his Teton brothers were friendly with these treacherous whites, his mission and identity would have to be kept secret. He knew that the wait would inspire tension and impatience, but it couldn't be helped.

The two warriors lay on their sleeping mats beneath the stars in a clear sky. Tomorrow would be a critical day. They needed sleep and rest, but both were evading them.

"A bad wind blows over our lands, Windrider," Bright Arrow stated solemnly in English. The closer he came to taking on the role of a white or half-white male, the more he practiced the language. "My spirit has been troubled for many days. I do not understand such feelings; I do not think they come from the white men who seek to show the way to invade our lands."

Believing Rebecca would soon belong to him, Windrider carefully listened to his friend's white words. "I will ride to my camp swiftly. My spirit has been restless for many mo— days," Windrider confessed, revealing a similar uneasiness. The eerie sensations were so powerful and intimidating that the Cheyenne warrior suggested, "Perhaps we should ride for my camp together on the new sun. The white men are gone; perhaps Grandfather does not wish you to follow them. Perhaps enemies are sneaking toward our camps and families."

Bright Arrow gravely considered his speculation. He had been wrong to suspect that his friend wanted him gone so he could be alone with his woman. If that were true, Windrider wouldn't be trying to persuade him to return to the Cheyenne camp. There was no doubt in Bright Arrow's mind that Windrider possessed strong, deep feelings for Rebecca. But he also felt that his friend would not betray him by enticing her to his mats while she was bound to another. Besides, Grandfather had chosen Bonnie Thorne as Windrider's new woman!

Bright Arrow informed him, "I must go on, my friend. I am sure the vision told me to uncover their evil plans and to destroy their messages to other whites. When you return home, guard our families until my return," he entreated.

"The path you travel is dangerous. What if you do not return home?" Windrider inquired seriously. "How many days will you travel with these white-eyes? How will we know if you are safe?"

"I will join the white-eyes in four days when they stop at the Brule camp. I am one man; they are many. I can travel faster. They will not leave the camp before I join them. I will return after one full moon has passed." He set a time limit of four weeks for his quest. "If I do not return by five days after the moon renews her face, it is the sign I will never return. You know what must be done," he hinted clearly and painfully. His dark eyes locked on Windrider's face as his friend nodded understanding and agreement.

Yet Bright Arrow's implication contradicted his heretofore confident feelings and beliefs. His charge to Windrider was the result of his mysterious qualms. If he died seeking this quest, he had to know that his family would be loved and cared for by a valiant and generous man like Windrider. Perhaps it was wrong or cruel to encourage Windrider's hopes and feelings, but he had no choice. Before this moment, he had not meant to imply that his friend take his beloved as a wife. But who could know what was in the mind and heart of the Great Spirit? Perhaps it was destined that Windrider's tepee should boast of two beautiful, brave white women. Perhaps Windrider's vision merely revealed Bonnie as a second wife, but that did not exclude Rebecca from being the first. After all, his friend had spoken of sending Sucoora away, as he had done with Kajihah. If only Grandfather would reveal all to him this very night! This dark confusion was frustrating. Just as a light had begun to reveal ways in which he could overcome his black situation, something or someone had doused it. Now all was in bewildering shadows once more.

One thing he knew for certain—if he couldn't have

Rebecca, he could think of no man better than Windrider to take his place! He lay quietly on his mat, his love and desire for Rebecca haunting him, as did an inexplicable and alarming feeling he might never view her beautiful face again. Or kiss those sweet lips again. Or make passionate and tender love to her. He longed to hear her sparkling laughter and devour her sunny smile, but he feared a future in which he could not gaze into those golden brown eyes or stroke that soft skin or flaming hair. He could not shake the eerie sensations, though he tried desperately to dispel them. Maybe this tension and foreboding were effects of fatigue, anxiety, and doubt. Maybe all was peaceful and happy in the Cheyenne camp. Maybe there was another explanation for fearing he had lost her. Maybe this cloudy premonition was a warning to prepare himself for his impending death . . .

Finally he succumbed to exhausted slumber, awakening a few hours later when the Minneconjou braves began to stir. A bargain was struck for a canoe; it had to be returned to their camp when he claimed his horse and he would have to relate any news about the expedition. When Bright Arrow accepted those terms, a brave was assigned to ride the horse along the riverbank to their camp. After the morning meal, Chief Black Buffalo and his braves packed the remaining canoe and headed home.

By noon, Bright Arrow had resumed his recently discarded Clay Rivera identity, thanks to a previous stop by the old cabin, where the last garments he had purchased had still been nestled in their hiding place. He was glad he had decided to conceal them and wondered if perhaps the clever idea had been placed in his mind by Grandfather for such a crucial purpose.

For this unique occasion, Bright Arrow was clad in brown buckskin breeches, a natural-colored heavy linen shirt, a brown felt tricornered hat, and brown boots. In the style of white frontiersmen, his shoulder length ebony hair was secured at the nape of his neck with a rawhide thong. He tied a sturdy rawhide sash around his waist to hold a leather sheath and very sharp hunting knife. In a leather parcleche slung around his neck, he carried the supplies for the long rifle in his hands. As an afterthought, he added the trader's tomahawk to his white weapons' collection, with which he hadn't felt completely safe or secure.

Windrider eyed him up and down several times, making sure they hadn't missed a single detail or item to ensure the safety and success of this charade. He had seen many Spanish trappers and traders in this area over the years; they had been the first white to come here. He grinned. "You can pass for half-white or a white of Spanish blood," he assured his friend.

Bright Arrow chuckled and remarked, "Have you forgotten? I do carry white blood from my mother's mother. Chief Black Cloud of the Blackfeet, my Sihasapa brothers, took a white slave to his mats. She was the mother of my mother. My mother does not look Indian. Her eyes are as green as newborn grass or leaves. Her hair flames as brightly as Rebecca's. Did you know Rebecca carries my mother's white name, Alisha? Did you know her father, Joe Kenny, was a friend to my parents? Did you know her mother and my mother were friends many years past?" he confided casually as he completed his tasks.

"I did not know such things about Rebecca. Why do they hate her and reject her, if such words are true?" he asked in puzzlement.

"It is a story that takes much time and strength. I must not waste either this day. When I return, I will reveal such truths to you. If I do not, ask Rebecca to reveal them. The Oglala are not wise or kind in the matter of Alisha Rebecca Kenny. I fight a battle that I do not understand fully or accept," he disclosed.

"You love and desire her greatly," Windrider remarked, dismayed by that undeniable fact. It was evident to him that Bright Arrow had not been pulling away from Rebecca because he no longer desired or loved her, but because he loved her so unselfishly.

Bright Arrow replied honestly, "Yes. I pray each day and night she will remain in my life-circle. With each passing sun, I fear it will not be so. We have shared too few seasons together!" he raged in exasperation. He confided unwillingly, "If I am defeated in this quest to keep her or if death claims me, she will turn to you for love and joy. This truth brings me anger and sadness and jealousy, but it also pleases me to know she will find new love and protection with one such as Windrider. I can trust you to love her and care for her as I would if these forces were not against our joining. Please do not draw her from my life-circle until it is over between us," he urged, stunning Windrider. He started to reveal the truth about Bonnie Thorne but changed his mind once more. "Return to your camp. The truth of your quest is there," he stated mysteriously.

Guilt chewed at Windrider's conscience. He fretted over his past, present, and future actions. What if he had been mistaken? What if he hadn't received a message from Grandfather to pass along warning words about these white-eyes and their expedition? Was he misguiding and fooling himself? Should he not have interfered in Bright Arrow's vision quest? Would his intrusion cause his friend's defeat and death? Was he selfishly sacrificing his friend's life to steal his woman? Could it be that the white woman with her face obscured in his own vision wasn't Rebecca? What if he were changing everyone's fates just to feed his ravenous desires? Wouldn't the Great Spirit prevent his friend's trek if it were wrong or lethal?

And there were other pressing matters for Windrider to consider. What if Weasel Tail exposed Windrider's intrusion into Bright Arrow's vision? What if Cloud Chaser revealed their original plot? What if Bright Arrow grasped victory for himself and Rebecca? Should he allow his feelings for her to run so wild and free before she was actually his? What if he lost her? What if he lost Bright Arrow's friendship and trust—or caused him to lose his life?

Bright Arrow observed his Cheyenne friend for a time. "What troubles you so deeply, Windrider?" he questioned.

"I fear I can no longer tell the difference between my wishes and those of Grandfather," he admitted openly, worriedly. "How does a man know if his desires overpower Grandfather's wishes? How does a man truly know when he is selfish or mistaken? How does he know when he follows his dreams and not the path of Grandfather?"

"If a man has the courage and honor to ask himself such questions, he need not worry over making a selfish or wrong decision. Why do such questions enter your mind this day?" Bright Arrow probed.

Windrider gave his imminent confession grave deliberation. He had no choice but to clear his conscience and possibly save his friend's life. "There is something I must tell you about the vision quest we shared. Before I returned to camp to prepare with you for the quest, Weasel Tail of the Sans Arc told me of the white-eyes and their journey into our lands. I did not know what to do with such facts. Grandfather held my tongue silent. He awoke me from the vision first instructing me to tell you of these strange white-eyes while you were held prisoner by the peyote. He told me you were the one chosen to defeat them. While you swayed under the powerful spell of the peyote, I put the news of them into your mind."

He sighed heavily. "Now I fear I followed my wishes to have you out of Rebecca's life, not the command of Grandfather. There are strange stirrings across our lands and in my mind. I fear my words will bring the death of my friend Bright Arrow. I fear this quest will cost me our friendship. You must be told this message of the whites came from Weasel Tail and me. Before you continue this journey, you must be certain this quest is commanded by Grandfather, not inspired by my words during your vision quest. We must be sure my words are a true message from Grandfather," he declared honestly.

Bright Arrow affectionately and proudly clasped his friend's shoulder, then genially encouraged, "Do not worry, my friend. Grandfather sends his messages in many strange ways. I feel in my heart and mind my quest is the will of Grandfather. Put your heart and mind at ease. Return home and seek the face from your vision." As soon as those last words left his mouth, he knew Windrider would misinterpret them. Yet he did not explain himself. In time, Grandfather would unblind his friend's eyes.

Bright Arrow placed his supplies in the canoe, stepped inside, and lifted the paddle. He smiled at Windrider, then pushed off from the riverbank. Just before he rounded a bend that would take him out of sight, Bright Arrow turned and waved farewell to his friend.

Windrider solemnly observed his friend until the canoe vanished, mutely praying for Bright Arrow's success and survival. Then he loaded his supplies and mounted up to head home. The sky was clear and warm. The signs on the land hinted at a late winter. It was time to return home and help with the last buffalo hunt of this season. In ten and two moons, he would enter his village. He would gaze into the warm eyes of the woman who was the answer to his dreams, to his vision. Excitement and eagerness surged through him. He had been honest with his friend. He had ceased all plots and games. He kneed his horse and rode eastward toward home, to his new love, and to his destiny.

Early that same morning, the Cheyenne camp had awakened to a frightening reality. Many bodies were consumed by fiery fever. Many lay prostrate on their mats, depending on the love and assistance of others. Some dark poison raced through their bodies, threatening to slay them while they lay helpless and weak. Too many were ill with the same symptoms for them to deny the truth spoken by the two white women. The bleak message of doom traveled rapidly through the camp. The horror of this illness touched each Cheyenne mind and heart, for there was no way to fight such a lethal and greedy foe.

Medicine Girl anxiously tended her father and her brother, Chief Yellow Robe and Big Crow. She forced down their dry throats a brew made from the feverwort bark, but the fever raged on, climbing higher. She steamed a liquid from the willow bark, which she had obtained from the Teton's Dakota brothers in the woodlands to the east. The fever and anguish did not subside. Medicine Girl worried over this strange condition that would not respond to any of her herbs and treatments.

Even the medicine chief, Running Elk, had no power to halt its swift progress in Medicine Girl's tepee or in any others. He went from tepee to tepee casting his spells, shaking his gourds, and singing his healing chants, performing the dance to drive out the evil spirits, giving herbs and aid, praying to all the spirits of the earth and heaven, and passing out sacred amulets to those who were the sickest. Nothing worked. The insidious illness consumed their bodies with fire and attacked more victims. In some tepees, all who lived there were struck down by the unseen enemy. Friends and families did all they could to comfort those laid low. Running Elk returned to his medicine lodge to fast and pray, calling on the Great Spirit to show him the path to free his people.

In the tepee of Windrider far from their camp, the scene and terror were much the same. Tansia, Pretty Rabbit, and Moon Eyes were engulfed by the fierce flames of high fever. All precautions had been taken since they learned of the possible contamination of the beads in Tansia's possession. Tashina and Silent Thunder had been kept away from the other girls. The four had not been allowed to touch anything that others touched or used. They had each been given their own drinking horn, eating container, garments, and sleeping mat, and their possessions had been kept separate from the women's and two smaller children's. Very early that morning, they discovered their caution had not been in vain.

In preparing for the possibility of illness striking their tepee, Rebecca and Bonnie had cut down small trees and constructed a lean-to a short distance away. Those who became ill would be taken there and tended. The air would help cool fiery bodies, and the distance would hopefully protect the healthy ones. Rebecca had continued her hunting and fishing to provide food for their camp. Sucoora had labored hard to dry as much meat and vegetables as possible for use later. In case of an emergency, extra wood and water had been collected.

Since Bonnie was safe from the disease, she insisted on caring for the stricken girls. She moved their possessions outside and, in turn, she lifted and carried each child to the lean-to and placed her on her mat. The girls were too weak and fuzzy headed to argue. For hours Bonnie bathed hot bodies and faces to soothe them. She used the herbs and medicines that Sucoora had transported in a parfleche. She knew all she could do was offer comfort and help, and she wept over the suffering of the small children and raged at her inability to cure them. All she could think about was helping these three girls and saving the five others from this dread disease. Would she be blamed if these girls died? she wondered dejectedly.

Rebecca sat rigidly near the tepee, her teary eyes glued on the tormenting sight at the lean-to. She had persuaded Sucoora to keep Tashina and Silent Thunder inside the tepee for their protection, and to keep Little Feet away from all of the other children. Rebecca wanted to help the children; she needed to help. But Bonnie had forbidden it, warning her of possible death and disfigurement. She told Rebecca that the girls and Bright Arrow would need her alive and well, that there was nothing she could do but become infected herself. Bonnie cleverly asked her who would care for the other children if Sucoora took ill. Or who would provide their game, water, and wood if Rebecca were attacked by this illness. Bonnie argued and debated Rebecca's persistent demands and pleas until the older woman was compelled to accept Bonnie's stern and logical orders. Bonnie had told her the girls would be contagious for nine more days! How could she sit and watch her little Moon Eyes suffer for ten days? How could she sit around and wait for Little Feet's reaction? She felt so useless, so terrified. She needed to get busy to distract herself!

Later that afternoon, White Antelope approached their somber camp. He told Rebecca she and the white captive had been right about the illness. He related Running Elk's confusion and lack of power to battle this unknown foe. Then he actually asked for their help and advice!

Enveloped by tension and fear, Rebecca wanted to scream at him that she had warned them about this vicious disease. But she realized that too many were suffering and would suffer, so she could not. She told him to seek answers from Bonnie, if there were any.

White Antelope said many people in the camp were angered and panicked; they were not thinking clearly. He pointed out the fact that a white man had brought this illness to their village, and that she and Bonnie also were white. He warned of impending danger for them if the disease did not cease. When White Antelope said many were suggesting it was an evil spell cast by the white women for revenge, Rebecca's anger briefly knew no limit. She couldn't believe what she was hearing, and she feared the hostility and power of an enraged mob. She couldn't understand why the Cheyenne suspected them of evil.

She shouted at him, "You can't be serious! How could we be blamed for this horrid event? We're not magicians or witches; we have no power to bring on illness or bad luck. Look there, White Antelope! My child could be dying. Windrider's girls could be dying! Would I slay my own child for vengeance? You spoke of madness? The madness lies in your camp and in the minds of your people. I warned your tribe this would happen. I tried to protect my family and Windrider's by moving out here, but unknowingly we brought the illness with us; Tansia found some trade beads that someone had dropped! I told Yellow Robe to burn the trader's body and all of his belongings, and that no one should touch them! I warned him to banish for twelve moons anyone who had touched the trader and his goods. If he had listened and obeyed, only those few would be ill and suffering now. He laughed at my words, called them crazy. He accused me of trying to trick the Cheyenne. The Cheyenne are not my enemies; they've helped Bright Arrow and his family. I tried to warn *you*, White Antelope. You also laughed at me and called me crazy. It's too late now; the illness has spread to Cheyenne bodies and possessions! If we possessed powerful magic, we would use it to help our girls. We are as helpless as you," she admitted hoarsely and sadly.

The Cheyenne warrior glanced over at the lean-to and observed the scene there. "She's the only one who can help them," Rebecca told him. "She's seen this illness before. She had it as a child and survived. It cannot attack her again. She's taking care of the girls so we won't be near it. Speak with her, White Antelope. Your cheeks burn now with the first signs of the fever. Ask her what you must do to live. You have been kind to us. I call you my friend. I wish to see no Cheyenne die; this I swear to you. The same is true of Bonnie. She does not hate her place here; she does not hate the Cheyenne. Tell no one, but she loves Windrider. She would do nothing to hurt him or his people," she vowed seriously.

When White Antelope hesitated, Rebecca boldly asked, "Do you recall Windrider's vision? Were you not at the council meeting the night he revealed it?" The Cheyenne warrior looked bewildered. Rebecca ordered firmly, "Look at her. Call Windrider's words to your mind as I speak. Spirits of the sky will send signs. Her eyes are as blue as the sky; her skin is as white as clouds; her hair is a blend of sunshine and moonlight; stars sparkle in her eyes. She shows much courage and acceptance. She came here following a great sacrifice, after losing her father and all she possessed. She knows the great pain and sadness that attack your camp; only she can help your people. Grandfather has chosen her for Windrider. Can you deny I speak the truth?" she challenged.

"Windrider did not speak of his captive at the meeting," he argued. "How do you know of his vision?" he asked suspiciously.

"He did not tell me. Do you think Grandfather speaks to no one but warriors? When it suits His purpose, he reveals signs in many ways. I know of his vision, and I know Bonnie is the answer to his quest. Grandfather has not opened his eyes to this truth yet. When he returns, he will see this message was about her. You must tell no one of my words. I revealed this secret to you for your help and understanding. Do not allow anyone to harm her, White Antelope, for she is the only hope for you and your people. Many will die; no one can prevent it. But she can save others if you follow her words. If you tell others she is the answer to his vision, they will doubt this truth; they will doubt her. They will not follow her advice, and many more will suffer. Please, hear her words and follow them," she urged.

White Antelope mused gravely on Rebecca's words and pleas. "I will speak with her. I cannot promise my people will listen to her words and follow them. But I will do as you ask; I will hold this secret."

White Antelope approached the lean-to and called Bonnie to speak with him. They talked for a long time. Finally White Antelope nodded in comprehension and left, while Bonnie returned to her task of mercy.

All day and night Bonnie forced life-sustaining soup and water down the parched throats of the three girls. She knew it was vital to keep liquid and nourishment inside a prostrate victim. She placed wet cloths on their foreheads and dribbed cool water over their slender frames. Once she had to hold a delirious Tansia down when she tried to rise and go to Sucoora for comfort. And the situation only worsened. Little Feet came down with a fever, and Bonnie took her to join the other sick girls. This same pattern continued until twilight the second day when Tansia and Moon Eyes broke out in a rash. Bonnie wept, then prayed for guidance and stamina, for she knew the rash stage should not occur until the third or fourth day after the onset of fever; an early rash indicated a severe case of smallpox, most frequently a lethal one.

With each passing night hour, the rash spread swiftly over both girls. Bonnie knew that two of the most painful areas would be the palms of the hands and the souls of the feet. She blended the mashed stems and leaves of the touch-me-not with a small amount of water. She spread the mixture on the worst areas of the rash to prevent excessive itching. To itch meant to scratch; to scratch meant possible infection. And infection and dehydration were two of the worst perils of this disease.

While the girls slept fitfully just after dawn, Bonnie checked the supply of herbs and plants that Sucoora had given her. There was milk vetch for watery rashes, yellow dock to bring about a discharge of pus from sores or boils, black willow bark to relieve pain and to lower fever, and water avens to dry out purulent sores. For fever, there was also creeping mohonia and western clematis. She wasn't sure what the bee plant and several other herbs would do, but she knew the water avens was the best treatment for smallpox. The supply was low. She would have to send Rebecca to the meadows or bogs for more. She dreaded to relate this dire change in their condition and decided to keep it a secret for another day or so.

Rebecca left the tepee just as the sun cleared the horizon. Walking as close as she dared to go, she asked Bonnie about the girls, and the younger woman said they were doing as well as could be expected. At a distance, Bonnie told Rebecca of her medicinal needs. Rebecca looked tired and depressed, and Bonnie was worried about her. Rebecca had been doing too much work, supplying all of their food and wood, tending the two horses. Now she had this added burden of gathering plants and preparing them.

Rebecca told her she would gather the plants as soon as she returned with food. The afternoon before, Rebecca had followed a stream that had forked off from the river, and she had dammed it. Now she asked for Sucoora's help with the rest of her plan. First they tied leashes around Tashina's and Silent Thunder's waists and secured them to a nearby tree. After walking to the river, which was low this time of year from lack of rain, they eased into the water. With Sucoora coming from one direction and Rebecca the other, they splashed and labored until they urged several fish to dart into the side stream. They quickly dropped logs and rocks Rebecca had gathered the day before into the narrow opening, trapping the fish between the two barriers. Now all they had to do was catch them, clean them, and prepare a stew.

Sucoora laughed and squealed in delight. She complimented Rebecca's cunning and intelligence. Rebecca asked Sucoora to check on the children while she used those wits to figure out how to catch the fish.

An idea came to mind, and she raced back to the tepee and grabbed Bright Arrow's lance. When she returned, Sucoora warned her of the insult and danger in touching a warrior's weapon. Rebecca frowned. "Is it better to starve and die or to risk his anger? I must use them. If I've stolen their magic, he can make others," she reasoned.

Sucoora watched as Rebecca speared the fish one by one and tossed them on the bank to die. When the task had been completed, they examined their prizes. There was one large trout, two good-sized bass, and four yellow perch. "You good hunter," Sucoora remarked with pride and affection. "I clean and cook fish. You get medicine plants." They suddenly noted each other's soaked condition and laughed.

After they had taken the two children and fish back to camp, Rebecca yelled to Bonnie that she was leaving to fetch the water avens. She related the success of their "fish hunt." Bonnie smiled and clapped her hands in pleasure and gratitude. Rebecca playfully bowed, then moved to saddle the horse. With luck, she would return before nightfall, she estimated. She mounted and rode away, after telling Sucoora to save her some fish.

Luck rode with Rebecca, for she found the plants without trouble or delay. She hurriedly pulled them, careful not to ruin the precious roots. She placed them inside her bag and rode for camp, arriving just in time to savor the fish that Sucoora had cooked. Rebecca watched from her safe spot as Bonnie force-fed the stew to the girls. She sensed a drastic change in Tansia, but was afraid to question it. Again sensations of utter helplessness and frustration assailed her.

Rebecca couldn't sleep that night. She was torn between praying for Bright Arrow's swift return and praying he would not return until this disease had ended. She tried not to blame him or his family for this tragic episode in their lives, but it was hard not to seek blame from some source. She was so afraid she would take ill and be unable to provide food and protection for her family and close friends. No one, except White Antelope, had approached their tiny camp since the monstrous illness had reared its ugly head and seized many victims in its sharp and lethal talons. Their survival appeared to be in her quivering hands. She unselfishly prayed that she would remain healthy and strong.

That next morning, the news from Bonnie was bad. Tansia was worse; Moon Eyes was weakening; Pretty Rabbit was covered in a rash; and Little Feet was still feverish. Rebecca panicked. Until now, she had never truly accepted the staggering reality that she could lose her middle child to death. She wanted to rush to Moon Eyes's side, but Bonnie demanded she stay clear of the infected area. She told her the child was too delirious to know her mother was there. Of all the girls, Little Feet was faring the best. Bonnie declared that they must not let the disease spread to the tepee, or lose their hunter.

Rebecca noticed Bonnie's fatigue and determination. Respect and affection for the sunny-haired girl filled her. She fretted over Windrider's return. They must watch for him and warn him of the danger in his camp. She was about to go hunting when Shooting Star and White Antelope suddenly appeared. From their expressions, she knew something was terribly wrong. She listened apprehensively.

Three Indians had died. Many were covered in a rash. Each day others were attacked by fever or redness on the skin. White Antelope knew he was coming down with the sickness. Shooting Star revealed that his wife and daughter were ill. They learned of others who were suffering. Rebecca asked White Antelope why he wasn't resting and taking care of himself. He told her he must get food for his family and for others who were too weak to hunt. She shook her head sadly and her eyes teared as he informed her of the chief's refusal to banish those stricken and to burn all things that had touched the white man or his belongings. She could easily detect the alarm in the man's voice.

"I'm sorry, White Antelope. The sickness lives on the trader's possessions and on the possessions of those who have touched him or his belongings. If you do not burn them, the sickness will spread to others. You must put up another camp. Take those who are ill there. Let no one enter or leave the new camp. Also send those who have touched the sickness of others. It is the only way to capture the disease. See how we keep our sick away? See how we are not attacked by it at this distance? I place food within their reach. You must do the same. We touch nothing they touch," she declared, pointing to those in the lean-to. "Anyone who gets well must tend the sick, as Bonnie does in our camp. You are safe from the enemy once you have conquered it. Do you understand?" she pressed.

The man wavered with fever and discomfort. Rebecca warned herself not to reach out and help him. "There is nothing more I can say or do, White Antelope. You must rest. Tell Yellow Buckskin Girl to force water and soup into your mouth if you go to sleep with fever."

The two warriors departed. Rebecca could not know

that this would be the last time she would look into the
face of Shooting Star. Never again would she see him or
his wife, White Bird, or their daughter, Prairie Flower,
who had tended and entertained Windrider's children
and her own many times. Nor did she suspect that she
would never speak with Yellow Buckskin Girl again.

Rebecca wearily mounted, then dismounted. She
wasn't trained to hunt on horseback, she realized. She
would only succeed in scaring off any game in her path.
She must travel by foot, cautiously and quietly. First she
would retrieve her rifle. She hadn't thought about it until
today. As she headed for the spot where she had hidden
it, sweat beaded on her forehead. She felt slightly dizzy
and trembly. When she reached the fallen tree, she sat
down to master her rapid respiration. Slowly she slid to
the ground and leaned against the rough bark to steady
her spinning head. She felt terrible. Her stomach was
churning and her eyes begged to close, if only for a few
moments.

When she opened them, there was a brawny warrior
standing in her line of vision. She knew he was not
Cheyenne. He was studying her closely. She eyed his
weapons, which were not drawn as yet. He neither
approached her, nor departed peacefully.

Summoning her courage and strength, she asked, "Do
you speak English?" When he didn't respond, she knew
his action might be from pride or reluctance. "If you do,
stay away from me and the Cheyenne camp. There is
much sickness and death there. Anyone who enters the
camp or touches us will be attacked by this powerful illness."

The warrior appeared not to understand her words.
Removing his parfleche, he dropped it to the ground. He
reached for his hunting knife; the sharp blade glistened

in the sun as he lifted it. His midnight eyes never left her face, which paled at his intimidating action.

"I swear to you it's the truth," she vowed faintly. "You must not touch me or go near their camp. You will take the sickness and death back to your people. Is my scalp and life worth the lives of your family and tribe? Please, I must hunt food for my children and those of Windrider. The braves are sick and cannot hunt. Windrider left with his friend Bright Arrow; they won't return for many days. If you kill me, there's no one to protect and feed our children. I have nothing to trade for my life . . . except your safety and survival." She made the Indian signs for peace and friend, with no reaction. In Sioux, she named herself Bright Arrow's woman. In Cheyenne, she asked for truce.

When he didn't reply or appear moved by her desperate words, she yelled at him, "Damn you! Answer me! I don't know how else to reach you, to make you understand! The Cheyenne camp is death to anyone who enters it. I'm death to anyone who touches me! Kill me if you wish, but you and your people will suffer and die for it."

He took a few steps. Then he raised the knife, slicing deftly and quickly through the skin into the tender meat. Blood ran between his strong fingers. As he held up the warm red flesh, he smiled . . .

Chapter Seventeen

On September nineteenth, Bright Arrow arrived in the Sicangu camp. He hoped none of his Teton brothers recognized him as the son of Gray Eagle, chief of the Teton Oglalas. It was alleged that the Teton Sioux ruled a long stretch of the big river in this territory. Farther north, the Arikaras lived in fear of their awesome Sioux prowess.

At mid-afternoon, Bright Arrow guided his canoe over to the shore near the Brule camp. He laid his oars aside and stepped out, securing the rope on his canoe to a small bush. He casually glanced around as he pretended to flex muscles that would be sore and stiff from a lengthy journey. A large keelboat and two pirogues were anchored in the middle of the river. From talk he had overheard, he had gleaned several facts. The two captains and a few men were meeting with the chief and his council; most of the white men had remained on the boats.

Seizing his possessions, he walked toward the Brule chief's lodge. Halfway there, he halted to stare at a man he was hopeful would recognize him as Clay Rivera. His dark eyes settled on James "Murray" Murdock. He had met Murray at Robert Dickson's trading post on Lake Traverse. Several times they had talked at the Englishman's post. If Murray or Dickson or any other white man present at the time had doubted his identity as Clay Rivera, no one had let on to him. Murray, a man known for his hunting skills and courage, seemed alert and smart. Bright Arrow would know soon if he had this amiable man fooled, for he was walking toward him with a grin on his face.

"Clay Rivera," he called out in his deep voice. "Good to see you. Been months. Where you been keeping yourself?"

Bright Arrow tested his false story on this man who had met him many times before. If Murray believed him, others would. "I worked with Jean Truteau in the summer. I got sick and had to stay behind. I'm trying to catch up before he reaches the Arikara camps. No work, no pay. When it gets cold, I'll go back to trapping. What are you doing up this way?" he questioned genially.

"I hired on to the Lewis and Clark expedition. I hunt for 'em and stand guard. You should forget about ole Truttie and join up with us," Murray encouraged. "They pay good," he added.

"Trappers?" Bright Arrow asked.

"Nope. They're here for the Great White Father," he teased mirthfully. "Supposed to map this area and make friends with the Injuns," he stated, though not in a derogatory tone.

Bright Arrow chuckled in the right places. "Are they?" he asked with a touch of humor, then put down his bundle to chat.

"So far, so good. Course, they're smart lads. Can't deny their courage and determination. They plan to ride the Missouri River all the way to the ocean. I guess you heard America bought this territory from the French," Murray added.

"How can they buy or sell what is not theirs? This land

is owned by the Sioux. Sounds like trouble to me," Bright Arrow observed, inwardly burning with rage.

"I don't think so," Murray ventured. "Lewis and Clark ain't here to fight or make trouble. They just want to draw maps, see new things, and find a water path to the ocean. They been collecting animals and plants they don't have in their territory. They been sending them back to the Great White Father. They got papers full of notes about ever'thing. I heard 'em say they wanted to learn all about the Indians hereabouts. They take this peace mission serious. You ain't worried about them causing trouble for your Crow friends and family?"

"I have nothing to do with the Crow; they're always stirring up trouble. I chose the white man's world. You say they mark papers about this land and people? It's a big land, a big chore."

Murray seemed eager to talk about his work. "They got lots of notebooks filled with pictures and words. Each one carries a pouch with him all the time to take notes. They got a map showing all the camps and how many Indians live in each. That map shows the rivers and mountains and plains and prairies. Lots of work if you ask me."

"Will they use such a map to make war on the Indians?"

"Nope. It's for settlers and traders and such. America owns this land now and she wants to see what's here," he declared with a laugh.

"How many men do you hunt for?" Bright Arrow inquired calmly.

"Around forty-five or fifty. Course most are soldiers. They got one black man with 'em, and one dog. The black's Clark's man, and the dog—Scammon or Scannon—belongs to Lewis. Ole Drouillard's traveling with 'em as a hunter and interpreter. They's real strict men, Clay. I heard they whipped two men for trying to run away."

"They are cruel men?" he questioned.

Murray shook his head. "Nope. They just don't allow no man to desert. Why them Rikaras cried like babies when they saw a man whipped. They told Clark and Lewis he should kill 'em, not lash 'em. They run a camp just like being in the army. They got lots of power, Clay. They can make peace or war for the whites. They's trying to take some of the chiefs back to Washington to visit with the President. I think they're crazy, but some's going. They won't know how to act or live in a big city. Probably scare off their breechclouts. Course they won't be in no danger, except of being teased and gawked at."

"Why did you join them?" Bright Arrow probed.

"The money first, then for the fun of it," Murray stated, chuckling. "It's been mighty exciting, Clay. Why don't you join up? They got some men can't find their ass from a hole in the ground. They get lost when they go to piss! Ole Drewyer and Shannon was lost for weeks in them woods. We sent Colter and two others after him. I'm surprised any of 'em got out alive. You shoulda seen them down at Spirit Mound; you'd think they believed all that Injun malarky about evil spirits and devils living there." He chuckled again.

"How long have you traveled with them?" Bright Arrow pressed.

"About five weeks. Them Yanktons asked 'em to send more traders with bullets and guns. They been meeting with councils and smoking peace pipes in every camp. Course some of them Injuns didn't take to 'em. A few times I thought there'd be fighting and killing. Had me plenty worried in The Partizan's camp. You been in this area since birth. I bet you know some of them Injun tongues and signs. They can use a man like you, Clay."

"I promised Truteau I would join him upriver. But I ain't much of a trader. You think I could earn more money with these men?" Bright Arrow asked, cleverly inspiring Murray to coax him to join the expedition.

"Yep. When I tell Clark and Lewis you can hunt, guide, and talk Injun, they'll hire you quicker'an a fly lands on flops," he vowed. "Clark's a happy-go-lucky feller. He knows lots about woods and Injuns. That Lewis is a strange man. Kind of moody and quiet. Course he knows more'an a medicine chief about plants and healing. He's the one who collects all them plants and roots and leaves. Sticks 'em right in a book and writes about 'em. Clark's the one who catches the animals and draws pictures about 'em. Come on, I'll get you hired."

The two men walked over to where several white men were giving out presents. They were passing out ribbons, mirrors, bells, beads, rings, and kettles to the women. To the men they gave tobacco, calico shirts, tomahawks, and knives. They gifted the chiefs with medals, flags, and whiskey. Sergeants Ordway and Pryor handled the gift-giving ceremony. George Drouillard observed the scene with amusement and interest, and McNeal and Fields stood by for protection.

As the action took place, Bright Arrow furtively watched and studied the two white leaders. Both men were in their thirties. The one called Clark had dark red hair. Both captains wore swords and knives and carried long rifles. Their shoulder pouches held shot, powder, and ball. Around each of their necks was a strap holding a leather satchel that contained papers and maps.

Bright Arrow observed the men more closely. Both had very pale skin and flushed cheeks. They had large

noses and serious expressions. Both men keenly observed their surroundings with hunter's looks in their
eyes, looks indicating cunning and intelligence. They
were also dressed similarly. One had a cocked hat, a dark
tricorn, and the other, a fur and felt hat. They wore
leather knee boots and snug breeches, and each carried
several weapons. Each wore a hunting shirt or smock
called a "wamus." The wamus was made like a tunic, to
be slipped over the head and laced down the front with
rawhide thongs. Its close-fitting sleeves and wide cape
were fringed, as was the tail; the fringe allowed the rain
to drip off and was also used for thongs. These smocks
were sometimes trimmed in fur, but those of Lewis and
Clark were made of light, warm buckskin, resistant to
wind and water.

As Bright Arrow watched and listened, he could not
help but be impressed by these two white explorers. Their
voices rang with the same honesty that gleamed in their
eyes. He had not expected such discoveries or feelings,
and he decided he would hold his judgment on these men
and their mission until later. If they posed no danger to
his lands and people, he could end his mission quickly. If
they posed no threats, they would be of no help in
earning him the *coups* needed to regain his former
position among his people. Yet the time and effort would
not be wasted. Each day his body and skills responded to
his demands on them. When it was time to return home,
he would go back a better man. *Home!* He wondered what
was happening far away from this camp . . .

Rebecca gaped at the copper-skinned male who spoke
to her in Oglala Sioux. As she had pleaded and demanded
of him, he did not come any nearer. Instead, he had

severed a large hunk of meat from his fresh kill and was offering it to her! Her fears turned to surprise and confusion.

"You Bright Arrow woman? Bright Arrow Oglala?" he inquired in broken English to test his understanding of her words and identity.

She pushed herself to a half-sitting position on the edge of the fallen tree. *"Sha,"* she responded affirmatively. Pointing to her chest and tapping it lightly, she said, "Rebecca Kenny, *Wanhinkpe Wiyakpa winyan,"* calling herself Bright Arrow's woman. *"Ni-ye Oglala?"*

"Sha, Oglala. You speak good Oglala tongue," he informed her, then smiled genially. "What death, sickness attack Cheyenne camp? Why you hunt? You weak. You sick?" he questioned.

Because she had forgotten many Oglala words, she spoke in broken English to help him understand. "White trader come. He bad sick. He die. I tell Chief Yellow Robe, burn body, burn possessions. They carry bad sickness. Cheyenne who touch trader and possessions get same sickness; many die. He no listen. He laugh, call Rebecca bad names. Sickness come. Many Cheyenne sick; some die. More will die. Chief sick. Children of Bright Arrow and Windrider sick," she told him, holding up four fingers. "We move Windrider tepee away from camp. Tansia find trader's beads. Beads have sickness. Windrider and Bright Arrow gone away many days; many suns before return. Camp say Rebecca and white captive bring sickness and death; many angry. They wrong. Rebecca hunt for Windrider tepee; protect it."

Rebecca inhaled deeply, for she had been speaking swiftly and breathlessly. "No go Cheyenne camp. All who sick or dead give sickness to others who touch them or their belongings. Must burn bodies and possessions to stop sickness. I no sick; Rebecca tired, afraid. No touch Rebecca; she near sick. Might carry sickness. White captive take children to lean-to; she tend them. We stay away. She white medicine chief's girl. She know much healing; Cheyenne no listen and believe. You go home; you and Oglalas be safe."

"Why Bright Arrow come Cheyenne camp? Where Bright Arrow, Windrider go? Why Cheyenne say you bring sickness?" he probed. He sat down cross-legged at a safe distance. He lay the freshly slain game on a hide, planning to leave it for her to take after he left, with some answers.

"Bright Arrow no happy in white land. He hunger to go home. He warrior. He no trapper. Whites bad. He lose spirit and prowess. He lose manhood. He come here to become man again before he go home. Tell no one he here. He go home when Great Spirit say time good. He man again. He seek way to help Oglala and all Indians. He seek *coups* to earn his path home. Bad whites come to Indian land. He go to defeat them. Must tell no one. He follow vision from Great Spirit. Cheyenne blame Rebecca and white captive Bonnie for sickness and death. We white; trader was white. We have no evil spells or bad magic. We no cure sickness; we tend it, to stop it. They no let us. If you tell others, they come to help Cheyenne brothers. They take sickness home to attack Oglalas. They no believe white females. Hold tongue, or many Oglalas die," she urged him gravely.

"I go. No talk sickness. I give elk Rebecca. I pull to river. You take meat home. Last many days. Six moons, I bring more deer; I give Rebecca. No come near camp," he informed her.

"Why are you being so kind? Don't you know your people hate me? They rejected me. They banished Bright

Arrow for taking me as his woman. I don't understand,"
she murmured, utterly bewildered.

"I know such things. I no agree council's vote. Bright
Arrow Oglala warrior; he belong home. I tell no one he
here; he come. I speak for him that sun. I no hate
Rebecca. You brave; you smart. You need food, rest. I
bring food six moons. You stay camp; safe."

He stood and retrieved the dead animal. Rebecca
realized he was very strong, for he draped the slain elk
over his shoulders as if it weighed very little. Then he
headed toward the river. Rebecca lifted the rifle and the
hide containing the hunk of meat. Staying within sight of
the generous and puzzling warrior, she followed him to
the river. He walked on until her small camp came into
view. Placing the elk on her side of the riverbank, he
turned, smiled, and waved a farewell to her.

Suddenly she realized she didn't even know his name.
She whirled around and called out, "Who are you?"

He halted, then chuckled. "Flaming Star, son of White
Arrow and Wandering Doe, adopted parents of Bright
Arrow. I wish his return. Tell no one I came. No tell my
friend and brother," he instructed. "I have vision: he
return home; you live at his side. Be happy." With that
startling statement, he vanished into the woods.

Rebecca hurried over to the tepee to ask Sucoora to
come help her with the elk. Between the two of them,
they skinned, gutted, and carved the animal into hunks.
They hauled the meat to the tepee where they would cook
some and dry the rest for use during the next week.
Rebecca didn't mention her meeting with or assistance
from Flaming Star. Yet she couldn't get his words and
kindness out of her mind. She prayed this was one vision
that would come true.

That following day was worse for everyone. The girls

were not getting better. Even from a distance, Rebecca could read the lines of worry and exhaustion on Bonnie's face. How she longed to help the unselfish woman and the sick children! Surely there was more she could do.

Bonnie didn't conceal the fact that the girls' rashes had changed to blisters, blisters that were rapidly filling with poisonous pus. The suppurative, pimplelike areas would soon mature and form the pustules that had covered the trader's body. This would be a dangerous stage of the disease, for infection could also attack the weakened body as those inflamed sores burst and secreted their vile fluid. Bonnie was deeply concerned over the too swift progress of the disease in Tansia and Moon Eyes, and she feared she could not save them.

By the next afternoon, Tansia was dead, as were many Cheyenne in the camp. Death scaffolds appeared against the fall horizon. Bonnie knew the disease was spreading rapidly in the camp, for the Indians still refused to burn infectious bodies and possessions. Bonnie labored hard to dig a grave for Tansia, for Sucoora couldn't bring herself to do it. It was Bonnie who wrapped the child in her sleeping mat and buried her with all of her belongings. It required all of Rebecca's strength and wits to prevent Sucoora from going to the dead child and holding her. When Bonnie's task was complete, she returned to care for the other girls.

Rebecca prayed as she had never prayed in her life. Tansia's death stirred new fears and panic to life. She could not imagine her own children dying over there without her comfort. Little Feet had a mild case; she did not understand why her friend had been placed in the earth and covered with dirt. She did not understand why her sister was so ill and full of pain. She did not understand her mother's distance.

Rebecca fought tears as Bonnie tried to explain the dread disease. The child wanted to go to her mother, and Rebecca pleaded with Little Feet to stay in Bonnie's area. Both feared the child might sneak over while Rebecca was away gathering wood or fetching water and Bonnie was distracted by the other girls. It was just as hard to protect Silent Thunder and Tashina, for they were too young to comprehend this evil. Bonnie was relieved that both were well-behaved children and had obeyed the orders of Rebecca and Sucoora to this point. She prayed they would not become overly curious or disobedient or forgetful. Rebecca prayed that Sucoora's grief would not blind her to her watchful guard over the two healthy children when she was out of camp.

It was cool that night. Two small fires lit the area of their camp. Little Feet, Silent Thunder, and Tashina were asleep. Moon Eyes and Pretty Rabbit struggled to hold on to life. The mentally and physically fatigued Bonnie worked automatically as she tended the three remaining girls in her care. All three women shuddered in consternation at the sounds of the death drums, which seemed to have been beating constantly since the sixth day of the insidious assault. The drums were a haunting reminder that they were helplessly caught in this vicious and lethal trap.

After two more days had passed, Moon Eyes was no longer able to resist the powerful illness. When Rebecca returned from gathering wood, she found that her daughter had been buried beside Tansia. In shock, she watched Bonnie as she burned the dead grass over the two graves, hoping to kill any infection that lived on the surface of those two mounds of dirt. Rebecca couldn't cry or pray or move or think. She was paralyzed with disbelief.

Bonnie called over to her, "I'm sorry, Rebecca. I did

all I could. Please stay over there. You have two other children to protect."

There was nothing she could do for Moon Eyes. Rebecca had to defend the others from this malicious enemy who could strike down innocent children. She sank to the ground on her knees, but she did not pray. She raged at the heavens and the cruelty that had taken her child's life. It wasn't fair. Fury had replaced her shock, but there was no one near to strike down in revenge. She didn't know who to blame first—herself, Bright Arrow, his parents, his people, the careless trader, the Cheyenne who had dropped the stolen beads, the chief and council who had refused to heed her warnings, nature, the Indians, the whites, their endless hostilities, God . . .

Tashina came and snuggled into her mother's arms, as if sensing Rebecca's anguish and need. Rebecca hugged her so tightly that Tashina squealed. As she covered her daughter's face with kisses, terror raced through her mind. What if Tashina took ill? What if Little Feet didn't conquer her illness? What if they all died? It was a horror too immense to ponder.

In the Cheyenne camp, during the next two days, the pustules of the first victims burst and crusted, and others joined the malevolent circle, either burning with fever, discovering a rash, or suffering from the purulent pus sacs that formed or grew. As the graveyard of death scaffolds increased its awesome size each day, the ominous murmurings against Rebecca and Bonnie mounted.

White Antelope left his mat to warn them to flee for their lives and safety. He was worried over the anger and accusations aimed at the white women. He could hardly walk on his sore feet, and he was covered in scabbed or oozing sores. Rebecca implored him not to approach their safe area. He halted and wavered as he stated his warning and the news from the camp.

The chief had died that morning. His son had died two days before. Shooting Star, White Bird, and Prairie Flower had died, wiping out his entire family. Medicine Girl was dying. His beloved wife, Yellow Buckskin Girl, had died. His daughter, Little Turtle, was very ill.

"Wanunhicum," Rebecca apologized for his agonies. She begged him to bring Little Turtle to their own camp for Bonnie to tend. She explained how important it was for the sick to have nourishing soup and water forced into them. She told him Bonnie had medicines to treat the sores and fevers. Then she told him of the deaths of Tansia and Moon Eyes, and that Pretty Rabbit was sinking but Little Feet was recovering. She showed him how they had remained safe by staying away from the ill and their belongings. She urged him to do the same in his camp. She urged him to at least bury those who had died and to burn their possessions.

White Antelope was intelligent. He realized the two white women were right. He went to speak with Bonnie, telling her he would try to force his people to follow her instructions. She asked him to return with his daughter so she could help them. Walking painfully, the warrior returned home.

Another day passed, and with it the life of Pretty Rabbit. After burying the child, Bonnie wept in anger and frustration. She was about to burn the infected area when White Antelope arrived with his daughter. She determined she would save these two people who had such faith in her. They were fortunate, for their cases were lighter, and they quickly responded to her treatments, as did Little Feet.

By late afternoon of the next day, hope and joy began

to fill Rebecca's little camp. No others had taken ill. Little Feet, White Antelope, and Little Turtle were stronger. Their sores had crusted; the oozing had ceased. The touch-me-not relieved their itching; the water avens was drying out the healing tissues. Their suffering had lessened; they had no fever. Bonnie's mood lightened and her confidence returned. She knew she would save three lives. By following her advice, the others in their small camp had remained well and safe. She wasn't a total failure. To save eight out of eleven lives must be viewed as a large victory! If only the Cheyenne would allow her to save others!

She told White Antelope that when he recovered he must go to the village and show others there was hope if they were treated properly. She told him he could not get the illness again for those who survived were safe. The survivors had to tend others and provide food. When they accepted the truth, they would bury the dead and destroy all things that carried the illness. White Antelope agreed to help her.

Those in the little camp slept better that night, never suspecting Windrider's impending arrival. Just after dawn, he frantically rode into the Cheyenne camp without warning. His astonished gaze took in the numerous death scaffolds, but not his tepee set far away from the camp. When he could not find it, he rushed to question the chief, only to learn he and his family were dead. He ran to another tepee, to learn Shooting Star and his family were gone forever. He could find no one in White Antelope's tepee. Fear such as he had never experienced tormented him. He sought answers from the ailing medicine chief, Running Elk, unaware of the terrible tales about to unfold, unaware of the lethal disease he was challenging . . .

Chapter Eighteen

In the Two Kettle camp, Bright Arrow decided he would cease this useless quest and head back to the Cheyenne camp. In the last ten days, he had learned of little, if anything, that would be perilous to his tribe. The group had traveled along the big river and halted at many Teton camps. He had keenly observed the two leaders and their actions and had seen the maps that the two captains marked. They did show the camps and numbers of Indians in each, but camp locations varied from season to season. By the time they returned to their lands, the maps would be of no use to white soldiers. Rivers and mountains could be seen with the eye, so it did not matter if they were marked on the captains' papers. Besides, Bright Arrow had become convinced that the maps were to be used for friendly purposes. And he was also convinced of the integrity and honor of the two captains. He truly believed he was wasting valuable time and energy.

Using Murray's influence, Bright Arrow had hired on as a guide, hunter, and translator. He had grudgingly come to admire the skills and courage of the two leaders. Their purpose here appeared honest and friendly. What did it matter if they falsely believed the whites owned this territory? There were enough warriors to defend it against a heavy white intrusion. In fact, he had learned much from the white men and had been able to teach them much about the Indians and their customs. The men had seemed eager to learn, in the name of peace. Soon they would leave the Sioux territory and enter the lands of the Arikara and Mandan. He had no desire to continue the trek with them.

If this quest was the will of Grandfather, its purpose was to prove that the expedition offered no harm to his people or their lands. It was late September, time to head home; his next quest was there, and he had to begin it before winter touched his lands. He would ride the Bad River past the Oglala camp without being seen. He would seek to trade with the Sans Arc for a horse, then ride for Windrider's tepee. There he would make his final plans.

After he spoke with Chief Turkey Head and Murray, he bid the group farewell. Now aware of his true identity, Murray chuckled when "Clay" stated humorously, "I'd rather not set eyes on my Arikara friends just now. Last time I was up that way, I lifted a few supplies and horses. I'd best head home and prepare my cabin and family for winter."

Lewis and Clark seemed reluctant to lose his help and company. They gave him many gifts, then thanked him and shook his hand. Clark stated, "We hate to lose a good man, Clay. Perhaps you can join us again when we pass this way. You have been most helpful in this region. I never forget a good friend. Godspeed." They clasped arms once more. Those on the expedition would head out the next morning, unaware that they would encounter and hire a female guide and interpreter named Sacajawea, who would become a legend and friend on their trip. The meeting would occur in mid-October, when the expedition arrived at Fort Mandan; there Lewis and Clark would meet a Frenchman named Charbonneau and his brave Shoshone wife.

In the Cheyenne camp, Windrider mounted and rode toward his solitary tepee. Sucoora saw him leave the camp and move in their way. She hurried out to meet him, warning him to stay clear of them. "You must not enter our little camp, husband. Black death rides with you. It has touched many here. Our warriors fall as dried leaves before this powerful evil. Our hearts grow heavier each sun." She revealed the horrors and ordeal that they had confronted and endured.

He listened to her words, then dismissed them. Bonnie shouted at him, telling him of the danger of his approach. "She speaks truthfully, Windrider! You must not enter this camp! Think of your children's lives," she urged him. "You have been in the camp and you carry the sickness. Come, and I will explain such matters to you."

He stared at the white captive who dared to raise her voice to him and issue orders. His keen eyes quickly scanned the small camp and observed both women. He was about to admonish Bonnie sternly when a soft voice touched his ears, and he whirled in the direction from which it had come.

Rebecca stepped from the forest calling his name, drawing his attention to her. "Windrider! If you've been to the camp, you must not go near the children in the tepee." She moved forward, maintaining a safe distance, then explained the dire situation to him. "We share a great sadness. Tansia, Pretty Rabbit, and Moon Eyes were attacked by the sickness. The Great Spirit freed them from their suffering and called them to walk at his side. We and the other children live only because Grandfather sent Bonnie to help us in this dark time." Then she related how Bonnie had helped them all. She told him he should speak with White Antelope and Bonnie, for he had been near the disease and more than likely carried it. She smiled encouragingly. "Bonnie is the only one who can save your life. She knows much powerful medicine, Windrider. Go to her. Let her help you, as she's done with others."

Unprepared for this crisis, Windrider argued her claims. "What foe can battle Windrider and the Cheyenne and win? Have I not slain countless enemies and stand alive to chant *coup?* I must hunt for my tribe and family and protect them while they are weak. I must look upon my children and the woman I love. I have great need to touch you and speak with you. We must return to camp and help others."

Rebecca shook her head and sighed wearily. "We have lost three children; we can lose no more. There are some forces more powerful than the great Windrider and his Cheyenne warriors. This is one. Even the Great Spirit has not found a way to defeat this foe and send him running from your camp. Many have died, Windrider. We must follow Bonnie's words so the tepee of Windrider loses no more family. Please do this for me and our children. I would not ask such a thing if I did not believe with all my heart that it was vital. Do not allow your pride to endanger your life and ours," she pleaded. Observing his face, she knew he believed her, although he didn't want to do so. She could sense his pain, his frustration, his helplessness. Like a child, at this grim time Windrider needed comfort and encouragement. Rebecca smiled and murmured very softly for his ears alone, "If I could enter the circle of your arms, I would do so, for I need to feel your strength and love. While you were gone, the days were as dark as the nights. We must accept our losses, for we cannot change them."

She had finally convinced him of the threat he posed to her, Sucoora, and the other two children. He agreed to follow her wishes and instructions. "I will challenge all devils who try to steal you and Silent Thunder from me. I do not understand, but I will obey your words."

Sucoora joined Rebecca. She extolled the flaming-haired woman's bravery and daring since the time this sickness took control of their lives. "Becca has more courage than the bear, my husband. She has hunted as the best brave. She has guarded your tepee and family as if they were her own. It is a shame women do not earn coup feathers, for Becca's would make a bonnet flowing to the face of Mother Earth." She went on to reveal many of the incidents involving Rebecca's skill and ingenuity.

Sucoora also related Bonnie's hard work, intelligence, healing arts, and bravery. She concluded with, "It is good Grandfather tossed the white captive into Windrider's path. She carries many healing secrets and shares them with us. She is wise and kind, husband. Grandfather has smiled on the tepee of Windrider, even in such dark times."

The warrior was amazed by the women's strength, cunning, and wisdom. "I will return to camp and hunt game for those too weak to ride or who have no one to hunt for them. And I will persuade my people to follow my captive's words. Then I will return and stay near the lean-to area until it is safe to approach my tepee."

His heart was heavy at the losses of his children and friends. How he yearned to hold Rebecca in his arms and comfort her. He also needed her solace, for now Silent Thunder was his only living child. He could not understand why the spirits had taken the lives of three of his children, but he trusted Rebecca. He would do as the women said to protect his son and love. He stared longingly at her for a time, then rode back to the camp. If he took ill, it wouldn't be for eleven moons, he realized. In that time, he would have to hunt and supply plenty of game for his family. He raged over this cruel situation, for he had never considered dying at such a young age and in top physical condition. It had never before mattered to him that death was a daily part of each warrior's life. He vowed that an early death was not for him!

Rebecca wondered if Flaming Star was well. He had returned with the game as promised. She prayed he had not come into contact with anyone ill or infected. He had said he would bring meat again in a week. She worried over Windrider. He had unsuspectingly visited the camp. She prayed he wouldn't get the disease, but if he did, that he would survive. At least he had Bonnie to care for him—in more than one way. How strange that the vision foretold an undeniable truth. Did that mean there was more to visions than she realized?

For two days, Windrider hunted game and brought it to the village. He talked and reasoned with the remaining council and warriors, convincing his tribe to bury their dead, to burn the scaffolds and all items belonging to those ill or dead, and to move the tepees of those not ill away from the camp. He told them that those who survived were safe to treat those who were ill. He warned those still healthy to avoid the sickness that lived unseen on bodies and possessions.

More Cheyenne took ill; others got well; many died. Within three more days, all Cheyenne either had the disease, had survived the disease, had died from the disease, or were immune to it for some unknown reason.

White Antelope and other warriors had healed sufficiently to help with the hunting. With the women who
were well and strong, they went on a buffalo hunt. The
tribe would need food and hides to survive the winter.
Those alive would share food, .chores, and new tepees
until the spring. It was agreed to burn all of the tepees
and belongings once the illness was conquered. They
wanted no infection to remain on any items to attack
others or to spread over their lands. It would be a harsh
and difficult season for them, but such drastic action
appeared necessary. Once all were healed, other tribes
could be inspired to share food, clothing, and supplies for
the water. There was no greater *coup* than unselfishness,
that generous spirit of charity that saved lives and
prevented immense hardships.

Those in the little camp anxiously waited to see if
Windrider would take ill. In five more days they would
know. The plan that Bonnie originally suggested had
worked; no one else in Windrider's tepee took ill. If they
could keep everyone away, Silent Thunder, Tashina,
Sucoora, and Rebecca were safe. Until the danger was
past, Windrider, Little Feet, Bonnie, White Antelope,
and Little Turtle would remain in the lean-to.

Windrider began to notice Bonnie more frequently
and intensely, especially when White Antelope started
showing subtle interest in her. The recovered warrior's
respect and admiration were highly visible, which oddly
annoyed Windrider. The white captive belonged to him!

Since coming home, Windrider had been told about
the women's actions, over and over. He was filled with
pride that those of his tepee had shown much courage
and wisdom. His tepee had helped the whole village, and
it was because of the white captive whom he had almost
traded! She knew the powers of healing. She wished to

377

help his people. Her heart was good and strong . . . and she was most pleasing to the eye.

Now he furtively glanced at Bonnie as she prepared their meal. She had helped his people in a time of great sadness and pain. His keen eyes slipped over her face and hair, and he noted for the first time that her coloring reflected the heavens and shades from nature. Suddenly he scowled. He wondered why he was comparing this white captive to the signs given in his vision! Rebecca was the answer to his quest; she was the one who caused his heart to beat fast and his body to burn with hunger! Then he boldly stared at the lovely and gentle Bonnie, recalling the vision in detail. He shook his head in disbelief and astonishment. It couldn't be . . .

Bright Arrow directed his canoe toward the bank two miles below the Oglala camp. He had thought at first that he had slipped by his tribe's camp without being noticed, but now he reluctantly responded to the signals from a Sioux warrior standing on the riverbank. As he paddled closer, he thought the warrior looked very familiar. When the boat touched shore, he asked the man's name.

"Do you forget your brother?" the twenty-one-year-old teased.

Bright Arrow's gaze eased up and down his frame, then settled on his ruggedly handsome face and dancing eyes. "You grow tall and strong, Flaming Star. You were ten and five winters old when I . . . left home. You are a man now, a warrior. Tell me of White Arrow and Wandering Doe," he entreated, tying the canoe rope to a rock.

When the response was given, Bright Arrow asked solemnly, "What of my father and mother? How does Sun Cloud grow?"

Flaming Star's expression altered. He hesitated briefly before saying, "Gray Eagle lies wounded. Sun Cloud is Crow captive. Many hunters gone on buffalo hunt. Many warriors fight Crow and Pawnee. I go to rescue Sun Cloud," he announced with vivid self-assurance.

"You return to camp. I will seek my brother," Bright Arrow argued. The news had brought anguish and torment to his mind and heart, and he felt he had to act.

"No. You go to Windrider. Sickness and death live in Cheyenne camp. Rebecca need food, protection. Moon Eyes very sick, dying." He spoke the facts as gently as possible. "I save brother."

Bright Arrow stared at him. "How do you know such things, Flaming Star?" he questioned anxiously, wondering if Rebecca had tried to contact his people again.

"I head to Cheyenne camp. I see woman hunting. I give meat. She tell me. She Rebecca. Many Cheyenne sick; many die. It bad. You go to tepee, not camp. I save Sun Cloud. No can help father."

"Will my father live?" Bright Arrow inquired hoarsely, finding it difficult to speak aloud such a heart-rending question. Again he was off somewhere while his families faced danger and death.

"Might live. Healing take many moons. Mother sad, afraid. Bright Arrow no go to Cheyenne camp. Attacked by sickness; die. Windrider tepee near river. I promise Rebecca more meat."

Bright Arrow was torn by the loyalty and love he felt for each of his separated families. His father could be dying; his mother was alone; his brother was a Crow slave; and his people were being attacked by two strong foes. Yet his woman was alone and afraid; one child was sick; they needed food and protection. Flaming Star insisted, "It is certain death to enter Cheyenne camp. No

379

man can fight invisible enemy. Rebecca has Windrider; your mother no one."

Bright Arrow felt he had to see Rebecca and explain his rescue mission. He charged Flaming Star, "Take word to my mother; tell her I am going after my brother. She is not to worry; I will bring Sun Cloud home safely. Then come to Windrider's tepee. Together we will seek revenge on the Crow and save my brother. But first I must see my woman and children."

"Why you not speak with Shalee and Gray Eagle?"

"It is not the time, Flaming Star. I will return when my brother is at my side. Hurry, I need your help. Join me in Windrider's camp."

The two locked hands and went their separate ways. At the Sans Arc camp, Bright Arrow exchanged the canoe and his gifts for a horse, then rode swiftly toward the Cheyenne camp, nearing it two days later. He observed the curious scene before him, seeing Windrider's tepee sitting apart from the camp. He noted another smaller camp of tepees farther away. Bright Arrow stared at the graveyard, a white man's custom, and he was confused and dismayed. As he rode toward the familiar tepee on the riverbank, his heart drummed wildly with fear.

Rebecca dropped her first load of wood near the tepee and saw a rider coming their way. As he drew nearer, she recognized him. Her heart raced with excitement and joy, then with fear and tension. She ran out to meet him. She had to warn him of the perils in their camp and in the Cheyenne village . . . and she knew she had to find the words to relate her tragic news about their daughter.

He reined in and dismounted. Without embracing or kissing Rebecca, he anxiously questioned her. "Why do you camp away from the village? Where is Windrider?" he probed in dread. Approaching from this side of camp, he had rebelled at the strange sight that had greeted his keen eyes. His astute mind instantly warned of some problem, for his senses had grasped many of the shocking sights and sounds.

Rebecca's happiness and relief at his unexpected arrival vanished. *No kiss? No hug? No warm and tender greeting?* Her smile faded. She dropped her entreating hands to her sides. "We're camped here for our survival, Bright Arrow. Windrider hunts for those too sick or weak to leave their tepees. It has been a terrible time. We needed you. A white trader brought smallpox to the camp the day after you left." As calmly as possible, she recounted most of the gloomy events.

"*Wicahanhan?*" He repeated the dreaded word. "You did not fall prey to this sickness?" he questioned, aware she appeared healthy.

"No. Bonnie told us how to battle it. But so many have suffered and died. The hardships have been nearly unbearable. Many times we went hungry. Many nights we stayed awake in fear. We couldn't allow anyone near our camp for fear they were contagious. All we could think about was protecting the children." Rebecca explained how they had survived. She didn't want to reveal their child's death until he had been calmed and prepared. She carefully observed his dismay and sympathy.

When he thought he knew all, he related his own bad news. "My brother Sun Cloud has been taken captive by our enemy the Crow. Three warriors sneaked into my father's camp and wounded him. He lies near death and cannot seek his son, my brother. I must do this before the Crow torture him or slay him. I will take you and our children to a safe place, then ride swiftly for the Crow camp. I will return for you when my brother sits in the tepee of Gray Eagle and Shalee. I cannot leave you here in danger. You must prepare yourself and our children while I speak with Windrider. We must leave this very sun."

Rebecca was startled by his unexpected and untimely news. She was trying to solve one crisis and he was introducing another one! She watched him pace unnaturally as he slipped into pensive planning. Her mind screamed, *You are leaving again? What about your family? Have I lost you too? Did you hear nothing I said?* He hadn't inquired about the children, or about who had lived or died. This troubled her deeply.

"To safety?" she echoed in bewilderment. "Where?"

"Flaming Star will take you to the camp of the Yanktons, where you and our children will be safe from this evil sickness. I will come for you after I rescue Sun Cloud and take him home. The Yanktons are friendly with whites; they know Bright Arrow. They will accept you and protect you until my return. You cannot remain near such evil."

Rebecca eyed him strangely. "You can leave us at a time like this? We have suffered much. We need you," she whispered raggedly.

"My father is dying; my brother is a slave to our enemies. My people are attacked by many foes. I must help them," he argued gently.

"Many have died and are dying here, too. We are being attacked by an evil foe who slays warriors and women and children. No one is safe. Even the chief has died. Shooting Star's whole family is gone. We need food and protection. We need hides and skins for garments and new tepees. You owe your people nothing! They turned their backs on us and banished us. If not for the Oglala, we would be safe and happy this day! The Cheyenne have helped us; you owe them much! This is the wrong time to choose your people over your family and friends. We need you here. Why must you do this? Surely another warrior can rescue one child? Surely the Crow would not slay a small boy, even if he is a slave," she reasoned irritably.

Her sharp words cut him deeply. "He is my brother! I must save his life. Do you wish me to remain here in danger from this illness? I can offer no help to fight an enemy that cannot be seen or touched. When I return, Sun Cloud will be safe and the illness will be conquered. I will help the Cheyenne when I return. The Crow will not know Bright Arrow as Clay Rivera. I will be able to enter their camp and steal Sun Cloud. He is the son of Gray Eagle, brother to Bright Arrow. To revenge themselves on us, they could torture or slay him. You are strong; you can take care of our family. He is but a child. You do not understand," he scolded her.

"I understand our daughter Moon Eyes is dead," she stated coldly. "It is too late for you to help her. Tansia and Pretty Rabbit are dead. Little Feet almost died. Our Cheyenne friends have died. We have gone hungry and quivered in fear. Many said Bonnie and I were responsible for the evil here; many wanted to kill us. We have done all we could to protect the other children from the illness. I have hunted and fished many days to provide food for our tepee. Now Windrider waits to see if the sickness has invaded his body."

Suddenly her tone and expression altered, and she told him with a sneer, "You are right; we do not need you. Go, Bright Arrow, we can survive without you. We have done so for many weeks." She whirled and ran back to the forest to finish gathering her wood. "Go," she had shouted over her shoulder, "I will seek another to fill the place you have abandoned." In her fury, disappointment, and anguish, she prayed he would leave before she returned to camp.

Bright Arrow sought out Windrider and conversed with him at a distance, at his friend's insistence. He told him about the expedition and his conclusions. Then he spoke with White Antelope and Sucoora. Soon the pieces to this monstrous puzzle fell into place. He couldn't believe what Rebecca and the others had been through since his departure. This had not been merely an illness; it had been a plague! He couldn't believe his little girl was dead. Pain knifed his heart and guilt pierced his mind. Once again he had almost lost his love and family to danger and death. Again, he had been away. Why was his fate so ensnared by tangled vines? he wondered sadly.

Bright Arrow explained the grim situation in the Oglala camp and told of his brother's capture. Windrider spoke clearly and strongly against their mutual foe. "You cannot leave the son of Gray Eagle and brother of Bright Arrow in the hands of our Crow enemies, hands stained with Sioux and Cheyenne blood. Show them that the firstborn son of Gray Eagle has the strength and courage to battle them, to cunningly take back what is his. This insult cannot be ignored. Their laughter will sing upon the winds. Soon all enemy tribes will know of this valuable captive. They will seek the life of your father while he lays weak and helpless. Your tribe faces great danger if you do not accept this challenge and overcome this enemy."

"You speak true words, my friend. But I have others to protect," Bright Arrow reminded him. "This is not an easy matter to settle. I did not know of the danger and sadness I would find when I rode here to share the dark news from my camp. I stand here with a heart and head divided, Windrider. Too many lives rest on my decision."

"The illness that attacked my camp grows weaker each sun. Windrider and your Cheyenne brothers will protect your family and provide for them. You cannot return life to Moon Eyes. There is nothing you can do here but watch others heal and wait for your brother to die. You must teach the Crow to fear the Oglala and the son of Gray Eagle. Without their chief and next chief, your tribe will lose its spirit and direction. You must offer your help and your life. This is why Grandfather called you home from the white man's journey. He seeks to return your honor and rank by your saving Sun Cloud and your tribe."

Flaming Star arrived. He told them, "Gray Eagle lives, but he is weak. He will not be able to trail Sun Cloud for many weeks. It will be too late. Your mother sends her love and prayers. She knows the dangers of seeking your brother. She fears losing two sons to the Crow. She does not ask you to save your brother, for she knows the Crow hate Bright Arrow more than Sun Cloud or Gray Eagle. I know the dangers, but I know the courage, daring, and cunning of Bright Arrow."

The four men talked. It was decided that Flaming Star would take Rebecca and the two girls to the Yankton camp, for the Crow would recognize Flaming Star. All knew that speed was vital. If Bright Arrow assumed his Clay Rivera disguise once more, he could fool them. He could enter their camp as a trader, then find a way to rescue Sun Cloud. Windrider asked Flaming Star to take his son Silent Thunder to safety with them. When this illness passed, he would go after them. White Antelope said he would help provide food and protection for Windrider's tepee. The four warriors agreed on the plan, and Bright Arrow left them to find Rebecca, to persuade her that the plan was best for all.

He found her in the woods, sitting near a stream and staring into the troubled water. He dropped to one knee beside her. "We must talk, Rebecca," he stated gently. "I know you have faced many dangers and torments, but I must make you understand and help me. I cannot change what has happened here. The danger had passed in the Cheyenne camp, but not for Sun Cloud or my father or the Oglala camp."

She stood up and glared down into his face. She declared icily, "I hate you. Go, and don't ever return." Tears filled her eyes and ran down her cheeks. Until now, she had locked the grief tightly inside. Until now, she had needed to be strong for others. Again she raced off into the forest to avoid his presence, tears blurring her vision.

Bright Arrow ran after her. When he grabbed her arm to stop her, they struggled until they fell to the ground. He pinned her beneath him. "You must hear my words!" he demanded urgently.

Rebecca fought wildly for freedom. "Let go of me! I hate you! I don't need you anymore!" she screamed at him.

"I need you. I love you," he asserted honestly and tenderly.

"You have a strange way of showing such feelings!" she shouted. "She's dead. Why weren't you here to save her?" she asked cruelly.

Bright Arrow sadly replied, "If I had been here, my heart, I could not have saved Moon Eyes. Is that not true? Perhaps I would be sick or dead. Is that what you wish for revenge—my life?" He sighed. "I loved her, as I love Little Feet and Tashina. I cannot bring her back, my heart. Do not punish us for her death." His dark eyes glistened with restrained tears, and his voice quavered. "Many nights I dreamed of you; I felt your spirit calling out to me. I longed to see you. I sensed danger in my lands. I was returning home to you when Flaming Star found me and told me of the sickness and death here. He told me of my father's wound and my brother's capture. I love you and need you, Rebecca. Must I sacrifice Sun Cloud's life and safety to prove it? Tell me why I am needed here more than another place, and I will remain. Do you wish their blood on our heads? If I refuse to help them, there would be no going back to my people in such dishonor and shame. Tell me what I must do to save our love."

Rebecca's writhing body halted its desperate movements. She could not ignore or deny the anguish on his face or in his voice. It was wrong to hurt him intentionally, spitefully. More tears gathered in her somber eyes and slipped into her hair. "Why must we be punished in this cruel way? Haven't we suffered enough? When will it be over, Bright Arrow? I hunger for peace and happiness once more."

"I know, my heart," he murmured tenderly. Drawing her into his comforting embrace, he held her tightly. "How I long to give you such things. I do all I can, but it is not enough. Tell me what path I must walk," he entreated, the words wrested from his soul.

Rebecca shifted to gaze up into his handsome face, now lined with worry and consternation. He was right; there was nothing vital he could do here. She sensed his turmoil. "I will do as you ask," she told him. "Perhaps saving Sun Cloud is the answer to ending our troubles."

"I cannot go if I will lose your love," he told her.

"I have loved you since we first met. I will love you forever. Forgive my harsh and cruel words; they were not true. Do what you must, my love, and return to me," she encouraged sincerely.

His lips covered hers in a kiss filled with deep love and gratitude. Their embrace lengthened until passions kindled within bodies too long denied of a union. At this time, they needed each other completely. He looked into her darkened eyes and asked, "Will you yield to me before we part?"

She smiled and nodded. He arose, took her hand, and pulled her to her feet. They walked a short distance to a more private place sheltered by trees. His fingers trembled as he undressed her. While spreading kisses over her face and each breast, he deftly removed his own garments. Gently he pressed her to the ground, and soon their bodies were lovingly entwined. As he teased and tantalized her quivering flesh, she pleaded for his entry. His manhood slipped into her moist and receptive body, and he moved gingerly, his passion raging wildly, almost uncontrollably.

The blissful tension mounted. Rebecca eagerly responded to his consuming kisses and stimulating movements. "Come, ride the stallion of love with me," he murmured huskily into her ear.

Their movements blended in a perfect rhythm, and as she moaned in anticipation, she heard an answering sound build in his throat. Each strived to pleasure the other, and soon, the rapturous peak was attained. They savored the triumphant moment as long as possible, then let it slowly fade away into peaceful contentment, remaining locked in each other's arms. They were bittersweetly aware that another such union would be long in coming, and they clung to this one until the afternoon shadows lengthened.

Later, they refreshed themselves in the stream, then redressed. Bright Arrow pulled Rebecca into his arms once more. Without words, he held her for a long time, then kissed her tenderly. "No matter what happens after this sun, I will never let you go. You are my life, my heart, my breath. If I must choose between you and my old life once more, I know I cannot live without my heart and breath. If my people refuse you in my life, I must refuse them. This I have learned and accepted since my return to my lands. Do you agree to remain my woman?"

Sheer ecstasy enveloped Rebecca, and tears of joy flooded her golden brown eyes. "I will always be your woman," she vowed, hugging him fiercely. "Please be careful, my love. If you do not return from the Crow camp, I will surely die without you. Why must I go so far away? Why can't I wait for you here?"

"I must know you and our children are safe from all evils. I give my word of honor to return safely to your side," he promised. He didn't want to spoil this beautiful moment by telling her his other motive—that he wanted her away from Windrider. He wanted his friend to be susceptible to Bonnie, the object of his vision quest. Once Windrider accepted Bonnie, his enchantment with Rebecca would end, and this would be best for all of them. Too, he feared the Crow might attack the Cheyenne while they were too weak to protect themselves and their camp. He didn't want Rebecca and his children taken captive or perhaps even slain during a raid; nor was he convinced that this disease was fully conquered. He couldn't leave them in peril again, for, to insure victory, he had to have his full attention on himself and Sun Cloud. Bright Arrow breathed a prayer of thanks to the Great Spirit that Rebecca was willing to leave.

Rebecca snuggled against his strong shoulder as they walked back toward camp. She smiled as she wondered if his jealousy of Windrider was behind his urgency to see her gone from the Cheyenne warrior's sight. Still, she would try to persuade him to leave her here. There was no danger of her falling in love with his friend, or of her succumbing to him. Even if she had to live here in another tepee and wait for occasional visits from her love, she would. She felt sure that, with persistence and intelligence, they would find a way to be together forever. She wanted to be close by when this new mission was over, for winter was approaching, and she didn't want them to be separated or stranded by it. She knew that traveling in winter could be as perilous as entering the Crow camp.

Chapter Nineteen

When Rebecca and Bright Arrow returned, the perceptive Windrider noted that something was different between them. On his arrival, Bright Arrow had been distant and cool toward Rebecca, for he had been distracted by other matters. But whatever Bright Arrow had said or done in the forest had brought to both countenances looks of love and commitment.

Windrider's spirits sagged, for he was now certain he would never have Rebecca Kenny. Clearly his two friends loved and needed each other, and this perception cooled some of his passion for her. He was a man accustomed to accepting the inevitable, the unchangeable. The possessive look he saw in Bright Arrow's eyes told Windrider that his Sioux friend would never discard this special woman. Windrider couldn't deny they were perfect for each other, and he resolved to find the strength and courage to master his feelings for her. Grandfather was never wrong; it was meant that he seek his new woman elsewhere.

He glanced over at Bonnie as she tended the last of Little Turtle's sores. He noticed the gentleness in her voice and touch. He allowed himself to study her intensely. She was beautiful. She was brave and smart. She, too, was a special woman. In astonishment, he realized his body was warming and responding to what he saw! He grinned in satisfaction, for the white girl belonged to him. Perhaps he had been drawn to Rebecca at a time when he was lonely and vulnerable, a time when she felt the same emotions and needs. Perhaps he had confused affection, respect, and physical appeal with love. Perhaps it was meant that Rebecca be nothing more than his friend, a comforter and helper during a hard time, a woman to open his eyes and senses to new feelings. He was acutely aware that budding affection for Bonnie was making his loss of Rebecca easier.

Windrider made a decision. While Rebecca and Bright Arrow were gone, he would delve into this mystery and learn more about Bonnie Thorne. He would discover how she affected him; he would see how he affected her. He had slain her people and destroyed her possessions; he had captured her and almost traded her. How did she view him? Was she the faceless woman in his vision? Had the heavens painted their signs on her as promised? How could he argue with the messages given for his quest? Everything in his vision pointed to Bonnie. Could he resist Grandfather's will? And now, did he want to?

The sun seemed to blaze to life within her hair, he mused, as if it had stolen some of that golden orb's glow and color. Her skin was as white as snow, as soft as a white ermine pelt, and her eyes were as blue and clear as Grandfather's sky covering. She only stood as high as his heart, small and delicate for one so strong. He was glad he had not been cruel to her. He recalled the terror in her sky eyes when he had pursued her into the woods and captured her. He remembered how she had bravely tried to flee from his tepee and her ensuing wisdom in bowing to his power. He was called a handsome and virile man and a great warrior. He could win her affection and respect! He could win her heart! He had to force his desire for Rebecca from his mind and body. She belonged to another, by her own will. He hoped the Sioux council would realize that Bright Arrow and Rebecca should remain together. If not, he would keep his word and take her into his tepee. Two special women would not be a burden for a strong and healthy male, but it would be best for each warrior to have his own unique woman.

Bright Arrow, Flaming Star, and White Antelope spent that next day hunting game for Windrider's camp. Rebecca gathered her belongings and prepared to leave early the next morning. Without getting too close, she spoke with Windrider, thanking him for all he had done. "I could not have survived these last months of trouble and sadness without your friendship and help. I shall miss you greatly, Windrider. Do not worry about the sickness; Bonnie will care for you and any others who become ill. She is a very special woman, with many good traits and talents. Be kind to her, my friend, and allow nothing and no one to harm her. She adds good fortune to your life and tepee. Until this dark evil has left your tepee and camp, please obey her words. I could not bear for this foe to take the life of one such as you."

Their gazes fused as they shared this bittersweet parting. "No matter the distance between us, our bond will always be strong and alive. I will pray for you to have all happy moons." Did she also feel Bonnie was the woman for him? he wondered. That speculation touched him. An unspoken message had passed between them, each feeling it was not meant that they share life together. They exchanged smiles. Both were glad they had not surrendered to their physical desires, to stolen ecstasy.

"You have renewed the life in my heart and body. I shall not forget our suns and moons. If death strikes my friend, return to my tepee," he told Rebecca. "Do you return my gift?" he mischievously asked, nodding toward Bonnie, who was too far away to overhear their words.

"Yes. She belongs at Windrider's side," she stated boldly, then blushed. "I will take care of Silent Thunder until our return," she hastily added, trying to change the subject in fear she had spoken too freely.

"Does she agree? Does she not hate the man who captured her?" he asked in such a way as to make his implication clear to her.

Rebecca laughed merrily. It felt wonderful to be happy once more. "Only as much as I hate the warrior who captured me," she teased. "You stole her eye and heart that first day! Let her love you, Windrider. Let yourself love her," she encouraged. "For you there will be much joy, for it does not matter to the Cheyenne that she is white. Send White Antelope and Little Turtle into your tepee; they are healed enough. Be alone with her; claim her."

"You are wise and kind, Rebecca Kenny. I am honored to know such a friend. I will do as you say. And if . . ." he began, then faltered as he wondered if he should mar her happiness by mentioning a looming possibility.

"If what?" she pressed, watching him closely.

"If the Oglalas reject you, you are welcome in my tepee," he offered as gently as he could.

She smiled. "You are generous and honorable, my friend, but Bright Arrow has told me he will not choose his tribe over his family. We will see what a new sun holds for us."

"It is good. Love is rare and powerful. It should not be tossed away at the blindness and selfishness of others. You opened my eyes to such truths and feelings. I will seek a love as you and Bright Arrow share. May Grandfather watch over you."

They parted, unaware of the perils they would face separately and together in the future . . .

Rebecca sought out Bonnie. Both woman wished they could hug each other in farewell and speak privately, but they dared not touch. They talked for a time, and Rebecca told her, "There is something you must know, Bonnie. I love Windrider only as a friend, nothing more. I will share my life and love only with Bright Arrow. Whatever happens in his camp, he will not desert me. Windrider also views me as his friend, nothing more," she added purposefully, then smiled.

Bonnie stared at her. "Do I hear you correctly? There is nothing between you and Windrider? He does not love and desire you?"

She playfully responded, "I know a lovely captive has captured his attention, but I think he's afraid she hates and fears him."

"That isn't true," Bonnie hastily protested. "Why didn't you tell him?" she implored nervously.

"I think it would be better if you showed him," Rebecca mischievously suggested. "He asked if White Antelope and Little Turtle were well enough to return to his tepee. I wonder if he wants to be alone with his enchanting doctor . . ." Rebecca shrugged and laughed.

"Please don't tease me, Rebecca. Whatever would I say to him while we're alone?" she asked modestly.

"Be yourself," Rebecca told her.

"What if he doesn't like me?" she fretted.

"It's too late for that. What's more romantic than sleeping together under the moon and stars? Take this chance and use it, Bonnie. If you want him, go after him," she advised seriously.

"I do want him," Bonnie dreamily confessed.

"Good, because I believe he wants you." Rebecca responded with confidence.

"I could hug you and kiss you, Rebecca Kenny. I will when you return. I need a bath and hair-washing," she stated wistfully.

"So do I. We'll stand guard for each other. We'll probably chill our fannies in that water, but it will be worth it. I'll fetch my things."

On October seventh, Bright Arrow, Rebecca, Flaming Star, and three children left Windrider's camp. They would travel together to the Sans Arc camp, and there Flaming Star would borrow a boat and hire several braves to accompany them on their journey to Yankton. Bright Arrow would become Clay Rivera and travel to the Crow camp.

In Windrider's camp, White Antelope and Little Turtle would scrub their bodies and burn all their belongings, then move into the tepee with Sucoora. Together, the three would begin preparing for winter. In the lean-to, Windrider and Bonnie would spend their first day in privacy, talking and subtly enticing each other. Their first night alone would be spent surrendering to fiery passions, passions that would inspire the planting of the seeds for Windrider's next child within her receptive body. Before the night passed, each would experience the birth of love and powerful desire. By the next morning, Windrider would yield to fiery fever as the disease challenged him and Bonnie to a vicious battle for his life.

The little group traveled all day, making only two stops for rest and food. Bright Arrow knew he was pushing his family hard, but he appreciated Rebecca's help and understanding. By the ninth, they had reached the Sans Arc camp. Hearing of the actions of the Crow, the chief and braves were angered and agreed to help. Arrangements were made for a boat and two braves. Bright Arrow bid his love and children farewell just before dusk. He told Rebecca he would have to ride all night to make up time. They hugged and kissed, then she watched silently as he rode away.

Flaming Star, Rebecca, Silent Thunder, and the two girls spent the night in the chief's tepee. Early the next morning, they stepped into a canoe loaded with supplies and began the next leg of their journey. They assumed that Bright Arrow would reach the Crow camp two days after they reached the Yankton village.

Flaming Star watched over Rebecca and the girls carefully. The trip down the Bad River to the Missouri, then down the Missouri to the Yankton village was an easy one, without trouble or discomfort. On their arrival, Flaming Star explained Bright Arrow's wishes to the Yankton.

Chief Red Tomahawk welcomed Rebecca and the girls to his tepee. He told them they could remain there with his wife while he and his son Six Feathers went to the fall trading camp between the James River and the Big Sioux River. There, members of many tribes would meet to bargain with each other and with white traders. They would smoke pipes, relate the news, and share plans for the winter. There would be games and contests, dances and a large feast.

Red Tomahawk told them of the great leaders who would soon assemble. Red Thunder of the Sisseton tribe would be present. Black Buffalo of the Minneconjou never missed a trading fair. Tamaha, the one-eyed Wahpeton chief, was coming this time. Wamdesapa, chief of the Wahpekute, hated whites but traded with them. Turkey Head of the Two Kettle would arrive with great show. Kicking Bear of the Brule would bring many warriors and women, as usual. Robert Dickson from the British trading post, Jean Truteau of the Spanish trading post, and other white traders would be there with many items. It was a festive time, the last before winter.

Rebecca and her girls were settled into Red Tomahawk's tepee, though she felt uncomfortable among these strangers. She begged Flaming Star to take them back to the Cheyenne camp, but he politely and firmly refused. He told her he would be leaving at first light to return to his camp and help his people battle their enemies. He promised to come for her as soon as Bright Arrow returned safely.

Before the sun rose above the horizon the next day, Flaming Star and the Sans Arc braves had gone, as had the chief and his son. Pierre Dorion, a Frenchman who had been living with the Yanktons since 1784, accompanied Red Tomahawk and Six Feathers.

Pierre hoped to see his old friends: Joseph Garreau, who lived with the Arikaras, James Murdock, who had promised to return this way when Lewis and Clark left the Dakota Territory, and Billy Culpepper. Pierre hadn't seen him since Billy had gone looking for Jess Thomas and Lester Paul, his best friends and fellow trappers, who had vanished mysteriously in early summer. Pierre had heard the three men talking at the trading post on Lake Traverse and he wondered if they had rashly gone after Clay Rivera's secret gold supply. If so, they were fools. Any one who had lived in this area all of his life should know who lurked behind that false identity and avoid him like a demon of Hell! Perhaps he should have warned

Billy to stay clear of "Clay Rivera." What Pierre Dorion couldn't figure out was why Rebecca Kenny was a guest of the Yankton chief. With a little nosing around at the trading camp, he was certain the answer would soon be his.

Along the Cheyenne River, Bright Arrow met with luck. He happened on the camp of a white trader and his Brule squaw. He knew what had to be done. He secretly waited until dark, then rendered both unconscious. He stole only enough trade goods to carry off his role, then swiftly put a great distance between the camp and himself. To prevent any recognition, Bright Arrow took a mirror and a sharp knife and cut his hair above the collar on his calico shirt, then he slipped into the dark breeches and black knee boots. He struggled to fasten the suspenders, finally succeeding. He pulled on a leather vest and black felt hat and checked himself up and down. Then he concealed all the items that would prove him "Indian." He was now Clay Rivera; he was ready.

Bright Arrow had one excellent advantage in this difficult situation; the Crow were friendly with most whites, especially traders. He had fooled whites for years with his claim of being half-Spanish and half-Indian. He spoke the white tongue fluently, and he did have a half-white heritage, which revealed itself even more in these clothes and hairstyle than in buckskins and braids. There was one slight disadvantage; he didn't know what his brother looked like, for he hadn't seen Sun Cloud since he was a small baby. Even that problem had a brighter side. His younger brother didn't know him either and therefore couldn't expose him to the Crow!

He wondered who Sun Cloud favored—his father or

mother. He cautioned himself to be patient, for he couldn't enter the camp asking too many suspicious questions. He would have to play the trader who was ready for a rest with his new friends. He would make certain his hatred and fury didn't reveal themselves. And even if he lost his life, he had to free his brother, the next Oglala chief.

There was nothing more he could do to prepare for his daring ruse. He mounted up, took the reins of the packmule, and headed for the Crow camp. A sense of adventure charged his body, for the thought of tricking the Crow brought him immense pleasure. Suspense and excitement coursed through his veins, and he had to keep reminding himself that this wasn't a casual mission, but a life-saving rescue.

Bright Arrow nonchalantly rode into the Crow camp. Women, children, and braves gathered around to see his wares. Dismounting near one of the trees scattered throughout the camp, he secured the reins of his horse and mule, unloaded the supplies, and spread them on blankets as he had seen the traders do countless times. He told the women to browse freely, then sat down and waited for the chief to appear. A trader never approached a chief; he had to wait for an invitation to speak and visit with such a powerful man.

It wasn't long before several warriors came over to him. "Clay Rivera" met Lone Horn, White Quiver, and Sly Hunter. He learned that the war chief, Big Thunder, was off on a raid of the Oglala camp. Bright Arrow warned himself to expose no emotion. Head chief Arapoosh joined them. He was dressed in buckskin breeches and a red shirt with ermine trim. They sat down to bargain.

As was normal, Bright Arrow gave Chief Arapoosh his

choice of a gift. The man took another red shirt, the sign of a Crow chief in battle. Bright Arrow tried to prevent his hands from shaking in eagerness to get around the throats of these foes! Rabbit Woman, wife to Sly Hunter, made her deal with Bright Arrow. She called over a small boy to carry the items to her tepee. Bright Arrow casually noticed the action, thinking nothing of it until the woman roughly shoved the child and called him insulting names.

The chief and warriors laughed and elbowed each other. "The son of Gray Eagle is weak and womanly," Sly Hunter taunted. "I will teach him more cowardice and his new place before I sell him," he boasted.

Bright Arrow tensed inside. He casually studied the child's face and noted which tepee he served. He swallowed his fury and declared, "You are a brave man, Sly Hunter. All say Gray Eagle is matchless. You prove such tales false. You must choose a gift for your courage and daring. I have met few such great warriors. If you wish to sell the boy, I am in need of a slave to help me and serve me."

Sly Hunter grinned, then invited the trader to share his evening meal. He selected a new hunting knife. Bright Arrow continued, "You must tell me of such a daring deed. Why has word of such a glorious warrior not spread over the land?" Bright Arrow inquired, feigning false respect and awe.

"I rode with my Pawnee friend Snake Tongue. We sneaked close to the Oglala camp. Gray Eagle was hunting with his son. Before I could slay them, Snake Tongue put an arrow through Gray Eagle's chest. I wished to take his scalp, but others came to help him. I seized the boy and rode away. We will use the boy to take the Oglala territory. If Gray Eagle still lives, we will trade the boy for him. We will torture him and make him plead for mercy. I will be the one to remove his skin and hair while he still lives. We will conquer them and enslave them. Sun Cloud will not become the Oglala chief. He will die as did his brother Bright Arrow," he sneered.

"I have not lived in this area many years. I did not know Gray Eagle had another son. He does not allow whites, or half-whites, to enter his camp," Bright Arrow added to further mislead his enemies.

The warriors laughed heartily. "Bright Arrow captured a white girl. His people would not let him keep her. He took her and ran away. She killed him and escaped to her people. He has been dead many winters. He would have been no match for Sly Hunter. His hunger for an enemy defeated him." Again, the men laughed and elbowed each other.

"When I return in the spring, I will seek Sly Hunter and his tribe on the lands of the Oglala," Bright Arrow remarked cleverly, flattering them.

"If Gray Eagle does not die, we will use his son as bait. We will lure him into our trap and capture him. If others join the Oglala to give them strength to battle the Crow, we will slay the boy before their eyes," Lone Horn snarled.

"We will conquer them before the winter snows cover our lands," White Quiver added.

Bright Arrow knew that many items were being stolen from his trader's pack, but he pretended not to notice. When he left this camp hurriedly, he would have to leave everything behind. He packed up the trade goods and stored them near the tree, supposedly showing his trust in the Crow. He told everyone present they could examine the goods on the new day and bargain for them, then followed Sly Hunter to his tepee.

It didn't take long for Bright Arrow to learn that Sun Cloud was not being brutalized by these enemies. Instead he was being teased, shoved roughly, insulted, mocked, and forced to labor. The boy noticed the trader but didn't realize who he was. He did as he was ordered, remaining proud and aloof. Bright Arrow was pleased with his brother's wisdom and courage. Gray Eagle had taught his sons well. In time, both would return safely to their father.

Bright Arrow longed to send a secret message to his brother, so that he would not worry or be afraid. He wanted to warn him to be ready to flee at a moment's notice, but he dared not expose himself and endanger them. During his conversation with Sly Hunter that evening, he tried to buy the child again. He offered Sly Hunter and his wife many goods in exchange for a slave who would be helpful and entertaining on his journeys. He claimed he wanted to use the boy to gain attention in other camps, perhaps force him to earn money or goods by performing tricks and dances. The idea of humiliating and abusing the child pleased Sly Hunter.

But the man refused to deal. When the hour grew late, Bright Arrow thanked Sly Hunter for the meal and talk. As he returned to Chief Arapoosh's tepee, he laughed inside at the stupidity of the Crow warrior. He had unknowingly entertained one of his worst enemies! Soon the Crow and all enemies would learn of Bright Arrow's return and his daring! There would be no more false talk, jokes, and laughter about him. He briefly wondered who had started such a false rumor.

Bright Arrow lay on the sleeping mat, thinking and planning. If he could trick Sly Hunter into selling Sun Cloud to him, they could get out of the camp without suspicion or danger. But he realized this was a fool's dream.

Sly Hunter would not trade the valuable son of Gray Eagle. The best thing was to befriend these Crow until they trusted him and ignored his presence. Then he would strike. He would steal his brother right from under their noses and make a daring though perilous escape. His only concern was acting before Sun Cloud was endangered. Lone Horn had joked he would send Gray Eagle a piece of his son each day until he surrendered. Bright Arrow knew his father was a great chief, and a great chief would never yield to foes for any reason. Lone Horn was cold and savage; he might convince the others to take his jest seriously. Proceeding with haste was crucial.

Rebecca had been in the Yankton camp for five days. As a good guest, she helped Laughing Face with her daily chores and her preparations for winter. The wife of Chief Red Tomahawk was a fat and jocular person. The woman often burst into girlish giggles for seemingly no reason, as if she shared some hilarious secret with nature. Because she spoke no English, there was little verbal communication between them.

Laughing Face had begun teaching Rebecca more sign language and a little Nakota. By the time her stay had ended Rebecca would know words in the Lakota and Nakota tongues; only the Dakota tongue would still be unfamiliar. As she studied, she wondered why the Sioux Nation had three dialects. She found that the vocabulary and grammar of the two tongues were similar, which made rudimentary achievements easy for her. The lessons were not complicated but they required patience and memory and practice.

Sign language was the "tongue" used by most tribes

when meeting or trading with others. These swift and deft hand motions were vital for communication during intertribal or international exchanges, for creating alliances, and for settling disputes.

Rebecca studied the signs naming the nearest tribes and practiced them. A slice across the throat with the right hand indicated the Sioux. Two fingers forming a V with the thumb and two smaller fingers folded into the palm on the right hand represented the Pawnee. Twice rubbing the back of the left hand was the sign for Indian. To say Cheyenne, a person made chopping movements on the left index finger from hand to fingertip. For Crow, a person held the flat part of a balled fist to the forehead, with the palm side outward. Laughing Face showed her many other signs, but those identifying tribes seemed the most important to Rebecca.

Little Feet continued to ask Rebecca questions about Moon Eyes; she could not comprehend the meaning of death, of never seeing her sister again. She wanted to know why she had been left behind, covered with dirt. No matter how Rebecca explained this loss, Little Feet talked and acted as if she expected to see her sister arriving at any moment. Each time the question was posed to her, Rebecca was plagued by anguish. She wondered how long it would take for her to accept such a tragedy, or if she ever would. Tashina noticed that her sister was gone, but she was too young to ask where or why. In time, both would forget Moon Eyes; living with death was one of the harsh, demanding terms of existence in the wilderness and on the prairies. Rebecca prayed for her sadness and grief to lessen, for there was no way to return her daughter to life. She had to stop tormenting herself with guilt and agony.

Rebecca hoped Flaming Star had reached home safely;

she had no way of knowing he had arrived that very morning. She couldn't free her mind of one of the conversations they had had during their journey to Red Tomahawk's camp. He had told her that he knew nothing of Cloud Chaser's alleged visits with Bright Arrow's parents and the council, insisting that she was terribly mistaken. He had said that the Oglala tribe knew nothing of her trip near their camp, and that no Oglala—family, friend, or tribesman—knew of Bright Arrow's return to his lands. Finally, he had claimed that the meeting at which she had supposedly been rejected for a second time had never taken place? This was an enigma that demanded questions and answers. Had Cloud Chaser tricked her? Had Windrider aided him in such deceit? It couldn't be true, she told herself. Windrider would never deceive her with words or actions. Yet she couldn't help recalling her initial suspicions about Windrider's motives . . .

Her troubled mind wandered to Bright Arrow. She prayed for his prompt return, for his survival, for his success. She tried to envision him in the camp of the Crow; she could not. She tried to imagine how he would act and what he would say. She worried that he would expose his hostility and fury. She fretted over Sun Cloud giving away his charade, then recalled that the child couldn't possibly recognize his older brother. She knew how Bright Arrow looked, for she had seen him as Clay Rivera many times. She became so deeply enmeshed in thoughts of Bright Arrow's safety and survival that she failed to notice the perils that were rapidly surrounding her . . .

Rebecca needn't have worried over Bright Arrow, for

his plan was progressing satisfactorily. It was his third day in the Crow village, the day for action. He had traded or given away many of the goods on the mule, and he no longer had a logical reason to remain in the Crow camp. He wished he could carry the trade furs to his Cheyenne friends who needed them, but the mule and goods would slow his pace during an escape. He would have to leave by the next day or risk exposing himself. Though he craved revenge on these cold-blooded warriors, his major concern was getting his brother home.

The Crow chief Arapoosh had gone on a raid, and Bright Arrow hungrily eyed his war shield. It was made of thick buffalo hide, and a painting of a man wearing an eagle-bone breastplate filled the center. *Coup* feathers, a rabbit's foot, and a weasel tail decorated the outer edges. Bright Arrow's longing gaze shifted to Arapoosh's eagle-feather warbonnet, which was worn only during major battles or special ceremonies. Indians of any tribe understood the markings and colors of other tribe's feathers; during a battle, the bravest warriors searched for the enemy warriors who wore large warbonnets or many *coup* feathers. Bright Arrow ached to steal either or both prized possessions before he escaped.

He reminisced on his days as a warrior. Following his accomplishment of a brave and daring deed, a warrior was questioned by the council. If he spoke the truth and had in fact performed a valiant deed, he was given a *coup* feather or permission to wear one of those he had collected. No matter how many feathers a brave collected, he could never wear them without first obtaining approval of the council following a special act of courage or daring. The same was true of eagle's talons or bear claws; a warrior had to verbally prove his right to wear them, for they were signs of immense prowess.

The most prized *coup* feather was from the golden eagle, a bird honored for its cunning, speed, and courage. *Coup* feathers were placed in a warrior's scalp lock or in a leather headband, and could be worn together or separately. The markings and colors on a *coup* feather revealed the nature of the deed the warrior had done to win it; a *coup* feather could relate the entire story of a daring exploit. When a warrior possessed enough *coup* feathers, he could make a warbonnet. This custom was confusing to many whites, for they erroneously believed that a warbonnet was worn only by a chief. Whites were also ignorant about the role of chief. A tribe had many chiefs: a head chief, a ceremonial chief, a war chief, a medicine chief, and sometimes more than one of each, with the exception of the position of head chief. Gray Eagle was a head chief.

When a brave first entered the Warrior Society and earned a *coup* feather, it was a happy occasion and was eagerly celebrated by all. At special ceremonies, the warrior or his best friend would chant his past deeds of glory. Even greater honor came in capturing an enemy's possessions while counting *coup* on him. An enemy's horse, his weapons, his prayer pipe, his medicine bundle, his ceremonial garments and sacred items, his necklace and armbands, or any other belongings clearly marked by his symbols and colors of ownership were highly prized. To capture Arapoosh's warbonnet of *coup* feathers or to steal those of other high-ranking Crow warriors would be a tremendous feat of cunning and daring. To also carry home shields, lances, and horses would bring Bright Arrow great honor and glory. To obtain a Crow medicine bundle from a Crow tepee would be a dream come true, a deed beyond imagination, a deed no Oglala could match, for to take a warrior's *pezuta wopahte* also meant to take his life and scalp lock.

The thrill of victory and the suspense and stimulation of danger throbbed within Bright Arrow's powerful and agile body. He was anxious to begin his daring game. As he had anticipated, Sly Hunter had refused to sell or make trade for Sun Cloud. Bright Arrow had chuckled and told him that the boy was probably too delicate and arrogant to make a good and strong helper. He hinted at his concern that some Oglala warrior might follow him and slay him to free the boy. He hadn't mentioned the boy again, though he had furtively observed his brother, his movements and his treatment. So far, the only harm had been to Sun Cloud's pride. Bright Arrow continued his vigilance, waiting for the perfect moment to begin his bold flight.

Luck aided him again. Sly Hunter and Lone Horn asked "Clay Rivera" to go hunting with them, suggesting he could use fresh game to trade for traveling supplies. Excitement and utter delight charged over him. The three mounted up and rode across the meadow toward the hills.

Bright Arrow knew what he was going to do on this hunting trip; he was going to kill both warriors. They rode for a time, entering an area where large rock formations covered much of the landscape. Sly Hunter instructed them to separate and search for a small group of elk or white-tail deer grazing in grassy areas between the boulders. The signal to be given to alert the other two hunters would be a bird call. Sly Hunter spent a few minutes teaching it to "Clay Rivera." When Bright Arrow pretended to give the whistle adequately, Sly Hunter warned him to be careful of his scent and noise. Then they went their separate ways.

Bright Arrow secured his horse's reins to a scraggly

bush and stealthily trailed Lone Horn on foot. The Sioux warrior silently and curiously observed the Crow warrior as he dismounted and gathered his weapons. It took but a moment to realize what the man intended—to circle around behind him and murder *him!* This hunt was a guileful trick! Bright Arrow eased behind a large boulder and, drawing his hunting knife, he waited for the devious Crow to approach his hiding place. As Lone Horn sneaked around the lofty rocks, Bright Arrow clapped a hand over his mouth and skillfully sliced through his jugular vein. Using his strength, skill, and resolve, he prevented the man's outcry and movement. The warrior struggled vainly for freedom and life. When he went limp, Bright Arrow let him slide silently to the ground. He shoved the body into a narrow opening in the rocks, planning to cover it with Sly Hunter's, then conceal both from view.

Bright Arrow knew that if Lone Horn was trying to ambush him, Sly Hunter must also be in on the scheme. He should have realized this hunting trip was a trap. He berated his lack of attention and caution. Slipping between the rocks, he kept alert for Sly Hunter's attack. As his keen ears detected a snap of a dead branch around the next boulder, he instantly flattened himself against the huge rock. He glimpsed a feather first, then a dark head of hair. But the man who stepped into view was not Sly Hunter; it was White Quiver. They had planned this trap cleverly, to kill the trader and divide his remaining goods. Again Bright Arrow seized his enemy by the mouth. This time, he angrily slammed his sharp hunting knife into the foe's back. He twisted the blade until the man's knees buckled. Fury surged through him, and he tossed the body aside to seek the leader, the man who had enslaved his brother and planned his death.

He could not allow Sly Hunter to escape and return to the village. If this were to happen, he would never be able to get near Sun Cloud. He strained to hear every sound. As he ducked behind a clump of dried bushes, he was careful not to cause their leaves to rustle. He listened, watched, and waited. Surely Sly Hunter would appear at any moment. Moments passed, and he knew he couldn't afford to hesitate longer. He went in search of his foe.

With a war cry, Sly Hunter jumped from atop a boulder and attacked Bright Arrow. Alert and nimble, the Sioux warrior threw himself aside, causing Sly Hunter to miss his target. Both men held knives. They crouched and circled each other, their acute senses alive with anticipation and perception. They studied each other, knowing it was best to pick out an opponent's weaknesses and strengths before rashly attacking him. Keen eyes analyzed the foe—his movements, his expressions, the situation.

When his friends did not appear after his loud shout, the astute Sly Hunter guessed why. He observed this deadly and skillful challenger. In broken English, Sly Hunter snarled, "You kill White Quiver, Lone Horn. Sly Hunter kill you. You no trader. You fight like soldier. You half-breed. Speak name before die."

"I killed my enemies Lone Horn and White Quiver," the Oglala warrior replied smugly. "I will take the life and scalp lock of Sly Hunter. I am Bright Arrow, son of Gray Eagle, brother to Sun Cloud. You will die, Crow dog," he warned ominously, his black eyes cold and confident.

A shudder of fear and disbelief washed over the man. "Bright Arrow dead. You lie," he declared nervously.

"Do I look dead, Sly Hunter?" he mocked. "I was

banished for taking a white woman to my mat and side. I have lived as a trapper for many winters. I have returned to my lands. I will avenge my father and my brother. No Crow will dare to attack us when they learn I have returned and slain three of their best warriors."

"Sly Hunter no die quick. I fight, slay two sons of Gray Eagle," he boasted, then lunged at his foe.

Bright Arrow stepped aside, causing the man to stagger past him. With a sharp blow from his elbow to the back of Sly Hunter's neck, he sent the Crow warrior sprawling roughly to the rocky ground. He rolled over, prepared for Bright Arrow's attack. Instead, he saw the Sioux warrior standing with his hands on his hips and grinning down at him. "If you are a man, stand and fight as one. Do not slither on the ground as a lowly snake," he taunted, then laughed insultingly.

The humiliated warrior jumped to his feet. He carelessly attacked Bright Arrow with blind hatred and distracting fury. They fought for a time, exchanging blows and shoves. Bright Arrow didn't want to end this enjoyable, thrilling experience too quickly. He was ecstatic to realize he had returned to his full potential and prowess. He felt unbeatable. His pride and self-assurance were limitless.

He played with Sly Hunter, increasing the man's rage. Finally he knew he had to head back to camp. The resting period was the best time to sneak away with his brother. It would be hours before anyone realized three warriors and a slave were missing. He ended the battle with Sly Hunter by stabbing him through his evil heart. He dragged the body over to join the other two, then removed the warriors' possessions from their horses and freed them. He broke all weapons and destroyed their shields and lances, tossing the ruined items on the bodies, satisfied the warriors could not be buried with them. He collected the scalp lock, medicine bundle, *coup* feathers, and necklace of each Crow warrior. Bright Arrow hid the items in the bundle on his horse, then concealed the bodies with brush and rode back to the Crow camp.

He couldn't risk stealing Arapoosh's shield and war-bonnet, much as he craved them. He wanted to enter the tepees of all three warriors and destroy any possessions there, but he dared not respond to that wild desire. He had avenged his family. Now he had to hurry. He would fetch his brother and leave this place. Nonchalantly, he headed for Sly Hunter's tepee. Fortunately, he met with no trouble. He ducked and entered the tepee, finding only two sleeping children; both were Crow.

He couldn't resist destroying Sly Hunter's belong-ings. To conceal the deed as long as possible, he covered them with a blanket. He sneaked outside, wondering where he could find Rabbit Woman and Sun Cloud. He casually strolled around the camp as he searched for them. When he saw the chubby woman trudging behind his brother, he stepped out of sight, just in case Sly Hunter had disclosed his plans to murder and rob him. He watched them enter the tepee and quickly followed.

The dull-witted woman stared at him. A person did not enter another's tepee without permission, but since the trader had become a friend of her husband's, there was no reason to be afraid or mean. She simply assumed he didn't know Indian customs and was seeking her husband. He approached her, smiling with false warmth, holding out a mirror in a gift-giving gesture. The woman grinned, revealing two missing teeth. As she ad-mired herself, Bright Arrow clubbed her lightly with a rock he had hidden behind his back. He caught her, al-

413

lowing her to sink quietly to the ground rather than fall roughly or noisily. He quickly bound the woman's ankles and wrists, then gagged her. He glanced at the two children; they were still slumbering peacefully.

Bright Arrow turned and smiled at the boy, then placed his finger over his lips for silence. Sun Cloud had been watching this man in great suspense and surprise. The man dropped to one knee before him and drew his ear close to his mouth. In Oglala, the fearless warrior revealed himself and his mission. "I am Bright Arrow, your brother. I come to take you home. You must obey my words without question or hesitation. It is good to see you alive and safe, my little brother."

The boy threw his arms round the man's neck and hugged him. "My brother is brave and cunning. Father was killed by a Pawnee when I was taken," he whispered sadly in a voice quavering with emotion.

In a low tone, Bright Arrow told him, "Father is wounded, but he lives, Sun Cloud. I have returned home to help my people against their enemies. Come, we must go quickly. You will be my trade bundle. Remain still and silent. Move for no reason—no reason, my brother. Breathing will be hard until we are out of the village. You are brave and strong. We will escape," he encouraged the child.

Again, he cautioned the astonished boy to keep quiet and obey his orders instantly. Sun Cloud obeyed fully and promptly. The Sioux warrior took a blanket and rolled Sun Cloud inside of it. He secured it with long thongs to make it appear to be a bundle of goods. Carefully he placed the precious burden over his shoulder, then calmly and casually walked to his horse, grateful it was the sluggish time of day. He loaded the priceless bundle on his horse, in case he had to make a run for safety. Then he mounted and led the mule from camp. Two miles away, he severed the thongs and freed his brother. Jumping to the ground, he unloaded the mule and set the beast loose.

He placed Sly Hunter's *wanapin* around Sun Cloud's neck. He didn't have to reveal the name or fate of its past owner. He showed his brother the items he had stolen, saying the medicine bundles were for Gray Eagle, to give him more power and strength. The boy was amazed by his brother's courage, daring, and cunning. Pride and love filled his heart. Taking only the necessary supplies and new possessions, Bright Arrow placed Sun Cloud before him and galloped toward home.

Chapter Twenty

Princess Shalee sat on the mat beside her sleeping husband, Gray Eagle. It had been twenty-three days since he had been wounded. For a time, she had believed and feared he would die. Never before had she been so afraid, so aware of her love and need for him. When he finally started responding to medicines and treatments, he had attempted to leave his mat and go after their youngest son. The only way she could keep him down was by drugging him lightly without his knowledge. She knew that if he rode off in this condition, he would never make it to the Crow camp, much less rescue their child. She despised tricking him, making him believe he was weaker than he actually was, but it was necessary, and she would continue doing so until he recovered fully. She could bear no more losses.

The woman who was once Gray Eagle's white captive, Alisha Williams, boldly asked the medicine chief to call the council together. It was past time to intervene for her oldest son, to halt this madness, to make a truce and to find peace for all! Mind-Who-Roams looked at her strangely, probingly, then smiled in comprehension. His instinctive understanding never ceased to amaze and mystify her. Seeing his expression, she smiled and ventured, "You know what must be done?"

He nodded, then affectionately patted her shoulder.

"It is time, Shalee. I will send out the call for council."

Shalee entered the ceremonial lodge, raising eyebrows and creating many a stare. Holding her head high and summoning her courage, she walked over to stand at Mind-Who-Roams' side. The medicine chief and visionary told the council that she wished to speak with them. The men listened reluctantly, yet with curiosity.

She prayed her voice would hold steady and positive during this crucial speech as she began, "I know a woman does not take part in the council meetings and votes. This time, it must be done. There is much I must say to you. My husband, your chief, lies wounded. Our son is a captive of our enemy the Crow. The Crow and Pawnee bite viciously at our camp. I have come to speak for mercy and truce."

The men exchanged bewildered glances, thinking she was referring to their two foes. "My other son was banished for choosing to love a white woman and share his life with her. Bright Arrow is in the Crow camp. He has dressed as a white trader and has gone to rescue his brother, your future chief if he survives. Have you forgotten all my first son has done for his people? Have you forgotten his love for us? He risks his life to help us, even after we turned our faces away from him. He is a warrior. He is an Oglala. He is the son of Gray Eagle. Where is your mercy? Where is your justice and kindness? Have you no understanding, love, or forgiveness for him? Is it so wrong to protect the woman you love? Do we choose who causes our hearts and bodies to burn with love and desire?" she challenged.

"Who among you can swear without a doubt that Rebecca was not chosen for Bright Arrow by the Great Spirit? And if this is so, can we resist Grandfather's wishes any longer? Why do you punish him for obeying

Grandfather, for following his guidance? Can such a pure and strong and unselfish love be evil? Who are you to judge Bright Arrow's actions and feelings? Have you forgotten his courage? His daring and cunning? Have you forgotten his blood and value?" Her entreating gaze went from one man to the next as she spoke from her heart.

"Can you deny Rebecca loves him beyond her own pride and life? Was she not willing to live among us, to call us friends and family? Was she not willing to accept our feelings and words against her in order to be at his side? Is not such love uncontrollable? Unselfish? Can she change her white skin? Can she cease her love for my son? Can he cease his love and need for her? Many winters have passed. Many have suffered from this punishment. Is it not time to halt the pain and sadness? Is it not time to open our hearts to forgiveness and understanding? Can we show no mercy and justice for him?"

She sank to her knees, not wishing to tower over them. Her voice held notes of pleading, firmness, urgency, and disappointment. She revealed Rebecca's help to the Cheyenne. "Is this the action of an enemy of the Indian? Why must we be cruel and blind? Grandfather should decide whether or not she lives at Bright Arrow's side. In his fevers, many times my husband has called for his sons. Why do you punish your chief by denying him his son, his happiness? Why do you make him choose between his son and his people? This is wrong."

She halted a moment to catch her breath. "Hear me, Oglala, you must unblind your eyes and open your hearts to understanding. You must show mercy and generosity. You have sent all whites from your village; you prevent others from coming. Is this one white girl a threat to us? Bright Arrow should be among his people. He should live by his customs and ways. He should ride at his father's side. He should help protect his people. He loves us. He longs to return. We destroy him by sending him into a white world. Do you hate him so much you wish to see him suffer and die alone? Why must you continue to do this cruel and evil thing? It is time for peace with his family and tribe. It is time for him to come home."

She dared not ponder the men's reactions and thoughts. She had to use her every means of cunning and daring to gain her son's return. "Is it not better to learn about the whites? One day many will enter these lands. The day will come when the Oglala must fight and kill many whites, or learn to make peace with them. Have you forgotten white blood flows in my veins? Have I not been loyal to my husband and his people? In your hearts, do you also hate me and reject me for this white blood? Do you wish to see me banished? You are strong and wise men. Why must you see this one girl as your enemy? Why must you hurt so many with this vote? It is not fair; it is not right."

She related Bright Arrow's experiences with the expedition. "Does a man who rejects his people seek to save them from enemies? He has not rejected us; we sent him away because he could not deny his love or cast her aside. How could you demand he do such a cruel thing?"

"If our sons die in the Crow camp and Gray Eagle does not survive, you will answer to Grandfather when you meet him on the Ghost Trail. What will you say when Grandfather asks why you interfered in his plans for Bright Arrow? Is your pride and hatred larger than Grandfather's power and wishes? How can you banish a great warrior and feel nothing? There are two more children with the blood of Gray Eagle flowing in them. Will you force them to become whites or despised half-breeds? If they had not been sent away, a third daughter would not be dead. We must tell Grandfather why Moon Eyes did not live to see five winters. We must tell Grandfather why a great Sioux warrior lives as a lonely and useless trapper. We must tell Grandfather why the noble and fearless Oglala allowed one tiny white girl to change so many lives, to cause such unnecessary suffering. We must tell Grandfather why we did not ask for his guidance in this grave matter, listening to our own hatred and fear instead of his voice. What will you tell Grandfather when he asks such questions?" she challenged, passing her defiant gaze over each man.

"Bright Arrow knows he cannot become chief. He walks the path he believes Grandfather has made for him. He also believes his place is here with his people. He wants to return to us. My son's daughters should live with us; they should be raised with their people. Do not punish them for their father's action. One has died; we must save the others. Rebecca is willing to send Bright Arrow and the girls home without her, if you once more demand it. Is this not unselfish and powerful love? Do you not remember how she risked her life to rescue him from the old fort? Do you not remember how gentle and kind she is? Do you not recall her obedience, respect, and skills? What more must she do to earn your approval? My son is an honorable man; he will not accept her rejection. To do so would go against Grandfather's message to him. He seeks to earn your forgiveness and acceptance, but he will not beg for them. Will you deny them? If you cannot do this for Bright Arrow, I beg you to do it for his children, for your chief, for Grandfather. In my heart and mind, I know she is the woman for my son. Let them return and join together. The day Rebecca proves unworthy of your trust and acceptance, you can take my life as payment and punishment," she stated bravely, her green eyes glittering with honesty and sincerity.

Shalee lowered her head. Mind-Who-Roams laid his hand on her shoulder and squeezed it comfortingly, declaring, "I say the words of Shalee are true and wise. I say this matter is for Grandfather to settle. The white girl is no threat to the Oglala. Bright Arrow's life and destiny are here with his people and his family. I say he returns." The medicine chief had firmly given his vote and opinion. "I say Bright Arrow rides at Gray Eagle's side until Sun Cloud becomes chief. In my dreams, I have seen these three warriors standing side by side and defending our camp. If it does not come to pass, the Oglala will be destroyed."

One warrior asked, "If we allow this white to enter our camp, others will try to enter. What of the white blood in his daughters?"

Shalee looked up and replied wearily, "Other whites cannot enter if you refuse them. The law against whites did not exist when Bright Arrow took her. His girls will join with Oglala braves; their children will join with Oglala. With each Oglala mating, the white blood will weaken until it is gone. I chose the Oglala over the whites. So will Rebecca if you allow it. Am I not Oglala in heart and mind and existence? It will be the same for Rebecca; I swear it on my life and honor. Do not deny my son his rightful destiny."

Plenty Coups inquired, "What if he does not escape the Crow camp alive? Do you ask us to accept his white woman and his children?"

"If he does not live, there is no need for a vote. Will you reject children of Gray Eagle's blood who are alone and helpless? Is it not true that children belong to the father's people? Rebecca could not care for them or protect them. She would give them to me," Shalee stated confidently, tormented by the possibility.

Cloud Chaser arose and suggested cleverly, "I say the vote belongs to Grandfather. If Bright Arrow escapes with Sun Cloud and returns to our camp, I say it is the sign for our brother's forgiveness and acceptance. I say we must agree with that sign. When we hear his words and deeds, we can vote on his woman." He sat down.

Flaming Star concurred. "I say Cloud Chaser speaks wisely. Grandfather must decide Bright Arrow's destiny." He had no doubt that his friend would succeed in his mission and return. The young warrior went on to reveal what he knew about Rebecca, remaining silent about his suspicions concerning Cloud Chaser. He vowed to watch the devious man carefully and closely, for he sensed something evil in him.

Standing Rock, Kajihah's father, stood up and scoffed, "I say the white girl is evil. She stole the eye of Windrider from my daughter. She casts her evil magic over a Cheyenne warrior, just as she did over Bright Arrow. I say she must not be allowed to enter our camp with her evil magic and potent spells. A great sickness and death came over the Cheyenne camp. Many say the two white women caused it."

Flaming Star jumped to his feet. "This is not so, Standing Rock. Your child fills your ears with lies. Windrider has chosen another woman, but it is not Rebecca. Rebecca loves and waits for Bright Arrow in the camp of the Yankton. The two white women knew the healing medicines. They helped the Cheyenne. If you do not believe this, go and ask the Cheyenne. They sing praises for the help of the white women. There is only friendship between Windrider and Rebecca. Did they not tell you of the evil of your child?" he asked, having heard the story from Rebecca as they had traveled downriver.

When the man remained huffy and antagonistic, Flaming Star exposed Kajihah's character and actions. Before the older warrior could debate them, Flaming Star craftily declared, "Ask any Cheyenne if these words are not true. You have been misguided, my friend."

The man grumbled but sat down. Walking Buffalo shifted on his sitting mat. Mind-Who-Roams looked at him and coaxed, "Speak your mind, *Tatankamani.*"

"When the white girl lived in our camp many winters ago, she was kind to me. My wife was sick; my children were small. Rebecca gathered wood and water each day. She brought us food. I did not speak out for her because too many were against her. It was wrong."

White Arrow, best friend to Gray Eagle since their youth and adopted father to Bright Arrow, spoke up, revealing, "It was this way for many. She has a good heart and kind spirit. I know of her great love for my other son. I was with her when she went to the fort to free him. She knew it might cost her her life; she did not care. She is the daughter of our old friend, Joe Kenny. He is one white we did not reject. Must we do this to his child? They have suffered too much. I wish my other son home."

Flaming Star looked at his father and smiled. White Arrow returned it, then paused to reflect on the past. White Arrow had been with Gray Eagle the day he had captured Alisha Williams. He had been at Gray Eagle's side during their times of joy and pains, watching their love increase with each new season. He had witnessed the day Bright Arrow had walked a similar path when he had captured Rebecca. Gray Eagle and Shalee had proven that skin colors did not prevent love and peace, that only the interference of others could cause anguish and trouble. He had watched Bright Arrow grow to be a man and become a great warrior. Such a loss to the tribe was intolerable. It was past time for the seeds of fury to be buried in the fertile earth to sprout into happiness and serenity.

During the pensive silence, Shalee pushed herself to her feet. She told the men, "I only ask for you to think and pray over this matter. You need not vote this sun. Search your hearts and minds for the truth, for mercy, for understanding and kindness. When my sons return to camp, the council can meet and vote," she suggested wisely, realizing that with so many men already in her favor, more time for them to think would be to Bright Arrow's advantage. Shalee thanked them for listening, then left.

After the council meeting, Cloud Chaser slipped from camp, unnoticed by all but Flaming Star. The younger warrior followed the stealthy Cloud Chaser until he was certain he was heading away from the direction in which Bright Arrow and Sun Cloud would appear. Evidently the man wanted to see someone or do something in private. Deciding the devious warrior was no threat to his two friends, he returned to camp to speak with Shalee. He would suggest that he head after Rebecca and the children, to have them nearby when Bright Arrow arrived. He felt that this trying matter should be settled promptly. As soon as the sickness left the Cheyenne camp, he needed to see Windrider again; his visit three days before had left him bewildered.

Far away, many things were happening. The tragic smallpox attack in the Cheyenne camp was nearly over. In all, three hundred and eleven of a little over seven hundred members of the Cheyenne camp had died. Of the two hundred tepees, all had experienced at least one fatality. Of just over three hundred warriors, only one hundred and eighty-nine had survived. Many of the fatalities had been children, elderly members, and women. But with Bonnie's warnings and guidance, the disease had not spread beyond their village.

Windrider was healing quickly and painlessly beneath Bonnie's glowing eyes and loving attention. It was decided they would join as soon as Windrider was totally well and on his feet again. Each night chants were sung in Bonnie's and Rebecca's names for their help and persistence. All felt that Bonnie was the answer to Windrider's vision, and she was accepted into his life and camp. In a few more days, he would no longer be infectious. He could help his people begin what they were calling a new life. Love and passion bloomed brightly and boldly between the Cheyenne warrior and his white captive. Yet there was one matter that troubled the man deeply . . .

Farther away, Bright Arrow and Sun Cloud were traveling a roundabout trail, which required more time and energy but was safer. The warrior knew that the Crow would head straight toward the Oglala camp the moment they discovered his deception and the bodies of their three warriors. They would think that the white trader, whoever he was, would gallop fast and furiously for the Sioux village, which lay southeast of their camp. His plan was to outsmart his foes by concealing his tracks and riding in a southwesterly direction until they reached the northwest border of the Black Hills. They would weave through the sacred mountains and come out near the Cheyenne River, just below Windrider's camp.

From there, Bright Arrow would sneak home with his brother, gingerly avoiding any Crow or Pawnee raiding parties or advance scouts.

Around dusk, Bright Arrow located a cave that he had visited many times in the past when his tribe had camped not far away during the winter. As a child, he had explored its deep, dark passages. He had been unaffected by the scary tales of ghostly spirits roaming the insides of this black hole. As he grew older, it had been a secret place to come and think. Allowing his stolen horse to water and graze, he and his brother hurriedly gathered plenty of wood for warmth and light. Then Bright Arrow led Sun Cloud and the trusty steed into the dark passage, where he built a small fire over which to roast a rabbit he had slain while collecting wood. As they waited for the fire to blaze, he tossed Sun Cloud a blanket to wrap around his body.

As the meal was cooking the boy asked, "Why did you dress as a white trader? Why did you scalp your hair?"

Bright Arrow laughed heartily. "To save my little brother from the hungry foes. They did not know me. It was a good trick. Hair will grow again; Sun Cloud cannot be replaced."

"My mother told me many stories about you. Why do you live with the whites? Why do you never come to visit us? Why do our people refuse to speak your name or chant your *coups?*" he asked eagerly.

As simply as possible, Bright Arrow truthfully explained the situation. When his little brother pressed for more answers, Bright Arrow revealed many things about himself and his past and present life. The boy was astounded by such facts and feats. "Will you bring Little Feet and Tashina to visit me? I will call them sister and protect them when you are gone," he offered, love and pride shining in his eyes.

When Bright Arrow agreed to fulfill his wishes, Sun Cloud asked inquisitively, "Will you come to live with us? Why did you join a white woman?"

Chuckling deeply, Bright Arrow tried to explain love and commitment. He told Sun Cloud all about Rebecca. He said his return home depended on the council's vote and their acceptance of Rebecca. Sun Cloud puffed out his chest and declared, "I will force them to obey. I will be chief when father dies. No one will defy my words. It is silly to fear a white girl. You are a great warrior, son of Gray Eagle and brother to Sun Cloud. You are brave and cunning. I will help you."

Bright Arrow watched his brother's expressions and listened closely to his words. For one so young, he knew many things, Bright Arrow mused. He would make a good chief for their people, and Gray Eagle was training and preparing him well. He was smart, quick-witted, alert, and brave.

Bright Arrow pleased him when he asked Sun Cloud to relate the news and events since his departure years ago. They talked far into the night, then slept for a few hours. Before dawn, they were up and gone from the cave. In three to five moons, they would be home.

The next day, Flaming Star and two braves began their journey to fetch Rebecca, Silent Thunder, and the two girls. They would follow the same plan as before, returning to the Oglala camp in twelve days.

Flaming Star was glad he had gone to see Windrider after returning from the trip to Yankton. After Rebecca's strange and shocking disclosure, he had needed to question Windrider about Cloud Chaser's alleged ride to the

Oglala camp and the mysterious council meeting that was supposed to have taken place. Windrider had been visibly astonished to learn there had been no such meeting, that no one had known about her quest or Bright Arrow's arrival nearby. An inexplicable expression had crossed Windrider's face, but because Flaming Star had stood at a required distance from the contagious Cheyenne warrior, Flaming Star had been unable to read it or understand it. Later he had wondered if it could have been a look of anger at a betrayal that Windrider had rapidly mastered and concealed.

It didn't make any sense to the Sioux warrior. He wondered what Cloud Chaser and Windrider had in common, other than Bright Arrow. He was already underway before he realized that Cloud Chaser had been heading toward Windrider's camp yesterday. He asked himself why Cloud Chaser would rush off to see Windrider after a council meeting about Bright Arrow and Rebecca. He pondered the Sioux warrior's motives for lying to Rebecca and Windrider and wondered why Windrider would have brought Rebecca to the Oglala camp secretly. Because Windrider's tale had matched hers, Flaming Star knew Cloud Chaser had to be lying, plotting. Yet he had spoken in favor of Bright Arrow's return. This strange matter would bear a closer look when he returned, he decided, unaware that his curiosity would forever remain unsated.

Cloud Chaser silently crept to Windrider's side as he sat on the riverbank trying to find ways to regain his strength and vitality. He was unaccustomed to a lazy life, and his mind whirled with distracting plans. The Cheyenne warrior jumped in surprise when a hand touched his shoulder; it was nearly impossible for any-thing or anyone to sneak up on him! He was stunned to find Cloud Chaser squatting there. How dare this traitorous, guileful foe calmly and boldly visit him! Fury surged through him, removing thoughts of everything but justified vengeance. The possibility that he had con-taminated Cloud Chaser never entered his warring mind.

Cloud Chaser appeared worried. He knew his plot would soon be uncovered, and he would be dishonored, shamed. He tried to think of a way to save himself, realizing now that the plot had been foolish and rash. He would offer Windrider a bargain—silence for silence. As these thoughts rushed through his mind, he was com-pletely unaware of Windrider's anger or contagion.

"Why do you come, Cloud Chaser?" Windrider asked frostily, laying aside his hunting knife and whetstone to stare intensely at the Sioux warrior.

"We must strike a bargain, Windrider. We must tell no one of our game to separate Bright Arrow and Rebecca. When he returns—if he does—they will take another vote. They are speaking of accepting his woman. It will cause trouble if they learn of our past trick to lure her from his side. Bright Arrow will be angry if he learns you tried to steal his woman while you played his friend and helper."

"I am his friend and helper. What trick and game do you speak of, Cloud Chaser. I did not lure Rebecca from his side. They are still mates. I have chosen another woman. Rebecca is my friend; I am her friend. There is no love or passion between us. She knows of my past desire for her. She has forgiven me. Why do you worry?" he asked innocently, placing the sharp knife in its sheath at his waist. "Come, let us walk in the forest and speak privately."

When they were hidden from all eyes and ears, Windrider asked, "Why did you lie to me, Cloud Chaser? You did not go to the camp and speak for her. Do you fear they will learn of your deceit?"

"Who told you such things?" he snarled guiltily.

"Flaming Star," the Cheyenne warrior replied.

"You told him of our game! You asked him about my meeting with the council? You are a fool, Windrider!" he thundered in alarm.

"You had no meeting with the Oglala council. Flaming Star learned of your deceit from Rebecca. He came to question me. I told him the truth. I told him you claimed you met with the council and they rejected her. He said there was no such meeting or vote. Why did you not tell me you were lying to her?" he demanded icily.

"You were a coward, Windrider. Your eyes and loins were captured by her. I said what you wished her to hear. You desired her. If you do not join me in this bargain, I will tell Bright Arrow and others of the nights you slept on her mat and the days you sneaked into the forest to roll on the earth in passion," he threatened venomously.

"You lie! I have not touched her!" Windrider shouted at him.

"I saw you kiss and hold each other in the forest. I saw you go to the river together on the trail. I saw you in camp while you awaited my return. Do not tell me you have never touched or desired her! You lie!" the malevolent warrior countered.

Windrider could not deny that he had kissed her, held her, enticed her, and desired her. But that was over. They had never yielded to wild passion. Each loved another. It had been a mistake, a brief moment when hunger and suffering had weakened and controlled them, a short time when loneliness and vulnerability had drawn them together, a tempting moon when touching and comforting had been needed by both. It had not been wrong or evil. He could not allow Cloud Chaser to make it appear that way.

Windrider suddenly comprehended another reality—what if he had infected this vicious male while they verbally battled? Cloud Chaser's unseen appearance at his side had given him no time for warning, and now there were other lives to consider. "You cannot return to your camp. I carry the death sickness. You have touched me and come near me. Now you carry it. You must remain here or you will carry it to your tribe. When you are well, we will go to see your people. We will confess our evil trick. We will beg for forgiveness and mercy."

"No," Cloud Chaser sneered. "If you speak against me, I will blacken the names of Windrider and Rebecca. When they question you, the guilt will show on your faces. This ugly secret will destroy your loves. I will say you lie about the meeting. I will say you lie about me. Kajihah will say I speak the truth. Sucoora and the white captive will prove my claims. All know of your lust for Rebecca. Why do you think Bright Arrow did not leave her here within your reach?" he taunted.

"You are evil, Cloud Chaser. I will not let you hurt others."

"If you try to stop me, I will slay all you love," the man warned. "Hold your tongue, Windrider, or your loved ones will feel my blade."

Cloud Chaser turned and walked away. Windrider called out for him to halt. He again warned of the danger of the disease, but Cloud Chaser laughed coldly and kept walking. Windrider drew the knife from his sheath and held it securely by the blade tip. He brought his arm over his shoulder, then jerked it forward, expertly releasing the knife. There was a dull thud as it entered the retreating man's back. Cloud Chaser pitched forward, dead when he struck the ground.

White Antelope arrived on the scene, having come in search of his friend. Windrider shook his head and informed him, "He refused to heed my warnings. I was too weak to fight him. I could not let him carry the sickness and death to the Oglala. He was frightened and tried to flee. I begged him to stop, to remain here until he was healed. I must bury him; he touched me. You ride to his camp and tell his people of his death."

"No," his friend argued. "I will bury him in secret. His death will cause panic and anger. He was a great warrior. We will tell no one."

Windrider cleared his mind of anger and his heart of hatred. He realized White Antelope was right, but for reasons only Windrider understood. He couldn't allow questions and suspicions to arise about this incident. The Sioux would never believe that Cloud Chaser would endanger their camp by taking the disease there. They would wonder why Cloud Chaser was afraid to remain with his friend Windrider. Murder—especially of a warrior from another tribe—was considered a grave act. Too many questions and doubts would arise from this deed. Windrider decided that Cloud Chaser's evil plot would have to be buried with him.

In the Yankton camp, Rebecca was helping Laughing Face near Red Tomahawk's tepee when a white man walked over to them. His hair had been recently cut and his face was clean shaven. She couldn't help but notice that his buckskins were freshly scrubbed and his body smelled of fragrant soap. Rebecca was quick to realize that he did not reek of whiskey or display crude manners and speech. The overall impression he conveyed was delightful to Rebecca—just as he had intended.

He spoke to the Indian woman, then introduced himself to Rebecca as James Murdock, a name familiar to her from many of her husband's conversations. He promptly and cheerfully added, "But ever'one calls me Murray. Laughing Face tells me yore a vis'ter. Shame, we don't gits many perty ladies down this here way. Sure would like to have you brighten this area fur a long spell," he remarked with politeness and geniality that couldn't be mistaken for anything else. He chuckled happily.

"I wuz asking Laughing Face if my friend Pierre Dorion wuz around. She tol' me he's gone to the trading fair with the chief and his son. Guess that means ole Murray'll hafta hang around till he returns. Course I kin use a rest and good vittles; don't git 'em on the trail. Here I go rattlin' me tongue likes we knowed each other. Sorry, Ma'am, ole Murray gits wound up when he's around folks agin. I'll be seein' ya," he stated pleasantly as he nodded his head, then walked away.

Rebecca watched the man approach a group of elderly Indians. He sat down and began to exchange tales with them. From his easy acceptance and the Indians' cordial manner, she assumed he was familiar to them, surely a good and respected friend. She returned to her chore, unaware of just how wrong and dangerous her conclusions were . . .

Billy Culpepper sneaked another look at his unsuspecting prey. She was pretty, but nothing to die for; and surely those two graves near her cabin belonged to his two reckless friends. She had bloody hands! Revenge was the law of the wilderness, and he must see it met. She was brighter than he had expected, he mused. Then again, she had defeated Lester and Jess. He cautioned himself to patience, congratulating himself on his first cunning and successful meeting . . .

Later that afternoon, Billy returned to Red Tomahawk's tepee. He told Rebecca he was a friend to the chief and his son, and she was readily convinced of his lie. Billy slyly asked, "Is there anything I kin do fur you an' the other womenfolk while the men are away—hunt fresh game or protect you all while you gather wood? This here area's perty safe, but you cain't ever tell when some bad seed's gonna drop in. I holds it my duty to take care of my friends and theys families."

Rebecca replied, "Thank you, Murray, but I think we have matters under control. These people are fortunate to have such a good friend as you." Oddly, she didn't think to tell him who her husband was, and it didn't seem necessary to warn him she was married, for he seemed perfectly behaved around her and the other women.

Billy hung around and chatted amiably, guilefully. He did some magic tricks for Rebecca's girls, causing them to laugh and smile. The two girls watched eagerly as he carved wooden dolls for them. He appeared to have an easy rapport with all the children. Since Laughing Face had seen this white man many times, she thought nothing unusual of his presence. She had no way of knowing that he had lied to Rebecca and was attempting to lure her away from the others to harm her. Tragically, she and the other Yanktons were aiding his evil plans.

Billy knew how to communicate in sign language and Nakota, the tongue Rebecca was presently learning. Any time Laughing Face was separated from Rebecca, Billy cleverly used the opportunity to converse and joke with the Chief's jocular wife. Observing this behavior,

Rebecca naturally assumed the two were well acquainted. She saw no reason to fear or avoid a close friend of the chief's. By the time two days had ended, Billy had Rebecca completely fooled. In a few more days, he would be able to spring his snare.

Billy carried out his plan with a patience and cunning unsuspected by anyone. He claimed to be waiting for Pierre Dorion's return from the trade fair. As he was a friend and sometime trapping partner of Pierre's, he was staying in his tepee with the Frenchman's family. That afternoon and the next day, he went with Rebecca and other women to gather wood and fetch water, giving his share to those of Pierre's tepee as gratitude for their hospitality. During these periods, he casually asked Rebecca many questions and related many interesting and amusing tales.

Rebecca's mind was too ensnared by personal thoughts and feelings to enable her to realize that "Murray" hadn't asked about "Clay." Winter was only weeks away, and there was much work to be done by the women. Rebecca had been trying very hard to keep busy, to repay her debt to these people and to keep her mind off her past and present dilemmas. Moon Eyes had been dead for over a month. She was relieved that her other daughter had stopped asking about her sister so frequently, understanding that a child's attention span was shorter at her age. After so many weeks and with many activities to fill her day, Little Feet unconsciously thought less and less about Moon Eyes as her mind began to heal itself from its sadness and suffering. As for Tashina, she was too young to recall a sister who had been absent for so long. To see their acceptance of Moon Eyes's death saddened Rebecca, yet she knew it was best. As much as she hated to admit it, Rebecca realized that the hardships and terror surrounding her child's death would be easier not to recall. At times reality seemed to all of them merely a thing of the moment.

Rebecca was glad to see her two daughters adapting so well to their new surroundings. They were enjoying their friends and the attention they received, and this made it simpler for Rebecca to immerse herself in mind-consuming and energy-draining labor. From Bright Arrow's words and the distance involved in his mission, she knew it would be at least a week or two before his return, and probably longer.

Clearly "Murray" was a good hunter; he brought in fresh game each day, game with lovely hides to cure for winter garments, hides that he passed out to the women to gain their affection and gratitude. He had brought along many gifts for the Yanktons, which he passed out in secret. These presents increased his excellent reception by the Indians, and he was invited to many tepees for meals and visits. He spent time with the other men, relating the news from other areas. Each day, he craftily wormed his way deeper into the villagers' lives and confidences. And still Rebecca had no idea this was merely a game with him.

Rebecca found the man affable and generous. She had been given no reason to mistrust or dislike or fear him. In her vulnerable and distracted state, Rebecca was too naïve and trusting where this man was concerned. After three days of close contact, she felt she knew him fairly well. Why should she be suspicious? He was accepted without a second thought in the camp.

As she and other women gathered wood the next day, "Murray" joined them. He talked with Rebecca about many things. She had told him that her husband was a guide and hunter for the Lewis and Clark expedition, to explain his absence. She had said he would return soon and they would head home to their cabin, to trap for the winter. When Billy asked his name, she said, "Clay Rivera."

"Yo're joshin' me!" he shrieked excitedly. "I knows Clay Rivery. Me 'n' him jawed lots of times when he came to the tradin' post or traders' camps. He shore knows how to trap 'n' hunt. Never seen prettier or better pelts 'n' hides. Course Clay's pretty much a loner, like me. Don't talk much when he comes in. 'Less it's to the second best trapper, which is me," he teased, then chuckled. "I wuz the one who give 'im that last knife he brung home. He came on me whilst two thieves wuz tryin' to take me whole winter cache. If'n it wuzn't fur Clay, I wouldn't be standin' here jawing with his wife."

He smiled at Rebecca and told her to thank Clay again for saving his life and cache. "He wouldn't e'en take narry a hide or gift. Ya gots yoreself a fine man in Clay Rivery. Shore would like to partner up with him. Trappin's hard these days, Rebecca. Too many doodlies tryin' to kill ya and rob ya. Ain't safe to trap alone likes in the old days. If'n ya gits a partner, ya hasta split right down the middle. Sometimes ya don't takes twixt as many with two trappers. It's downright hard to makes a good livin' these days," he muttered, then sighed dejectedly. "Course trappin's in me blood." He laughed merrily.

Rebecca halted to tie up her bundle of wood. "Where do you live and trap, Murray?" she inquired, glancing over at him.

"Up the Missouri, toward the Two Kettle camp. Old Turkey Head don't mind white trappers. Ya takes Wamdesapa and The Partizan; they don't likes whites. They'd kilt ya if'n ya turns ya back to 'em. It's good trappin' in Red Thunder's area; he's chief of them Sissetons 'round

Lake Traverse. That Minneconjou Black Buffalo ain't bad."

Billy helped her position the wood sling on her back, then retrieved the other one to carry. "Thanks, Murray. Who is this Wam . . . whatever?" she asked, having heard of the other chiefs and tribes.

"Wamdesapa. He's real bad, Rebecca. He hates all whites, like them Sioux. He's chief of the Wahpekutes, over that way," he informed her, pointing northeast. "I got meself outa them woodlands. Yessiree, I tries to stay outa them Wahpekutes' way."

"Most Indian tribes don't bother you, do they?" she asked.

"Naw. Course I been here since I wuz a pup. They knows me, knows they kin trust old James Murdock. I kin go most places and trap. If I gits sick or lonesome, I got me friends ever'where in these parts. Ya knows what I means. Sometimes a trapper don't see nobody fur months. One of these here days I guess I'll git me a woman like Pierre and Clay done and settles down in a fine cabin. I shore ain't gittin' no younger or prettier," he jested, then roared with laughter.

Rebecca laughed at his humorous expression and words. He added conspiratorially in a whisper, "I got me eye and heart set on this fine Blackfoot girl. She's perty as a flower and real smart. I've knowed her fur years. Me 'n' her pa's good friends. He knows she feels the same 'bout me. I stops by theys camp ever time I'm 'round. She comes of marryin' age next spring. If'n I has me a good cache this winter, I'm gonna trade fur'er," he announced smugly. "A good man shouldn't live alone, now should he, Rebecca?" he teased comically.

"No, Murray, a man shouldn't live alone," she replied mirthfully.

Early the next day, the jovial man returned to camp with an elk. He told Rebecca she could have the hide to make fur moccasins and garments for her children. After he carefully skinned the animal, he sliced off hunks of meat for Red Tomahawk's tepee. As he worked, he asked, "Clay ever takes ya to that Spirit Mound downriver a piece?" he questioned nonchalantly. Knowing her identity and predicament from Pierre, he guilefully began to set his irresistible trap. When she shook her head, he whistled eerily. "Won't no Indians go near it. They's sceered to death of it. Says it's a place with powerful, bad magic 'n' evil. Theys believes devils 'n' demons live there. Theys says them devils 'n' demons got little bodies," he murmured, holding his hand near his knees, "and great big heads," he added, curving his arms around his head to indicate an immense circle.

While Rebecca waited for him to complete his chore so she could carry the meat to Laughing Face, he casually continued his tale. "It ain't just the Yanktons afeared of that place; no Indian tribe or member will put a toe on that spot. Theys says them devils 'n' demons got magic bows 'n' arrows. Theys think they kin kill anybody who comes miles near that spot. Ain't nothing kin make an Indian go near Spirit Mound. Theys says if any white goes there and comes back alive, it means they's got powerful magic; they's protected by the heaven spirits. No one harms a man who's been to Spirit Mound."

Billy knew he had caught her interest and full attention. "I been there twice, and I got me a bag of them rocks. I give 'em as gifts to chiefs and warriors. Theys thinks Murray ain't afeared of nothing. Theys afeared to do me harm. Theys let me comes and goes as I wants. Nobody tangles with someone who's been to Spirit Mound and returned alive. Yessiree, them rocks makes good gifts and weapons. You oughta gits old Clay to takes you; it's somethin' to see. Ya mights has needs of some of them magic rocks one day," he hinted provocatively.

"Isn't that dangerous?" she questioned, her curiosity rising.

"Nope. 'Cause no one dares to go near it. Theys thinks I passes my powerful magic to them rocks. Theys carries 'em around as good-luck charms. That's how I gots away from them Wahpekutes. Ever'body knows Murray's been to Spirit Mound and survived. Theys respects me, and fears me. When I had me two bad trappin' seasons, I used them rocks to trade fur food and weapons. You 'n' Clay oughta gits some to carry home. Cain't tell when ya mights needs somethin' valuable to trade, or to sceer off enemies. Ask Laughing Face; theys powerful afeared of such magic. Won't nobody turns theys backs on me, or anyone who comes outa there alive," he declared confidently.

It was true that Murray had been there twice; it was true that the Indians feared and avoided that location. If she questioned anyone about his claims, he knew his words would seem accurate and honest. His story was a great temptation to someone trying to earn acceptance and respect from Indians.

"I'm heading over there tomorrow. Ya wants me to bring ya a few rocks?" he offered. "If'n ya wants, ya kin comes along."

Rebecca contemplated this intriguing possibility. "How far is Spirit Mound?" she asked, recalling her love's acquaintance with Murray. He had spoken highly and affectionately of that white man.

"About two hours' canoe ride. I'll be going and coming afore the sun's overhead. Ain't no need to sleep there again. I dun proved my courage and magic. Ya wants to go see 'er?" he invited cordially.

Laughing Face joined them. In the Yankton tongue, Billy told the woman his plans. Fear and tension lined the woman's face. When Billy said that Rebecca might go with him to prove her courage and magic, the woman fretted and shuddered. She warned Rebecca to stay away from that evil place. Billy laughingly translated the woman's words, then craftily asked the woman to show Rebecca her magic rock. Laughing Face pulled the small rock from beneath her buckskin dress. It was imprisoned by thongs on a long tie and worn as a necklace.

Billy told Rebecca the woman always wore it to ward off evil and danger. He claimed he had given it to her. Rebecca was hooked on his devious line. She knew that Bright Arrow would win his return home with his actions. She knew the Oglala would accept the two girls. She concluded that her visit to Spirit Mound could ensure her own acceptance and respect. Too much had happened lately, and she wasn't thinking wisely or clearly. And Billy had won her trust.

That night, Rebecca lay awake for many hours. She couldn't believe she had agreed to go on a trip to Spirit Mound, even with a trusted friend of Bright Arrow's and the Yanktons, and even if the trip only required one day and night. She was a brave and daring person, but she was a married woman. Reservations filled her. Her decision had been too hasty and impulsive. The idea was marvelous, but it should be carried out with Bright Arrow and not his friend. It wasn't that she couldn't leave the girls in the care of the Yankton women, and it wasn't that she expected her husband to return any time soon, and it wasn't that she was afraid of Murray. It just didn't seem proper for her to spend the night alone with another man. After all, look what trouble had come from her trip with

Windrider—and they hadn't exactly been alone! Tomorrow she would tell Murray she had changed her mind. She closed her eyes and slept peacefully.

Rebecca returned from the river with two bags of fresh water. It was very early and few tepees had stirred to life. Laughing Face was preparing a fire to cook the morning meal when the others awakened. She was chatting with Murray as Rebecca approached them.

He swept off his fur hat and nodded his head in respect. He smiled lightheartedly and greeted her. "Mornin' Rebecca. I wuz just telling Laughing Face our plans. She thinks yore the bravest woman she knows. You'll hafta make sure you give her one of yore magic rocks." He had spoken with the Indian woman for a time, clearly arguing Rebecca's incredible decision when the woman disagreed with it. Billy explained why Rebecca wanted to go—to win acceptance and approval from the Oglala. Cleverly playing both sides of this game, Billy convinced the woman it was a good idea, claiming he would protect Rebecca from any harm. The woman grudgingly yielded, as it was not her place to command this white visitor. Besides, Rebecca would return in one day, and this man was Rebecca's trusted friend.

While Laughing Face focused her attention on her task, Rebecca gave Billy her distressing and unacceptable news. She smiled ruefully and told him she had changed her mind. "I can't go, Murray. There's so much work to be done here. I can't ask busy women to look after my children while I go collecting magic rocks. When Clay returns, I'll have him take me before we head home."

The finality in her tone was unmistakably clear. Billy had suspected she might change her mind. He was pre-

443

pared not to expose his dark feelings but to switch to his backup plan. He smiled in sunny resignation and told her it was fine, for he had other matters to handle.

His tone was almost musical as he lightly replied, "Ain't no never mind. Be more fun with Clay and yore girls. Pierre's wife and daughter are heading to pick some medicine plants upriver. I wuz gonna guard 'em in the woods afore we left. I came over to say we couldn't leave till later. Thought Laughing Face might need some healing herbs. You wanna go along and git some for her? Won't take more'n an hour."

Rebecca said it was fine with her if Laughing Face needed and wanted the plants. In the Nakota tongue, which Rebecca had not yet mastered, Billy deceitfully asked Laughing Face if she wanted Rebecca to bring her any magic tokens from Spirit Mound. The woman went into the tepee and brought out a leather bag. She smiled her gratitude and handed it to Rebecca as Billy told the unsuspecting white girl it was for the medicine plants.

Rebecca Kenny and Billy Culpepper set out for the riverbank where Billy said Pierre's wife and daughter would join them. When they reached it, Billy pointed upstream and said the women were waiting in a clearing not far away. They walked for a time, and Rebecca gradually realized they had traveled much too long. She wondered why they were continuing and if there were some mix-up in the meeting place. "Murray" had told her the location wasn't far. "Murray, haven't we—" As she turned to question her companion, Billy's pistol butt landed across her temple, cutting off her words and rendering her unconscious.

Billy glanced around, finding no one in sight. He would have slain anyone who tried to interfere with his evil scheme. Lifting Rebecca's limp frame, he carried her into the woods. After locating a sizable hollow tree, he bound and gagged her, then shoved her inside the dark confinement. He placed large rocks and heavy brush at both ends, trapping her in a helpless position should she awaken. He eyed his clever handiwork and chuckled satanically. Everyone would believe she was heading for Spirit Mound, so she wouldn't be missed for two days, which would give him a considerable head start. She couldn't get out of her wooden prison, and she wouldn't be heard through it and her gag. She was his helpless captive. He crept back to the camp, careful to stay out of Laughing Face's sight.

While most Yanktons were busy starting the new day, Billy gathered his belongings and two horses. He bid Pierre's family farewell and left. When he returned to where he had concealed Rebecca, he found she was still unconscious. He tossed her over the other horse and secured her to the Army saddle. His chilling laughter filled the silence in the forest, as he anticipated that this woman of Bright Arrow's would make a nice gift for his Crow friend, Chief Arapoosh . . .

Chapter Twenty-One

Rebecca slowly came back to awareness. Her face flamed and blood whirled madly inside her head. She seemed to be suffering from a strange and uncomfortable rocking motion that tormented her stomach, hipbones, and breasts. Her arms and legs were cramped and strained, and her fingers were almost numb. She forced her eyes to open and saw the upside-down landscape moving dizzyingly. Her fuzzy brain told her she was lying across the back of a moving horse. As her sherry-colored eyes touched on her arms, which dandled over the horse's side, she noted that her hands were bound.

She tried to sit up and free herself. She couldn't. A rope was wrapped securely around her waist and attached to the saddle and horn. It prevented her from slipping off the saddle, from sitting up, and from getting free. She was someone's prisoner! She lifted her bound wrists to her face and studied the tight knot; it would be impossible to untangle it with her teeth. Her actions alerted Billy to her arousal, and he reined in the horses and dismounted. He came over to her. Seizing a handful of auburn hair, he lifted her head and stared into her confused features. She shrieked in pain and surprise as she confronted her captor.

"Yur position a mite touchy, Mrs. Bright Arrow?" he taunted maliciously, jerking on her hair again as he laughed ominously.

Tears burned in her tawny eyes and she yelped in new pain. "Why are you doing this?" she panted in mounting alarm. Terror had chilled her body at the name he had called her. She didn't challenge his claim as to who she was; instead she waited anxiously for him to reveal his motive.

"I owes me Crow brothers a favor. Cain't think of nuthin' better than givin' 'em a valuable slave. Gittin' old Bright Arrow's squaw oughta sit real good with Chief Arapoosh. He'll probably makes me his blood brother. Them Crow don't hates no Injun worse'n the Eagle and his baby bird. Afore anybody knows what happened to Rebecca, she'll be givin' ole Arapoosh great pleasure on his mats. He loves frisky, fightin' women under him. Ever time I gits me a white captive, I trade 'er to him or his bucks. Course, Bright Arrow's squaw is a real prize."

Rebecca was horrified by his malevolent intentions. "You can't do this, Murray!" she protested fearfully. "Untie me this instant!"

"Murray my arse! I'm Billy Culpepper. Ya see this scar right here?" he asked hatefully, shoving his hand under her nose. "Yur man gave it to me fur pickin' up one of his nuggets to study. Put his knife right through me hand. Ya thinks I don't knows ya and him kilt me friends Lester and Jess? Yessiree, ya gonna pay big," he threatened harshly, yanking her hair once more. As he pinched her cheek and brought forth a wince, he chuckled maliciously and added, "If'n I liked females, I'd punish ya meself. Cain't stand 'em. I'll let old Arapoosh git revenge fur me. If'n ya don't gives him a good fight, he'll make ya. He's a real mean'un on the mats, worse'n Lester."

"I'll be missed! They'll come after us!" she shrieked in panic.

"Ha!" he sneered. "They won't be looking no time soon. I told that Injun bitch we wuz going to the Mound, just like we planned—not plant pickin'. By the time theys misses you, we'll be long gone."

Rebecca was alarmed by his ominous disclosure. "Bright Arrow will track you down and kill you for this!" she bravely warned.

"I'm tremblin' in me moccasins," he mocked her, flipping his fingers and shaking his knees wildly. "Don't matter if'n he does come after us. Them Crow will be waitin' fur him. He'll makes a better prize than a piece of pretty tail."

"Can I sit up?" she asked softly, cautioning herself not to antagonize or provoke this dangerous and evil man.

"I likes ya just like that," he stated, walking around to strike her forcefully on the rear several times. She thrashed and cried out in smarting torment. Billy laughed and laughed as he repeated the rough spanking. He lewdly rubbed his hand over her burning rump. "Yep, ole Arapoosh is shore gonna enjoy this sweet tail. You just full of lusty fight, ain't ya?" He remounted and galloped off at a merciless pace for Rebecca's tender undersides and clattering teeth.

After an hour or so, Billy slowed his mount. Rebecca knew he was trying to torture her with pain and fear. Her body ached; her teeth were sore; her head pounded, and her buttocks still stung. She was utterly helpless, at the complete mercy of this villain. Billy was determined to make her suffer as much as possible before he delivered her to a horrid fate. She knew there would be no timely rescue for her, for no one realized she was missing. No one knew where to look. No one who cared was around to discover her misfortune and to track her.

Rebecca tried to retain her wits and courage. She had

to be ready to spring on Billy and escape if an opportune moment presented itself. She feared Billy was too clever and wicked to thwart, but she knew she had to retain hope; she had to remain on guard; she had to endure. She prayed and wept as the monstrous trip continued.

Billy seemed to know where each tribe camped and avoided those areas. Rebecca wondered how long it would take to reach the Crow camp. She tried to remember Bright Arrow's schedule, though she realized he could be in a different Crow camp. Even if she escaped from Billy before they reached the camp, she would face many dangers trying to get home. She didn't know this area or these Indians. If she was too inquisitive or cooperative, Billy would become suspicious and watchful. If she got away from him, she would confront more danger. Rather than ask help from a possible foe of the Oglala, she would have to survive on her own wits. It all seemed so hopeless . . .

That night when they camped, Billy kept her hands and ankles bound. He tossed her practically raw meat, as if she were some wild dog. He made her lie on her stomach near the stream to drink, refusing to share his canteen. As she did so, he cruelly mashed her face into the mud. He howled with laughter as she squirmed to free herself, then sat up choking and gasping for breath. When Billy hunkered down to observe her dirtied face, Rebecca almost spit into his; but she wisely controlled that impulsive action, knowing he could slay her without a second thought.

"Yep, ya looks just like a little black slave," he remarked.

"You're mean and cruel, Billy Culpepper. God will punish you for your wickedness," she warned him softly, spitting the dirt and mud from her mouth. She cupped water with her bound hands and washed it from her face. She dared not mention his dead friends, even to claim innocence in their deaths. Arguing and pleading would only fuel his vengeful fire.

"God shouldn't made no womenfolk and theys wouldn't be no trouble," he scoffed. "My ma weren't worth spittin' on. Pa punished her good ever'day. When she wuz real bad, he kilt her to stop her evil."

It was evident that this man was insane—crazy and evil and brutal. He hated women. Rebecca was in more danger than she had realized. The sooner she got free of this demon, the better. But how, unless she killed him? And how could she carry out that incredible feat?

He let the small fire go out. Then he unrolled his sleeping bag and snuggled into it, for the night air was moist and crisp. Rebecca was forced to lie on the ground uncovered, and by midnight she was cold and damp. She shivered and curled into a tight ball. Nothing helped. Her body throbbed. She was miserable, assailed by the dew and the brisk night air. Only through sheer exhaustion did she get any sleep, though the few hours of fitful tossing did nothing to provide the rest she needed. When Billy nudged her roughly with his foot the next morning, her clothes and hair were wet. She shuddered from the chill; her teeth chattered. Billy eyed her up and down, then laughed sardonically.

Anger charged through her, and fear was briefly forgotten. "If you treat me like this for many days and nights, I won't reach the Crow camp alive!" she snapped at him.

He was surprised by her outburst and logic. "What do ya care?" he queried.

"I have found that any life is better than none, Billy," she scoffed deviously. "Who knows, perhaps I'll like this powerful chief."

"Just like a whore!" he snarled at her. "Ya don't cares who beds ya as long as he feeds and tends ya! Ya ain't no different from Ma."

Rebecca could imagine what that poor woman had gone through, living with this man and his comparable father. She was probably delighted to find death and peace! Her hatred and repulsion for Billy increased. How could she ever have thought him a decent, honorable trapper?

That day, Billy tied Rebecca's hands to the saddle horn and her feet to the stirrups. He knew if she bolted, she would be sorry. There was no way to get free of those bindings. He took her reins and galloped off, with Rebecca hanging on tightly and nervously.

Bright Arrow and Sun Cloud reached their father's camp just before noon. The Oglala surrounded them in excitement and joy. Shalee rushed out to greet her two sons. With Sun Cloud hugging her legs, she gazed with teary eyes upon Bright Arrow. She flung herself into his arms and embraced him fiercely. He lay his cheek atop her head and held her tenderly and lovingly for a long time.

Shalee leaned backward and studied his handsome face, which almost mirrored a younger Gray Eagle's. Love and pride flooded her. "It has been too long, my son. You are home where you belong. Never will we allow you to leave us again. How I have loved you and missed you," she murmured, hugging him tightly.

Bright Arrow lifted Sun Cloud in his arms. "You have a brave second son, my mother. You must be proud of his courage and strength. We must see father. Does he get better?" he asked worriedly.

Shalee beamed with joy. Surely the heavens had watched over her this day. She had not drugged her husband since two days before. He was stronger and clear headed today. She told the others they could speak with her sons later. Taking them by their hands, she led them into their tepee. Gray Eagle was standing beside his mat, dressing and preparing to investigate the commotion outside.

Sun Cloud ran to him and hugged his knees. Gray Eagle hunkered down and pulled the boy close to his chest. With great animation and excitement, Sun Cloud began to relate his brother's deeds. He left out nothing of the bold adventure. Gray Eagle listened intensely to his son's stirring account, then he stood and faced Bright Arrow. Pride and love glimmered in his eyes, but Bright Arrow hesitated in uncertainty. Gray Eagle made the first move. He walked over to his older son. Their eyes met and locked. Gray Eagle put his arms around Bright Arrow's shoulders and drew him close in a loving and grateful embrace.

"My son is home. My love and pride are great this day, Bright Arrow. You have returned my life and joy. It was wrong to allow our people to send you away. All have suffered. The day has come for your return home. Flaming Star seeks your woman and children. When they return, you will join. You will ride at my side. Your people need you. I need you," he admitted hoarsely.

Bright Arrow fought back the tears that threatened to spill forth. "I love you, Father. I have missed you and my life here. I feared I would never look into your face and the face of my mother again. I will accept my place here. I will follow you as chief, then my brother Sun Cloud. I will make you proud to call me son and brother."

"I am proud to call you son. Life will be good again for the Oglala. We must have council. There is much you must tell us."

"Yes, Father, there is much to tell," he agreed solemnly.

"First, you must rest and eat," Shalee insisted, slipping her arm around Bright Arrow's waist. She called Sun Cloud over to them. Bright Arrow lifted the boy in his arms. The four locked arms and exchanged smiles. "My husband heals more each day. Soon he will be well and strong. My sons have been returned to me," she murmured, kissing each one. "Flaming Star will return with Rebecca, Little Feet, and Tashina. We are a family once more. Together we are strong. Nothing and no one will ever separate us again," Shalee vowed.

The three men smiled, then laughed and agreed. They sat down to share their first meal in years. As if no time had passed or anguish had existed, talk flowed freely and merrily. All believed their sufferings and separations were over.

That night in the council meeting, Bright Arrow was readmitted into the Warrior Society. The council listened eagerly, astonished by his tales. He showed them the Crow weapons and possessions he had stolen. He held up the three scalp locks. He revealed the name of the Pawnee warrior who had wounded Gray Eagle, vowing revenge. He swore his loyalty, help, and prowess to his tribe.

The vote for Rebecca's acceptance was taken. Each council member held two sticks, one black for no and one white for yes. Bright Arrow couldn't watch as the pile grew with one predominate color. When the voting was done, he dared to glance at the evidence. Gray Eagle and White Arrow smiled at their exhilarated son as he observed that all were white sticks except one, Standing

Rock's. Mind-Who-Roams stared at the stubborn man who was being tricked by his daughter. He reminded the man that the council vote had to be accepted by all.

Standing Rock nodded, then left. The others remained to hear more about Bright Arrow's recent journeys and feats. They also needed to plan their strategy for revenge against the raids of the Crow and Pawnee. When Bright Arrow made several cunning suggestions, they approved them. He was appointed one of the band leaders. Finally the council was dismissed. Gray Eagle and his son returned to their tepee where Sun Cloud and Shalee eagerly awaited them and the news.

That night, Sun Cloud slept on the mat with his brother. The child was fascinated and gratified by this change in his life. He claimed he had the bravest and cleverest brother alive. It pleased Shalee and Gray Eagle to see their sons so taken with each other.

Far away from the Oglala camp and its celebratory air, Rebecca tossed and turned, in danger and dejection. At least she had a blanket to lie on and one to cover her body. Billy had fed her better that day and had been easier on her. Yet she knew it was only the result of her remark that morning. She was bone weary and sore, but sleep eluded her. She couldn't help but fear she had seen her family for the last time. Billy guarded her as the most valuable prize that had ever existed. Unless he lessened his watchfulness, she would never have a chance to escape. She knew he would not. It seemed she had just closed her eyes and surrendered to slumber when Billy was forcing her to rise and continue the agonizing trek.

In the Cheyenne camp, Windrider was healed. He and

Bonnie were talking softly on the mat they now shared.
Her face rested against his shoulder as she listened to his
stirring words. "It comes time for our joining moon, Sky
Eyes. All must know I have chosen you as my honored
wife. You have done much for my people; they will be
pleased with our union. They will be honored to call Sky
Eyes a Cheyenne."

"And I," Bonnie murmured contentedly, "will be
honored to become the envied wife of Windrider. I have
loved no man but you. You have brought such happiness
into my life."

"And pleasure to your body?" he teased huskily,
recalling how she had responded so passionately to his
lovemaking just minutes before.

Velvety laughter filled his ears. "I cannot deny such
truth from the lips of my future husband. You have but
to touch me or look at me and I go wild with a craving to
have you. We will be happy, my love."

"Yes, it is so. But before we join, I must visit the Oglala
camp. I must know the fate of my friend and brother,
Bright Arrow. He has walked a painful and difficult trail
for many seasons. I pray his demanding journey is past. If
he does not survive to flee the Crow camp, plans must be
made for others," he remarked gravely.

Bonnie did not realize he was referring to Rebecca, for
Windrider felt a deep commitment to her safety and
happiness. In truth, he loved her, but not in the same way
as Bonnie. "If they have not returned, I will go after
Silent Thunder and Rebecca. Winter comes, and it is not
good to be so far from family and home."

Bonnie persuaded him to wait another day or so, to
regain more strength. "I have taken much care to see you
healed. I will not lose you to a foe while your body still
seeks its full power. Two more moons cannot change

what Fate has decided. Stay, my love."

He smiled into her sky-blue eyes and relented. "How can I regain my strength when you force me to work and not rest?" he jested merrily before taking her again. They couldn't seem to get enough time or privacy since he had gotten well. Though Rebecca was out of Windrider's life, Sucoora couldn't have been happier with her replacement.

Flaming Star and three Oglala braves reached the Yankton camp to make a stunning discovery: Rebecca had disappeared! He was told she had gone to Spirit Mound to prove her worth and mettle but had never returned. "It cannot be so," he argued in disbelief. He knew Rebecca was brave and daring, but she was not foolish or stupid. "This matter does not smell sweet, my friends. We must seek the facts. I sense she is in grave danger. Some call the man who took her away Murray, but others call him Billy Culpepper. Both names are known to us," the alarmed warrior stated grimly. "It is strange she took nothing but a bag with her." With Flaming Star's tedious investigation and keen intelligence, the alarming truth was unfolded, and he raged at the twist of fate.

Pierre Dorion had returned. He had intended to warn Billy to stay clear of the camp while Bright Arrow's arrival was imminent, not inspire him to treachery against an innocent female. Angered by his friend's deceit, he supplied the Oglala with an idea of Billy's plans. Billy had talked about kidnapping Rebecca and giving her to Arapoosh, but Pierre had not taken him seriously. He chided himself, "I should have listened closer. His eyes were bright with mischief, but I thought he feared the man too much to steal his woman. Surely he is crazy. You must stop him and save the girl. He will never be welcomed in my tepee or this camp again. Do not fear for her safety along the trail; Billy would never touch a woman," he informed them.

"Come, we must ride quickly. We will slay him and free her." Flaming Star took Bright Arrow's daughters and Windrider's son and headed home at a rapid pace.

Three grueling days passed for Rebecca. Winter threatened to overtake the land within the next few weeks. Once it struck with its cold and snows, she would be out of the reach of a rescue party until spring, even if anyone guessed her whereabouts. She couldn't imagine spending any amount of time, let alone the whole winter, in an enemy camp as a brutal man's slave. She would rather die. But if she forced them to slay her or if she took her own life, she would forever be out of her love's reach. Could she endure such degradation and cruelty with the hope of being returned to her love one day? What would she be like after enduring such a vile experience? How would Bright Arrow feel about a soiled, abused woman? How strong was his love? How large was his understanding?

She sank into exhaustion and depression. She didn't speak unless Billy demanded some response. Because thinking of her predicament caused panic and tears, she tried to keep her mind blank. She mechanically obeyed Billy's orders, ignoring his taunts, insults, and lewd remarks. Her body became numb to Billy's harsh demands on it, and she gradually lost all hope and vitality. And still the journey went on and on.

*   *   *

Two days later, Windrider rode into the Oglala camp. He had cunningly avoided two Pawnee scouts and immediately warned Gray Eagle of their position. After three warriors sneaked behind them and captured them, Windrider met with Bright Arrow. The two exchanged tales, and each was happy for the joy of the other. Sun Cloud joined the two to revel in stories about his brother's prowess and adventures. When Windrider learned of Flaming Star's impending arrival with Rebecca and the children, he agreed to wait for his son there.

The next morning, several bands of Oglala warriors left to attack small camps of Pawnee and Crow warriors. They vowed to end these hostile attacks, at least for this season, by driving their enemies back to their lands, where winter would hold them away until the spring. Bright Arrow rode out as one of the four band leaders. To his surprise, most warriors wanted to ride with him, but the four groups had to be divided equally to ensure victory. The bands eagerly charged their foes and put them on the run. Determined not to allow further attacks, the Oglala continued to chase their enemies for miles.

Having just ridden for four days, Windrider awaited their return in the camp. No one realized two of the bands would be gone for several days, one of those being Bright Arrow's. The leader of the band he was pursuing was the Pawnee Snake Tongue. He and his band resolved to slay the man who had wounded their chief. They would carry his scalp lock and medicine bundle back to Gray Eagle.

As Windrider was strolling around the Oglala camp, Flaming Star and two braves returned. Windrider felt a stab of foreboding when he saw that Rebecca was not with the small group. He hurried over to greet his son and to question Rebecca's absence. Flaming Star related his dire news.

Shalee and Gray Eagle came out to meet Flaming Star. They were distressed over his revelations. Shalee took the two girls inside to calm them after their frightening race to camp. It was the first time she had ever seen her granddaughters, and she was saddened by the fact she would never view Moon Eyes. She silently prayed for Rebecca's survival and grieved over Moon Eyes's tragic death.

Shalee placed furry sitting mats on the ground for the two girls. "I am Shalee, your father's mother, your grandmother," she informed the wide-eyed Little Feet. "Soon your father will come home. He will be happy to see his girls. I am told you are Little Feet and your sister is Tashina. I have known your mother for many years, long before you were born. You are as pretty as Rebecca. When your mother and father come, we will have a feast and celebrate their return home."

"A bad man took Mama away," the child murmured with quivering lips and teary eyes, surprising Shalee with her knowledge and openness.

"You must not worry, Little Feet. Many friends are trailing them. They will rescue your mother and bring her home to you. Your mother is very brave and smart; she will not be harmed. You will see."

"I want my papa," Little Feet stated anxiously.

Shalee wanted to draw the confused child into her arms and comfort her, but she feared it might be too soon. After all, they were strangers. "Your father will be here soon; do not worry. I promise your mother will be holding you in your lap very soon," she vowed confidently. She tried to change the subject to distract the older girl. "I have missed my son and his daughters. Your father says you will live here with us now. You will have many friends to play with and plenty of things to do. Do you know what a chief is, Little Feet?"

When the girl nodded, Shalee explained, "Your father's Indian name is Bright Arrow. He is the son of Gray Eagle, the chief. Do you know you have an uncle called Sun Cloud? He is your father's brother. He is seven years old. He is happy to have you come live with us. When your father and mother return, we will build a tepee for you. You will be happy here, little ones. You must be tired and hungry. I will prepare food for you, then you can nap. When you awaken, Sun Cloud will show you around our camp and you will meet many new friends. Do not cry or be sad, Little Feet. This is your home."

Tashina was drawn to Shalee by her silky voice and gentle manner. She crawled into Shalee's lap and snuggled to her breast. Shalee held her tightly and smiled, stroking Tashina's shiny black hair. Fear left both of the girls, and Little Feet slowly inched over to them. Shalee closed her arm around the girl and hugged both affectionately. It was good to have her grandchildren with her, where they belonged.

Gray Eagle told Flaming Star that Bright Arrow had gone on a raid, and that he expected the bands to return that afternoon. The men discussed this crucial matter, imagining what Arapoosh would do to the woman of Bright Arrow. Gray Eagle voiced his fears aloud. "It will be bad for her. They will be angry over Bright Arrow's daring rescue of Sun Cloud. They will take this fury and hatred out on his woman. We must not allow her to reach the Crow camp. Why do such troubles attack my camp and family while I am not a whole man?" he raged in frustration.

Gray Eagle was still too weak to risk a long ride and

battle; he angrily and reluctantly accepted this fact. Flaming Star would need to rest at least one day before he headed off again, for he had rushed home and was exhausted. Also, supplies had to be gathered for a long, hard ride. He hoped Bright Arrow would return that day and they could start their pursuit early in the morning.

"Do not worry, my chief," Flaming Star declared. "Rebecca will not fall into the hands of our enemies. Grandfather will provide a way to rescue her and defeat them again. I go to prepare supplies and horses. When Bright Arrow returns, we will seek her."

Windrider couldn't wait. Rebecca meant a great deal to him, and he knew that by morning Culpepper and Rebecca would be more miles ahead of their present location. He sought out Shalee to give him supplies and to watch after Silent Thunder. He did not reveal that he was heading out alone. "I will ride ahead and scout their trail," he told her. "I will leave signs for others to follow. We must act quickly, or lose her to them."

"May Grandfather watch over you, Windrider. Bring her home to us. She is loved and needed here," Shalee whispered urgently.

While Flaming Star was seeing to his horses and making plans, Windrider prepared himself and set out toward the Crow camp of Arapoosh. Shalee was busy with her grandchildren and did not notice his solitary departure. By the time Flaming Star learned of Windrider's intention, the Cheyenne warrior was long gone and it was getting dark. He and his father, White Arrow, made plans to leave at dawn. It was a long, tormenting night in the Oglala camp.

Windrider halted only for rest and nourishment for

himself and his horse. He headed straight for the Crow village, planning to lie in wait for the white devil who had captured Rebecca. Estimating the distance she and Culpepper must have traveled since her abduction, he knew he would be hard-pressed to get near the camp before they arrived in the area. Flaming Star had made good time on the river and had been told that Culpepper was traveling by horse, with a captive to slow him down. Therefore, Windrider assumed, he might be able to overtake the white devil. If he raced like the wind, there was hope. Yet, after two days on the trail, Windrider had to yield to his lagging energy and strength. Clearly he was not fully recovered from the white man's illness.

Flaming Star and White Arrow had joined forces with two Blackfeet warriors who were visiting their camp. One of their great chiefs, Black Cloud, had been the father of Shalee and grandfather to Bright Arrow. His son Brave Bear had been slain years ago in a battle with the Crow. Brave Bear's wife Chela, daughter of a past Oglala medicine chief, had died in childbirth three years before his death. Their daughter Singing Wind was now the adopted daughter of the Blackfeet chief, Medicine Bear. Revenge for Brave Bear's death had long escaped the Blackfeet, and because of their strong ties with the Oglala, Brave Bull and Running Horse now insisted they ride with the Oglala warriors. The four set out at first light.

Two days went by at such a snaillike pace that Shalee feared her newly returned son had met with death. Sun Cloud encouraged her, saying his brother could not be conquered or defeated. When Bright Arrow finally rode victoriously into camp the next day, Sun Cloud beamed with smugness and pride. When Gray Eagle came out to speak with him, Bright Arrow grinned and tossed him the scalp lock, medicine bundle, and war shield of the man who had wounded him. Before his father could get a word in, the braves in his band bubbled with tales of Bright Arrow's cunning and daring. They said he had used many tricks and traps to thwart their enemies. The chase had ended in hand-to-hand combat between Bright Arrow and Snake Tongue. The band insisted on a feast and celebration in Bright Arrow's honor, and the warriors boldly argued over who was going to sing his *coup* chant.

Suddenly Bright Arrow noticed his father's distracted expression and reserve, sensing his father was being too quiet and unresponsive for such a momentous occasion. His inquisitive gaze shifted quickly to his mother's worry-lined face. He knew something was terribly wrong and questioned this alarming mood. "What new evil walks in our lives this sun, my father?" he inquired, fearing he didn't want to hear his father's reply.

"I would yield my *coups* not to utter such tormenting words, my son, but they must be spoken," Gray Eagle began reluctantly.

When the facts were exposed, Bright Arrow was stunned and dismayed. "It cannot be true! Grandfather would not allow it! I have proven my courage and loyalty many times over. I should be rewarded, not punished!" he thundered furiously. This couldn't be happening to him and his love—not now, not when everything was finally working in their favor! Surely he had misunderstood!

His daughters came running out to greet him. Little Feet eagerly asked, "Where is Mama? Did you save her from the bad man?"

Bright Arrow grimaced in pain and disbelief. He

464

encouraged his child gently, "Mama will return soon, little one. You must stay with Grandmother while I go after her. You are a big girl; you will be brave for Papa, won't you? You will help Grandmother with her chores?" When the child nodded both times, Bright Arrow kissed her cheek and nuzzled her neck, bringing forth laughter from both girls.

To calm them and to reassure them, he took precious time and energy to play with them for a few moments. Afterward, he placed them in his mother's care and watched as Shalee led the girls inside her tepee, where Sun Cloud was playing with Silent Thunder.

It was almost dusk and he was weary. Still he knew he must mount up and go after his love. Thinking a chilling swim might revitalize him, he hurried to the stream and tossed off his garments, then dove into the nippy water. He knew he had to build up a new supply of energy and stamina. He felt terribly depleted and depressed by this new assault on his happiness. Suddenly he wanted to weep but realized such an act would be childish and of no value. He left the water and donned his garments, wetting them, then forced his slumped shoulders to straighten. He was determined not to give in to such hopelessness and fatigue. His heart began beating swiftly as panic crept into his thoughts. He couldn't lose Rebecca—not now, not ever. Why was Fate so cruel to them? He anxiously prayed this was not a soul-staggering message from the Great Spirit. Rebecca belonged at his side, and he would fight the devils of all lands to rescue her! He would slay anyone in his path!

Suddenly scouts rushed over to Gray Eagle to warn him of a sneak attack by more Pawnee war parties. No time could be worse, for the Oglala had not expected another attack! Bright Arrow made sure his children were safely in his mother's care, then he and his band seized their weapons and headed to meet this new and deadly challenge. He had no choice in this matter, for he would have to defend his camp and life, or die. As he rushed to meet these foes, he prayed his love would not be lost to him. At least Windrider, Flaming Star, White Arrow, Brave Bull, and Running Horse were on her trail. He begged *Wakantanka* to guide them to Rebecca and to help them save her.

Windrider had been on the trail for five days and was nearing the outskirts of the Crow territory. Perhaps it was wrong for him to hope that many Crow warriors were battling the Oglala in Sioux territory, but it certainly would aid his cause. The more warriors missing from this area, the better it would be for him and Rebecca. He rested just after noon, then mounted up to bravely and stealthily sneak into their domain.

Billy Culpepper halted his exhausting trek early that evening, knowing he and his captive would reach the Crow village in one more day. He set up camp near a large pond that was partially enclosed by trees, then ordered Rebecca, "Now, white squaw, get off them clothes and scrub that body and wash yer hair. I don't wants to give a stinkin', smelly present to Chief Arapoosh."

Rebecca was appalled by his command, and by this time she was too fatigued to obey it. She weakly lifted her head and spat, "I won't go there in front of you and wash!"

Billy retorted, "I'm jest too tired myself to put up

with yore arguin' and ya better do as I says before ya rile my temper!"

Some of Rebecca's spunk and courage returned. She clenched her teeth, shook her head, and rashly held her ground. She had endured too much from this brutal beast. She would not strip naked before him and bathe. If her ankles and wrists hadn't been bound, she would have physically attacked him!

Billy drew his knife and stormed over to her. "If'n ya don't wants me to cut them clothes off'n yore body, ya best obey me, squaw! If'n I cuts it off, ya'll haveta ride naked into the Crow camp." The petrifying threat was one Rebecca knew he would fulfill.

"How can you be so cruel and sinful, Billy?" Rebecca murmured in a ragged voice. "Please don't do this awful thing. I've never done anything to you. If it's gold you want, Bright Arrow will get it for you. Please let him pay for my release," she tempted him.

Billy rubbed his bristly chin and jawline as he pondered her offer. He was afraid of Bright Arrow and didn't trust the clever, strong warrior. He was certain he wouldn't get two feet from that exchange before his body was full of arrows. Billy liked young boys between the ages of ten and fourteen, and the Crow warriors traded them for the female captives he supplied. This female ought to be worth two or three ripe youngsters, he calculated greedily. It was getting close to winter, and he planned to take over Bright Arrow's cabin. The winter would pass blissfully with a slave or two in his possession. Of course he had never told the Crow why he wanted young boys, and he certainly wasn't going to tell her!

"Nope. I got no use for gold. 'Sides, I don't trust the Arrow. I'll gits just what I wants and needs by trading you," he stated with finality. "Now gits them rags off and git washed. I wants ya clean and pretty for me friend. And wash them stinky clothes."

There was no other choice but to follow his instructions. At least she would be clean. Billy hated women, so she knew he wouldn't try anything with her. She yielded to the humiliating situation. "Untie me."

"If'n ya tries anything funny, I kin think of ways to torture ya afore I gives ya to Arapoosh," he threatened.

After Billy severed her bonds, he stepped back to prevent her from doing anything rash, such as trying to seize his knife or knee him in his privates. He had captured many women, and he knew all of their tricks. He watched her with an eagle eye.

Rebecca walked to the edge of the pond and stared into the untroubled surface, knowing the water would be cold. Billy shouted for her to hurry and tossed her a small cloth and soap. She stared at them, surprised that he carried such items. No doubt he did so for moments such as this. She gritted her teeth and entered the water quickly, before she lost her courage.

Billy howled with laughter as she struggled to undress beneath the water's chilling cover. She turned her back to him and, using the soap, she washed her dress and breechclout, knowing the buckskin would require days to dry. She didn't want to put them on the bank, fearing the satanically malicious Billy might snatch them. Yet she couldn't hold them and bathe. When they were clean and wrung, she reluctantly tossed them on the dead grass, then tried to shut out reality. She scrubbed her hair and body, rubbing hard to provide some warmth and circulation. Eventually she was compelled to leave the security and concealment of the water and longingly eyed the opposite bank.

As if reading her desperate mind, Billy called out, "If'n ya swims over there to runs away, it'll be naked, Rebecca. How ya gonna gits home with no cothes. Git out. I'm tired and hungry."

"I need a blanket for drying off," she told him. "I'm freezing."

Billy walked over and dropped a blanket beside her garments. He didn't move away. Despite the chill, Rebecca's face flamed with color and warmth. "Turn around," she ordered frostily.

Billy chuckled and refused to move or give her privacy. "I don't wants none of yore tail. But ya'd better git it out here afore I gits mad."

"You sorry bastard," she sneered angrily. "One day somebody's going to kill you, with great pleasure. I'll stand here until I turn to ice before I'll let your wicked eyes touch me."

He picked up her garments and threatened to slice them to pieces. God, how she wanted to scream, *Go ahead, you low-down dog!* But she kept thinking of riding naked into a camp filled with hostile Crow. Billy had no conscience. He had no mercy or pity or morals. She had no doubt that he would parade her nude through the camp.

Rebecca didn't want to cry; she didn't want to show anguish and weakness, but she couldn't help herself. Her life was over; her world was lost. Let him kill her. What did it matter? She had wanted to live; she had wanted her love to have time to rescue her. But could she stall at such a price? Exist at such a cost? And if rescued, in what condition?

Her gaze met his. The moment of truth and decision had arrived. At first she shook her head very slowly, then the speed increased as her mettle and determination mounted. "No, Billy. I can't do as you say. It ends here, and now. If you take me into the Crow camp, it will be as a dead body. If you don't accept my offer of gold, you'll have nothing for your time and trouble. Kill me, or turn around."

"Whoring bitch!" he yelled at her. "Ya gits one minute to bring yore arse outta that water. Ya thinks I don't knows how to hurts a woman? When I finishes with yore body, won't be nuthin' left for Arapoosh. I'll git me gun and see how long ya kin dodge me fire. Course I'll just wounds ya a mite. Don't want to spoil me fun fer later."

Still, Rebecca did not relent. Her hands were crossed over her bosom, her face a picture of courage and obstinancy. She knew she had issued a death challenge. She would not submit to evil.

Billy turned to fetch his rifle and shot pouch. With the speed and flash of a single bolt of lightning, two arrows thudded forcefully into Billy's shoulders. He instantly dropped the knife and lost use of both arms. He spun and fell, though neither of the arrows had struck a lethal blow. He squirmed in agony and attempted to stand. All he could manage was a sitting position. The arrows had been placed perfectly, right through the muscles that provided strength and control.

Billy glanced around, trying to locate his attacker. A warrior stepped from behind a tree, fifty yards away. His garments and patterns were Cheyenne. The warrior headed for the wounded Billy, and the man tried to back away on his seat. An ominous sneer curled up one side of the warrior's lips, and his dark eyes warned of impending death. Billy licked his dry lips, then pleaded for mercy. He offered the girl in the water in exchange for his life.

Windrider glanced at the stunned Rebecca who hadn't moved or spoken. As if in shock, she merely stared at him in disbelief. Windrider said, "She is mine. I will take her. You will die for stealing her and abusing her."

"Ya knows her?" Billy murmured in rising terror.

Windrider smiled mischievously. "She was a gift from Bright Arrow, son of Gray Eagle. She is to be my wife. I am Windrider of the Cheyenne. No man takes what is mine."

Windrider placed an arrow nock against his bow-string. He pulled the string and released the arrow. Horrified, Billy watched his death in progress, unable to flee. The arrow pierced the villain's heart, and Billy fell back to the ground. As if needing more release from his anxiety and fury, Windrider buried four more arrows in Billy's body.

He turned and walked toward the pond, smiling and calling Rebecca to him. Without modesty or thought, she rushed into his entreating arms, where she sobbed and clung to him, finding it difficult to believe her ordeal had ended. Windrider seized the blanket and wrapped it around her shivering frame, then held her tightly and silently. This was not a time for words. She needed warmth and the assurance of safety—comforts he was providing, not Bright Arrow . . .

After a long time, she mastered her tears. Windrider's warmth had spread to her body, and she felt protected and calm. Looking up into his face, she smiled faintly. "You're well. I'm so glad, Windrider; I've been so worried about you. Did you know I was kidnapped by that devil?" she questioned, hugging him in affection and gratitude. When he nodded, she probed, "How did you find me?"

"I was in the Oglala camp when Flaming Star

returned with the news. My son and the girls are safe with Shalee. Gray Eagle will soon heal. Bright Arrow and Sun Cloud are safe; they are home. I rode out as soon as Flaming Star told me of your danger and destination."

Windrider explained the mystery and how Flaming Star had solved it. He quickly related Bright Arrow's recent adventure in the Crow camp. He told her they must hurry, as it was dangerous to linger in this area. He said he would take her home to her family.

Rebecca listened to his words. She was bewildered by one overwhelming fact—Bright Arrow was not here. "Was Bright Arrow wounded during Sun Cloud's rescue?" she asked in dread, unable to comprehend his absence. When Windrider assured her they were both fine and safe, her perplexity increased. "Where is Bright Arrow? Why didn't he come with you?" she inquired, knowing her love must be aware of her abduction and danger if he had returned to the Oglala camp.

"He returned from the Crow camp after Flaming Star left to bring you to camp. Shalee sent Flaming Star after you and the children."

"If he reached home safely, why didn't he come after me?"

"Many Pawnee and Crow attack the Oglala camp. Bright Arrow and all warriors battle them. He is an Oglala warrior again. They made him band leader. He claims victory over many foes. He protects his camp and people."

"Did he send you after me?" she pressed in rising dismay, shuddering in apprehension that Windrider mistook for chills. He tucked the blanket around her and drew her close to share his body heat.

"No. I came as soon as the words left Flaming Star's mouth." Windrider was unaware of the erroneous direction of Rebecca's thoughts and feelings; his omission of many vital facts and clues had been unintentional.

Rebecca was confused and pained by this information. Her love knew of her kidnapping and peril, yet he hadn't come to save her. The camp couldn't be completely surrounded by enemies; otherwise Windrider could not have gotten away safely. And if he had come, why not Bright Arrow? Was he more concerned over his tribe's safety and survival than hers? What she thought was the truth suddenly dawned on her. Windrider had said that he had been taken back into the tribe, into the Warrior Society. He was probably now reveling in the glory of Sun Cloud's rescue! He was a band leader! Why should he take the time and effort to search for her? He had what he wanted. He had regained his rank, his honor, his daring adventures, his people, his family, his Oglala life. He probably assumed she had already been ravished and soiled. No doubt the council had met and discussed her. Evidently he had made that long-awaited and dreaded choice—his rank and tribe over her—even though he had promised he wouldn't.

She looked up into Windrider's face. His smile was encouraging. He was handsome. He had saved her life and honor, risking his own life to come after her. Her hand reached up to caress his cheek, and she smiled into his gentle eyes. He had once desired her and wanted her. Had he changed his mind? She felt she had nothing and no one. Her family was lost to her. Could she rekindle those flames of desire in him?

Her eyes softened and glowed, and her hand slipped behind his head and pulled it down to fuse her lips to his. She kissed him feverishly, pressing her body snugly against his. She was tormented and bewildered; she wasn't thinking clearly or wisely. After all she had endured these past months, and weeks, and days, she needed comfort from the man who had saved her life, the man who was sharing the climax of this hellish episode. She needed to feel loved, and clean, and valuable.

Windrider was surprised and affected by her action. Passion and hunger called out to him from her lips and body. He had grown accustomed to sharing fiery passion each night with Bonnie. For many days, his body had been denied that regular feeding. He caught her shoulders and pushed her away. He stared down at her. She was beautiful and vulnerable. She was tempting and enticing. "What of Bright Arrow?" he reminded her gently, though his loins throbbed with hunger.

"He no longer exists for me. You are the man I love and desire," she murmured in desperate deceit. "You have saved my life; it is yours now. I give myself to you, Windrider. Please do not reject me."

Windrider was utterly astounded by her words and behavior. She was a powerful temptation. As her mouth skillfully assailed him and blurred his senses, friendships were forgotten. Bonnie was forgotten. Danger was ignored. Their perilous location ceased to concern him. He didn't consider right or wrong, just his raging passion.

His arms went around her and pinned her tightly to his chest. His body burned with desire for this fascinating and enchanting creature. Their mouths meshed greedily and fiercely, as they sank to the hard, damp ground. The blanket slipped away, allowing warm coppery flesh to make stirring contact with chilly white skin.

Chapter Twenty-Two

A brief moment of reality flashed across Windrider's mind. He knew he had to be honest with this special woman. He could not reject her, but his feelings had changed since meeting and knowing his white captive. He could love and desire both women in varying measures, but the whites were known for taking only one mate, as Rebecca had reminded him not long ago. He could not lose Bonnie because of Rebecca. Yet he didn't want to hurt Rebecca. She had suffered so much. He had enticed her first. It would be wrong to reject her after his snare had worked. Before it was too late to turn aside from this passionate madness, he huskily asked Rebecca, "Why do you come to me now when my love and desire for another are stronger than my feelings for you? Are you willing to share me and my tepee with Bonnie?"

His words struck her like icy water. She looked up into his serious expression. "You and Bonnie?" she asked dumbly.

"Yes. We have shared many nights on my mat. She waits for my return so that we might join. I know the white way of one mate. I do not wish to lose her," he stated honestly, almost regretfully.

Rebecca pushed him aside and sat up, clutching the blanket around her trembling body. Shame and guilt assailed her. What was she doing? How could she have behaved so wantonly, so deceitfully? Why was she using Windrider to mask her anguish over Bright Arrow? Why was she trying to punish herself for loving Bright Arrow? What madness had stolen her mind? She didn't want this man; she wanted and loved Bright Arrow. During those wild moments, she had imagined she had yielded to her love, not Windrider. Such a pretense had been wrong. How could her love have betrayed her in this cruel manner? How could she have retaliated so wickedly? Tears flowed down her cheeks as she comprehended the truth of her actions.

Windrider misunderstood her pain. "Many times I tried to make you mine, to steal you from Bright Arrow. It is wrong to turn from you when I have won this battle. If you cannot share me with another, I will send her away," he vowed in tormented sincerity. He had made this trap, and now he would pay for his mistake.

Rebecca turned her head and looked at him. "No, Windrider. You owe me nothing. You are my friend. You saved my life. Many times you were there when I needed something or someone. Bonnie loves you, and you love her. You must join with her, as it should be. I should not tempt you because madness fills my mind this day. Please forgive me for behaving so badly," she entreated tearfully.

"Do you speak truthfully?" he demanded.

She smiled faintly. "Yes, I speak the truth. You are a tempting man, but I love Bright Arrow. I was angry because he did not come for me. I was afraid and confused. I'm fine now. Forgive me."

"Come, let us ride home," he suggested.

She inhaled deeply. Yes, she would ride to Bright Arrow's camp and force him to say farewell face to face. She would see her girls one last time, then seek a new life.

Where and how, she did not know. But she knew she could not interfere in Windrider and Bonnie's entwined destiny. "Let's go."

Windrider searched Billy's possessions. He handed Rebecca a flannel shirt and a pair of buckskin pants. "These will keep you warm. Dress quickly. We must leave this place."

He turned his back while Rebecca slipped into the garments. She used a rawhide thong to hold the pants in place. If one could be grateful for small favors, she was glad Billy was slender. The garments would be fine. Windrider took what supplies and possessions he needed from Billy's pack and helped Rebecca mount Billy's horse. Windrider mounted his own steed and grasped the reins of the other animal. They rode out, heading south at a steady pace.

They traveled for two days, seeing no one. On the third afternoon, Rebecca's horse stepped into a gopher hole and broke his leg. Rebecca was thrown from his back and landed roughly on the ground. Windrider reined up and jumped off his horse. As he hurried over to her, he saw she was hunched over on her knees, gripping her abdomen and rocking in pain. Windrider dropped to a knee beside her and questioned her agony.

"I don't know. I feel sick. It hurts right here," she told him, her flat palm circling her lower abdomen just above her groin. "I think I'm going to faint," she warned him just before falling over into his arms.

Windrider studied her face; it was white and damp. He checked her arms and legs for breaks, finding none. He gingerly pressed her collarbone, hipbones, and ribs. They seemed fine. She had a few scratches here and there, and he knew she would be bruised and sore, but he couldn't understand her suffering and loss of consciousness. The

Blackfeet camp was a few miles off to the east, and he decided to take her there.

He held her in his arms as he rode toward Chief Medicine Bear's village. When she did not awaken, he worried over her strange reaction to the fall. Something was wrong.

They reached the camp before nightfall, and he immediately requested that the medicine chief see her. She was taken to his lodge and placed on a mat. The Blackfoot shaman began to check her over from head to foot.

Windrider paced nervously. He called a brave over to him, offering him many gifts to ride to the Oglala camp and speak with Bright Arrow. The man nodded, accepted the gifts, and rode out of camp within the hour. Windrider sighed in relief. He estimated Bright Arrow would arrive within a few days. If Rebecca healed quickly, they would meet on the trail. It seemed imperative that he coax Bright Arrow to her side. He had begun to suspect that Rebecca doubted Bright Arrow's loyalty and love. He should have realized this was the reason she had reached out to him at the pond! She probably thought Bright Arrow was putting his people's safety before her survival! For all he knew, the Sioux warrior could be searching for her at this very moment. Considering the scant information he had imparted, Windrider could understand Rebecca's misconception. She didn't know the Oglala had accepted her. She didn't know Bright Arrow hadn't been in camp when he had left. Bright Arrow loved her and wanted her. When she awoke, he would explain matters to her more clearly and tell her she was wrong.

Rebecca was more than wrong. She was suffering a miscarriage of a child she hadn't known she was carrying, a child conceived in the forest near Windrider's camp, a child conceived in early September just before Bright Arrow left to join the Lewis and Clark expedition.

The shaman informed Windrider of Rebecca's condition and problem, and he grieved over the loss of this second child of his two friends. He knew what it was to lose a child, more than one child. He raged at her new torment, and he blamed himself. He bemoaned his carelessness on the trail, and in fear he asked the shaman, "Will she live?"

The man shrugged, replying, "Most women survive such an injury."

Windrider prayed that Bright Arrow would rush to her side. She would need him. If he didn't arrive to share this crucial time with her, he dreaded to imagine what it would do to their love. Too many times Fate had kept Bright Arrow from being by her side when Rebecca needed him the most. Would she understand and accept another rejection?

The Blackfeet brave rode slowly toward the Oglala camp. His journey would cause more damage and pain. He was a *heyoka*, a "contrary." A *heyoka* was a warrior who had experienced a vision of thunder. Such a warrior could not refuse his destiny as a "contrary," which demanded that he do everything backward and opposite. To answer affirmatively, he must respond negatively. To get him to act in a certain way, one had to ask the reverse of the desired behavior or deed. "Go" meant "stay," and "stay" meant "go." This often-confusing conduct ruled his life. Such men were accepted and many were revered. *Heyokas* were considered brave and daring warriors. No one laughed at them, to their faces or behind their backs.

Windrider had not realized that Thunder Head was a *Heyoka* when he had asked the Blackfeet warrior for assistance. He had been too upset and frantic to see that the man was dirty because he "bathed" in dust, not water. He had been unaware that the man wore his garments inside out. He had failed to notice that the man moved backward toward his tepee, for Windrider had already turned to reenter the medicine lodge.

Thunder Head did the opposite of what had been requested. He rode slowly rather than swiftly. He recalled Windrider's message, so he could reverse the words and follow the man's odd instructions. He would speak with Gray Eagle, not his son. He would say Rebecca was well, not ill. He would say she was safe, not injured. He would say she didn't wish to come home to him. He would say she didn't want him to come after her. He would say she didn't love Bright Arrow or wish to see him. He would say she was in the Crow camp. He would say she wanted to remain there. He would say an enemy sent these words to Gray Eagle. Thunder Head could not understand why Windrider was sending such strange and dishonest words to another warrior, but he had been paid well to deliver the deceitful message. Perhaps there was some reason for this game, these lies. It was not for him to intrude. He would swear his words were truthful. The statements from Windrider would be transformed into exact opposites of their meanings, as was expected and demanded of a *heyoka*.

When Rebecca regained consciousness, she was taken to Chief Medicine Bear's tepee. She would remain there and be tended carefully until Bright Arrow came for her. She was depressed by the loss of another child, and her spirits brightened only when Windrider told her he had sent for Bright Arrow. He told her to rest and heal, that all would be good again. She closed her eyes and surrendered to needed sleep.

A few days later, a Cheyenne warrior galloped into camp to beg for help from his Blackfeet brothers. He was relieved to find Windrider there. He quickly told Windrider of savage attacks on their camp by Pawnee raiding parties. He reassured Windrider that Bonnie was safe and was being guarded by White Antelope. Windrider didn't want to upset Rebecca with such alarming news; instead, he went to her and told her he was riding home to check on his family and tribe. He assured her he would return as soon as possible to make certain Bright Arrow had arrived safely. Knowing he had to leave with further delay, he told her not to worry and to get well quickly.

Rebecca hugged him. She thanked him once more for saving her life. "I'll be fine, Windrider. You've done so much for me. Tell Bonnie I think of her each day. Tell her I wish you both much happiness. You don't need to return here. Just marry Bonnie and begin a new life. You two can visit me in the Oglala camp," she stated wistfully.

Windrider didn't want to give away Bright Arrow's good news about her acceptance, so he kept silent. She would know very soon, for surely Bright Arrow was responding to his message. He kissed her lightly on the forehead and departed.

Four days passed without word or sign of Bright Arrow. Her concern deepened over his delay, especially when she was told that Thunder Head had returned to camp after delivering Windrider's message. She wondered why her love hadn't raced to her side. Singing Wind, the nine-year-old daughter of Chela and Brave Bear, was delighted to wait upon Bright Arrow's woman.

She was a pretty, strong-willed child, and Rebecca had no way of knowing that one day Singing Wind would play a major role in the life of Sun Cloud and Bright Arrow.

Five more days passed. Rebecca's fears and doubts increased. She asked Singing Wind to go see Thunder Head, to make certain he had talked with Bright Arrow, to make certain her beloved was alive and well. She sent questions about the enemy raids on the camp. The child raced to carry out this important mission for her new friend. When she returned to Rebecca's mat, she smiled and informed her that Bright Arrow had been in his father's tepee and that he had heard Thunder Head's words. He said the enemies had been driven off the Sioux lands. Singing Wind didn't tell Rebecca how much she enjoyed the word games with Thunder Head, as it was evil to laugh over such matters.

Rebecca was recovering rapidly. She could get up and walk for short periods. Her weakness was fading gradually. Medicine Bear, his wife, family, and the Blackfeet tribe members were kind and friendly toward her. She ate, rested, exercised, and slept for many more days. This routine, and Singing Wind's childish encouragement had a favorable effect on her health. It had been almost three weeks since her fall and miscarriage, yet it seemed ages ago to her. She was nervous and miserable. She was tired of lying around and waiting for something to happen. She knew she had to face reality—if Bright Arrow had not come by now, he was never coming. She had to make some plans. The weather had turned cold and damp; the sky hinted at snow any day now. Tears burned her eyes as she mentally rationalized, *Better to be trapped here for the winter than in the Crow camp!*

*   *   *

In the winter camp of the Oglala, Bright Arrow stared moodily into space. He was wearing leggings, breechclout, knee moccasins, and vest. A bow and quiver of arrows were slung over his shoulder; he was supposedly hunting. He didn't notice the chill on his flesh as he walked in solitary silence around the black rock formations, spooking several deer and rabbits, which he ignored. He and his fellow warriors had finally driven off their enemies and moved their camp from the Plains to the base of the Black Hills. In sheltered canyons, there was winter grass to feed the horses and towering boulders and cliffs to block the worst of the harsh weather. All appeared peaceful; all were ready to face the demands of nature—all but Bright Arrow.

White Arrow and Flaming Star had returned to the camp the day before. Rebecca was not with them. They told of finding a white man's decaying body near the old Crow camp; they spoke of signs of a woman's presence. They had found severed bonds and Rebecca's tattered dress—ominous signs. They had sneaked toward the Crow camp, only to discover it had been moved for the winter. The Crow were too far ahead of them for pursuit. They had no choice but to call off their frantic search. There was nothing more they could do this winter. They apologized for their failure to locate and rescue her, but they had done their best. They had searched for weeks without victory. They sadly told him he had to face and accept the staggering reality. If Rebecca was with the Crow, she was lost to him, at least for now.

When Bright Arrow described the visit from Thunder Head, Flaming Star disputed the man's message. "It is not so, Bright Arrow. I have seen the love in her eyes for my brother. If she sends such words, it is to stop my brother from riding into a trap to save her. You must not lose hope, my brother and friend. She is your woman. When the snows melt and the Crow return to their summer camp, we will find her and bring her home. We will seek vengeance for this deed."

Bright Arrow was lonely and distressed. Even if he could track his enemies' cold trail, he reflected, how could he get her out of camp alive and uninjured? Surely the Crow would be watching and waiting for him. This was a large territory. His foes could be camped anywhere. Where should he look? How could he search with winter breathing coldly on his neck and offering a perilous journey? As much as he loved her, was he willing to sacrifice his life on a rash and surely futile venture? And yet, could he do nothing? He was plagued by helplessness. For three days, he grieved for her as if she were dead.

Shalee observed her son's dilemma and his misery, and she asked, "Why do you punish yourself this way, my son? If you love her and cannot exist without her, go after her," she reluctantly advised. "Grandfather will guide your feet and watch over you. Why do you accept Thunder Head's words so easily and blindly? Who told him such things? If the Crow have vanished, where did he get such words? How does he know they are true?" she reasoned cleverly, earnestly.

Bright Arrow straightened. His eyes glittered with new life. Was he a fool? A blind weakling? A defeated man? Why hadn't he asked himself such questions? Where were his wits? He needed more answers! "On the new sun, I will ride to the Blackfeet camp. I will know such things before three moons have passed. She is mine, and I will save her. You will not see me until I find her, or at least know the truth."

* * *

Just after dawn the next morning, two people rode away to seek answers—Rebecca toward the Cheyenne camp and Bright Arrow toward the Blackfeet camp. Rebecca had decided to question Windrider about Bright Arrow and his recent words and behavior. She was going to beg for his assistance in winning back her love. She couldn't give Bright Arrow up without a desperate fight. Medicine Bear loaned her a horse and two braves for protection. She had learned that the Cheyenne had moved their camp near the northeastern base of the Black Hills, and knew she could reach it within two days. There she would demand answers and help!

Two days later, Rebecca turned the horse over to the Blackfeet braves and thanked them for their protection along the trail. The two men rode away. Rebecca inhaled deeply, summoning her courage. She walked towards the colorful tepee with Windrider's coups painted on the outside. She hoped he would understand and forgive her intrusion.

In the Blackfeet camp, Bright Arrow was receiving unexpected and startling news. He spoke with Thunder Head once more, demanding to know who had sent the message to him. He learned it was from Windrider and Rebecca, and from this very camp! He wondered how that was possible.

He was impatient with the man's contradictory speech. He wanted the facts immediately and clearly. When he discovered that Rebecca had been carrying a child and had lost it, he couldn't understand why she hadn't shared such happy news with him. What possible reason could she have had to withhold the fact he was going to be a father for a fourth time, especially after they had lost Moon Eyes? He discovered that she had been traveling with Windrider and that the Cheyenne warrior had been called home during a crisis. As soon as Rebecca had recovered, she had ridden after Windrider, instead of coming to him! He asked himself why. Harsh suspicions began breeding in his warring mind. He didn't like the way these clues and facts were mounting against his love and his friend.

Bright Arrow glared at the "contrary," trying to pick the truth from his converse statements. Consternation racked his brain. He was too tense and tormented to unravel this mystery, and fury kindled within him toward Windrider and Rebecca. If they had been this close, why hadn't Windrider come for him? he asked himself. Why hadn't she come home after healing? How had she gotten away from the Crow? When? Why would they send him such a devious and tormenting message? He feared he had been tricked. She had not summoned him to her side! She had not told him about the child. She had gone to Windrider for comfort and love! Anguish and mistrust chewed at his heart and mind.

How could she betray him, torment him, desert him? She had not waited for the council's vote. If she had asked Windrider about it, then she knew of their favorable answer. Unless Windrider had deceived her . . . Was it possible that Windrider was determined to have her? Was it possible she had been tricked, deluded? In her state of mind, after her many ordeals, perhaps she wasn't thinking clearly. Was his friend luring her away from him? Did Windrider hope to make it appear she was choosing his friend over him? All warriors knew it would show weakness to race after a woman and beg her to return home. When a wife left her mate, he was expected to retain his pride and courage. He was expected to let her go without a fuss or outward show of grief and sadness. He was not to pursue her, or fight over her, or expose any regret over her loss.

Bright Arrow considered all he knew. He couldn't lose a woman like Rebecca without knowing why, and he didn't care what others said or thought. She was his by first right! She was his by a willing commitment of love! She couldn't toss away what they had between them without a good reason! She owed him an explanation! She owed him a farewell! If it were a trick, he would slay the traitor who called himself friend!

Bright Arrow was on the trail early the next morning. He debated the possibilities over and over in his mind. Many times he almost turned back, but he couldn't. Perhaps he was to blame for losing her. He had to fight for her, or forever regret her loss. There had to be an answer for them and an answer to this puzzling mystery. Too many times he had placed her in danger, danger that someone else had overcome in his place. Too many times he had hurt her and disappointed her. He had spent so much time, energy, and effort on others' problems, seemingly to ignoring theirs. If she had chosen Windrider, she would have to convince him it was for love. Only then would he accept her decision.

As he rode along, he reflected on Sun Cloud's rescue and his battles with the Crow and Pawnee to defend his camp. He pondered Rebecca's impulsive decision to go to Spirit Mound to prove her value and courage to his people. He did not know she had not left the Yankton camp willingly to head to the Mound. If she didn't love him, why would she risk such danger and evil? He recalled what she had done for the Cheyenne during that terrible time of sickness and death. She was a rare creature, a special woman, a beautiful one.

He had made peace with his tribe. He had regained his honor and rank. He had accepted the fact that Sun Cloud would become the next Oglala chief, not him. All he wanted was to be a warrior, to live with his family and people, and to have Rebecca. Only then could he enjoy real peace, love, and honor. Was this too much to expect from life? Was this being too greedy and selfish?

In the Cheyenne camp, Rebecca and Bonnie were talking. "Do you think Windrider can make him understand?" Bonnie asked sadly. She hated to see her friend so miserable and lonely.

"I'm afraid to hope and pray for something that might not happen, Bonnie. I'm the one who doesn't understand. This isn't like Bright Arrow. Why didn't he come to me in the Blackfeet camp? I know he's not wounded or away on some critical mission. Even if he's still helping to battle their enemies, he could take time to come after me, couldn't he? It doesn't require nearly a month to make a two-day ride—not after what I've been through!" she exploded angrily from anguish and confusion. "My God, he didn't even search for me after he got the news of my kidnapping! If it hadn't been for Windrider . . ." Her voice trailed off and she shuddered.

"Something must be wrong, Rebecca. I can't believe he would turn his back on you. We've got to wait until Windrider returns. Then we'll know why Bright Arrow's behaving this way."

Rebecca smiled at Bonnie. "You're happy with Windrider, aren't you?" she asked unnecessarily, for Bonnie's face was a mirror of love.

"I haven't told him yet, but I think I'm—" She instantly halted her statement, recalling Rebecca's recent miscarriage.

Her hand had gone to her abdomen in a loving caress, alerting Rebecca to the truth as well as to why Bonnie hesitated. She smiled at her blue-eyed friend. "It's all right, Bonnie. I didn't have time to get used to the baby; I didn't even know I was pregnant. I hope this doesn't sound awful, but it's hard to miss something that doesn't seem real. Maybe the Blackfeet shaman was wrong. Maybe I just hurt myself when I fell. I have to believe it wasn't meant to be. Don't spoil your joy. I'm sure Windrider will be ecstatic."

"You think so?" she murmured optimistically.

"I'm positive. I can just imagine a new Windrider with blue eyes. He'll be a collector of young girls' hearts—Indian *and* white," she teased to lighten her gloomy mood. Even though she was miserable, she wouldn't spoil the joy and peace of her friends. She was honestly happy for them.

They shared laughter. "Do you know how good it feels to be safe, to be smiling and laughing? For a while there, I thought I would die a horrible death. I've never met any man so evil and cruel as Billy Culpepper, and I knew I couldn't become a Crow slave." Tears dampened Rebecca's lashes. "I don't know what I'll do if Bright Arrow doesn't return with Windrider. I'm so frightened, Bonnie," she confessed nervously.

"He will, Rebecca." Bonnie sought to ease her fears and doubts, though the younger woman fretted over his inexplicable and cruel behavior toward her friend. She hoped Windrider would bring Bright Arrow back to settle matters with Rebecca—for selfish and unselfish reasons. Sucoora had become the wife of White Antelope, and Bonnie wanted to be alone with her love. Yet she longed for Rebecca's joy and peace.

With agonizing sincerity, Rebecca replied, "I'm not so sure, Bonnie. Bright Arrow's changed so much this last year. He's been so contradictory and bewildering. Now that he's back with his people and a skilled warrior once more, he might not want me to complicate his life and

emotions any more. Besides . . ." she began, then
blushed and halted.

"Besides, what?" Bonnie entreated.

"You know how men are about their women. What if
he thinks I've been . . . abused by that terrible Billy Culpepper? What if he thinks I was ravished by Crow before
Windrider rescued me? The Sioux despise the Crow.
Who knows, maybe he's suffering from bruised pride or
false suspicions about me and Windrider. I have no idea
what he's thinking or feeling," she declared in frustration and dismay.

"Even if that were true, Rebecca, it wouldn't have
been your fault. How could he possibly blame you or
reject you for being kidnapped or raped?" Bonnie reasoned.

"Men are funny about such things, Bonnie," she
remarked.

"But that man didn't touch you. And you never
reached the Crow camp," Bonnie argued. "When Bright
Arrow comes, you can tell him."

Rebecca wasn't convinced. Bright Arrow had been told
where she was and in what condition. There was no way
she could explain his behavior. He knew she wouldn't
ride into the Oglala camp after he had ignored her completely for weeks. This had to be his way of telling her
good-bye, of implying it was over for them. Confronting
him would only cause her embarrassment and suffering.
She shouldn't have sent Windrider to the Oglala camp.

Bonnie watched Rebecca's pensive features. She
inquired, "What are you thinking?"

"I'm a bloody fool for sending Windrider on such a
futile mission. It's clear Bright Arrow doesn't want me
back. He would have come by now or sent me a message. I
shouldn't have drawn Windrider and you into this prob-

lem. I've got to get away from here, Bonnie. I can't be here when he returns. I know what he's going to say. There's no need to put either of us through a painful scene like that. Can you loan me a few supplies and a weapon?" she asked, shocking her friend.

"Rebecca Kenny, you can't ride off alone, especially with winter just around the corner!" Bonnie fearfully protested.

"I must. I can't bear any more torment. I've lost everything, Bonnie. I should have understood his message from the first! I'm not staying here to be ripped apart again! With or without your help, I'm leaving in the morning," she declared firmly.

Bonnie knew she was serious, and she shivered in panic. She had to find a way to stop Rebecca's reckless flight. Until she reasoned out a plan, she would feign cooperation. "I don't like this," she argued. "It's dangerous and foolish, Rebecca Kenny. Where will you go? How will you survive? What about enemies? And food and shelter?"

"I can take care of myself," the flaming-haired woman stated.

"Like you did in the Yankton camp?" Bonnie unthinkingly scoffed.

Rebecca grimaced. "That was a valuable lesson—trust no man! I've lived in the wilderness most of my life. If I don't know enough to survive, then I don't deserve to do so. I'm going to St. Louis."

Windrider couldn't believe what he had discovered from Shalee in the Oglala camp. Now he related his own tale to the worried woman. At Shalee's insistence, he would spend the night in the Oglala camp and head home in the morning. Both assumed that Bright Arrow was on his way from the Blackfeet camp to the Cheyenne camp. Soon, they hoped, this confusing and painful situation would be a thing of the past.

Rebecca knew Bonnie would try to trick her into staying in the camp. She realized that Bonnie wasn't beyond using force or help from another warrior to hold her captive until Windrider returned. During the night, she crept out of the tepee, taking with her a knife and a few supplies, including a buffalo robe for warmth during the cold days and to sleep on at night. She didn't feel too guilty about taking the supplies; many tribes had come to the aid of their Cheyenne friends by providing food, weapons, garments, and hides for tepees.

At the edge of camp, she turned and glanced backward, struggling to prevent tears from flowing. She whispered sadly, "Good-bye, Bonnie, my good friend. Be happy with Windrider and the new baby. One day I'll repay you for these supplies and your kindness." To herself she said, "Well, Rebecca Kenny, you're on your own now. Let's see if you can make St. Louis before spring." She looked up at the full moon, and a strangled sob was torn from her very soul. "Farewell, my traitorous love," she softly cried. "Perhaps we'll meet again someday. Fate has a way of traveling in circles."

She turned and determinedly began her journey toward a new life. It was early December. It was cold and lonely. Snowflakes began to fall ever so gently, the first of the season. Regardless of her efforts to hold them back, tears began to slip down her icy cheeks. The snow would make everything pure and white and beautiful again, everything except her life and love.

Chapter Twenty-Three

Rebecca walked for an hour, making very little progress. The cold attacked her moccasin-clad feet; the light snow flurries hindered her vision and chillingly teased at her face. As her hands gripped the buffalo robe she wore to keep her body warm, they became numb and icy. She tried not to cry, for she knew tears would freeze on her cheeks. Yet she was dejected, for even Nature was proclaiming herself an enemy during this tragic time.

Rebecca realized it would take her several hours more to get past the rocks and evergreens of the Black Hills. Afterward, she would be in the open. It would require days, perhaps weeks, to conquer the grasslands and prairies before she could reach more protective forests. She wondered how she would find food on that wide span of nothingness during the winter. She sadly concluded that maybe Bonnie had been right; it had been stupid and dangerous to run away. Yet she walked for another half hour, unable to force herself to return and hear her love's verbal rejection.

Under these demanding conditions, Rebecca tired easily and quickly. She longed for a fire to warm her flesh and a rest to appease her weary bones. Evidently she hadn't regained as much strength and energy as she had thought. But she knew that if she halted the cold would be worse. She wondered whether it was too early in the season for a blizzard.

Far away, Rebecca could hear the howls of a lonely wolf, perhaps calling to his mate. She could envision other animals, two by two, huddled snugly and affectionately in their various abodes. She wanted to scream at the heavens, to demand to know why she had been singled out for such punishment and anguish. She hadn't done anything wrong! Why was she being forced to suffer in this cruel and dangerous manner?

The snow flurries ceased, having left a light sprinkling of white on the ground, tree limbs, and black rocks. The wind settled down, halting its brisk and chilling assault. The sky was brightening gradually. Within an hour it would be dawn, Rebecca mused, a new day of misery!

Bonnie was alarmed when a man appeared near her sleeping mat and shook her roughly to awaken her. He had entered the tepee without asking permission, and she feared he was an enemy. Then the intruder's words and face revealed his identity.

"Where are Rebecca and Windrider?" he stormed angrily. His ebony eyes glittered with emotions that frightened the white woman.

Bonnie rubbed her sleepy eyes and glanced over to where Rebecca had been sleeping. She sat up and looked around in confusion. "I don't know, Bright Arrow. She was sleeping there last night. Windrider went to your camp to fetch you. He left yesterday, after Rebecca's arrival. Why are you being so cruel to her?" she blurted, the question involuntarily spilling from her mouth and heart.

It was the Sioux warrior's turn to show and experience confusion. "I have done nothing to her. She betrays me

494

for another man," he accused irately, although he doubted his own words.

Bright Arrow's first statement caught Bonnie's attention; his second went unheard. "Nothing!" she sneered incredulously. If he believed that, then why was he here? she asked herself. To pour more torment on Rebecca? "You betray her, reject her, abandon her, torment her, and call it nothing? You are a wicked, cruel man," she declared.

Silent Thunder had been aroused by their harsh voices. Bonnie comforted him and told him to return to sleep. She refocused her attention on the virile man at her other side who was demanding that she explain her daring insults.

"I explain?" she scoffed, her own anger increasing by the minute. "You are the one who should explain your cruelties to her. She loves you! How could you be so heartless and mean?" she asked.

"If she loves me, why did she run to Windrider's side when she healed? Why didn't she return to me?" he argued bitterly.

Bonnie couldn't believe what she was hearing. "What did you expect from her after you ignored her for weeks? She was very sick. She went through awful times with that kidnapper. She needed you. Surely it was easier for you to ride to the Blackfeet camp than for her to ride to you in her condition! At least you could have sent her a message! All those weeks without a word or a sign from you!"

"Where is she?" he questioned sternly. This woman's words made no sense to him. Rebecca was the one to explain her actions.

"I told you I don't know." Suddenly Bonnie paled and shivered. "Surely she wouldn't . . . My stars!" she shrieked as the obvious truth touched her mind. "She's run away to St. Louis. Yesterday she said she would leave before Windrider brought her news of your rejection."

"Your words confuse me," Bright Arrow declared impatiently. "Why did Windrider go to my camp? Why would Rebecca leave him?"

"You're confused?" she replied, shaking her head. "So am I. Windrider wouldn't have had time to reach you before your arrival. How did you know to come here for her?"

"Chief Medicine Bear of the Blackfeet told me she ran into the arms of Windrider, my treacherous friend," he snarled bitterly.

"She what?" Bonnie inquired skeptically. His jealous anger dawned on her. "That isn't true. She came here to plead for Windrider's help. Windrider left her in the Blackfeet camp waiting for you to take her home. She said you never came for her there. You never even sent her a message. She asked Windrider to go to you, to beg for an explanation for your rejection."

"I have not rejected her," he protested.

"What do you call your behavior? She sends you a message to come after her, and you never arrive. She doesn't hear a word from you. What is she supposed to think and feel? The Blackfeet warrior told her you were in camp, that you weren't wounded. You had no excuse not to go see her," she retorted.

"I was told she was a captive of the Crow. They have moved their camp. My friends searched for her many weeks. She could not be found. I rode to the Blackfeet camp to ask more questions. They told me of her injury. I knew nothing of such things. I feared she was lost to me, enslaved by my enemies. When I learned she had been in the Blackfeet camp for many weeks, I was hurt and confused. When I learned she had come to Windrider, I was angry."

"This doesn't make sense, Bright Arrow. Who would tell you such lies?" Bonnie probed in irritation and dismay. From the man's tone and expression, she sensed he was telling the truth.

Bonnie was shocked and disturbed when he confidently accused, "Windrider sent the message to me. I did not know it was from him until I reached the Blackfeet camp. He sent many lies to mislead me."

"That isn't true!" she panted defensively. "Windrider is trying to get her back into *your* arms and tepee, not his! He loves me. We're joined. I carry his child. He has gone to bring you here to solve this matter. There is nothing but friendship between my husband and your . . . Rebecca. This is also true for her. She loves you and wants you. For weeks she has suffered from your rejection. She does not understand why you have turned your back on her. She left to avoid hearing what you have shown her with actions. You are wrong, Bright Arrow. Your lies and mistrust have cost you a woman who would have given her life for you."

"Quickly, you must tell me all," he insisted worriedly. Now he needed to find Rebecca; later he would seek the truth.

After the two hurriedly compared stories, both were appalled by the misunderstandings. "I must go after her. When my friend returns, tell him all will go good for Bright Arrow and Rebecca. Tell him I feel shame for speaking such false words against him. It is clear he did not know the man he sent to me was a *heyoka*. When I learned of Thunder Head's identity in the Blackfeet camp, I thought my friend had intentionally used him to trick me. It was only a terrible misunderstanding. I will send word of her safety and our return to my people."

Bonnie smiled. "Hurry, it is cold and dangerous in the hills."

Bright Arrow chose the most likely trail toward the east. He rode for a short time, then dismounted to check for her signs. The light snow was concealing any markings on the stony ground. He had to trust his instincts and tracking skills to locate her before nightfall. The sky hinted at more snow and colder weather.

Before noon, Rebecca halted to rest. She ate strips of dried meat without any appetite. Her only thought was of obtaining energy for her trek. She was depressed, which only added weariness to her already exhausted body and mind. She leaned against a boulder and closed her eyes, trying to envision a cabin with a warm fire and hot food. The problem was that Bright Arrow and her children were also in the cozy scene.

As her tears began to flow again, she lowered her head to hide her face in the folds of the buffalo robe. She was snuggled tightly in a ball, attempting to warm and soothe her body. Her eyelids drooped. Slowly she sank to the ground, fast asleep.

From a short distance, Bright Arrow saw the little bundle. Fear gripped his senses. After the snow had ceased, her tracks had been easy to locate and follow. He jumped off Tasia's back and raced over to Rebecca's prone, limp body. He gently lifted her to a sitting position and thankfully locked her in a possessive yet tender embrace. He spread kisses over her hair and face, murmuring her name and thanking *Wakantanka*.

Rebecca awoke in this stirring and bewildering position. She looked up into his face, lined with tenderness and concern. *"Taku ca yacin hwo? Tokiyatanhan yahi hwo?"* she whispered hazily in Oglala, asking, "What do you want? Where did you come from?"

"I tracked you for the beautiful prey you are, because I love you and cannot lose you," he responded, relieved and happy she was alive.

"It took you four weeks to come to those conclusions?" she asked in a solemn tone as Bright Arrow examined her beloved features. Her tawny eyes revealed anguish and doubt. Her white skin was flushed from the wind and snow. Her flaming curls were mussed and tangled, so fiery against the white background.

"I was told you were a Crow captive. The Blackfeet warrior you sent to me is a *heyoka*," he informed her, then explained the warrior society of "contraries." He smiled and hugged her tightly. "I did not know you were near until I rode to the Blackfeet camp to ask more questions." He explained about the search for her, the misleading message from Thunder Head, and his urgent quest to find more clues.

"You didn't come to me because you didn't know I was in the Blackfeet camp?" she probed, needing to make certain she was hearing him correctly. Had all of her suffering been merely a horrid mistake?

His dark eyes were studying the ominous signs in the sky. *"Osniyelo,"* he announced, needlessly telling her it was cold. "We must find shelter. The snows come before nightfall. There is a cave nearby. We will go there to camp and talk. There is much for us to settle. Know this, woman. I love you and need you. I will not allow you to leave me."

With that stimulating confession, he scooped her up into his strong arms and headed for his horse. Placing her shaky legs on the ground, he mounted agilely then he reached down and lifted her to sit before him. His infectious smile warmed and enticed her.

She smiled up into his tender gaze. She expressed her joy at his arrival. *"Tanyan yahi yelo.* I love you, Bright Arrow," she murmured, then fused her lips to his. His arms encircled her fiercely as they savored each other's response. Tingles ran over her body. Hot blood flowed swiftly through her veins and warmed her. How could she have doubted his love and commitment? She should have known something was wrong!

Her thoughts turned to their daughters and, in answer to her maternal inquiry, he assured her they were safe and happy with their grandmother. Comforted by his words, she nestled contentedly in his arms as he guided Tasia through the trees and around the rocks. Every so often, he dropped a kiss on her head and squeezed her affectionately. Her face rested against his drumming heart, the rhythm of hers joining its wild beat.

When they reached the cave, he slid off the animal's back, then helped Rebecca down. Cupping her head between his hands, he searched her face with his searing gaze as if he couldn't believe he was staring into it once more. He lightly brushed her lips with his. "We must hurry, my rash heart. I will build you a fire and fetch more wood. Then I will hobble Tasia nearby to graze. Come, you are cold and weak."

Bright Arrow grasped her chilly hand and Tasia's reins. He led both inside the cave and unloaded his supplies. He knew there should be wood left from the time he and Sun Cloud had used this same cave during their escape from the Crow. He stacked brush and small limbs inside the rock enclosure. Soon he had a bright fire going. He placed larger pieces of wood nearby so that Rebecca could feed the hungry blaze while he was gone.

He would bring more wood, to dry for use later when the temperature dropped. He estimated they could be trapped here for days.

Bright Arrow handed Rebecca his water bag and a pouch of pemmican. He told her to eat, rest, and get warm. Then he took Tasia's reins and led him to the edge of the cave, glancing over his shoulder at Rebecca. "If we are lucky, I will find game for a hot meal. Tasia will graze while I find wood and meat. I will return soon, my beautiful heart."

She watched him lead the horse to an area where winter grass was showing. He took a pine brush and moved aside the thin blanket of snow, then hobbled Tasia's two front legs. After retrieving his bow and quiver of arrows, Bright Arrow headed into a stand of trees and waved to her. Rebecca leaned against the wall and watched him vanish from sight. She went to the fire to await her love's return. Her mind was spinning happily. She was eager to know everything.

Rebecca laughed merrily when Bright Arrow returned. He was carrying two rabbits and a small deer. She teased, "Either you think we're starving, or you plan to stay here a long time."

His gaze smoldered with leashed passion as he trained his midnight eyes on her beaming face. "We must wait out the storm. Will you mind being alone with me for several days?" he teased in return, his white teeth gleaming in the firelight. Like an adoring woman's hand, the colorful flames lovingly caressed the bronze planes of his arresting face and the muscular ripples on his bulging arms. His deep voice was mellow and provocative.

Rebecca realized how good these past months and rigorous activities had been for her love's body and spirit. He was a man, a warrior. He exuded self-assurance and prowess. Even his stance revealed confidence. He was a bronze and black god who controlled her emotions and fate. It was sheer heaven to be so near to him. His sensual mood tantalized her. She shrugged and sighed playfully. "I suppose I can endure it, if I must," she jested lightly, then grinned at him.

"You must," he retorted, chuckling in high spirits.

Her tone waxed serious as she replied, "I can think of nothing I would enjoy more. I was so afraid I would never see you again," she told him, her voice strained with emotion and her eyes misty.

He laid the game aside and went to her, gathering her into his arms and holding her. "It is over, my heart. My people say you can live at my side, as my wife."

She looked up into his face. "You mean it?"

"The vote was cast when I returned with Sun Cloud. I was waiting for Flaming Star to bring you home to me. I was not in camp when he arrived with the news of your capture by the white man. That is why Windrider came alone for you. Our camp was under attack by many foes. White Arrow, Flaming Star, and two Blackfeet warriors searched for you. They looked many weeks. When they returned, they told me you were with the Crow. The Crow had left their old camp; they did not know where to seek the new one. I feared you lost to me forever. Thunder Head's confused words confirmed their findings."

Her hand rested over his heart. She looked into his intense gaze. "I didn't know such things, my love. I could not understand why you refused to come to my side. I was so alone and afraid."

"When the Blackfeet told me you had gone to the Cheyenne camp, I was hurt. I thought you had chosen Windrider over me. I rode swiftly to force the truth from your lips. You were gone. I was too late. I was wrong," he admitted hoarsely. Remorse and guilt were reflected in his midnight orbs.

She inquired about Gray Eagle's health. *"Niyate kin toketu hwo?"*

"Tanyan yelo," he replied, informing her of his father's recovery. His hand reached up to caress her cheek. "What is my life without you at my side? Will you join to me, Rebecca? Will you end our pain and separation? *Winyeya nanka hwo?"* He asked if she were ready.

"Han, winyeya mankelo. Do you even need to ask?" she murmured, lacing her fingers behind his neck. She raised herself to kiss him, murmuring, "Yes, yes, yes," before meshing her lips to his.

Her breath was stolen by the feverish kiss and their fierce embrace. He tasted her response, her eagerness, her unbridled passion, her love and commitment. She needed to touch him, to feel his flesh against hers. Her hands unlaced the ties on his shirt. She drew away to remove it, tossing it to the ground. She laid her face against smooth, coppery flesh that was hard and vital. Her lips placed kisses over his heart her tongue mischievously flicked over his taut nipples.

Bright Arrow groaned in desire. His loins throbbed with instant arousal at her stimulating touch. He needed to touch her. He unlaced her garment and removed it. He untied the thongs of her breechclout and let it drop to the ground at her feet. He bent forward and captured a light brown peak in his mouth, then feasted on both for a time.

"That feels so good," she murmured. Rebecca's head arched backward as she savored the blissful sensations. His hands drifted skillfully over her responsive body. She moaned in rising need to sate the ravenous demands of her womanhood. Her fingers played in his silky hair and mapped his shoulders. Bright Arrow grasped her buttocks and pressed her against his hard and aching manhood. Their burning bodies rubbed provocatively against each other as their mouths blended.

"I want you, my heart. Is it too soon?" he asked cautiously, his manhood firm and erect, its heat calling out to her.

"No, my love, the time is perfect. I shall die of starvation if you do not feed me this moment," she coaxed as her palm rubbed over the bulging area in his breech-clout.

He spread the buffalo mats near the fire, adding more wood, then he held out his hand entreatingly. She took it and allowed him to pull her over to the mats. She lay down, sending him a visual invitation that sent fire coursing wildly through his whole body. He sat down beside her, passing his igneous gaze over her full length. Soon their hopes and dreams would be realized, and they would be united for all time. Such thoughts and emotions increased his rampant desire.

"I love you, Rebecca Kenny," he suddenly declared, leaning over to fasten his mouth to a tantalizing breast.

Bright Arrow worked slowly and carefully, drawing out this special moment as long as possible. His hand tingled over her abdomen and slipped into an auburn forest, to play around a sensitive peak. His hand caressed the smoothness of her inner thighs. His lips nibbled at her collarbone and ears. His movements became more serious and deft, and he stimulated her senses to mindless, instinctive response.

Finally, Rebecca could stand this rapturous torment no longer without giving him something in return. She rolled Bright Arrow to his back and removed his breech-clout. Then she covered his face with kisses. She worked her way down his chest, her tongue teasing each hard mound and tiny dip on his well-developed body. She drifted lower, surrounding his groin with kisses and caresses. She drew soft, throaty groans from him as she stirred his passion to a mindless level. Up and down his pulsing shaft she dropped moist kisses. His manhood quivered as he writhed under her ministrations. He could barely master this rearing stallion that longed to gallop wildly into her dark canyon. She lovingly and excitedly worked until he shuddered with urgency.

Turning her over, he pressed her gently to the soft mat. His mouth fused with hers as his hungry shaft sought appeasement. He entered and withdrew only three times before he halted briefly to cool the flames that she had kindled. With a tenuous hold on his passion, he continued his movements. She arched and matched his rhythm, and their bodies labored in ecstatic unison.

Rebecca's legs encircled his body and held him possessively. "Take me," she murmured into his mouth, grinding her lower body against his.

Bright Arrow increased his pace and power. She held him tightly as the blissful climax stirringly racked her senses. Her entire body experienced a rush of heat and tingling. The instant she tensed and indicated her release, he joined her, knowing there would be no retreat or denial for either. Together they rode out the wild and wonderful sensations. He continued his deft actions until every seed had been delivered into her enticing body and had blended with her release. They shared tender kisses and gentle caresses until their breathing slowed and contentment filled them, and they lay locked in each other's arms for a long time.

The cold had been forgotten in the heat of their passion. When Rebecca shivered, Bright Arrow propped himself up and gazed down at her. He smiled. Rebecca returned it. "I must see to Tasia and our game," he stated reluctantly, not wishing to move from this delightful position. He cupped a breast and fondled it. He kissed the tips of her shoulders, then her chin and nose. "You are much too tempting, my wild heart."

Her fingernail teased down his chest to circle his sated manhood. "Not as much as you are. We have the rest of the day and all night," she responded with a provocative grin.

"No, *mitawa cante,*" he laughingly corrected her. "We have the rest of our lives together. You are mine, woman."

She sighed peacefully. He hadn't called her "my heart" in a long time. "Our dream is coming true, my love," she whispered.

"Yes," he happily concurred. "Did I not tell you many times you were meant to be in my life-circle? Now all know this and agree."

"We always knew it. We simply had a difficult time convincing everyone else," she merrily retorted, joining in his playful mood.

"When the storm passes, we will return to my camp. You will become my wife. It cannot come swiftly enough for me."

"Nor for me. Can it truly be over, Bright Arrow?" she inquired anxiously. "We've faced so many fences that I fear another will be built before we can enjoy our freedom."

"Do not worry, my heart. I will let nothing and no one come between us. I give you my word," he vowed honestly.

"I believe you. How I do love you, my fierce and handsome warrior. I am the luckiest woman alive." She sat up to hug him, then nestled into the curve of his shoulder.

"Rest and warm yourself. I will return shortly." He pulled on his garments, then left the cave.

Rebecca tossed two pieces of wood on the dwindling fire. She snuggled into the mat, drawing a blanket over her naked body, and stared into the colorful flames. She was so happy and content. She closed her eyes as needed slumber claimed her serene mind.

Bright Arrow secured Tasia's reins to a pointed rock near the entrance, then he walked over and gazed down at his sleeping love. He watched her for a time, relishing his victory. He inhaled deeply as the same sense of tranquility filled his mind, and he turned to prepare the game. He then placed the cleaned deer on a high rock where it would be protected from animals. The cold weather would keep it from spoiling. He constructed a forked holder and placed it over the fire, then skewered the rabbits to roast. When his love awakened, the meal would be ready to eat.

Bright Arrow sat on a leather pouch across the fire from Rebecca. He couldn't seem to look at her enough. He was the lucky one. He had everything he wanted and needed. From Rebecca's actions and words, he knew she, too, was content. They would share a long and happy life together.

It was two hours before Rebecca stretched and sighed. She opened her eyes to find her love's warm gaze on her, and a radiant smile greeted him. She smelled the fragrant rabbit, and she grinned. "Now I know what woke me up," she told him, sitting up as the blanket fell away from her nude form.

"I had to tempt you. I was hungry," he announced. Yet his greedy eyes were feasting on her body, not the roasting meat. "*Loyacin hwo?*" he asked playfully, inquiring if she were hungry.

507

She laughed. "I am as ravenous as you, my love." Her expression matched his; both radiated reborn passion and deep love.

They joined in laughter. He cut a hunk of tender rabbit and passed it to her quivering hands. Glancing first at the meat, then at him, she giggled. "I thought you meant a different kind of hunger," she teased, devouring the delectable tidbit.

"I did. But we'll need stamina to feed it." He cut her another morsel. His laughing eyes surveyed her heart-rending beauty.

"How long can we stay here?" she asked suggestively.

"Not long enough," he replied. "A few days, as long as the storm is bad. I don't want anyone out searching for us in this weather. I will give you a critical mission," he announced mysteriously.

"A mission?" she echoed as she nibbled at the roasted game.

"I must send you into a marriage with a greedy and possessive warrior. You must make him happy for life. You must take care of his needs and hungers," he ordered between chuckles and bites.

"And what of my needs and hungers, my demanding captor?" she inquired as girlish giggles spilled forth to amuse him.

"Perhaps he will find a way to satisfy them. Do you think he can accomplish such a large task?"

"Yes," she replied dreamily. Her gaze wandered over his face and frame. "Oh, yes, I'm positive he can."

"Then you will be a good match for this warrior," he concluded, tugging on a fiery curl, then tickling her nose with it.

"I am unskilled and inexperienced on the mats. I will require many lessons and much practice. Do you think I can learn to please him?" she questioned with feigned innocence. She moved closer to him and passed her hand over his smooth chest with its two scars from the Sun Dance. Her fingers traced little patterns on his bronze flesh.

"Oh, yes, you positively can," he said as he watched the whitened fingernail-drawn heart slowly vanish from his chest.

They laughed and talked while they finished their meal. The winds howled around the entrance to the cave, and the snow began to fall again. It was as if they were sealed inside a private haven. The air was chilly, but the fire shared its warmth and light. Tasia seemed perfectly calm. They had food and wood. It seemed an enchanted time for them.

"How large is this cave?" Rebecca asked, staring into the blackness that appeared to stretch for a long distance.

"It is big and deep. It runs beneath the mountain. There is a stream back there. We will have plenty of water."

"A stream?" she echoed excitedly. He nodded. "Can I have a bath?" she asked with almost childlike enthusiasm.

"The water is cold, my heart," he warned her.

"I've had plenty of cold baths. I have soap in my pack. Please," she entreated, as if needing his permission. She hadn't had a real bath since Billy Culpepper had forced her to take one in that pond. She had washed off, but that wasn't the same. She didn't care if the water were freezing, for she knew an excellent way to warm up afterward.

"I will light a torch," he agreed. He took a large, dry piece of wood and held it in the flames until the end was burning.

Rebecca gathered her things and followed him into the dark recess. It was a spooky place. The torchlight danced eerily on the cave walls of midnight rock. They reached a circular area where water ran down the wall and flowed into a small pool. She squealed with delight. After testing the water with her finger, she said, "It isn't so cold." Quickly she dropped her things and disrobed.

Rebecca stepped down into the pool, delighted to find it was only waist deep. She didn't wash her hair, as she knew it would remain wet too long and she might catch a chill, but she scrubbed her body from face to toes. She hummed merrily as she worked, perhaps to give her the courage to remain in the water long enough to complete her task.

Bright Arrow observed her and his body alerted him to his rising desire. Her sun-kissed flesh still held its summer glow; it glistened with moisture. She smiled dreamily as she labored. When her tawny eyes landed on him, they darkened and reflected her own desire. He hunkered down beside the pool and watched her as overwhelming passion coursed through them both.

He stripped off his garments and joined her in the small pool. The coldness closed around him, but it soon faded as his body adjusted to the temperature. He took the hunk of soap from her hand and began slowly and enticingly to bathe her. She did the same for him. His lathered hands slipped over her breasts, kneeding the nipples between his thumb and forefinger. Her hands moved with slippery pleasure over his chest and shoulders. His head bent forward as his probing tongue touched hers; they savored the taste of each other.

His hands squeezed the pleading mounds and sweetly tormented the thrusting peaks. His hands slid around her back and grasped her buttocks. As he fondled them, he

pressed her snugly against his rapidly enlarging maleness. Bright Arrow caught Rebecca's shoulders and
pulled them beneath the surface to rinse away the soap.
After he raised her upper torso above the water's surface,
his tongue circled her nipples and inflamed her senses.

Bright Arrow's hands teased down her sides, over her
hips, and parted to go in separate directions. One hand
caressed her buttocks as the other moved into her auburn
triangle to gently stroke the straining peak there. He
could feel the tension and throbbing within that pleasure
point. As he lavished warm moisture and delight on her
nipples, his finger entered her entreating womanhood.
He moved expertly until her head thrashed wildly with
mounting desire.

Rebecca's hands roved the hard, smooth body before
her. They played over the taut, sinewy muscles across his
chest and lining his shoulders. They roamed over and
around his slim, flat stomach. Her fingertips playfully
grazed his hips, then wandered to examine his firm buttocks. His actions were stealing her senses and control.
Her hands shifted to weave through his groin area. She
caressed the two round knobs beneath his blood-
engorged shaft. Her hands ran up and down its length. It
was so smooth and firm, so full of skill and need.

Bright Arrow was starving for her. He lifted her and sat
her on the edge of the pool, then he grabbed the blanket
and tossed it beneath her. Their eyes met; she comprehended his sensual intention. She smiled and tingled
with anticipation. He pushed her down upon the rumpled
blanket. In the heat of their passion, the frigid water and
cold air were ignored. She inhaled deeply to control the
building suspense and her eagerness. She snuggled her
back against the blanket, closed her eyes, and allowed
him free rein over her body and senses.

511

Bright Arrow's gaze locked on her womanhood, its appeal calling out to him. He visually explored her most private area. His hand reached out to gently stimulate the tiny mound. He smiled when she trembled at his stirring touch. A finger eased within her secret recess to find it moist and eager. Heady power and pleasure surged through him.

His other hand wandered up and down her silky thighs. He was fascinated by the beauty of his stimulation. He passed his tongue over his lips, and his manhood pulsed with a response. He pushed her fuzzy hair aside as his finger moved upward to make blissful contact with that peak, and he deftly massaged it until her hips undulated and she moaned unceasingly. His head bent forward and his tongue replaced his finger. He teased the extremely sensitive peak with his teeth, giving her exquisite pleasure.

Rebecca groaned and her head thrashed against the blanket. Tension built within her. She wanted to relax, but couldn't. Her stomach muscles tightened in almost painful anticipation. She was engulfed by passion's flames. The peak throbbed and pulsed as Bright Arrow continued his erotic attack on her mindless senses.

His tongue flicked and circled, sometimes slowly, sometimes swiftly. His finger slipped within her body. Together it worked with his tongue to bring her to the point of torturously sweet rapture. She cried out his name and arched her hips upward as the spasms rocked her body. Bright Arrow increased his endeavors to give her supreme pleasure. As soon as she settled down, he climbed out of the water and hovered over her. Then he captured her lips and entered her slippery haven.

His self-control was sorely tested. He was surprised when she rapidly responded to him, as if insatiable. He thrust gingerly until she arched and matched his pattern. Bright Arrow didn't have to labor hard or long. He sensed her urgency and increased his pace.

His mouth went from nipple to nipple as he drove into her body and retreated rhythmically. Another explosion of rapture assailed Rebecca. She clung to her love tightly and fiercely. Bright Arrow cast aside caution and control. Together they scaled the heights and power of the heavens. Ever so slowly they drifted back to reality, remained entwined until they grew chilled.

"Does your captor please you?" he asked casually. Merriment and joy radiated from his twinkling eyes. "Was that not a good lesson and good practice?" he jested, grinning beguilingly at her.

"However shall you hunt for us and protect our lives when I force you to remain inside your tepee for more such lessons and practice?" she ventured seductively.

"I shall feast on your body and passion. And what better place to die than in your arms and body?" he smilingly retorted.

"You sorely tempt me to take on this critical mission. How soon will you have a tepee of your own?" she asked, playfully reminding him of their imminent lack of privacy. A walk in the forest to share passion would be impossible when the ground was covered by snow.

"At this moment, my parents and friends build a tepee for Bright Arrow and his wife. It is their gift to us for all we have done for them and our brothers. Does that please you, my greedy heart?" he murmured tenderly. His finger rubbed back and forth over her lips.

"Very much," she replied, cuddling up to him.

They washed off, gathered their belongings, and returned to the fire. For three more days, they talked, laughed, shared, and loved. When travel was possible,

Bright Arrow told her they must head for his camp. Aside from his concern that someone might search for them, he wanted to make her his wife as quickly as possible. Only then could he be certain that she would share his life-circle, that nothing would come between them to vanquish this dream come true. He wouldn't be satisfied or convinced until she belonged to him.

For some inexplicable reason, dread and tension chewed at him every time he thought about or mentioned returning to camp. There was no reason for his tribe or the council to take back its vote and acceptance of her. She loved him, and he loved her. Both agreed to this marriage and a life together. His family desired her return to his side. Windrider loved another, and was joined to her. The Crow and Pawnee were far away at their winter grounds. His enemies were dead or defeated. He had avenged his father and brother. He had proven his warrior rank and prowess. His family was safe. His beloved was in his possession. The weather was clearing steadily. So why was he haunted by an uneasy feeling? he anxiously wondered. Why was he reluctant to leave this secure and happy place? What could possibly go wrong now?

Heyab iya yo, wakansica woniya, his mind commanded, ordering the evil spirits to cease disrupting his peace of mind.

Chapter Twenty-Four

As Rebecca rode nestled against her love, she inquired with curiosity, "Why did your people change their minds about me? After what Cloud Chaser told me, I didn't think they would ever allow us to be together."

Bright Arrow stiffened in renewed anger against that treacherous man. If Cloud Chaser hadn't vanished, he would call him to a challenge. Evidently the malicious Sioux warrior had met with death or capture. Bright Arrow couldn't grieve over his loss, but he knew that if Cloud Chaser ever returned to camp, he would slay him with his bare hands!

He leashed his fury, explaining "He lied to you and Windrider. He never told my people you wished to speak with them. The council did not meet that day. They did not talk of you or vote against you as he claimed. Cloud Chaser told no one of your visit or my approaching return. He has fled in fear of my vengeance. If he returns, I will punish him for his lies, which cut your heart deeply." He didn't add that he knew such lies had almost driven her into the arms and tepee of Windrider. It was best to forget that difficult and painful episode. Bright Arrow didn't know about his friend's original plot against Rebecca, and he never would.

He blamed their mutual attraction on vulnerability, on intense needs, on loneliness, on desperation, on his own

515

foolish behavior. He knew there was nothing to explain or forgive. Rebecca and Windrider were friends, nothing more. Bright Arrow knew this fact without a doubt.

This was their second day on the trail. The day before had passed in light conversation or serene silence. This day, they spoke more seriously. Now Rebecca leaned away to stare at him in disbelief. "It was all lies? A vicious trick? Why?" She wanted an explanation. Bright Arrow gave her the only one he could imagine—jealousy and hatred of him. She frowned. "Is he the only one who hates me and resents my return?"

"It was me he hated and resented," he gently corrected. He avoided answering her question, praying she had no foe in his camp.

"Why must people be so cruel and evil?" she mused aloud. "Why must they intrude in others' lives? Why must they feed on the suffering of others? It's wrong! It's mean and wicked!" she stated angrily. She couldn't help but imagine what Cloud Chaser's mischief had almost done to her life. She had unwisely trusted two men—one white and one Indian. One had almost stolen her love, and the other had almost taken her life. She would not be so trusting and gullible in the future. Yet she despised the idea of suspecting each person of harboring evil intentions. In the past, she had been a good judge of character. This last year, with all its pain and troubles, had blunted her instincts and keen wits. Surely her problems and suffering had ceased . . .

Bright Arrow knew Rebecca wasn't asking questions to which she expected answers from him. She was right; it was hard to understand or explain such treachery and evil. People made mistakes; they might follow a wrong trail; they could be duped or snared or tempted by wicked forces. But misleading or tormenting a friend or tribe member was unspeakable evil. It could not be accepted or forgiven; it could not go unpunished.

That night, they camped beneath a heavy overhang of spruce branches. After a satisfying meal they snuggled together to stay warm. As the moon sprinkled her light upon them through the boughs, they made love passionately and freely. Afterward, their bodies remained entwined as they slept.

Shortly after midday, the Oglala camp came into view. Bright Arrow reined in Tasia. He searched Rebecca's face for any sign of anxiety or indecision. She smiled knowingly. "I'm fine, my love. This time I enter your camp as your bride, not as your white captive. One day, everyone will forget the troubles of these past years. We must show our courage, and love, and determination."

He grinned and hugged her. "Yes, my heart, you are ready to confront my people and win their affection and respect. We will be happy, Rebecca Kenny," he stated confidently.

"Han," she playfully responded in Sioux.

"Waste cedake," he murmured, speaking his love for her.

"Oihanke wanil?" she teased, caressing his strong jawline.

"Yes, always, forever, *Cante Peta,*" he stressed, tenderly calling her the fire in his heart.

"My heart, my life, my body," she murmured seductively, then added, *"Lena oyas'in cic'u kte,"* vowing she had given all these things to him.

He kissed her thoroughly. When their lips parted, their gazes remained joined. He clutched her to his body and rode into his camp.

They were greeted by many friends, his family, and curious tribe members. Shalee hurriedly stepped forward. As her green gaze slipped over Rebecca, she smiled in relief and affection. "Welcome home," she declared joyfully, then embraced the younger woman.

Over Shalee's shoulder, Rebecca's eyes met those of Chief Gray Eagle. He smiled warmly and greeted her, "It is good to have you back at my son's side. You will be called my daughter. It is as it should be."

Rebecca's eyes misted. It's true, she thought joyfully. They are going to accept me.

Shalee informed her, "I have made you a joining dress. The tepee is finished. We will have a feast and share your happiness."

"Where are my children?" she inquired eagerly.

"They sleep. They are lovely girls, Rebecca. My son and his family will know peace here. Come, you must rest and eat," she invited.

The group entered the tepee of the legendary Gray Eagle and Princess Shalee, the beautiful woman who had once been enslaved by this still handsome and valiant man. Rebecca noted that the years had been good to them, for neither seemed to have aged appreciably, and the looks of affection that passed between them hinted at a love still strong. They all sat on small mats and leaned against backrests, careful not to disturb the sleeping children. The small girls were accustomed to sleeping during noisy periods, and they did not awaken. Wanting to savor this long-awaited reunion, Rebecca left them in peaceful slumber.

She could no longer deny this reality, for the proof surrounded her. Yet she couldn't help but wish she could turn back the clock a few years, to prevent their suffering and to have another chance to save her child's life. She resolved to let go of such feelings and thoughts, for she knew she would have to give her best, her all, to this new chance for them.

The joining ceremony was planned for the next night. Shalee offered to keep the children that night and the next, giving the couple time alone after their reunion and wedding. Bright Arrow readily agreed, so eagerly and instantly that Rebecca blushed shyly. But when he playfully cuffed her chin and visually devoured her, she couldn't suppress the desire that danced in her tawny eyes.

Shalee and Gray Eagle exchanged knowing smiles. It was good to see such powerful and passionate love between their son and his chosen woman. If it hadn't been real or potent, it wouldn't have lasted so long and endured so many trials. It was good to have them home where they belonged.

Gray Eagle reached out to take Shalee's hand. He squeezed it meaningfully. What did it matter that he was fifty-three winters old and his love was forty-eight? When the right moment presented itself, their passion could burn as brightly and fiercely as Rebecca and Bright Arrow's. He warmed just knowing what beauty and sensuality lay beneath her chamois dress. In two nights, they would be alone again, if Bright Arrow would return their favor by keeping Sun Cloud. With that heady thought, his passions were kindled to a cautious and smoldering level. He would feed them and allow them to burst into roaring flames in three days . . . As if reading his thoughts, Shalee smiled and nodded.

The next day passed in busy preparation for the joining ceremony and feast. The girls did not understand the meaning of the Indian wedding; they only realized that their parents were involved in something exciting and

special. Windrider and Bonnie arrived as welcome
guests. Each member of the tribe offered something for
the joining, or the feast, or their new tepee. It was a
joyous time for everyone, especially for the second gen-
eration of lovers and their family.

The crisp December evening seemed perfect for the
occasion. The sky was clear. The moon was full. Millions
of stars glittered across the indigo heavens. The brisk
wind had ceased, and the winter air was far from unpleasant. It was a beautiful night for a wedding.

Flaming Star, Gray Eagle, Windrider, and White
Arrow were helping Bright Arrow to prepare himself.
Gray Eagle had insisted that his son wear his long robe of
multicolored feathers, his most richly decorated buckskins, and his deftly quilled moccasins. His ebony hair
had grown long enough for braids that brushed his
shoulders, but to give the appearance of greater length,
they attached feathers, tufts, and beaded thongs to the
edges. At last, the bridegroom was fully attired. He
presented a handsome and stirring image.

Bright Arrow's tension was obvious to the other men.
They laughed and joked with him. They talked of olden
days and past adventures and future times as they waited
for the signal from the ceremonial chief.

Mind-Who-Roams, the medicine chief and visionary,
entered the tepee. He informed Bright Arrow that he and
his wife would be very happy, that the Great Spirit would
guide and protect this special union. He embraced the
younger warrior. Then, in turn, each man embraced him
and offered last words of advice or congratulations. He
accepted all with gratitude and happiness.

In another tepee, Rebecca was donning a beautiful

wiyan heyake, a dress of the softest and whitest elkskin. She wore matching beaded, knee-length moccasins. The bodice of the dress was exquisitely decorated with beads of red, white, blue, and green. It was heavily fringed on the arms, yoke, and hem. She was given a tuft adorned with beads and feathers, which she placed in her fiery chestnut hair. She was radiant.

Little Feet, Tashina, and Sun Cloud were with Wandering Doe, wife to White Arrow and mother to Flaming Star. She had had a hard time controlling the children, so eager were they for the activities to begin. When all was ready, she took them to observe the dancing and singing, which was taking place near the center of camp. They were soon caught up in the excitement of the celebration. The girls were enjoying their new life in the Oglala camp. They liked having grandparents and friends.

When the drumming began, Shalee looked at Rebecca and told her it was time to join the others. Rebecca hugged Shalee and Bonnie, then thanked them for their assistance and friendship. Joyfully, the three women left the tepee and walked toward the large campfire. Rebecca saw that Bright Arrow and the other men were waiting for them, and she noted that the children were standing nearby. The kettle drum ceased for a time. It seemed a perfect moment.

Suddenly a wild scream rent the still air, startling everyone. Kajihah burst from the tepee behind the three women. Her frenzied yell had caused all three to whirl around and face her, and they were horrified by the sight that greeted them. Two knives were raised high over the crazed woman's shoulders, and the sharp blades glistened ominously in the firelight as she prepared to release the deadly weapons. There was little, if any, time to react. Panic and confusion engulfed the crowd surrounding the four women. Almost in the flicker of an eye, both blades were deeply buried within feminine flesh. It was over as rapidly as it had begun. Registering disbelief and shock, all eyes locked onto the grisly sight.

Standing Rock swayed back and forth on his knees and openly wept. He stared at the bright red liquid on his hands, his own child's blood. Yet he had been forced to seize her hands and drive the blades into her body. He could not have allowed her to murder two innocent women. Until tonight, he had denied the warnings and indications of her madness and wickedness. He had been unable to ignore the horrible glow in her eyes as she had sharpened the two hunting knives, all the while murmuring the names of the two white women and cursing them. She had been crazed by her hatred and jealousy. Now it was over; Kajihah was dead.

Standing Rock lifted the bloody, lifeless body and vanished into the darkness. The three women remained frozen in place. Gray Eagle nodded to the eight men surrounding the kettle drum. They began to beat out the joining song. Others obeyed the chief's silent command; they began to sing and to smile. Gray Eagle strode to his wife Shalee, drew her close, and escorted her to her place beside him. His jet eyes caressed his emerald-eyed love of twenty-eight-and-a-half years.

The final seed of fury had been destroyed. Bright Arrow's adoring eyes never left Rebecca Kenny's glowing face as he sought her hand and led her to the ceremonial chief. She gripped his hand tightly, smiling nervously into his tender gaze. No one had to wonder if they loved each other; it was apparent to all.

Windrider walked over to Bonnie and slipped his arm around her waist. Their eyes met, blackish brown melting into sky blue. He knew beyond all doubt that she was the answer to his quest. They exchanged smiles and expressions of love, certain they would share a bright and happy future.

Flaming Star grinned. He nudged his father, who had been Gray Eagle's friend since childhood. He wistfully ventured, "I pray I will find a woman as beautiful as Rebecca and Shalee. I would be happy with a love only half as powerful and unconquerable as theirs."

White Arrow nodded his agreement as he slipped his arm around Wandering Doe's waist. He grasped his son's arm and squeezed it lovingly, proudly. He had witnessed the births, the pains, the joys, the defeats, and the triumphs of two loves between white women and Sioux warriors. At last there would be only happiness, peace, and serenity for Gray Eagle and Shalee and for Bright Arrow and Rebecca. Watching the four tonight, White Arrow had no doubts about their futures.

The joining ceremony began. It was a lengthy and exhilarating rite. Joining necklaces were blessed and exchanged. The couple vowed their love and commitment to each other. When it was over, Bright Arrow pulled Rebecca into his powerful arms beneath the flowing robe of feathers, and their eyes fused. It was an embrace much like the one Gray Eagle and Alisha Williams had shared many years ago. Then Bright Arrow's lips covered Rebecca's, sealing their love and vows for all time.

Princess Shalee snuggled against her husband's side. She was consumed by ecstasy as she and Gray Eagle exchanged intoxicating smiles. Suddenly, Sun Cloud wriggled between his parents' bodies. They looked down at their young son, attempting to envision the destiny and love awaiting him. But that's another story. . . .

A NOTE FROM THE AUTHOR

I do hope you enjoyed this sixth book in the SAVAGE ECSTASY series. I am grateful that you and other readers have made these characters and stories so popular. I am also grateful to ZEBRA BOOKS for continuing this saga for nine books. When it is time for major characters to "pass away," it will occur between books. I have worked with these characters for so long that they are like my family, and I hate to part with them. Please write and let me know which of the books is your favorite, and why. I would also like to know which characters, major or secondary, you find most appealing. Write to me at: Janelle Taylor Enterprises, 4366 Deerwood Lane; Suite 6E; Evans, Georgia, 30809. As quickly as possible, I will answer your letter. If you have missed one of the books in the series and cannot find it at your local bookstore, you can obtain it from ZEBRA BOOKS, at the address listed near the front. For a "Janelle Taylor Newsletter," send a self-addressed stamped envelope to the address above. Thanks for your support and interest. Until SAVAGE ECSTASY saga #7 . . .

HISTORICAL ROMANCES BY PHOEBE CONN

FOR THE STEAMIEST READS, NOTHING BEATS THE PROSE OF CONN . . .

ARIZONA ANGEL	(3872, $4.50/$5.50)
CAPTIVE HEART	(3871, $4.50/$5.50)
DESIRE	(4086, $5.99/$6.99)
EMERALD FIRE	(4243, $4.99/$5.99)
LOVE ME 'TIL DAWN	(3593, $5.99/$6.99)
LOVING FURY	(3870, $4.50/$5.50)
NO SWEETER ECSTASY	(3064, $4.95/$5.95)
STARLIT ECSTASY	(2134, $3.95/$4.95)
SWEPT AWAY	(4487-9, $4.99/$5.99)
TEMPT ME WITH KISSES	(3296, $4.95/$5.95)
TENDER SAVAGE	(3559, $4.95/$5.95)

Available wherever paperbacks are sold, or order direct from the Publisher. Send cover price plus 50¢ per copy for mailing and handling to Penguin USA, P.O. Box 999, c/o Dept. 17109, Bergenfield, NJ 07621.Residents of New York and Tennessee must include sales tax. DO NOT SEND CASH.